BY MY HAND

Maurizio de Giovanni

BY MY HAND
THE CHRISTMAS
OF COMMISSARIO RICCIARDI

Translated from the Italian
by Antony Shugaar

Europa
editions

Europa Editions
214 West 29th Street
New York, N.Y. 10001
www.europaeditions.com
info@europaeditions.com

Copyright © 2011 by Giulio Einaudi Editore SpA, Torino
This edition published in arrangement with Grandi & Associati
First Publication 2014 by Europa Editions

Translation by Antony Shugaar
Original title: *Per mano mia. Il Natale del commissario Ricciardi*
Translation copyright © 2014 by Europa Editions

Library of Congress Cataloging in Publication Data is available
ISBN 978-1-60945-206-3

de Giovanni, Maurizio
By My Hand

Book design by Emanuele Ragnisco
www.mekkanografici.com
Cover photo © Angelafoto/iStock

Prepress by Grafica Punto Print – Rome

Printed in the USA

Paola
every beginning
no end.

BY MY HAND

The murderous hands work unhurriedly in the dim light. They have no recollection of the blood that was spilled. They stir the little pot of glue that is heating over the fire, careful to keep lumps from forming. One hand grips the handle of the pot, the other stirs with the wooden spoon, gently, clockwise; the glue closes up immediately in the spoon's wake, like a dense sea.

Now the murderous hands check the wooden structure, testing the joints, proofing its strength. They realize that one corner piece hasn't been nailed securely; they pick up a hammer and strike, carefully, accurately.

They go back to the little pot over the fire, tipping it slightly to one side without removing it from the flame. They touch the cork, weighing it, assessing the size of the pieces, the curve of the bark. They know that the way the materials are prepared and the quality of the components are the most important thing, and that they have to get those details right.

The same hands that have ravaged human flesh with one clean motion now move over the statuettes, lined up neatly on the table; they count them one by one, arrange them in crucial, rigorous order. First the architectural elements, columns, ruined temples, huts, and houses; after them, the various objects, butchers' counters with meats on display, fish vendors' stands, carriages, fruit carts and carts of salami, and chairs, furniture of all kinds. Then the animals, sheep of different sizes to give the illusion of distance, horses, cows, hens, roosters, and baby chicks.

And also camels, elephants, and ostriches in an incongruous menagerie, drawn from within the boundaries of tales and traditions, not of continents and nations.

Now the murderous hands arrange the human figures, carefully, painstakingly. Shepherds, shopkeepers, housemaids and slaves, old men playing cards and old women gossiping, confiding secrets. The men on one side, the women on the other.

The murderous hands run lightly over the contours of the faces and the limbs, searching for chips and cracks in need of repair, identifying in the semidarkness the pieces requiring touching up, a little paint or a dab of terra-cotta. Every so often, one of the murderous hands will brush against the other; as if to underscore a thought, the fingernails of one hand will lightly scratch the back of the other. If not love, these murderous hands at least show respect for each other.

Just as they have sliced open veins and gushing arteries, just as they have disfigured and slaughtered, the murderous hands now carefully arrange on the table the last missing statuettes. The three kings, in their richly colored attire, with their exotic complexions, their golden crowns. Their mounts, caparisoned in red, double humps on their backs, with leather harnesses and reins. Gold, frankincense, and myrrh.

As if awakening from a dream, the murderous hands clap lightly and hurry back to the glue pot, stirring rapidly; then they turn to the straw-lined crate, now almost empty. They pull out a sad-eyed reclining ox and an ass the same size, the long hairy ears painted with fanatical care. The two animals join the others on the table, at the head of the army behind them, like a pair of captains waiting for their generals.

The murderous hands, which never so much as trembled as they choked off a life in the gurgle of one last blood-spattered gasp, now betray a moment of emotion. As if stalling to put off a momentous decision, they hurry over to stir the glue pot again, then they jump to another shelf to briefly caress the fabrics and colored paper. They smooth the creases, fold down the corners of the blue and yellow sheets of paper that will become sky and stars. They have raised the knife high and brought it down cruelly, stabbing hearts and lungs, extinguishing dreams and thoughts, but now they can't seem to bring themselves to plunge one last time into the straw that lines the wooden crate.

At last, the murderous hands, with all of the delicacy of which they are capable, without a thought for the lives they have cut short, pull out a Holy Mother with a sweet and loving face, wrapped in a sky-blue cloak. Both the murderous hands cradle the figurine, though it's as light as a feather. They set her down in front of all the others, at the center of the table, safe from all harm. In front of her, exactly where her gaze would fall if it were real, they place a Newborn Babe, its sad eyes already looking out upon the world, with a crown upon its head emanating beams of light, rosy cheeks, and a swaddling blanket.

Last of all, the murderous hands pull out a kneeling man, a staff with a curved crook in his hand, his long beard streaked with gray, wearing a dark brown cloak. After setting the man down next to the woman, one of the hands caresses him gently; the thumb runs over the man's chest, as if testing its consistency. So perhaps a vague memory of blood may still persist, after all, in these murderous hands.

Outside, suddenly, a bagpipe moans and a horn emits a long, lamenting wail.

The murderous hands grip the table's edge, their knuckles white from the strain.

In the piercing memory of blood.

I

Brigadier Raffaele Maione, trudging through the cold, wondered for the thousandth time who could possibly feel like committing a murder just a week before Christmas.

Not that anyone should ever feel like killing another person, to be clear: murder is madness, the worst thing a human being can do. Still, Maione thought to himself, it was somehow even worse at this time of year, when the children were so eager and excited that they couldn't sleep, now that people were greeting one another on the street, wreathed in smiles, trying to decide what to make for the Christmas Eve banquet. Now that the shops were decked out for the holidays, now that the churches were all vying to display the most spectacular manger scene, now that every conversation began and ended with best wishes for the season. Who could want to commit murder at a time like this?

And yet someone had done it. So here I am—the brigadier said to himself—trudging toward Mergellina, in this icy wind that cuts into my bones, running the risk of spending this Christmas in bed with a raging fever.

Behind him walked the uniformed patrolmen Camarda and Cesarano, their faces buried in the lapels of their overcoats, caps pulled down to cover their reddened ears. The two of them weren't even ribbing each other the way they almost invariably did, clearly both thinking the same thing as the brigadier. The mobile squad, they call us, thought Maione.

Mobile on our feet, mobile in our boots. Two automobiles assigned to police headquarters, and one of them's always in the repair shop, while the other one's assigned to His Honor the Chief of Police for official business. And here we are, raising blisters on our feet, hustling back and forth from one end of the city to the other.

A few steps ahead of him he saw Commissario Ricciardi, his hair tossing in the wind. Hatless as always. How the devil the man managed not to come down with some illness, God only knew.

Above the commissario's ear he could see a purplish cut, a shaven area, and a few stitches. Maione remembered the car crash his superior officer had been involved in on the Day of the Dead, nearly two months earlier, and a shiver ran down his spine as he reflected on what a miracle it was that he had survived. The woman who was driving the car that had skidded off the road had been killed on impact, after the car tumbled fifty feet down, and the commissario had emerged with little more than a scratch.

Walking along behind the commissario through the narrow lanes of the seaside neighborhood of Chiaia, Maione remembered when the man had awakened, in the hospital: the brigadier was sitting by his bedside, determined to watch over him all night long, when Ricciardi had suddenly opened his eyes.

His gaze was alert: he was completely conscious, and those unsettling, transparent green eyes, in which you could discern neither his thoughts nor his state of mind, were focused on Maione. Then, in a low, worried voice: "Do you see me? Do you see me, Maione? Are you able to see me?" "Of course I can see you, Commissa'," Maione had replied. "I'm right here, sitting next to you, why on earth wouldn't I be able to see you?"

The commissario had sighed. Then he had settled back on his pillow and fallen asleep again.

Maione saw him again at police headquarters seven days later, his wound bandaged inexpertly. Not that he'd really expected to see Ricciardi stay in bed for the month the doctor had recommended. And now the commissario was striding along ahead of him, heading for Mergellina, where the call had come from earlier that morning. Maione wondered what thoughts were going through that mind of his.

Ricciardi was thinking about the dead.

He was thinking that, Christmas or no Christmas, holiday season or no holiday season, goodwill or no goodwill, there was always someone dying, and it fell to him to witness the blood and the devastation.

When the car had skidded into thin air, he thought that he was about to die, and a part of his soul had almost wished for it: it would mean an end to the dark suffering that had always tormented him. Then he'd be nothing more than a fading image on a rock spur, condemned to utter one mute thought over and over into the wind, heard by no one, unless some other unfortunate man burdened by the same curse happened to be looking out at the sea from Posillipo.

But instead here I am, he mused. Once again heading out into the breach, as if nothing had happened. As if I hadn't died just a little more, the way I do every time I discover just how black a human soul can be. As if I were still alive.

Mergellina was changing: from a fishing village set off from the center of town, it was now primed to become an expensive neighborhood. New apartment buildings, shops here and there, wet nurses and governesses, doormen in livery, but it was a quarter still swathed in the look and the smell of the ways of old, with the odor of fish and stale cabbage, and women wrapped in black shawls mending torn fishnets.

As a rule, as soon as the platoon of policemen was spotted

coming in the distance, a small gang of *scugnizzi* rushed toward them shouting. These street urchins were at once the sentinels and the Greek chorus accompanying every event, ready to cluster around to celebrate or to protest, to obtain some slight advantage from every situation, the beneficiaries of a tossed coin or a mouthful of food; shoeless, tattered, their skin dark and callused, gap-toothed mouths open in a soundless, perennial scream. The *scugnizzi* stepped aside for Ricciardi without so much as a wave from him, while Maione and the two patrolmen did their best to swat them away like so many buzzing pests. But they did serve one purpose: they made it easy to find, without having to remember the address, the place where the crime they'd been summoned to investigate had taken place. It was a recently built, somewhat out-of-the-way apartment building; a small knot of rubberneckers were milling around in front of the street door, hiding the entrance from view. There was a strange silence. The wind coming off the salt water was sharp and chilly, but no one seemed disposed to budge from the vantage point they'd conquered.

As they got closer, a man broke away from the crowd—red-faced, dressed in sloppily buttoned footman's livery, a hat askew on his head. He approached Maione and took him by the arm.

"Brigadie', you're finally here. It's a bloodbath, just a bloodbath! You have no idea! I can't imagine, none of us can imagine who it could have been. They were a distinguished family, such a distinguished family! And now of all times, just as Christmas is approaching, I don't understand, I just don't understand . . ."

Assailed by the smell of rancid wine wafting out of the man's mouth and irritated by his tone, Maione shoved him away.

"Calm down, calm down. I'm not following a word you're saying. Step back, catch your breath, and tell me who you are and what you're talking about."

The man, nonplussed, took a step back and a deep breath.

"You're quite right, Brigadie', forgive me. It's just that the whole thing has me so upset. My name is Ferro, Beniamino Ferro, at your service, I'm the doorman of this building."

The crowd had shifted its attention from the front door of the apartment building to the conversation between Maione and the doorman. Ricciardi walked over to the two men.

"I'm Commissario Ricciardi from the mobile squad, and this is Brigadier Maione. Tell me what happened."

Ferro blinked rapidly, made uneasy by Ricciardi's gaze and the low voice with which he'd spoken. He grew cautious and whispered:

"I don't know what happened, Commissa'. That is, I know, I saw and . . . *Madonna mia*, there was so much blood . . . but I don't know how it happened, I mean. That is, I didn't have anything to do with it, let me make that clear. I went upstairs, when the *zampognaro* called for me, and I went to see, but I only looked from outside the door—I know that you're not supposed to touch anything." He'd referred to a *zampognaro*, a traditional Christmas bagpiper.

Ricciardi listened patiently, then said:

"What did you see from outside the door? What is it you're not supposed to touch?"

"I know, because I used to work at a construction site up in Vomero and one time a buddy of mine fell off a balcony, and they told us not to touch anything until they showed up . . . until you all showed up, in other words. The dead, Commissa'. Dead people, lying on the ground—that's what you're not supposed to touch."

The man's words fell into the silence like a rock into a deep well. The people at the front of the crowd that had surrounded the interview took a step back. A woman raised her hand to her mouth and her eyes grew round.

"Dead people, did you say? What dead people?"

Now Ferro seemed to have lost all interest in talking. He stared back at Ricciardi, wide-eyed, silently muttering those last words over and over again, the dead, the dead, as if he had only now just understood their meaning.

"Dead. They're dead. The signora, and the captain, too. They're dead."

He repeated the phrase several times, in a low voice, glancing around. The man's eyes glittered with the absolute terror and bewilderment that were washing over him; the rubberneckers looked away. From the nearby waterfront came the sound of a wave breaking over the rocks.

Ricciardi still hadn't taken his hands out of his overcoat pockets. The wind was tousling the hair that hung down over his forehead, his eyes gazed, almost unblinking. He was trying to piece out how much of the doorman's agitation was real and how much of it might be camouflaging a lie.

"What makes you say that this signora and this captain might be dead? Did you see them? Where are they?"

Ferro seemed to snap out of it.

"Forgive me, Commissa' . . . It's just that I still hadn't fully realized. I saw . . . I saw the signora, through the open door. I didn't go in; I called out for the captain, I called for him over and over but there was no reply. I thought . . . I just thought that if he wasn't answering, then that must mean that he was dead, too."

"And you're sure that he's home? He couldn't have gone out?"

"No, no . . . he's home. I always see him leave, for the port, in the afternoon. But at this time of day he's always at home."

Maione intervened.

"A minute ago, you said that the *zampognaro* called for you. What do you mean by that?"

"The two *zampognari* had gone upstairs to play the novena, for the third day. They came back down right away; one wasn't talking and he's still not talking even now. He's over there, you can see him, sitting in that chair, so pale he looks like a dead man himself. The other one, who's older, he came to get me, and he said, 'Signor Doorman, hurry upstairs, something awful has happened.' I would have believed anything, except that I'd go upstairs and find . . . what I found."

Ricciardi nodded, lost in thought. Then he said:

"All right then. Let's go take a look. Ferro, you can walk the brigadier and me upstairs. Cesarano, you keep an eye on the two *zampognari* and don't move from there; we'll talk to them afterward. And you, Camarda, I want you to stand guard at the front entrance. I don't want to see anyone go into the building, not even the people who live here, until I say so. Let's go."

II

F erro walked ahead of Ricciardi and Maione, leading the way into the building. The lobby was spacious and clean, reasonably warm and well lit; it was clear that the building aspired to a certain tone, as did many in this new neighborhood growing at the foot of the hill. Ricciardi addressed the man.

"How many people live in this building?"

"There are three families, Commissa'. The Garofalos, the ones . . . well, where I'm taking you now, the Marras, a childless couple who are out at this time of day because they both work, and the accountant Finelli on the top floor, a widower with five children who all go to their grandmother's, not far from here, when he's at the bank where he works."

Maione puffed as he heaved his 265 pounds up the stairs:

"So in other words, at this time of day there's no one else in the building but the Garofalos, is that it? And they don't have any children?"

"A little girl, Brigadie'. Her name is Benedetta and she's at school with her aunt, who's a nun. The aunt comes to get her every morning. That's lucky: if not, then she, too . . ."

He stopped on the last step, just before the third-floor landing, without turning the corner, his eyes fixed on the large window overlooking the courtyard.

"You'll have to forgive me: I just can't do it. I just can't see all that blood again."

Ricciardi and Maione walked past him. In the half light,

they were able to make out two doors, one closed and the other one left ajar, from which there came a shaft of a white light. They could glimpse a section of wall, flowered wallpaper, half a hanging mirror, a console table with a vase, and a framed photograph. They stopped, then Maione, according to a well-established routine, turned away, facing the stairs. The first encounter with the crime scene was always and exclusively the commissario's prerogative.

Ricciardi took a step forward, opening the door to the apartment a crack more. The light came from inside, the chilly December afternoon sunlight streaming through the windows in the other rooms. At first he saw nothing; then he realized that what he had at first taken for a decorative floral pattern on the wallpaper was actually an array of blood spatters. He leaned forward, taking care as to where he put his feet. On the floor there was a broad dark stain, in the middle of which was the head of a woman whose body lay behind the door.

The commissario understood immediately that all the blood he saw, the blood that had terrified the doorman and spattered and stained the carpet and the wallpaper, had sprayed from the woman's throat when it had been sliced open by a single blow from a razor-sharp blade. He observed the expression on her face, the half-closed eyes, the wide-open mouth. In the puddle of blood, the print of the toe of a heavy boot: someone had come in, but they hadn't ventured any further, probably the *zampognaro* or even the doorman himself.

He took a step forward, being careful not to step on the pool of blood, and half-closed the door behind him. He looked around: from the front hall, spacious and elegantly furnished, he could see a sitting room with two armchairs and a low table. He again looked at the corpse, then followed the trajectory of its dull gaze.

In the opposite corner, some six feet from the woman's

dead body, standing in the dying light of the day, the same woman was smiling in his direction, eyes downcast as she welcomed him to her home with the pleasure of a perfect hostess. She was murmuring: *Hat and gloves?* Her hand was slightly extended, as if to take her visitor's articles of outerwear and show him in properly, with grace and pleasure. *Hat and gloves?*

Under the smile, from the gaping wound in the throat, sliced open from one ear to the other, blood pumped out in small black waves, dripping unremittingly onto the flowered dress, muddying the woman's chest horribly. *Hat and gloves?* she kept saying. Ricciardi heaved a sigh.

He spotted a few black drops far from the corpse, on the floor; they didn't match up with the direction of the spatters that had hit the wall. Someone had walked away, probably unconcerned about the fact that the weapon used to cut the woman's throat was still dripping with her blood. He started following the tracks, passing through the sitting room and ending up in the bedroom.

The sight that greeted him there was overwhelming. The bed was drenched with blood, a horrifying amount of it: the sheets had turned black, the liquid had oozed onto the bedside rug, the light-colored wood headboard was spattered. At the foot of the bed, two long streaks. The murderer had cleaned the blade before leaving the scene.

At the center of the bed, and of the broad patch of his own blood, lay a man's corpse. His head was just starting to go bald and he had a drooping salt-and-pepper mustache. He might have been forty years old. The mouth gaped open as if trying to take in one last gulp of air; the hands were clenched in fists at his sides. Ricciardi understood, from the quantity of blood and the absence of visible wounds, that the man had been covered up as he lay dying and that he'd gone on bleeding for a good long while.

The commissario glimpsed the image of the man on the

bed, sitting beside his corpse and bleeding from a countless array of knife wounds. He was reminded of a painting of Saint Sebastian that hung in one of the classrooms of the high school he'd attended; he remembered how often, during the boring sermons he'd been forced to sit through, he'd counted the arrows piercing the martyr's body, twenty-three to be exact. Judging by the sight of him, Ricciardi felt pretty sure that the man on the bed had rung up a higher total than the Christian martyr.

He was saying over and over: *I don't owe a thing, not a thing.* Grim-faced, eyebrows knit, teeth clenched, glaring furiously: *I don't owe a thing, not a thing.* Ricciardi met the dead man's glare, then turned his back on all that blood and returned to the front door to let Maione in.

As always, so as not to run the risk of inadvertently moving some important piece of evidence, they held off on performing an in-depth examination of the crime scene until the medical examiner arrived. Leaving an irritated Cesarano at the front door of the apartment, the commissario and the brigadier went downstairs to interview the doorman and the *zampognari*. They'd tried to persuade the three of them to come back upstairs, but without success: nobody was willing to face that scene of mayhem a second time.

Ferro was having a hard time smoking, his hand was shaking so badly. Ricciardi said to him:

"Well, you were right: the man's dead, too. What were the victims' names?"

"Garofalo was their surname, Commissa'. Captain Emanuele Garofalo, and the signora was Costanza. I don't know what her maiden name was."

"Captain, you said; was he in the military?"

"Yes . . . uh, no, not exactly. He worked at the harbor, a member of one of those voluntary militias, those new Fascist institutions. He wasn't really a captain; he must have told me a hundred times but I never understood, something else, um, maybe it was a centurion. In the end he gave up and he just said to me, 'Beniami', let's do this: why don't you call me captain, which is the corresponding rank in the army, and we won't have to discuss it again.'"

Maione commented:

"In fact, our friend here isn't entirely wrong, Commissa'. They create a new one of these militias every few months, and you can't make heads or tails of it. Anyway, if he worked at the harbor it must have been the port milita, the one that's in charge of cargo and fishing."

"That's right, Brigadie', in charge of fishing, too," Ferro broke in, "and in fact we'd often have fishermen showing up here with gifts for him, but he'd always turn them away; he said that they were trying to buy his silence with a basket of fish, but that he couldn't let himself be corrupted in any way. He was a model of honesty, a real straight shooter. And now just look what's become of him."

Ricciardi brought the conversation back to the main topic:

"You didn't leave the building, all morning long?"

"No, Commissa'. Well, that is, I did go over to the trattoria across the way, just for a bit, no more than half an hour, and I kept my eye on the front door the whole time. You feel how cold it is out here, and the wind that's blowing, no? At a certain point a man has a right to get warmed up a little."

With a shudder Maione remembered the man's breath, reeking with the foul stench of cheap wine.

"Half an hour, eh? And you never took your eye off the front door the whole time. And the whole time, you never saw anyone go in?"

"No, certainly not, Brigadie'. The last one to leave the building was the accountant Finelli, then the captain came home, and he always goes out again in the afternoon, but that was it. I keep a sharp lookout, you know: a fly couldn't get inside without me knowing."

Maione shook his head.

"With the exception of two *zampognari*, complete with musical instruments, whom you neglected to mention. As invisible as a couple of big shiny bluebottle flies, I'd say. You didn't see them when they went in?"

Ferro opened and shut his mouth a couple of times. Then he admitted:

"No, Brigadie', I didn't see them. They managed to get by me. They must have gone in just as I was getting my money out to pay and I looked away for a moment."

Maione and Ricciardi exchanged a glance: even if they hadn't noticed the alcohol on his breath, it was obvious from his red nose and bloodshot eyes that good old Ferro liked to lift an elbow, whether or not it was cold out. Anyone who knew the doorman's habits could simply have waited for their chance to slip past him.

"All right. Let's go have a chat with the two *zampognari* then. We'll see what they have to say for themselves."

III

The *zampognari* were clearly father and son. The resemblance was unmistakable: same eyes, same features, same movements.

Ferro had let them into the small apartment where he lived, on the ground floor, right behind the doorman's little booth, in the lobby of the apartment building; most of the room was occupied by a wooden table on which a manger scene was in the process of being assembled. The doorman apologized for the clutter.

"Excuse the disorder, Commissa'; I still haven't found the time to finish it. I want to put it at the entrance of the building for Christmas. That is, I wanted to put it out, but now I'm not sure it would be in good taste. Certainly, the accountant Finelli's children would have loved it, and I even promised them that I would; they'll be so disappointed. But with two people dead, and with the horrible way they died, it seems like a bad idea, don't you agree, Brigadie'?"

Maione shrugged his shoulders. Ricciardi focused on the two men waiting off to one side of the room, as if they were hoping to be swallowed up by the shadows. The son, sitting in a chair, was pale in the face, trembling; next to him his father, his face baked by the sun, had put a hand on the young man's shoulder. An acrid odor wafted off the pair of them.

They wore the distinctive clothing of their trade: pointed hats, sheepskin jackets, thigh-high lace-up boots. The young man held the *zampogna* in his arms, an animal-skin bag from which protruded three pipes of different lengths. The older man had set his own instrument down on the floor; it was a sort of double horn. The father's calm air served as a counterpoint to the son's terrified expression, almost as if they were playing an emotional duet as well.

Ricciardi spoke to the man standing by his son.

"Now then, what's your name? And where do you come from?"

To his surprise, it was the boy who replied, his voice shaky but confident.

"Our name is Lupo, Commissa'. I'm Tullio, and my father is Arnaldo. We come from Baronissi, near Avellino. We play the novena. This is . . . was the third day, the Friday before Christmas Eve."

"Tell me what happened. What time did you get here?"

"The times we play in the homes change, the ladies like to do things their way and they tell us to come in the mornings, the afternoons, or the evenings, whatever suits them. We make our rounds; we have four different homes to go to, but they're not close and we really have to hustle. Signora Garofalo . . . poor lady, *mamma mia* . . . had asked us to come around lunchtime, so her husband would be there. The little girl was kind of afraid of us; children are strange, some of them clap their hands when we play and start singing along with us, others get frightened, clap their hands over their ears, and run off."

Ricciardi nodded, remembering the discomfort that he'd felt as a boy at the ear-splitting sound of the horn and the dull rumble of the *zampogna*, the bagpipe.

"So the little girl wasn't there, is that right?"

"No, that's why the signora asked us to come at one. And also because her husband was coming home from work, and he wanted to hear us play, too."

Maione listened carefully. He asked:

"And when you got here, was the front door open downstairs? Did anyone see you come in?"

The two men exchanged a quick glance, then shot a quizzical look in the doorman's direction. Maione explained:

"We already know that the doorman was . . . otherwise occupied. Don't worry about getting him in trouble. Just answer the question, please. And tell the truth."

The father answered, in a deep, low voice that reverberated in the small bedroom.

"There was no one there. No one saw us. We went upstairs to the landing. I knocked, I called out, and there was no answer. The door opened partway; my son looked in. And then we came downstairs, to summon the doorman. That's all there is to tell."

"And you saw no one come up or go down? You heard no sounds in the apartment, or outside?"

"Nothing. We heard nothing and we saw no one."

His tone had been conclusive, firm. Exact wording aside, the man had just said: We had nothing to do with this; we were here just to do our job. Ricciardi nodded.

"I see. So it was your son who saw the signora's corpse, is that right?"

The young man ran his hand over his eyes.

"That's right, Commissa', it was me. And I'll never forget it as long as I live, that poor woman lying in all that blood."

His father gripped his son's shoulder and said:

"You have to understand, he'd never seen blood before, only the blood of the lambs at Easter. And even that upsets him."

Maione looked hard at him.

"What about you? Does blood not upset you particularly?"

The waves roared in the wind, not far off.

"I fought in the war, Brigadie'. I fought in the war, and I was at the front. And when I was a boy there were still bandits where I grew up. No, Brigadie', blood doesn't bother me. And it hasn't bothered me in a long, long time."

Another crashing wave in the sea below resounded like the thunder of a distant cannon. Ricciardi thought to himself that blood still hadn't stopped upsetting him, no matter how much of it he saw.

"Give your particulars to the officer, including the address of wherever you're staying here in Naples, and your address back in Baronissi. Don't leave the city until we let you know it's all right; make sure we can get in touch with you if we need to, in other words. For now, you're free to go."

When they were alone again, Maione said to Ricciardi:

"Commissa', I think you were right to let them go. It's true that no one saw them come in, they're the only ones who saw the corpses, the door was open and not tampered with, which means that whoever killed the signora, she let them into the apartment herself. If it had been them, would they have killed the Garofalos and then gone to the tavern to summon the doorman, without taking any valuables, instead of simply running away? And the bootprint in the blood is proof that when the young fellow poked his head in, the woman was already dead."

"No, I don't think they did it either, and in any case, we know their names and addresses; we can track them down when we want to. You know I don't like throwing people in jail if I can possibly avoid it. Let's wait and try to find out a little more about what happened. Have the doctor and the photographer arrived?"

"Not yet, Commissa'. I had calls put in to both of them from headquarters before we headed out, so they'll be here any minute. And as usual I made a special request for Doctor Modo, and no one else."

Ricciardi agreed.

"You did the right thing. I don't trust anyone else; the others inevitably make a mess of things. Why don't you ask that Ferro, the doorman, to come in here for a minute. There's something I want to ask him."

The doorman seemed to have regained some degree of confidence, Ricciardi thought; his jacket was buttoned more neatly, his hat was on straight, and the man had even combed his hair.

"Commissa', here I am, at your service. I sent the rubberneckers home, with the help of your officer. They're all fishermen. Nothing much ever happens around here; I don't even know what it is they had hoped to see."

"I wanted to ask about the little girl, the Garofalos' daughter. How old is she, and what are the hours of her school?"

"Well then, Commissa', the little girl is named Benedetta, like I told you before. She's eight or nine and she goes to school with the nuns, on Riviera di Chiaia, not far away but not so nearby that she could go there on her own. Her aunt, Sister Veronica, comes to pick her up. That's her mother's sister; she teaches girls Benedetta's age."

Ricciardi chose to focus on this.

"What time did her aunt come to get her this morning?"

"As always, quite early, around eight o'clock. I was here, I said hello to her—she's a jolly nun—then she took the little girl and they left together. That one, Sister Veronica, she has a voice that's very . . . very odd, piercing. She never stops talking. If you ask me, she stuns that poor child into obedience."

"It all checks out, then. At eight o'clock they were still alive, and at one o'clock, when the *zampognari* got here, they were dead. But did you see the captain leave for work?"

Ferro avoided Ricciardi's gaze.

"I don't remember, Commissa'. A couple of times I might have stepped away. A man has to use the facilities every so often, after all; then I watered the plants in the courtyard, I went to pick up some groceries . . . No, I don't remember seeing him leave, or for that matter come home."

Maione bore in, shoulders thrust forward.

"Clearly, Ferro, with you on the job a person can rest assured that nothing will slip through the cracks, eh?"

"What can I say, Brigadie', I'm all alone. I have no wife to help me, no children to lend a hand."

Maione looked over at Ricciardi and threw his arms open helplessly.

"Well, that's that, Commissa'. If we want to find out anything about what happened here, or when it happened, we'll have to wait for Dr. Modo."

IV

And Dr. Modo arrived, his face bundled up in a scarf and his hat pulled down over his ears to ward off the biting winter wind, followed by the police photographer, and just as furious as ever.

"Ah, it's you, I knew it; I knew it'd be the two of you behind this. Now then, gentlemen, it's time for us to come to an understanding once and for all and put an end to these summonses by name. What have things come to when I have to be afraid of the switchboard operator at the hospital? When that devil of a telephone contraption goes off, ringing its bell, it always means trouble, and that trouble always seems to have your names on it!"

Maione snickered.

"Dotto', what can we do about it, it's your fault for always being around for us to call. Why don't you try taking a few days off sometime; then we'll have to work with one of your colleagues and we'll finally get it through our skulls that there are better doctors than you around."

Modo shook his fist in Maione's direction.

"Well, then I'll just have to shut up and take it, because there's nobody around who's a better doctor than me. But excuse me, did you make some kind of pact with Lucifer so that the bloodiest murders would always happen when it's cold as a witch's tit out? Or else when it's pouring rain, like with that poor little boy two months ago, or when the wind is so icy it'll slice your ears off your head? And every time, I have to walk clear across town, thanks to you two!"

Ricciardi hadn't so much as blinked.

"Now, there's an idea worth looking into. Maione, make a note: let's arrange to have the next murder take place in the hospital waiting room, that way the good doctor won't have to go out in the rain. The truth is that we ought to be more understanding when we're dealing with white-haired senior citizens."

The doctor stood, arms akimbo, in a combative stance.

"Listen here, Ricciardi. It just so happens that I'm one of those guys who just gets better with age; and my hair turned white before I turned forty. You on the other hand: I was hoping that the blow to your head might have set your sense of humor straight, but instead here I find that you're no better off than you were before. Next time I have you under the scalpel I won't be able to resist the temptation to open up your head so I can tidy things up in there."

Ricciardi snorted dismissively.

"All you did was give me a few stitches. It'd take a lot more than a windshield to crack my head; I'm a country boy, and you know our skulls are a lot tougher than you city types'. But I have to say, Christmas hasn't put you in a particularly good mood."

"Aside from the fact that, as you know, I'm an atheist, I've always found Christmas to be sort of depressing, if you want to know the truth. All these families gathering together to pretend they love one another, whereas you and I see day after day how much they hate one another in actuality; all this exchanging of smiles and best wishes, only to insult one another and wish one another ill as soon as they turn their backs; this flaunting of wealth and prosperity, only to plunge back into the grimmest poverty in the days that follow. It disgusts me."

Maione laughed.

"Oh, *mamma mia*, Dotto'—there's a nice bit of optimism! Listen, come over to our house on Christmas Eve: we'll see if you can resist the broccoli, the vermicelli with clam sauce, and the big pan of eel my Lucia makes, with a couple of liters of wine from Gragnano, which a friend of mine who works down there brings me. Shall we make it interesting, a little cash bet that the Maione family can make you like Christmas?"

"*Grazie*, Maio'. Thanks especially because, as far as I can tell, you don't listen to a word I say: Haven't I told you that gorging yourself like that is bad for your health? Will you get it through your head that you need to start living a healthier life?"

"I give up, Dotto': there's just no way to put a smile on your face today. Christmas must just really get you down."

"It's not Christmas, it's humanity's sheer evil that gets me down. This morning, before you called and invited me to join you at your murder victims' social club here, I had to stitch up another couple of skulls because your friends from the Fascist Party were letting off steam by strolling around town cracking people over the head with bats. Whether you call this Year Nine of the Fascist Era or 1931, it doesn't change the fact that those who have power use it to crush the powerless underfoot."

Ricciardi looked at his watch.

"How about that: we'd been talking for almost three minutes and politics still hadn't come up. That may be a record. Why can't you get it through your head that if you keep talking like this you'll wind up with a fractured skull yourself?"

Modo grinned, slyly.

"Because the police can't protect me, that's why. Neither me nor any other honest citizen. Speaking of which, would you care to show me your new clients, my dear Commissario Dracula? Your thirst for blood has brought us all down to the seashore: So who's dead now, some fisherman? Or have you found a comely mermaid murderess?"

"Come with me, I'll take you upstairs and introduce you to a handsome couple. I'll also have you know that we have a brand-new orphan on our hands, an eight-year-old girl who still doesn't know, so it's nothing to joke about."

Standing off to one side of the room while Modo, the photographer, Maione, and the two police officers performed the usual minuet that is always danced around corpses, Ricciardi mulled over the feelings that the murder scene filled him with. He was curious about the phrase that the dead woman kept uttering—*Hat and gloves?*—in a tone both affectionate and deferential; the commissario sensed a familiarity, a straightforward warmth underlying the formality of the words. The man in the bedroom, on the other hand, had been brusque and peremptory; his words—*I don't owe a thing, not a thing*—clearly referred to a debt he refused to acknowledge. Money and affection, mistrust and warmth, scorn and reverence. It was a sharp contrast. The man had thought about money, the woman about cordially welcoming a visitor into their home.

The commissario had always recognized that hunger and love, and their various, countless derivations, were the root causes of every murder. Hunger gave rise to ambition, envy, and vendetta; love was the mother of jealousy, hatred, and rage. The two great enemies, allies until the first drop of blood was spilled. This time Ricciardi would have to wait for the evidence he needed to identify which of the two corrupt passions had played the leading role in the performance he was observing.

Maione called him, taking him out of his thoughts.

"Commissa', come take a look."

The brigadier's voice reached Ricciardi from elsewhere in the apartment, a little sitting room next to the bedroom. The room was decorated for Christmas with garlands and cockades. In the center, on a wooden table, stood a large manger scene. It was really extraordinary, complete with all the traditional touches; Ricciardi was no expert, but he could appreciate a finely detailed landscape, with animals and human figures and architectural elements all arranged so as to give the impression that the scene covered more ground and was more expansive than it actually was. He spoke to Maione.

"Very nice. But what's special about it, in particular?"

"According to tradition, the *zampognari* play the novena right in front of the manger scene," the brigadier replied, "nine times, that is, in front of the Christ Child. Which means that the Lupos, father and son, would have been ushered into this very room. Now, we have no way of knowing with certainty, but it looks to me like nothing is missing. These Garofalos were well-to-do, the apartment is upscale, the furniture and decorations are new and handsome, there are even a number of pieces of silver serving ware still in their places. And aside from the mayhem visited upon the bodies, there's nothing broken, no sign of forced entry."

Ricciardi waited for the punch line.

"So? Why did you tell me to come over here?"

Maione smiled cunningly.

"The reason why is right here, Commissa'. Just crouch down and look under the tablecloth on the table with the manger scene."

Ricciardi noticed that under the landscape constructed on the wooden table there was a heavy red linen tablecloth decorated with embroidered stars, the edges of which reached almost all the way to the floor. He kneeled down next to Maione, who lifted a section of tablecloth, and spotted some broken shards. He picked up a few of them and held them up to the light.

Among the other shards, he made out half a bearded face and the curved handle of a staff, with a small hand attached to it. He turned to look at the manger scene again, and before he could even articulate the question, Maione answered:

"That's right, Commissa'. Everyone's in the manger scene except for Saint Joseph."

V

They remained on their knees before the manger scene, Ricciardi holding a handful of pieces of the statuette of Saint Joseph, looking at each other, perplexed. Finally, the commissario said to the brigadier:

"So what's its significance? Maybe one of the Garofalos dropped it, and it just broke by accident."

Maione scratched his head, lifting his cap an inch or two.

"Well, Commissa', I don't know. If I drop something at home, I pick up the pieces and toss them in the garbage if there's no way to fix them. I don't throw them under a carpet or a tablecloth, the way someone did here. It looks to me like something that was done intentionally."

"So what's the meaning of it? I could understand if they'd taken it, or broken it out of spite; but then they'd have left it on the floor, in plain view. Instead, someone tried to conceal it. What does it mean?"

The brigadier spread his arms wide in frustration.

"Like I said, I don't know. It might not mean anything. Maybe I'm running past the manger scene and I knock over one of the shepherds, I'm in a rush so I don't stop to pick up the pieces. After all, with all that blood . . . Something like that, I guess."

Thinking out loud, Ricciardi said:

"But this room isn't on the way from the door to the bedroom: you'd have to come here on purpose. No, if it was the murderer, he was trying to say something. But what?"

Dr. Modo appeared in the doorway. His shirtsleeves were rolled up, his white hair was unkempt, and his hands were stained with blood.

"Here you are, the two of you, in the full throes of a mystical crisis, kneeling before a nativity scene. What a moving sight to behold, the conversion of two hardboiled cops. What will the two of you do now, get thee to a monastery and cultivate your gardens?"

Ricciardi easily got to his feet, and Maione struggled to do the same.

"Bruno, I'm happy to know that you appreciate spirituality. Why don't you do like us and choose a mission of your own? I'm sure you convert the hundred or so Mary Magdalenes that you patronize on a weekly basis."

Modo laughed.

"Can you imagine the faces of the young ladies, if I were to show up at the bordello with a cross in my hand? Maybe I'll actually do it, just to see their reactions. Do you know how heartbreaking that would be for them, to lose a man like me?"

"And one of their primary sources of income as well, I'd have to guess. Well, have you found something?"

The doctor began cleaning his hands on a handkerchief.

"Well, I'll tell you, the autopsy of the woman by the front door was pretty straightforward. Someone, using an extremely sharp blade, decided to give her a nice second smile an inch or two below the one she was born with. A single blow, from someone standing in front of her, using the right hand. Incredible power behind it: just a little more and it would have taken her head off. It sliced through everything, larynx, sternomastoid, carotid artery. That's where all the blood came from. It must have been quite a spurt."

Maione broke in.

"So, Dotto', that means there's a good chance the murderer got blood on himself, no?"

Modo nodded.

"No doubt, Brigadie'. Unless he was quick enough to jump out of the way, he must have gotten some blood on his face and on his clothing. In any case, she died immediately, a matter of seconds. She didn't even have the time to understand what was happening, fortunately. What I'm not so sure about is the husband. That's a different matter."

"What's different about it?" Ricciardi asked.

"I'll explain. In his case, the fury behind the attack was spectacular. The body has about sixty stab wounds, many of them inflicted after death, I believe at least half. The murderers must have had some very grave reason to hate him. They assaulted him while he was asleep, or half asleep; there's no sign of struggle or resistance. I'll have to do a close examination during the autopsy, but from what I can tell the victim's nails are intact and there are no marks on the hands. However, and this is one of the curious things, after all this violence they laid him out neatly, straight as a board, and covered him with the sheet. Showing a respect they clearly lacked when they killed him."

The change from singular to plural wasn't lost on Ricciardi.

"Excuse me, Bruno: when you were talking about the woman you said 'the murderer,' as in one person, acting alone. But for the man, you said 'the murderers.' Why is that?"

"The old bloodhound doesn't miss a thing, does he? You're right, I used the plural. I'll have to do the autopsy; then I'll have more information. But judging from appearances, just based on an initial examination, it seems to me that the wounds on the man's body must have been inflicted by different hands."

Maione looked from the doctor to the commissario, baffled.

"What are you talking about, Dotto'? What do you mean 'by different hands'?"

"Well, there's the angle, first of all," Modo replied. "Some of the stab wounds were made by a blow from right to left, others from left to right. A right-handed stabber and a left-handed one. Then there's the force of the blows. Some stab wounds are deep, in fact I think there were even some broken ribs. Others are shallow, made by just the tip of the blade. I couldn't say how many weapons were used, but it's my impression that at least two different hands were at work."

Silence fell. Then Ricciardi said:

"What about the time of death, is there anything you can tell us there?"

Modo shook his head.

"You see, this place is very warm in comparison with the exterior. Can you feel how toasty it is in here? There are several heaters going full blast; the couple must have suffered the cold even worse than I do. That tends to alter the time line for the changes that take place postmortem: the cooling of the body, for instance. Generally speaking, however, I think I can narrow the window down: our friends died sometime between seven and one, considering that it's now five in the afternoon."

"Dotto', can't you be a little more precise?" Maione asked. "Seven in the morning is one thing, one in the afternoon is another!"

Modo snapped a brusque reply:

"Why of course, I'll just grab my crystal ball, Merlin-the-Magician-style. *Abracadabra!* Tell me the exact time, because Brigadier Maione wishes to know. What do you think, that I'm some kind of charlatan? I'm a scientist, goddammit! It's already quite an achievement, narrowing the window that much, without an autopsy!"

"All right, Dotto', don't fly into a temper. Just so long as we can say with certainty that Signore and Signora Garofalo are dead. Can we at least say that much?"

Modo threw up his hands, feigning resignation.

"I surrender. I killed them both myself, I confess: I'm tired of carrying on this charade. Listen, I'm hoping to get you more information once I've done the autopsy. The morgue attendants are here, and I'm going to have these two unlucky souls taken to the hospital, now that the photographer says he's finished. Are you coming downstairs with me?"

At the main entrance to the building, they found Ferro surrounded by a small group of people.

"Commissa', these are the tenants from the other apartments; I detained them here because I didn't know if I could let them in. Can they go up?"

"Yes, you can all go upstairs. Just stop to talk with Brigadier Maione, here, for a moment; he'll have a few questions for you, but it won't take long."

He turned to Maione, murmuring under his breath, "Try to find out something about Signore Garofalo: his routines, his bad habits, acquaintances, friends. Sometimes neighbors know a little something more than the relatives."

Maione nodded.

"Certainly, Commissa', don't worry. I'll take care of it. I also sent Cesarano to the school the little girl attends, to alert them to what's happened. I thought it was best to make sure the kid didn't come home and find that bloodbath. Did I do the right thing?"

"Yes, certainly. It would be better for the child to stay there tonight. Tomorrow morning we'll go talk to her aunt and, if possible, to the little girl, too."

As Maione began the process of questioning the neighbors, Ricciardi walked the doctor to the front door.

"You know, Bruno, I feel the same way you do about Christmas. The whole holiday just doesn't mean that much to me. But for whatever reason, seeing something like this this time of year in particular makes me feel more depressed than usual."

"I know what you mean, and you're not wrong. Maybe it's because it's a little easier during the holidays to fool yourself into thinking that human nature might be better than it really is."

Once they were out on the street, Ricciardi noticed a dark shape moving toward them along the wall before stopping some ten feet away.

"But isn't that . . ."

The doctor seemed embarrassed.

"Yes, it's the dog of that little boy, the one who died in November, who you brought to me to be autopsied, the boy who was poisoned. The dog just kept on circling the hospital, but he would never come close. A few *scugnizzi* threw rocks at him; he'd go away but he'd always turn up again. Who knows, maybe he hoped his little friend would come back. Eventually I gave him a piece of bread, and he ate it when he saw me leave. The next day he came over to me, and he let me pet him. So then I . . . well, both of us are alone, no? I figured that maybe we could sort of keep each other company. He followed me home, but he wouldn't come inside. He sleeps in the courtyard garden, and that's where I find him the next morning. He follows me around, he never bothers me. There's nothing wrong with that, is there?"

Ricciardi made a wry face.

"No, Bruno. There's nothing wrong with that."

Ricciardi looked at the dog, which returned his gaze with its warm chestnut-brown eyes, its coat white with brown spots, its muzzle angular, one ear cocked, the other flat. A dog, like any other. Or, perhaps, unique.

"I remember him. He was sitting by the little boy when we found him. I'm happy to see he's made a new friend. You have to admit, Doctor: it's nice to have a friend, especially at Christmas."

Modo laughed.

"Nonsense. Let's go, dog; let's get out of here, it's windy. *Ciao*, Ricciardi. Come see me at the hospital the day after tomorrow and I'll let you know the results of the autopsies."

And he walked off under the wobbly glow of the street-lamps tossing in the wind, followed by the dog half in shadow.

VI

A little boy came from Mergellina to tell everyone about it. He ran barefoot, along the shore, through the wind and the spray, the soles of his feet tough as leather on the sharp rocks that stuck up from the sand, leaping over the jagged shoals.

He came running as fast as he could, to deliver the news.

I was carving wood, getting ready to glue the cut-out figures from the Stella sheet on top of it; even my children need to have a manger scene. All four of them were crowded around me to witness the creation of the ox, the ass, and the Three Kings. I have to paint a few of the figures myself, because certain shepherds are missing from the sheet: Cicci Bacco, Uncle Vicienzo and Uncle Pascale, Stefania, and the Monacone, the "Big Monk." And the fishermen, of course. The children have to see the fishermen in the manger scene. They have to know that the uncles and friends are there, too. The father. Everyone has to be in the manger scene. Everyone has the right to be there.

The children were clustered around me, watching me carve, while the waves pounded right up against the walls of the castle, like an animal trying to butt down a door with its head. The castle protects the borgo, the little fishing village, that's the way it's always been. The black castle, and the borgo hidden behind it.

The little boy arrived; he called up from the piazzetta. We all ran outside, all of us who were waiting for it to be time to take the boats out, waiting for another night with heavy seas, another night to find something to eat, another night when the women wait, praying to find out whether their men will make it home.

The little boy arrived, out of breath, and we all ran over and asked him what had happened. And the little boy took a small drink of water, and then he told us about the blood. He told us about the knife wounds, he told us about the police and the doctor, he told us what he heard someone say from behind a wall, words carried to his ears by the icy wind.

We listened, we who had trembled at the sound of that name, we who had seen him arrive a hundred times, and a hundred times we had thought about that blood, the blood that had now finally been shed.

When the little boy was done telling his story, everyone went home. Not me. I went down to the wharf, where we keep our boats tied up, waiting for the night's heavy seas to settle. I went down to look at the sea, with the knife still in my hand, the knife I had been using to carve the wood for the manger scene: the ox, the ass, Cicci Bacco.

I sat down on a mooring bollard, with the spray in my face and the wind in my ears.

I looked down at my hand, still gripping the knife.

And I started to laugh, and laugh, and laugh.

Until tears came to my eyes.

VII

Ricciardi retired to his bedroom. From outside his door, which he'd left ajar, he could hear the music of the orchestra that was playing on the radio, the lament of a tango whose notes spoke of loneliness and jealousy. From farther away came the noise of the dinner dishes that Tata Rosa was washing in the kitchen sink.

He went over to the window, with the usual pressure in his chest, the familiar sense of disquiet. He opened his eyes, realizing only then that they had been closed, and looked. Nothing. The shutters of the third floor of the building across the way, on the other side of the narrow lane leading up to Materdei, were locked shut. From between the slats filtered the light from the kitchen of the Colombo home. Every so often he could see a shadow go by. He knew those movements; he'd watched them, enthralled, for months, one performance every evening, the sole concession to normalcy for the soul of a man who knew there was nothing normal about him.

Why did you close the shutters? he wondered for the thousandth time. Standing there, his arms wrapped around his ribs, his green eyes glittering in the dark like a cat's, seeking an answer that he couldn't find.

He missed Enrica. Even though he'd never spoken to her in any real sense, unless he counted that awkward, clumsy police interview the previous spring; even though he'd never looked into her eyes, with the exception of a few desperate fleeting moments; even though he'd never abandoned her in his thoughts, except for that one time, two months earlier, when he'd allowed his loneliness to overwhelm him.

He missed that normal young woman, a little too tall, who wore long, hoplessly unfashionable skirts and tortoiseshell spectacles, whose left hand embroidered by the light of a table lamp with calm, methodical gestures every evening, for his eyes alone as he watched her from the darkness.

He missed finding in the serenity of her movements—as she made dinner for her parents and siblings, or read or cleared the table, listened to music or tutored children at home—a haven from the blood and sorrow that assailed him at every street corner, a respite from the pain that serenaded him, and him alone, with its horrible song.

He couldn't figure out why she would close even that narrowest of openings that had once allowed him to observe her life, knowing that there was no other way he could take part in it. He had discovered that she knew he was watching her thanks to a single short-lived correspondence. He remembered how long it had taken him to write his letter to her—his difficulties, his hesitation. So much time and effort to produce just a few formal lines, in which he asked her for permission to greet her, even if only from a distance. And her reply, calm and unruffled, in which she informed him that she would be pleased, very pleased indeed, to be greeted by him.

Everything had been moving smoothly toward a greater closeness, a friendship. And then there had been the accident, the hospital: and not a single visit, not a single letter in all those days. Then when he returned home, the shutters were locked tight.

As the tango outside his door gave way to a melancholy waltz, Ricciardi's thoughts returned to the blood of the Garofalos, strewn all over their seaside apartment; and to how brief life could be, how wrong it was to cast off one's feelings. He thought about himself, how he was treading the boundary between life and death without ever truly taking part in either, and about the life he led, caught between profound silences and deafening noises.

He looked up, toward the darkened windows of the fourth floor of Enrica's apartment building. Through one of those windows he saw clearly, translucent and dangling as always, the hanged bride.

A very particular case, in the context of his visions. She appeared and vanished, from one period to another, haunting the apartment where she had put an end to her life; as if her final emotion had come in on a wind, and had then been swept away again into the darkness, to await its return. He could see her clearly, on that chilly December night, the neck elongated by the dislocation of the vertebrae, the eyes bulging out of their sockets, the black tongue lolling out of her mouth, open wide as it gasped for air. And her voice, hoarse and grating: *"You damned whore, you took my love and my life."* A betrayal, an abandonment, an inability to survive in her solitude.

Ricciardi turned his back on the closed window and on the open one above it: the living woman who refused to let herself be seen, and the woman who was no longer alive but who presented herself to the eyes of his soul in all her grief and suffering. He went over to his desk, he sat down, and he pulled out a sheet of paper. He would write to her, this time without the assistance of the book entitled *Moderno segretario galante*, without a model letter, without an outline. He would write to her, and he would tell his story to someone who knew nothing about it.

Dear Enrica,

Ever since I returned home from the hospital you've denied me the sight of you. I know that you heard about the accident; Rosa told me that you were there with her in the first, terrifying moments, when no one knew whether I'd survive. I'm all right now, in case you were interested to know: nothing much, just a scratch on the head, the occasional dizziness. But I'm all right.

I don't blame you for the closed window, for the silence. You're right: a young woman has hopes, aspirations, desires. A young woman wants to be courted, taken to the movies, taken out dancing. A young woman would like a man she could introduce to her parents, invite over for Sunday dinner. A young woman wants to be loved.

I love you, Enrica. Please don't doubt that. If love is a heartbeat, if love is waiting, if love is a faint suffering, then I love you. And my mind and my heart never abandon you, for a moment.

But love isn't a luxury that I can afford. I wasn't born to experience emotions, to try to be happy. I'm a condemned man.

I see the dead. On every street corner, at every window, I see the dead. I see them as they were when they died their violent deaths, their bodies ravaged, blood pouring, bones jutting out from their torn flesh. I see suicides, murder victims, those who were run over by carriages, those who drowned in the sea. I see them, and I hear them obsessively repeating the last obtuse thought of their broken lives. I see them, until they dissolve into thin air, to find a peace that may or may not exist, I don't know where. And I feel their immense pain at abandoning love, for all time.

I'm a condemned man. I've carried this mark upon me since I was a child, and I have reason to believe that my mother suffered from the same terrible malady, and she died a raving lunatic.

I love you, Enrica. And if loving someone means wanting what's best for them, how can I condemn you to a life with me? How can I force you to share the existence of a man who walks among the dead? You who don't have to see them, you who can smile happily in a place where I see shrieking corpses just paces from where I stand: would you want to be condemned to have a man like me by your side?

I love you, Enrica. And there's nothing in the world I'd like more than to hold you in my arms, safeguard your dreams, kiss your smiling lips. But precisely because I love you, I have to stay away from you. And believe me when I tell you that it hurts me more to condemn myself to life without you than it does to see, in this very instant, the ghost of a hanged woman who calls out for her lost love.

I'm heartbroken at the sight of your shuttered windows; but I'm happy because they protect you from me.

I love you, Enrica. And I'll always love you, in the darkness of my soul.

A gust of wind rattled the windowpanes.

His eyes gazing into the middle distance, Ricciardi slowly picked up the letter he'd written and tore it into a thousand pieces. Then he stood up, opened the window, and gave the shreds of paper to the chilly night wind.

VIII

The morning of the Saturday before Christmas was special. Venerable traditions mingled gleefully with new customs, and women with enormous baskets of eggs balanced on their heads walked along followed by swarms of children dressed in junior Fascist *balilla* uniforms, on their way to attend the rally in the square.

On the sidewalks along the more expensive shopping streets there were hundred of stalls selling everything imaginable, robbing space from pedestrians and therefore actually depriving themselves of customers. Chinese vases, wartime relics such as binoculars and spyglasses, combat boots and bayonets, military shoulder patches and hats: each vendor shouting the merits of his wares at the top of his lungs so as to be heard over the roar of the waves.

Maione and Ricciardi walked against the chilly wind along the Via Santa Maria in Portico. As they went past, the beggars and vendors, recognizing the brigadier's uniform, stepped aside, looking away and lowering their voices. It was as if a black wing were sweeping through the market.

Neither of them was in a particularly good mood. They were on their way to the convent of the Reparatrix Sisters of the Sorrow of the Blessed Virgin, which was where the Garofalos' daughter attended school; the idea of coming face-to-face with a little girl who'd just lost both her parents wasn't an appealing prospect.

Ricciardi asked, without breaking step:

"What did you find out yesterday, from the neighbors? Any interesting information about the lives of Signor and Signora Garofalo?"

"No leads, Commissa'. Apparently he, Emanuele Garofalo, was a centurion of the port militia: you know, that Fascist agency that's based down at the harbor and oversees the transit of goods as well as monitoring fishing. He'd been promoted a couple of years ago, the accountant was telling me, that Finelli. It seems that the promotion was for special merits, though he didn't know what they might have been."

Ricciardi nodded, and went on walking.

"Merits, these days, means that he spied on someone. Well, what else?"

Maione continued, huffing and puffing to keep up with his commanding officer.

"The neighbors confirm the family's complete integrity and respectability. I would guess that, since he was a member of the Fascist voluntary militia, they were afraid to say anything bad about him. I heard too many lines like 'he was a wonderful person,' and 'respectable people.' All too perfect, in other words. Even the doorman, that Ferro, was far too deferential. Could it be, Commissa': not a single piece of gossip, no backbiting at all?"

Ricciardi shrugged his shoulders, thinking of the courteous welcome that the woman's corpse, its throat cut, went on offering: *Hat and gloves?*

"Maybe it's the truth, how can we know? Was there anyone who went to see them?"

"Not many. Her sister, a few of his colleagues, dressed in those odd new uniforms with the tassel on the hat, suppliers of various kinds. They entertained little if at all, according to what the neighbors had to say."

"What about the woman? What was she like, what kind of personality?"

Maione waved his hand vaguely.

"Ah, they had even less to say about her. A fine woman, serene, always smiling, unfailingly polite. She went out only with her husband, she was very attached to her daughter, a good housewife. No one ever heard a raised voice or even a loud conversation coming from that apartment."

"So, no news," Ricciardi snapped. "Everything was perfect, all peace and quiet, no trouble in this family's life. Until one fine morning just before Christmas someone walks in, stabs them both to death and floods the house with blood, breaks the Saint Joseph in the manger, and leaves. A slight flaw, a wrinkle in an otherwise orderly day."

"Isn't that the way it always is, Commissa'?" Maione remarked bitterly. "Everything's fine, until something goes wrong. And the one who's left in the lurch is this poor child, who has no one on earth but an aunt who's a nun. She'll have to live in the convent, and maybe she'll become a nun herself."

"Or maybe not, Maione. What can you tell me about the aunt?"

"Nothing, Commissa'. She seems to be a fairly unusual sort, to judge from what I could gather from the half-statements of Ferro and the neighbors. A petite but energetic woman, always on the move, with a strange voice, like a trumpet. She's Garofalo's wife's older sister: no other siblings, and he had no siblings either. In other words, this aunt is the only family that little girl has left."

The convent entrance was a small doorway set in a very tall gray wall, in an narrow lane running toward the Villa Nazionale. The incessant sound of waves crashing against the breakwaters could be heard from down by the beach.

After showing their badges through a peephole, Ricciardi and Maione were welcomed at the entrance by a novice who led them to a freezing waiting room, bare of all furnishings save for a prie-dieu in front of a painting of the Madonna. A window looked out onto a large garden, with tall trees tossed by the wind. A faint gray light filtered in.

After a few minutes, during which Ricciardi looked out the window and Maione inspected his fingernails, the door opened and a nun entered the room. The woman said nothing; she walked to the middle of the room, appraised Maione dismissively with a quick glance, and rested her gaze on Ricciardi. After a long silence, Maione coughed awkwardly and ventured:

"Good morning, Sister. I'm Maione, Brigadier Maione, and the commissario here is Commissario Ricciardi, from the Naples police mobile squad. We're here to see Sister Veronica, the sister of Signora Garofalo, Costanza Garofalo. There is supposed to be a little girl, as well, and . . ."

Keeping her gaze fixed on Ricciardi, the nun spoke. And she spoke in a shrill, piercing voice, very much like fingernails dragging across a blackboard.

"The little girl is named Benedetta, and she's my niece. I'm Sister Veronica, of the Reparatrix Sisters of the Sorrow of the Blessed Virgin."

The woman looked nothing like her sister, who had been slender and of average height, with features that even in the rigor of death could be seen to be delicate and refined. The nun, in contrast, was short and stout, red-faced with a snub nose. Her voice and her posture—her body wobbled slightly back and forth—served to complete a fairly comical picture.

Maione, to break the tension, approached her and respectfully extended his hand.

"Sister, our condolences for your loss."

After a moment's hesitation, the nun offered him her hand and the brigadier bowed to kiss it. He found himself touching a small thing clammy with sweat, whose stubby fingers barely protruded from the sleeve of the black habit, and he had to overcome a surge of disgust and the temptation to drop it after a quick squeeze. He got away with miming a kiss an inch or so above the hand, and then he took a quick step back, abandoning the field to Ricciardi. Maione had been excessively heroic as it was, and now he was done.

"Sister, we sent an officer yesterday to inform you of what had happened at your sister's home."

"Yes, and just in time, because I was about to take Benedetta back to her parents. This isn't the first time I've had to keep the child here with me; I let her sleep on a cot in my room. She's always happy to stay, we're very close."

Ricciardi studied the nun's face, trying to read her emotions.

"Could you tell us about any of your sister and your brother-in-law's acquaintances? Anything that could put us on the right track . . ."

"I don't know a thing about my sister and her husband's life. He was an ambitious man, he thought about nothing but his work, and they didn't do a lot of socializing. I was in charge of the child and her education, in collaboration with my sister. That's all."

The shrill sound of her voice, childish and earsplitting, contrasted with the adult harshness of her words. Ricciardi persisted.

"But your sister might have told you something in confidence, I don't know, she might have talked to you about threats or disagreements that she or her husband may have had with someone."

The nun went on wobbling, and then said:

"Commissario, I had nothing to do with the affairs of my sister and her husband. I saw him rarely, and then only in passing; he was always at work, as I told you. And since my sister lived very much in his shadow, I never discussed anything with him but a single topic: my niece. And her education."

Ricciardi met the nun's gaze and held it. Maione dragged his foot over the floor, like a restless mule.

"Would I be mistaken if I guessed that you didn't much like your brother-in-law, Sister?"

The nun's round red face opened up in a sad smile.

"To dislike someone you have to know them, Commissario. And I doubt I saw my brother-in-law more than four or five times in all. What with the party assemblies and his work for the militia, he was never home. And now he's dead, and it's his fault that my poor sister is dead, too, and my niece will now have no one but me, a nun."

Ricciardi focused on this last sentence.

"Why do you say 'it's his fault'?"

Sister Veronica held his gaze.

"He was the man of the household; he was the important one. As I told you, my sister was nothing more than a shadow in their home. Whoever it was, you can be certain that they had it in for him, and if they killed my sister, too, it's only because she happened to be in the way. Your officer yesterday told me something about how they were found: my poor Costanza merely answered the door. The one they wanted was him."

The wind reverberated in the garden. The temperature in the room seemed to go down even further.

"What are you going to do now, with your niece?" Ricciardi asked. "What are you going to tell her?"

The nun looked out the window.

"She's a strong little girl. I'll tell her that her parents have gone away on a trip, and then little by little I'll give her some hints, and eventually I'll tell her that they were both killed in an accident, something romantic, a ship that sank, a train that ran off the tracks in some far-off exotic country. And in the meantime, I'll try to give her the best life possible."

She stopped for a moment, then turned her gaze on Ricciardi again.

"My sister was very sweet, you know, Commissario. She was a delicate, peaceable, educated woman. She deserved a long life, grandchildren, a comfortable old age. I prayed for her, and for my brother-in-law, all night long. It seems impossible that I'll never see her again."

Silent tears began to run down her face. She pulled an enormous handkerchief out of her habit and blew her nose, with the grotesque sound of a toy horn at Carnival; but neither Maione nor Ricciardi felt like smiling.

After a pause, she asked:

"Do you have to . . . do you want to talk to the little girl? I beg you, I'd like her to find out the way that I told you before. She's so small, only eight years old. Her world consists of fairy-tales and heroes. I don't want her first experience of the real world to be confronting the blood of her parents."

Maione looked at Ricciardi, who nodded.

"Don't worry, Sister," Maione said. "We have no need to speak with the little girl, and even if we did need to ask her a few questions, we wouldn't have to tell her what's happened. Keep her here, in any case. We might need to talk to her in the coming days."

"*Grazie*, Brigadier. It won't be easy. Christmas is coming, and she'll want to know why she can't return home. I'll send someone to gather her things: her clothing, a few dolls. It won't be easy."

Ricciardi began to take his leave.

"Let us know, Sister, if there's anything you need. You or the little girl."

"There *is* something we need, in fact," Sister Veronica replied, quietly. "We need for whoever did this to pay, and to pay dearly. So, Commissario, what I'd ask of you, on behalf of my niece and myself, is to find the men who killed my sister and my brother-in-law."

When they got outside the wind had stiffened and the sea roared, invisible, from beyond the Villa Nazionale, but they both felt they were in a pleasant and hospitable place.

"*Mamma mia*, Commissa'," Maione said, "that voice cracks your eardrums. And that hand . . . you have no idea! Phew . . . disgusting, damp, squishy. Poor little kid, the daughter; she's been left to stay with a strange creature."

Ricciardi sighed.

"But at least one who loves her. A better fate than that of so many of the *scugnizzi* that we see on the street. Let's not waste any time, Raffaele. We have to decide what line of action we're going to take, and we don't have much to go on. You heard what Sister Veronica said, no? We have to find the murderers."

IX

He knew he'd find him there, and sure enough, there he was. Sitting at the far end of the big room, his eyes lost in the empty air, a glass in hand, while the others sang around a cracked, out-of-tune guitar.

He crossed the tavern to reach him, waited for an invitation to sit down that never came, and then took a seat on a stool. The clamor of the merrymaking was deafening. A tavern down a narrow lane near the harbor on a Saturday night.

He looked at him for a long time, then he said:

"You could at least say hello to me. Do you know the risk I'm running, coming here? They could see me."

The other man replied, slurring his words, without lifting his gaze from the empty air.

"Well, who asked you to run that risk? Go on, get out of here. That's what you do best, the lot of you."

The newly arrived man slammed his fist on the table, making the bottle clink.

"And what you do best is whine and complain. I'm here to ask you just one question: Was it you? I have to hear it from your lips."

"I don't know what you're talking about," the drunk murmured. "And I'm not interested to find out. I told you before, get out of here and leave me alone."

The music broke off suddenly and two men started arguing furiously. The tavernkeeper moved fast, grabbing them both by the shoulders and tossing them out into the street. The guitarist resumed playing.

"So, was it you? The wife, Anto' . . . was that necessary, the wife, too? And did it have to be done that way?"

In the eyes of the man who had been called Antonio there was a gleam of interest.

"What are you talking about? Speak plainly!"

"I can't tell if you're toying with me or not. All things considered, maybe it's better that I not know. So let's just pretend that you don't know anything, and I'll go ahead and tell you. Yesterday morning Garofalo and his wife were found murdered. Stabbed to death, the pair of them. Is that clear, now? Now you know. If I were you, I'd get out of town; the first freighter for America, and it's goodnight Irene. That's what I came here to tell you, and now my conscience is clear. Good night, Anto'. You can finish getting drunk now."

He stood up and left, shoving his way through the drunken dancers.

Antonio sat there, his gaze once again lost in the darkness. He gently shook his head and murmured:

"This, too. This, too, you stole from me. Damn your soul."

X

The week before Christmas the center of the city became one huge marketplace; and police headquarters was right in the center of the center. To reach their office Ricciardi and Maione now had to pass hundreds of beggars, lottery sellers, junkmen, water carriers, shoeshine boys, all busy trying to steal their rivals' clients. The air was rife with odors, the smell of fried foods, pizza, macaroni, seafood, and candied almonds. You had to take care not to step on the merchandise that was laid out on filthy sheets on the ground: vases, glasses, silverware, and other utensils.

Maione had to dance a pretty elaborate jig, on the toe tips of his boots, to keep from stepping on the open hand, resting on the pavement, of a begging gypsy girl.

"Damn it, it's becoming impossible to even get through here on foot! And then, all these wonderful smells, how is a poor devil supposed to eat only at meals, and not in continuously?"

Ricciardi, thanks to his considerably smaller build, managed to maneuver with less difficulty.

"Christmas is conspiring against us, too. This investigation is going to be no easy matter, let me tell you. We're going to wear out a lot of shoe leather, and we're going to have to make our way through this market more than once."

When they got to the office, they found, waiting for them at the foot of the staircase, none other than Ponte, assistant to the deputy chief of police Garzo, head of the mobile squad. Like almost the entire staff at police headquarters, Ponte was convinced that Ricciardi brought bad luck, that he had some obscure link to the devil or some other dark deity: because of the unorthodox way he conducted his investigations; because of his complete lack of friends, or of even rudimentary communication with any of his colleagues aside from Maione; because of his disinterest in advancing his career, in spite of his many successes.

Strange, inexplicable things. Which for Ponte, a cowardly and superstitious little man, translated to a simple imperative: to avoid, as much as was possible, having anything to do with him. And to avoid looking into his incredible green eyes, which, as far as he could tell, were a direct portal to hell itself.

"*Buongiorno*, Commissario. Brigadier . . ."

Maione made no effort to conceal his repulsion for that policeman who had chosen to become the deputy police chief's butler; and, knowing the reason why the man spoke without looking his superior officer in the eye, a superior officer of whom he was very fond, Maione became openly hostile.

"Well, look who just crawled out of the sewer. What do you want, Ponte? We're busy, we're working a murder, if you can remember what that is."

Ponte let the irony fall flat; he was a master at sidestepping fights. Looking at a vague point on the floor, he said:

"I know, I know, Brigadie'. And that's exactly why I'm here. The deputy chief of police would like to see you both immediately."

"Incredible: we still don't really know what happened, and Garzo's already asking for a report. Let's get it over with and go see him immediately. That way we can get to work."

The deputy chief of police Angelo Garzo felt certain that he possessed a superior talent for diplomacy. He'd built his career on it, on his diplomacy, although the colleagues he'd surpassed—thanks to various whispering campaigns and personal favors leveraged through influence and connections—might well have seen matters differently.

To tell the truth, his wife's blood ties to the prefect of nearby Salerno had also played a role. But Garzo preferred to see his personal qualities and determination to reach the top as the chief factors in his professional trajectory.

As he waited for Ricciardi he shot a glance at himself in the mirror, and he liked what he saw. His mustache was his latest innovation. He'd given it plenty of thought. He didn't want to give the impression that he was someone who took excessive care when it came to grooming; those types are usually loafers, he'd decided. Then, as his sideburns started to frost over with a pepper-and-salt coloration, he gradually came to the conclusion that a mustache would make a perfect companion piece, endowing him with distinction and authority, and he'd nurtured it like a rose garden. The result, he had to admit, was quite satisfactory.

Ah, Ricciardi, Ricciardi. His albatross and his prized possession. Uncontrollable, independent, undisciplined; but also a guarantee of success. With the inestimable added advantage of being entirely indifferent about the advancement of his career. In other words, Ricciardi had no interest in taking his job the way that Garzo, in fact, had set his sights on the police chief's. This meant that Garzo could claim the commissario's brilliant sleuthing as his own in the eyes of his superiors, especially those at the ministry in Rome.

Certainly, more than once they'd had a hard time of it: that time that someone murdered the great tenor who was a personal friend of Il Duce, for instance; and even though he had a magnificent confession safely in the bag, Ricciardi had insisted on continuing to investigate until he'd established that the singer was anything but a sterling individual. Vezzi, his name had been. And his widow, who was friends with Il Duce's daugher, had later come to live in Naples; Garzo suspected that she'd fallen for Ricciardi of all people, the Good Lord alone knew why.

In other words, he was a tiger that had to be ridden, this commissario with his unsettling green eyes. And Garzo was the man to ride him, especially now that he had a new mustache.

Ponte knocked discreetly and poked his head into Garzo's office.

"Dottore, Commissario Ricciardi and Brigadier Maione, as you requested."

Maione shot him a venomous glare and hissed:

"Well, look at that, a talking lapdog. But can it bow?"

Garzo put on a jovial, conciliatory air.

"Oh, here he is, the man of the hour! *Caro, carissimo* Ricciardi, *prego*, come in and have a seat. Brigadier, *buongiorno*."

Ricciardi entered but remained standing.

"*Buongiorno*, Dottore. You'll have to excuse us, but we don't have much time. We're investigating a double homicide, and as you've always taught me, the first forty-eight hours are crucial."

The deputy chief of police's jaw dropped. How dare he, this ridiculous underling, come in and tell him that he didn't have time for him? Diplomacy, he thought. Remember to be diplomatic.

"In fact, that's exactly what I wanted to talk to you about. Ponte informed me that it was during your shift that the call came in for the Garofalo case."

Addressing Ponte, who was gazing at the ceiling with great interest, Maione murmured:

"Ah, nothing eludes the notice of the secret police."

"He—by which I mean Garofalo, of course—was an officer of the port militia," Garzo went on.

"A centurion, to be exact. Which would correspond . . ."

Ricciardi broke in:

". . . to the rank of captain, from what we've been told."

Garzo smiled, pleasantly surprised.

"I see that the infallible machinery of the mobile squad has already been set in motion. Now, tell me, what do you know about the port militia?"

Ricciardi shrugged his shoulders. He hadn't taken his hands out of his overcoat pockets, except to push back the rebellious lock of hair that kept falling over his forehead.

"We know that it's in charge of the movement of cargo and the regulation of fishing."

"Precisely," said Garzo, with a smile of approval. "Which, in a major seaport like the one we live in, makes it one of the most important police agencies."

Maione furrowed his brow.

"Police? I thought that they were only concerned with administrative irregularities."

The deputy chief of police wasn't pleased to have a mere noncommissioned officer worm his way into the conversation, but he was determined not to be rude.

"No, they provide support as an allied police agency to the coast guard when it comes to fishing and freight, with identical jurisdiction and responsibilities, even if they don't possess their own watercraft. In any case, the point is this: like any other agency under the command of the national volunteer militia, the port militia is a branch of the *fascio*, the national Fascist party. They report to the Blackshirts, and the Blackshirts report to Rome."

Ricciardi smirked.

"I'm beginning to understand. This means that our dead centurion, Emanuele Garofalo, is quite the excellent cadaver."

Garzo stiffened his jaw: a gesture that worked especially well since he'd grown his mustache, and one that he'd practiced repeatedly in the mirror.

"I don't know what you're trying to say with that tone: but yes, it's true, this is an important murder. The man was spoken of as a likely future consul, I'm told. He'd been promoted for special merits, and he was widely respected for his integrity and sense of duty."

There was a moment of silence, during which Ricciardi scratched his chin.

"I'm sorry, Dottore. Are you trying to offer me some unofficial advice?"

Garzo began to lose his patience.

"I have no unofficial advice for you. I just wanted to tell you that . . . well, to make a long story short, we've just received a dispatch from Rome that unofficially advises"—Garzo faltered as he realized that he'd used the same phrase twice in two completely contradictory sentences—"that is, that suggests that we conduct the investigation with great care and caution."

Ricciardi hadn't moved a muscle, but Maione knew that he was enjoying himself immensely.

"I'll devote great care to the investigation, Dottore, as I'm sure you know. The same amount of care that we devote to every investigation. But caution? What exactly do we need to be cautious about?"

Garzo felt as if he had his back to the wall. He stroked his mustache with his forefinger, but that offered scarce comfort.

"Caution, caution. Using caution to avoid stepping on certain toes, as you have the unfortunate habit of doing; to avoid being arrogant, to keep from annoying prominent citizens. For once in your life, Ricciardi, caution!"

The commissario bowed his head.

"Don't worry about a thing, Dottore. We'll use all our . . . caution. May we go?"

With the unpleasant sensation that he'd been beaten once again, though he couldn't quite put his finger on what game they'd been playing, Garzo waved his hand in annoyance and dismissed them.

On his way out, ostensibly by accident, Maione stepped on Ponte's foot, who took it without so much as a whimper.

XI

I've decided: this year I'm going to make another hill. I'll put it right over here, to the side, like Posillipo with the Vomero. That way I can make the countryside, the flock of sheep, a few houses lit up from within. The children like that—lambs and shepherds.

Maybe it won't be as densely populated as what's already there, but that doesn't matter. It's like the city, after all: there are some parts with more people and other places with less.

I don't even have to rebuild the structure with wooden sticks; all it takes is a slightly larger piece of cork, the moss for the grass, and a few wire trees. Here's the cork. I'll have to cut it, to make a rectangle to nail down.

The knife is in my hand. And I think of flesh.

Flesh isn't like cork: it's so easy to cut, so very easy. All it takes is one quick clean slash. The problem is making up your mind to cut it.

But now I know how it works. You lay the blade down, and then you press.

The flesh takes in the blade, it's elastic; it gives a little.

But then the blade cuts through the surface.

And that's when you can no longer turn back.

XII

Maione was frothing with fury.

"That idiotic buffoon. He wants to tell us how to do our jobs! How dare he? Him and that incompetent Ponte, as God is my witness, one of these days I'll slam my fist into his head so hard I'll make him forget his address! And another thing, does he think that those scraps of whore-bush he's grown on his upper lip have somehow made him any less of a moron?"

Ricciardi, sunk comfortably in his old leather office chair behind his desk, was fiddling pensively with his paperweight, made from a fragment of mortar shell.

"On the contrary, this time more than ever before, good old Garzo has been a great help to us. He's given us an important lead, you know."

Maione wasn't ready to calm down.

"Commissa', that guy's never going to give us any useful information, because he himself is a completely useless individual. Did I tell you that Antonelli, who was temporarily assigned to switchboard duty, told me that he overheard him telling his wife on the phone: 'Ricciardi, he knows how to catch criminals because he understands the way they think. Which means that he's a criminal himself.' To justify the fact that he doesn't understand criminals, or anything else!"

"Think about it, Raffae'. The bodies are still warm, and the party apparatus has already sprung into action. Garzo does nothing on his own initiative, ever, unless somebody tells him to. So why did the militia intervene immediately? I have a feeling that the stroll we need to take over to the barracks where Garofalo worked is going to provide us with some interesting pieces of information."

Maione scratched his head.

"You think? Then we'd better get strolling, sooner rather than later. That's what you always say, isn't it, that the first few hours are the most important, no?"

Livia Lucani, the widow Vezzi, was thoroughly enjoying the Christmas atmosphere in her new city.

All of the qualities and details that made Naples so unique and interesting multiplied a hundredfold this time of year. Waking up to the calls of the strolling vendors, the noise rising from the streets, the songs. And the smells, the thousands of pots bubbling busily away, the thousands of frying pans sizzling, the pastry shops competing to present their masterpieces. Everyone had dreamed up a calling, a profession; every one of them was trying to eke out a living.

Livia's impression was one of generalized good cheer, but with a strain of sadness running through it. It was as if the citizens of that special place were constantly telling one another, It's hard, terribly terribly hard. But we'll make it all the same.

Just the day before she'd spotted a strange individual from the window of the car, a man wearing a bicorne hat à la Napoléon Bonaparte, a long, loose coat, a thousand chains of all sizes as well as fake medals, and a brightly colored walking stick with bells on the end of it. He was walking along with an eccentric gait, hopping and leaping, followed by the usual procession of barefoot urchins. He was shouting something that Livia couldn't make out.

When she'd asked her driver just who that character might be, he'd replied with a wry laugh:

"Signo', that's the Pazzariello. He's a sort of walking newspaper, a town crier. He goes through every street in the quarter to announce that a new shop has just opened, or maybe that someone's lost their dog and is looking for it, or that a young couple is finally getting married. He announces his news singing and dancing, and dressed the way you see him, so that he's sure to attract attention."

Livia saw four women dressed in black emerge from a *basso*, one of the dark, dank street-level apartments of the poor; they listened attentively to what the Pazzariello had to say, burst out laughing, and went back inside. Over the door of the *basso* hung a black cloth. The driver didn't miss his passenger's observation.

"Ah, Signora, no one can resist the Pazzariello; even if they're holding a wake for the dead, they come out and listen to what he has to say."

Livia was falling in love with that city a little more with every day that passed. It was the city where, a little at a time, she'd rediscovered her will to live.

She still received very long phone calls, during which her Roman girlfriends tried to persuade her to return to the capital. When she had she left, four months ago now, she'd told them that she was just going to spend a few days at the seaside; and then she'd never gone back.

These days the idea of the social life she'd led for years in Rome was intolerable to her: false smiles, backbiting, gossip. An endless footrace to earn the favor of the newly powerful, a performance that was alien to her very nature. Precisely because of her indifference to that game, and her basic sincerity, she had become a close friend of Il Duce's rebellious daughter, a young woman who concealed her great emotional fragility behind an exterior of apparent aggressivity and masculine ways.

She was always delighted to receive Edda's phone calls, but not even she had been able to change Livia's mind: she had no intention of moving back to Rome. And since it amused Livia to watch everyone she knew rack their brains to figure out the real reason the Italian capital had lost its most enchanting dinner guest, the life and soul of Roman social life, she was careful to keep it to herself.

Making its way through the armies of strolling vendors and beggars, blasting its horn, Livia's car pulled into the courtyard of police headquarters. The guard at the door saluted deferentially, and the woman nodded. By now she was a habitual guest.

Without signaling to her chauffeur that she wished to get out of the car, she started counting under her breath. When she got to eight, Garzo appeared, panting, having burst through the main door that led to the offices without even an overcoat.

"Signora, why, what an honor, what a pleasure! You're a ray of sunlight in our day. We're certainly very lucky to have you as our visitor."

Livia took the deputy chief of police's proffered arm.

"*Caro* Dottore, believe me, the pleasure is all mine. And to be welcomed by such a gallant gentleman really is a delight. But do my eyes deceive me? You've grown a mustache! It looks just wonderful on you."

Garzo seemed embarrassed.

"Well, you know, Signora, as one gets older it's sometimes a good idea to try to look a little more authoritative, don't you think?"

Livia laughed.

"And authority's what you care about most, isn't it?"

"Absolutely right. Those juvenile delinquents who report to me, it's no easy matter to keep them in line. I was just saying so to your friend Ricciardi and his brigadier."

Livia immediately turned serious.

"Why, is there some problem? He was determined to return

to the job such a short time after the accident; he won't listen to anybody but himself."

"Yes, he's one hard-headed individual, *una bella capa tosta*, as we like to say here in Naples. And in every sense of the phrase, if you follow me. In any case, you won't find him here, he just stepped out with Maione a few minutes ago. He's working on a fairly sensitive investigation. As you may certainly have the opportunity to inform your friends in Rome, if the topic happens to come up, we always pay the closest and most careful attention to anything that concerns Fascist Party members."

Livia's disappointment at having missed Ricciardi had ruined her mood so suddenly and completely that she hadn't heard a word that Garzo had said.

"Ah, I understand. Well, perhaps you'll do me the courtesy of telling him . . . no, don't tell him a thing. Perhaps I'll come back later."

Garzo put on his most dazzling smile.

"Why, of course, Signora. He'll no doubt be very happy to see you."

As she found herself in her car again moving slowly through the crowd, Livia felt her good mood returning. And she decided that the real reason she'd moved down here had to be that man with the sea-green eyes, those eyes so full of despair; that man she'd finally succeeded in holding in her arms just two months earlier.

What would her girlfriends back in Rome say, if they ever found out?

XIII

While out on the streets the chaos that preceded Christmas was suffocating and anarchic, inside the port the picture was quite the opposite. The freight traffic and the passenger traffic were kept neatly separated, and thousands of people worked efficiently, moving as if guided by a shrewdly conceived choreography.

The port was the nation's largest and it seemed to be aware of its unrivaled standing. Crews of longshoremen crossed paths with the crews of freighters newly landed or about to ship out, dozens of stevedores were continuously at work loading or unloading immense cargo holds, huge trucks and horse-drawn carts lined up at the exit, the draft horses snorting vapor into the wind as their drivers waited for their loads to be checked. Passengers debarking from the huge ocean liners were greeted by lovely uniformed auxiliaries stationed at the pedestrian exits. Maione thought of the shock they'd have once they left the port and found themselves in the terrifying disorder and noise of the city itself.

Ricciardi walked quickly, hands in his pockets and hair tousled, his gaze fixed straight ahead of him. Aside from the human bustle and activity all around him, other beings appeared to the eyes of his soul.

A young man stood on the wharf, his arm shorn clean off by a whipping cable, the blood pumping out powerfully through the open artery with each heartbeat, murmuring: *Mamma, Mamma, help me, Mamma.* A man sitting on the ground next to a freight-unloading site, currently occupied by a team of stevedores cheerfully singing a popular ditty, had been crushed by a falling crate or something of the like: there was a vast depression in his chest and it was clear from the angle of his head that his spinal cord had been severed. He was muttering: *This last one, I'll just do this last one and then I'll head home.* What a shame, mused the commissario. If the one before had been your last for the day, maybe now you'd be with your children. You just wanted too much. Too bad for you. And maybe too bad for me, too, he thought to himself.

Among the many uniformed men supervising the harbor's operations, it was easy to identify the members of the port militia: the gray-green felt hat, the jacket of the same color with a half-belt in back. Active, precise, energetic. As Ricciardi made his way to the barracks with Maione, he thought that a military organization parallel to the administration of the state but answerable to a political party was potentially dangerous. But then it was also true that the party in question had won the most recent elections with more than ninety percent of the votes, and so it was hard to tell the Fascist party apart from the state itself.

As far as he was concerned, and as he tried to make Dr. Modo understand whenever he tried to pull Ricciardi into one of his angry anti-Fascist tirades, politics was entirely uninteresting. He believed that, when all was said and done, the root of all problems was human nature: and for that there was no remedy.

The militia barracks was not centrally located, but it was located strategically, not far from the tracks along which the freight trains ran from the docked ships up to the station. The civilian personnel tended to steer clear of the place, perhaps instinctively. They seemd to prefer to take the long way around rather than walk along the barracks walls, which only added to the sense of its extraneousness from the colorful world of the Naples harbor.

The two policemen walked around the building's perimeter, in search of the main entrance. It was a three-story building, spartan and solid, in keeping with the architecture of the regime. Over the entrance, between the second and third floors, was a large sign: MUSSOLINI BARRACKS. Ricciardi remembered the inauguration, years earlier: Il Duce had come to Naples in person, and Garzo had been so anxious that he had almost tipped over into hysteria, as was typical of him on such high-pressure occasions.

The militiaman at the front door asked them to identify themselves, then muttered something into a modern-looking intercom; Maione thought sadly of the miles of stairs and hallways that the officers were forced to walk at police headquarters just to deliver routine messages. A minute later, a junior officer appeared and, raising his arm in a rigid Roman salute, welcomed them and introduced himself.

"First squad leader Catello Precchia. Please, come this way."

The militiaman headed up the staircase at a run. Maione and Ricciardi exchanged a glance of sympathetic amusement, and followed him at as quick a pace as they could manage; the commissario thought he could hear the brigadier inwardly cursing as he struggled to make it up the steps. On their way up they crossed paths with a large number of soldiers running at the same enthusiastic clip, each of them snapping a sharp Roman salute. Ricciardi spitefully wished that one of them would trip in his eagerness and tumble all the way down to the ground floor. He'd have gladly pulled out his wallet and put cash on the barrelhead to see such a sight.

The first squad leader came to a sudden halt in front of a tall dark hardwood door, where an usher stood at attention next to a desk. The man didn't even have a chair. The militiaman knocked just once at the door and then showed them in.

The office they'd just entered was enormous. The marble floor had no other decoration apart from small tiles of various colors. On one wall hung an outsized painting of the Port of Naples during the Middle Ages and, on the opposite wall, there was a large-format print of a photograph of Il Duce inaugurating the barracks. Behind a massive desk made out of the most magnificent wood hung the two regulation portraits: the head of government and the king. In one corner, next to a large French window that led out to a balcony, stood a gilt flagstaff with an elaborate spear tip, and from it hung the Italian tricolor with the Savoy shield.

No cross in sight; around here, Ricciardi mused, they worship only one god. But he noticed with surprise, and with a hint of disquiet, that partly concealed behind the open curtain there was a painting of Saint Sebastian much like the one at his boarding school, and which he'd been reminded of just the day before, as he stood looking at Garofalo's corpse.

From the far end of the room, an officer walked toward him. The junior officer who had accompanied them performed a synchronized heel-click and Roman salute that was nearly perfect, right down to the hiss of his gloved hand whisking through the air. The officer returned the salute absentmindedly, then turned to speak to Ricciardi and Maione.

"Please, have a seat. I'm Consul Freda di Scanziano, commandant of the second legion of the port militia. Precchia, you may go, *grazie*."

"Yes sir, Signor Consul. I'll be right outside the door, if you have need of me."

Another heel-click with whisking hand followed by a second heel-click, about-face, and door-click. Maione decided that the first squad leader would have made an excellent tango dancer if he had chosen to pursue a different career.

The consul looked like an actor out of the moving pictures, the type that's usually cast as a grand duke or the father of the wealthy young noblewoman who falls in love with a rootless but good-hearted young man. All except for his eyes, looking out from under the fez emblazoned with the Fascist lictor's staff, anchor, and crown, which expressed an unmistakable curiosity and intelligence.

The gray-green uniform, with a sky-blue sash hanging diagonally across the chest, was bedecked with a dozen medals.

"Well, gentlemen: what can I do for you?"

Ricciardi and Maione were caught off guard. They'd been ready to work their way through various ranks of officers, from junior to senior, and to be thwarted by a wall of curt sentences and owlish silences. They certainly hadn't expected to be received immediately, and directly by the consul and commandant of the legion himself.

Maione was the first to recover.

"Signor Consul, thank you for agreeing to see us. I'm Brigadier Maione of the mobile squad of the royal police, and this is my direct superior, Commissario Ricciardi. We're here about . . ."

The consul interrupted him:

"Yes, yes, Brigadier. Unfortunately, I know why you're here. And I'd like to thank you first of all for what you're doing to bring justice to bear on the cowardly murderers who have made that poor little girl an orphan."

Ricciardi studied the officer's face, trying to work out his real intentions; but all he saw was what the man's words had already expressed.

"Signor Consul, that's why we're here. You must be well aware that the work that Garofalo . . . that Centurion Garofalo did, his work could have been . . . in fact, in all likelihood *was* the reason for which he and his wife were so savagely murdered. That's why we're starting from this office. We'd be grateful for any information about him: names of colleagues, a list of the most recent cases he'd worked on, any eventual disagreements or quarrels, threats he might have received. Everything."

Freda nodded. Then, unexpectedly, he got to his feet and, hands clasped behind his back, walked over to the balcony, from which could be seen the salt water of the harbor. The cargos of several ships were being unloaded.

"Commissario, what do you know about our organization? About the port militia, I mean to say?"

Ricciardi looked at Maione, then shrugged his shoulders.

"No more than what everyone knows. That you oversee the loading and unloading of freight as well as fishing. That you're a corps of judicial police, operating in the port and along the coast."

"No, that's not what I was asking. How we recruit, do you know anything about that? Who we are, in other words."

"I know that young men can opt to join the militia, as an alternative to the draft. That you're paid a daily indemnity, which makes it easier for you to staff your ranks. That you're fairly selective as far as the criteria for enlistment are concerned."

Freda continued to look out at the sea.

"Yes, everything you've said is true. But there's more." He turned to look at his two guests, without moving from where he stood by the balcony. "You know that this is a relatively new corps, founded only in 1923. In the immediate aftermath of the March on Rome, in other words. 'Mussolini's military prosthesis,' as one journalist described it. Of course, that journalist is no longer writing."

"I imagined as much," Maione murmured.

Freda smiled.

"Exactly right. Il Duce said that *squadrismo*, the uncontrolled strong-arm activism which was the heart and soul of the March on Rome and of the very birth of the Fascist movement, must be kept alive. And so he founded this corps, the militia, which was then divided into its various forms: the forestry militia, the railroad militia, the postal and telegraphic militia. And us, the port militia."

Ricciardi wondered where the consul was heading with all this.

"Alongside the volunteers, who often had no military experience, and the pioneers of Fascism, who were full of ardor but also, from certain points of view, potentially dangerous, it was decided that genuine soldiers were needed to lead the corps. I for example was a captain in the Italian navy. I had commanded a cruiser, and my life was out there, on the open sea. You can't imagine how much I miss it, the fresh salt air."

"If I'm not being indiscreet, Consul, why did you accept?" Maione asked.

"Do you really need to ask, Brigadier?" Freda replied, looking out again at the sea. "There are certain . . . proposals that you can't refuse. I was told in no uncertain terms that in any case I'd be assigned to administrative duties, on shore. And that my indemnity would be sufficient, if I chose to accept, to keep my family in a manner far better than what they'd been accustomed to. I was told that it would only be for a few months, perhaps a year, and then I could return to sea, with a more prestigious command. But it's been six years now, and I don't see any changes in the offing."

Maione and Ricciardi exchanged another glance. They'd hadn't even expected to be received, and now here they were, the recipients of the personal confidences of the commandant of the legion.

"This is just to make it clear to you that ours is no ordinary corps of volunteers, much less an auxiliary structure attached to the port authority. Other . . . organizations collaborate with us, and report to the same high officials, in Rome. We have very special duties, of which not everyone is aware."

Ricciardi wondered once again just where the consul was heading with this line of conversation.

"Forgive me, Signor Consul; our visit today has nothing to do with any inquiry into your operations here, nor into those of the late Signor Garofalo. We just wanted to ask a few questions to find out whether anyone had any resentment toward him. That's all."

Freda nodded, in the direction of the water. Then he turned around and looked at the commissario, expressionless.

"How are you feeling, Ricciardi? The accident on the Day of the Dead didn't have any unfortunate consequences, aside from the wound to the back of your head that Dr. Modo sewed up with six stitches?"

XIV

Last night I dreamed. It must have been because of all that wine.

I dreamed that I was climbing the stairs to your apartment; that strange doorman was out cold, drunk as usual, and he didn't see me go by. My steps didn't make a sound, as if I were barefoot.

I was knocking at your door. Your wife came to answer; she recognized me, and she smiled at me. Oh, how furious that smile made me: it was as if she didn't know what had happened, what you had done to me.

I dreamed that I had the knife in my hand, the regulation knife. And I got your wife out of the way with a single slash, without pleasure, but also without remorse. Then I found you, in your bedroom, with my bloody knife dripping on the floor. And you looked at me, and you laughed, unafraid. You were telling me that that's life, that those who can take will take. That's what you always said.

And I stabbed you. Once, ten times, a hundred times I stabbed you. And every cut was an arrow, just like the ones piercing Saint Sebastian's body, you remember? We wondered that a hundred times, why they had chosen Saint Sebastian.

At the end of the dream, you were dead, but you went on laughing anyway. I woke up, and there was no blood on my hands.

God, what a lovely dream. It must have been the wine.

XV

A leaden silence followed the consul's words. From the window came the sound of a siren announcing an arrival or departure in the harbor.

Maione's mouth snapped shut and he swallowed with a gulp. Then he said:

"Just what is that supposed to mean? What do you know about the commissario's accident?"

Freda approached the desk and sat down calmly, then put on a pair of half-lens reading glasses with a gilt frame and, picking up a sheet of paper, read in a faint voice:

"Now, let's see: Raffaele Maione, fifty-one years of age. Promoted to brigadier five years ago. Three distinguished service citations, one meritorious service notice, and two favorable mentions. Congratulations, that's an outstanding record. Married to Signora Lucia Caputo, resident at Vico Concordia, 16. Five living children, three sons and two daughters. The eldest, Luca, likewise a member of the police force, deceased three and a half years ago in the line of duty, during a police roundup—I'm very sorry, please accept my condolences. Weaknesses: he likes to eat with gusto and drink, in moderation. There's also a note about a friend of yours, a signora who lives in Vico del Fico, the victim of a face-slashing in the spring of this year, but just a friend."

Maione had had the wind knocked out of him. He went on staring at the consul, wide-eyed and breathing heavily. The man went on.

"You're the favorite associate, the only one apparently, of Commissario Luigi Alfredo Ricciardi, thirty-one years of age, born in Fortino, in the province of Salerno, near the Lucania border. Your details, Commissario, are even more interesting. You're wealthy, quite wealthy indeed; but your funds, your farmland, and the properties you own in your hometown are all under the management of Rosa Vaglio, your childhood nanny, who also lives with you. All the same, a couple of foremen are embezzling freely; the poor woman can't catch everything. If you like, I have the names, and I'd be glad to give them to you."

Ricciardi looked the man in the face, expressionless, both hands clenching the armrests of his chair. Freda continued.

"Particularly brilliant on the job, no friendships with any of your colleagues as far as we know; in fact, they don't much like you, as far as we can tell, with the exception of Brigadier Maione here. No career ambitions, to the delight of your superior officer, Deputy Chief of Police Garzo, who is an incompetent."

Maione, who was just recovering, murmured:

"That's in the report, too?"

"Yes, that's in here, too. As well as the friendship . . . the devotion, I dare say . . . of the Signora Lucani Vezzi, who is a personal friend of the Mussolini family no less, and a former opera singer. That's something that plays to your advantage; whereas something that plays to your distinct disadvantage, in contrast—and in fact it's even underscored in red—is your friendship with Dr. Bruno Modo, suspected of militant anti-Fascism, though he is a respected doctor at the Pellegrini hospital. You have successfully solved a number of noteworthy cases, such as for instance the murder of the tenor Vezzi, who was the husband of the lady I just mentioned; the case of the Duchess Musso di Camparino; and so on. I imagine everything here is correct."

Ricciardi replied promptly:

"Why this display of information, Consul? What is it you're trying to tell us?"

Freda held his gaze for quite some time, then replied:

"This report, addressed to my personal attention, was delivered by a man dressed in black, about an hour ago. He told the guard downstairs that you'd be here in forty minutes, and you arrived exactly thirty-eight minutes later. The man said that it would be best to receive you immediately. This is how they do it, every time: to report some fraud that bears investigation, to alert us to some transaction that might appear aboveboard but which in fact conceals something. Other times, we're only asked to monitor a shipment, or else the movements of a particular person: a specific name departing for a given destination, someone else passing through the port."

Maione was disconcerted.

"And they don't even tell you why? And who are they, for that matter? Who are these people who know everybody's business?"

"No one's ever told me explicitly, Brigadier. Neither me nor any of the other commandants of the legion. Officially they don't exist, and they never will; but in reality, they are the ones pulling the strings of a great many marionettes. Commissario, I simply wanted to show you that this murder, which took place here, on our home turf, is a much more serious case even than it appears; because it's actually an assault on the uniform, this uniform, and against the very regime this uniform represents."

Ricciardi drilled in.

"So just what is all this supposed to mean? In what way should the scope of this crime weigh on our investigation?"

Freda fiddled with his spectacles, then replied:

"If, as we believe, the murder has to do with Garofalo's work, the performance of his duties, then I would ask you to report that to us; that would give us a chance to put things back where they belong, to make sure that the outside world doesn't get the impression that there might be any flaws in our operation. That would be serious, very grave indeed."

Ricciardi shook his head.

"So that you can do what, exactly, Signor Consul? To give you, or the gentleman dressed in black who brings you these dispatches, an opportunity to beat the law to the punch, thus avoiding a trial that might make public some inconvenient details and lead to riots in the streets?"

Freda suddenly slammed his fist down on his desk, causing pens, inkwell, and blotter to rattle. Maione leaped in his chair, while Ricciardi, as usual, didn't bat an eye.

"Ah, then you refuse to understand! Let me explain to you: This is the most important port in the nation, the busiest in terms of both passengers and freight. We must supervise the wharves, the warehouses, the adjoining waters, and the ocean liners and steamers as they arrive and depart. It is our duty to monitor all the cargo before it's loaded aboard, including railroad cars; we perform political surveillance on both crews and passengers, and we're responsible for public safety during boarding and disembarking. We are the first face of the nation's armed forces that foreigners encounter, and the last when they leave. When one of our officers is murdered, it isn't a common street crime; it's an affair of state!"

Ricciardi didn't change his tone.

"And what is that supposed to mean? Every murder victim is a very serious matter to us. Every single murder victim screams out for help, and demands that we set things right. If you want to push us aside, you only need to call Rome and arrange for the case to be assigned to the military police. Why don't you?"

Now Freda had lost his aplomb.

"You know perfectly well that that's not possible!" he

roared. "On paper my men are volunteers, no different in status from any other civilians. This was a choice made by the party to avoid being subjected to the rules of recruitment that apply to the army and the navy. Also, Garofalo wasn't murdered in the barracks, he was killed at home, in his bed. This places the murder entirely outside of our jurisdiction, blast it!"

Ricciardi decided to be conciliatory. He'd appreciated the consul's approach, the way he'd shared with them the difficulty in which he found himself.

"Don't worry, Consul. I assure you that, if and when we capture the guilty party, you will be informed immediately; you have my word on that. But only after their arrest, let me be perfectly clear, not before. I don't want to find myself with a suspicious suicide on my hands. Then it will become a matter to be settled between you and the highest levels at police headquarters, and knowing them I have no doubt that you'll be able to come to an understanding; I'm uninterested in communicating with press outlets and public opinion."

Maione shot him a look. He was accustomed to not immediately grasping the commissario's strategies, but this struck him as too far removed from the principles that he shared and understood. It was obvious: Garzo would consider it a heaven-sent opportunity to gift wrap the murderers and hand them over to the secret police or who knows who else, as long as it meant a pat on the back from on high. And so much for justice.

The consul nodded his head slowly: the solution offered by Ricciardi struck him as acceptable.

"All right. But I'm warning you, Ricciardi: don't try to wriggle out of your end of the bargain. It says here that you're a man of your word, but this matter is much bigger than this legion. Remember that we will stop at nothing in our quest to preserve our role."

Ricciardi nodded agreement.

"Fine. Then we have a deal. We want full freedom of action within your organization, though. We'll have to speak with those who worked with Garofalo, as well as those who knew his professional history, how he advanced his career, what his past was like: the people he talked to, who he confided in. And what kind of investigations he worked on, which ones he'd been working on recently."

Freda stood up.

"Yes, of course. I'll call someone right away who can accompany you to Garofalo's office and answer all these questions. Unfortunately, I wasn't in direct contact with him very often and, to tell you the truth, I didn't much like him. He was too cloying and obsequious; I find that people like that are always dangerous. Then there was the matter of his promotion . . . But Seniore Spasiano, Garofalo's direct superior officer, can tell you all about that. I'll summon him now, you can even wait here if you like."

Ricciardi got to his feet in turn.

"*Grazie*, Signor Consul; we'll wait just outside the door, we don't want to intrude any longer."

They saluted; then on the way out the commissario stopped and asked:

"Sorry, one last thing: Why the painting of Saint Sebastian?"

The consul, who already had the intercom in hand, seemed surprised at the question; then he turned and looked at the painting, as if he were seeing it for the first time.

"Ah, that? He's the patron saint of the national volunteer militia. Only the Good Lord knows why."

XVI

Maione exploded the minute they were alone in the hallway.

"Commissa', this one you're really going to have to explain to me," he hissed, looking out of the corner of his eye at the usher, who stood to attention, motionless behind the desk, some ten feet away. "Why would you promise to alert these fanatics when we catch the murderers? We might as well just give them a call when we think we know who it is, that way we can save ourselves the effort and risk of carrying out the arrest ourselves. For all we know, it was one of them: if so, they can sing the song and accompany themselves on guitar. What could be more convenient?"

Ricciardi smirked.

"You see, Raffae', I had to think on my feet. It occurred to me that if I told him no, as would normally have been my instinct, they'd simply take us off the case and some innocent citizen might have paid the price. These folks aren't kidding around: if there's the slightest doubt people just vanish and no one ever knows what became of them. So I decided it was the best course of action to make that promise, so that it might allow us to find out what happened and who did it. Besides, as you know, once we've made the arrest, what happens next is out of our hands anyway; and do you think that someone like Garzo wouldn't do his best to make these maniacs happy, if there was anything he could do for them?"

Maione stood shaking his big head, still unconvinced.

"I don't know, Commissa'; your line of reasoning makes sense, I can't argue with you, but I just don't like cutting deals with these people. They scare me. Did you hear how they knew every detail of our lives? Even what happened with poor Filomena; to hear them tell it, she was practically my lover. And all about your financial situation, and Signora Rosa. Those damned spies!"

Ricciardi sighed.

"They must have a vast network of informers. They even have someone at police headquarters; otherwise, how could they have known that we were coming here?"

The question went unanswered, because the sharp sound of heels clicking just a few inches away made them both jump.

"Seniore Renato Spasiano, at your orders. The Signor Consul told me to take you to the office of Centurion Garofalo and to answer your questions. Please, come with me."

And he set off, it goes without saying, at a run. Maione rolled his eyes.

The office where Garofalo had worked was on the third floor, the top floor of the barracks building. The window looked out on the area opposite the wharves, offering a grim panorama of dead tracks and abandoned railcars. To make up for that, the noises that reached it from both the port and the street were quite muffled.

There was another officer seated at the desk, and when Seniore Spasiano entered the room this officer leaped to his feet with the usual perfect heel-click and Roman salute.

"This is Platoon Leader Criscuolo. He's going over the cases that Centurion Garofalo was working on, for anything urgent that may require action. Go ahead, Criscuolo, you may speak freely. These gentlemen are from the mobile squad, and they're looking into the accident."

"The accident," thought Maione. "Accident," my foot.

Garofalo just slipped and fell on a knife. He slipped and fell on it a good thirty times.

Criscuolo, a strapping big man with a ridiculous-looking ultrathin black mustache, replied:

"Seniore, I've reviewed all the documentation on the cases still under way. As you know, Centurion Garofalo was in charge of monitoring small-scale fishing on the city coastline, an area that extends from the port to the island of Nisida. There are reports on inspection up to this month, as required, including the quantities of fish and an inspection of the fishing areas. Detailed lists of the equipment on the individual boats, minutes of the meetings of the district commission. Human error aside, I found no irregularities awaiting report."

Ricciardi broke in, as a fascinated Maione watched the movement of the mustache on Platoon Leader Criscuolo's upper lip, a mustache that seemed to move independently of the lip itself.

"Excuse me, but what does 'irregularities awaiting report' mean?"

Spasiano explained:

"As you may know, the legion performs a number of duties, among them, monitoring fishing. There are large fishing boats, the ones with crews consisting of many men, which, because of their size, operate here in the port, at specially designated wharves. Then there are the smaller boats, which is to say boats owned and operated by families, which dock at the beaches of the *borghi*, near Castel dell'Ovo, in Mergellina, in Bagnoli, and so on. Centurion Garofalo was assigned to inspect these small fishing boats. The platoon leader, who worked with him, has checked to see that the centurion didn't have any pending investigations, irregularities detected that had yet to be reported. It's important to be timely, to avoid giving those who have committed some violation the time to rectify it and thus elude further inquiry."

Ricciardi nodded, pensively.

"I understand. And had Centurion Garofalo recently reported any major irregularities, as a result of which major proceedings would have been undertaken against anyone?"

Spasiano tipped his head in Criscuolo's direction, passing him the ball. The mustache leaped and dived on the motionless lip, like a cat's whiskers.

"No, Signore. Little things, the kind of things you see all the time: non-regulation nets, minor incursions into private waters. Slight infractions. The centurion was highly respected and feared for his strictness; the fishermen knew it and toed the line."

Ricciardi turned and spoke once again to Spasiano.

"The Signor Consul, earlier, made some reference to Garofalo's promotion to centurion: to be exact, to the way in which that promotion was obtained. What can you tell me about that?"

The Seniore was caught off guard. He looked at Criscuolo, who, apart from a vibration that ran through his mustache, didn't move a muscle. He reddened, opened his mouth, and snapped it shut. Ricciardi decided to lend him a hand.

"The Signor Consul told me that I could ask you for any information that I might find useful. If there are problems, we can just go speak with him."

Maione smiled warmly. Ricciardi's ability to slip into the cracks of a given bureaucracy was unequaled. Spasiano blinked and gave in immediately.

"Garofalo was the deputy platoon leader. The corresponding rank in the army is second lieutenant. This means that he worked with a superior officer, an officer assigned to a specific area: a sector to be monitored, in other words."

He stopped, looking down at the toes of his boots. Ricciardi and Maione waited. Criscuolo moved a sheet of paper on the dead man's desk. From outside came the mournful sound of a siren, carried by the stiffening wind. Spasiano went on with his story.

"This officer was the platoon leader Antonio Lomunno. One of the youngest men to hold that rank, ready to be awarded another promotion. The inspection area he was assigned to was smuggling, a terrible problem especially where tobacco and spices are concerned, and with coffee in particular. They were a hardworking team, and they'd uncovered a lot of smuggling operations."

Another silence. This time they could hear Criscuolo sigh, a sigh accompanied by a quiver in his cat whiskers that didn't escape Maione's notice. The Seniore was clearly having a hard time continuing. His voice dropped an octave.

"One day, Garofalo knocked at the door of the consul's office, without even stopping to speak to the usher first. He said that he had something he needed to show someone, and that he could reveal it only in the presence of the highest officer of the legion. The consul summoned me as a witness, so that if needed I could testify concerning this act of insubordination. Garofalo announced that he had uncovered a large-scale coffee smuggling ring that had been active for many months, perhaps for years. He said that he'd informed his superior officer, Lomunno, of his discovery, but that he'd been told to say nothing about it."

Maione looked at Criscuolo and saw that the man was staring at Spasiano with a silent note of accusation in his eyes.

"Why would this Lomunno have ordered Garofalo not to say anything?" Ricciardi asked.

Spasiano went on.

"Exactly. The Signor Consul asked the same question. Garofalo reported that he'd even been threatened with disciplinary sanctions by his superior officer if he talked, and that he'd been unable to understand the reason under the circumstances. Later he said that he'd stopped some of the smugglers and that one of them, in order to gain his release, had declared that he paid a monthly sum to Lomunno in order to be allowed to continue his smuggling without interference."

Criscuolo sighed again.

"I'm sorry, but did this Garofalo produce even a shred of evidence?" Maione asked. "Or is it enough to lodge an accusation when you feel like it, from one day to the next?"

"Of course he did, Brigadier," Spasiano replied. "We're not savages. Foremost among our considerations was the fact that Lomunno's service record was perfect, as I've told you; he was one of the finest officers in the legion, skillful and knowledgeable, with great instincts and intelligence. But Garofalo said that the smuggler, on condition of anonymity, had revealed the exact date on which he paid his monthly kickback to Lomunno, and that as it happened it was that same day. Garofalo invited us to question the officer, who had just returned to the barracks from an inspection."

Maione sat openmouthed.

"And you believed him?"

Spasiano shrugged.

"What else could we do? The Signor Consul told Garofalo that, if his charges proved to be unfounded, he'd be punished with expulsion from the corps and that he might well face proceedings for defamation of an officer of the National Volunteer Militia."

"And what did he say in response?" asked Maione.

"He asked, 'And if it's true? What would be my reward?'"

Criscuolo puffed out his cheeks, then said:

"May I go, Seniore? I'll finish after my inspection, that way you can . . ."

"No, don't leave, Criscuolo," Spasiano replied. "It's better that someone else be present to hear the story I'm about to tell. The order comes from the consul, but still, this is privileged information."

"At your orders, Seniore."

Ricciardi had listened carefully to this exchange. Criscuolo seemed to be in some discomfort hearing the story, which, in any case, he must have known quite well. Spasiano continued.

"We were so sure that the accusation was false that the consul said in my presence, 'If it were true, he'd receive the maximum punishment allowable. Corruption is a cancer that the legion cannot allow to spread. You, on the other hand, would be promoted, for having had the courage to . . . to accuse an unworthy colleague."

A cold drizzle had started to fall, tapping against the windowpanes.

"And what happened?" asked Maione, more than anything else to break the silence.

"Lomunno was found in his office with a large sum of money on his person. In cash. He wasn't able to explain where that money had come from, and he was arrested. Garofalo's testimony was decisive, and Lomunno was dishonorably discharged from the militia and served a year and a half in prison."

Ricciardi had listened attentively.

"So what happened is that Garofalo ruined his superior officer and took his place."

"There's more. He took the post to which Lomunno was about to be promoted, the rank of centurion. To place that in the context of ranks in the army, his promotion was the equivalent of going from second lieutenant to captain, in a single leap and without respecting the years of minimum seniority for the ranks in question. It was something unprecedented."

Maione couldn't believe his ears.

"Excuse me, maybe I missed something. What did Lomunno say?"

"Of course, he swore he was an honest man, but he refused to reveal the provenance of that money. He said it was his, his whole life's savings, and that he was going to use it to finally buy a house of his own."

"So, really, wasn't it just his word against Garofalo's?"

"Yes, but no one carries some ten thousand lire in cash around with them. And in any case, it takes a lot less in this corps to merit disciplinary proceedings. His wife, when questioned by several of our officers, knew nothing about the money, and that was considered further evidence against him."

Ricciardi stared at Spasiano.

"There's more, isn't there? An epilogue."

Spasiano looked at Criscuolo, who in turn looked down at the floor. Maione had the impression that he was clenching his fists.

"While Lomunno was in prison, his wife killed herself. She threw herself off the balcony of their apartment, the day she learned they were being evicted. She left behind two children, who stayed with a neighbor woman until their father was released."

Wind and rain on the window, and the roar of the sea. Ricciardi thought to himself that, as usual, it was the innocents who paid the price.

"What became of them?"

Spasiano shrugged.

"These events date back three years, more or less. We don't have any more recent information, in part because, Commissario, I have to confess to you, we're not very fond of remembering it, and for more than one reason. First of all, we don't like to think that we were completely wrong in our evaluation of Lomunno, who was very well liked in the barracks. And, second, we don't like to think that one of our own officers, and one of the best, for that matter, might have been corrupt. But above all, though I would never admit this outside of this room, we don't like the way the matter ended."

Maione broke in.

"And you did nothing for the family of this Lomunno? The wife and children, what did they live on while he was in prison?"

The raw nerve. Criscuolo jerked his head up, started to say something, and then looked back down at the floor. Spasiano replied:

"No. It was as if we were dealing with lepers. None of us had the courage to give them a hand. We're all partly to blame for what happened."

Ricciardi brushed aside the lock of hair that had fallen over his forehead, with the usual quick swipe of his slender hand. Then he asked:

"Where are Lomunno and his children now?"

XVII

The little one was the first to notice, in spite of the rain and the wind, and the incessant roar of the waves.

"Papa, don't you hear? Someone's knocking at the door."

The man stopped what he was doing, set down the knife and the piece of wood he was carving, and went to open the door. When he saw who it was, he turned around and went back to the table, leaving the door wide open.

The visitor closed the door behind him. He looked around.

"Do you realize it's colder in here than it is outside? Can't you feel how freezing it is?"

The man had gone back to his carving.

"It's a hovel. It's drafty, the wind cuts right through the wood; and the fire goes out quickly, of course. What do you want? If you're cold, go home, where it's nice and warm. And take your conscience with you."

The visitor opened a bag he'd brought with him, pulled out some clothing, and gave it to the little girl.

"Here, Adelina, this red one's for you, it's a nice heavy sweater. The blue one ought to be Vittorio's size, you see if it fits him. And here are two wool hats, my wife made them, and two scarves. Make sure you bundle up, now."

The woodcarver barely looked up from the piece of wood he was working on.

"Who asked you for anything? When their mother needed you or any of my other so-called friends, where were you? And when she decided to . . ."

The other man broke in forcefully, his eyes darting to the children.

"Anto', for the love of God! That's enough! Have you lost your mind? In front of the children!"

"Why, didn't she do it in front of them? Not even she believed me, her own husband. Not even she had the strength to help me prove that I was telling the truth."

"Anto', listen to me. The trouble you're about to be in is serious. Today two policemen came in, a commissario and a brigadier. Smart people, very good at what they do. Spasiano got orders to tell them the whole story."

"Are you sure?"

"Of course I'm sure. I was right there. And they listened, and the first thing they asked when they'd heard everything was if we knew where you were."

Antonio Lomunno slammed the knife down on the table. The little girl, who was stirring a pot on the stove with a wooden spoon, jumped at the sound.

"Damn him, damn him! This thing will never end, never!"

Criscuolo took a step toward him.

"But you can say that you were out on the water when it happened. You can say that you were on the fishing boat, you can say . . ."

"'You can say'? But—that means you think I did it! And you don't realize that if I'd wanted to . . ."

He shot a quick glance at his son, who was staring at him openmouthed.

". . . I'd have done it then and there, on the spot, in front of everyone. That coward, that bastard. I'd have done it then, and goodnight Irene."

Criscuolo grabbed him by the arm, whispering with a hiss:

"Don't say that, even as a joke. You wouldn't be the man you are, if you'd done it. And we helped Maria, not enough, but we did help her, while you were locked up. We couldn't have done more than what we did; you know the way it works. If they'd seen us—and they were watching her all the time— they'd have taken us for accomplices, and we would have wound up like you. We had families, too, and we still do."

Lomunno looked at him, grinding his teeth, his eyes brimming over with tears.

"And you still have your families . . . And look at what I have, a poor little twelve-year-old girl who has to be a mother to her eight-year-old brother, because her father's out on the water trying to earn two pennies' worth of stale flour and a scrap of pilfered fish. That's my family."

"Yes, that's your family. And you need to care for your family, support them, because that's what they deserve, instead of going to the tavern to fry your brains and your liver with cheap wine. Most of all, you have to stay out of jail, because if you wind up behind bars again what's going to happen to these kids?"

Lomunno let himself drop back into his chair.

"All right. Tell me what you think I ought to do."

Criscuolo told him.

When he was done, Lomunno put his hands over his face.

"Do you realize what you're asking me to do? It's the same thing that he did to me."

Criscuolo, sitting next to him, took his hand.

"No, Anto', no. It's not the same thing at all. He was lying and you won't be. And you might not have to do it. Or maybe it wasn't even them, and they can prove it, and no one will be the worse for it. But in the meantime, you'll get them off your back."

"I don't know if I can bring myself to do it. I just don't know."

"You're going to have to, Antonio. You have to bring yourself to do this for them, for your children. And for Maria, who was fragile and couldn't take it."

As he was getting ready to leave, Criscuolo looked at the piece of wood that Lomunno was carving and realized that he was building a nativity scene.

"You're making a manger, eh? Good for you, that way the children know it's Christmas. In a few days I'll come back with something good for you to eat on Christmas Eve. Ciao, *bambini*, give me a kiss goodbye."

As he left, he heard Lomunno's voice calling him.

"Pasqua' . . ."

"What is it, Anto'? Tell me."

His friend's eyes were glistening in the half-light of his shack. He opened his mouth, and shut it again. It's hard to say thank you to someone when you can't admit to yourself that you care about them.

At last, Lomunno spoke:

"Shave that mustache off. You look ridiculous."

Criscuolo smiled, intentionally making his mustache quiver.

"You're wrong; it's magnificent."

And he turned and left.

By the time Ricciardi and Maione found themselves outside the barracks it was nightfall. It was no longer raining, but the wind was blowing hard again, hurting their ears. They raised the lapels and collars of their overcoats.

The brigadier put on his gloves and clapped his hands together.

"*Mammama'*, there's a cold wind tonight. But then again, if it weren't cold what kind of Christmas would it be, eh, Commissa'? Well, all told, we learned a few things today about this Garofalo."

Ricciardi, his hair tossing in the wind, replied pensively:

"And about ourselves, as far as I can tell."

Maione nodded.

"And to think that there are some people who say that the secret police don't exist. Unbelievable."

"And it was because of the secret police that Lomunno was ruined so easily. The militia *is* the party, and they can't afford for there to be even the suspicion of a scandal. No question, Garofalo was putting it all on a single roll of the dice; if his claims hadn't checked out, he would have been in a world of pain."

Ricciardi had set off toward police headquarters, walking at a fast clip.

"That must mean he felt he was making a safe bet. In any case, he ruined his colleague's life, not just his career. Just think of that man's wife, jumping out the window in her despair over losing her home, her husband, and her dignity."

Maione was puffing out clouds of steam as he walked behind Ricciardi, like a small locomotive.

"You're quite right, Commissa'. It's possible to steal someone's life, their dreams and hopes. That's the worst crime of all: the theft of hope."

Ricciardi shot a sidelong glance at the longshoreman who'd been crushed under the last load of the day, now standing alone on the wharf: abandoned by the living, who'd all gone home.

"Hope may even be the last thing to die, but it does die sometimes. At any rate we, at the end of our first day on the case, have more than just the name of Antonio Lomunno, ex-militiaman and ex-convict, in hand."

"Oh, we do, Commissa'? What else do we have?"

Ricciardi was looking straight ahead, walking fast because of the wind blowing against his back.

"We have Saint Joseph, and Saint Sebastian."

"We have San Gennaro, too, if we're counting our saints . . . But what are you talking about?"

"The broken Saint Joseph: if it was broken on purpose, there must have been a reason. We need to figure out what that reason might have been. As for Saint Sebastian, that's just an idea I have, and I want to check it out. But we'll need to talk to a couple of experts, because you and I don't know much about saints."

Maione thought it over for minute, then said:

"As far as I can remember, Commissa', the only expert on saints that we have is Don Pierino, from the Parish Church of San Ferdinando."

"Yes, I was thinking the same thing. Maybe tomorrow I'll swing by and see him, but only for Saint Joseph. For Saint Sebastian, on the other hand, I'll need to talk to another expert: Dr. Modo."

Maione burst out laughing into the wind.

"Commissa', that Dr. Modo knows even less about saints than we do; that is, if we leave aside his cursing and oaths, when I'd say he knows quite a few of them, considering how many of their names he calls out. Anyway, I'm always delighted to see him."

"No," replied Ricciardi as they were entering the courtyard of police headquarters, finally sheltered from the cutting northern wind. "I'll go, both to see Don Pierino and to see Modo. But what I'd appreciate is if you'd do me the favor of going to call on your informer, the famous Bambinella, and ask her to nose around and find out what she can about both Lomunno and Garofalo. Maybe all that integrity was nothing but a front."

Maione stopped to think, then said:

"At your orders, Commissa'. If I want to see Bambinella I have to catch her early in the morning or late at night, otherwise she'll be out going about her business, making her rounds in the city's *vicoli* and *vicarielli*. But if you want, I'll go by her place tonight."

"No, it's late and we've had a hard day. Come on up for a moment to sign the reports, then you head home. After all, in a few days it'll be Christmas."

"And I still have to finish my nativity scene. What can I do, I have to do it, it's a tradition, but I never have the time. It makes me think of Luca, when he was little; he always wanted to work on it with me. Sometimes I still think I can see him, you know that? Ah well, let's not get blue about it. *Grazie,* Commissa'. Tomorrow's another day."

XVIII

C hristmas is an emotion.
It can last for a whole year, in the anticipation of a gift, a kiss from a new love, a pastry to be eaten by the light of red candles.

It has the flavor of almonds and cinnamon, silver sugar dragées and chicken broth.

Christmas is an emotion.

It runs on the light of a thousand tiny bulbs, along electric wires painted black to make them look like so many stars falling from the sky, tossing in the wind.

It's reflected in the countless voices exchanging false affection, forgotten embraces, and season's wishes for all good things.

Christmas is an emotion.

Anticipation, finally, of something new.

Or perhaps simply of a return home, with cardboard suitcases tied up with twine in overcrowded, stinking passenger cars, from the places we work to the places of our age-old loves, which become new again when viewed from so great a distance.

Christmas is an emotion.

It's strong, like the yearning for home in the cold and the wind, and yet faint, like the sound of an accordion in a tavern to someone hurrying past, without any clear destination in mind.

Christmas is an emotion.

You can wait for it day after day, from when the sirocco dies down under the blows of the cold northern wind, but it catches you unprepared all the same, like a runaway horse covered with plumes and bells.

Christmas is an emotion.

It's as strong as a pounding heart, as light as a fluttering eyelash.

But it can be swept away by a gust of wind, and never come at all.

Maione, having finished writing his reports, was hurrying down the big staircase of police headquarters, finally heading home. Why hide it? He was a happy man.

Those three years hadn't been easy. In fact, to tell the truth, they'd been the three most painful years of his life.

First of all, losing Luca. The terrible way it all happened, a phone call, a desperate race through the *vicoli*, a thousand eyes watching him pass from the shadows of the doorways, the crevices and alcoves, the lobbies and atriums, and no one on the streets. The usual little knot of people gathered around the entrance to the cellar, where he'd insisted on venturing in alone, poor little stupid beloved son of mine, I wasn't even able to teach you the basic caution that every good policeman needs to have. And the dozens, the hundreds of hands reaching out to restrain Maione, to keep him from going in: Brigadie', let it be, remember him the way he was, alive.

It seemed like just the other day, but it had been more than three years. The clear green eyes of Deputy Officer Ricciardi, whom he'd always avoided because he didn't like his long silences, chatterbox that he was. Deputy Officer Ricciardi, the Jonah, the albatross, the jinx, as everyone said at police headquarters. But that day Ricciardi had come later, at the same time as Maione: Luca had brought his own bad luck. Ricciardi had gone down into the cellar, stayed a few minutes, and then emerged, taking Maione aside and saying: He loved you. He loved his big-belly papa, his *papà panzone*.

Even tonight, as he walked out the front entrance with a wave to the sentinel standing guard, Maione wondered how Ricciardi could have known that Luca, inside the four walls of their apartment and with that off-kilter, loopy laugh of his, always called him that, *papà panzone*, with irreverent affection. And why he'd believed him immediately, why he'd sensed that Luca had chosen Ricciardi to convey the farewell that he hadn't had time to whisper to him with his last breath.

The snow-scented wind slapped at him, but Maione was still reliving the days after the murder in his head, when the only one at his side had been the tireless, unstoppable Ricciardi; their strange friendship, the affection that bound them together, cemented then during the long stakeouts, the interviews, the trail that had gone cold and then heated up again, finally leading them to the murderer. And to send him where he belonged: behind bars.

What Brigadier Maione hadn't known at the time was that the worst was still to come, that it was beginning at that very moment, when his energy and his rage could no longer be channeled into his search for his son's murderer; when he would find himself in an apartment submerged in a new silence, without hope, with a wife on the verge of madness, and he himself, with Luca's five younger brothers and sisters, teetering on the brink of the abyss, staring wide-eyed into the void.

How many times had the slender thread that bound them together been on the verge of snapping. How many times had the ghost of their love been about to dissolve into the dark fog that surrounded his lovely wife, reduced to a phantom, sitting in an armchair and staring out the window at the sky.

Then, that spring, something had happened. The spark of almost forgotten feelings had rekindled a new and wonderful passion, and in the warmth of that revitalized love, their home had reawakened, like a flower buried in the snow. And now, for the first time in ages, Maione could look forward to the coming Christmas as a time of joy and good cheer, instead of as yet another exhumation of his grief and pain.

As he was remembering that he needed to order the fish for Christmas Eve—or else his supplier wouldn't be able to set aside the finest cuts—his heart suddenly lurched.

At first he thought he must be mistaken; his eyes, squinting in the wind, must have mistaken the silhouette, a trick of the light from the wildly swinging streetlamp. But when the man waiting for him at the corner of Vicolo della Tofa, seeing him approach, discarded his cigarette butt and crushed it underfoot, Maione knew it was him.

Franco Massa and Raffaele Maione had been inseparable ever since they were boys. They tormented everyone in Piazzetta Concordia and the surrounding area with pranks and hijinks, but they were lovable and all the shopkeepers of the neighborhood were always happy to see the odd pair, one of them as skinny as a rail, with an enormous schnozzola in the middle of his gaunt face, the other a big strapping boy, always ready to burst out laughing, with a noise like a cartful of pots and pans crashing down a staircase. It was hard not to love those two, even though they never got tired of dreaming up mischief.

And inseparable they had remained. Long after they'd stopped running around barefoot, chasing after the Pazzariello or clinging precariously to the outside of the trolley as it rattled over the tracks, on their way out to the seaside, where they would dive off the rocks of Via Caracciolo. They were together as adolescents, waiting for the girls to come out of the Catholic school in Piazza Dante; and as young men, sharing the same ticket to the Salone Margherita, where the dancers hiked their skirts, one of them distracting the usher at the door while the other would crouch down and sneak in among the legs of all the well-to-do boys dressed in tailcoats.

Raffaele Maione, known as *Orso*, the Bear, for his size, and

Franco Massa, known as *Cicogna*, the Stork, for his long, skinny legs and a nose that made him tip forward slightly as he walked. One of those friendships that know no bounds, that expand to fill an entire lifetime, with one imitating the other without realizing it, until no one can remember which is the original and which is the copy.

When Lucia came along, the blonde angel who would become the mother of Maione's six children, Franco didn't disappear, as too often happens. He just became Uncle Franco, and the children grew to love him as a second father. Most of all Luca, for whom Franco naturally acted as godfather. The Stork kept a photo from the day of Luca's baptism on his bedside table, with him proudly and awkwardly holding that bundle in his arms, and Raffaele and Lucia, smiling and overcome with emotion, at his side.

He'd been a conscientious and caring godfather. He'd watched Luca closely, sternly monitoring his friendships and activities. Often the boy even asked his father to intercede with Uncle Franco, in order to obtain his permission to stay out late or skip school.

Both friends had chosen to wear the uniform, the Bear as a policeman and the Stork as a prison guard. It was only natural that Luca should make the same choice. Natural and tragic.

Luca's death had been devastating for Raffaele, of course, but it had been every bit as painful for Franco. He had no family of his own, no special love in his life: his desire to be a father had been satisfied by that loudmouthed handsome blond boy, with his eyes the color of the sea and that hee-hawing laugh like his father's. Luca's death had shattered something inside him; it had extinguished a flame that would never be reignited.

After the first few months, it became harder and harder for the two old friends to meet. After a moment of silence, Franco inevitably broke down in tears. He wept silently, without changing expression; big hot tears would streak down his face, as if from some sudden rain.

Little by little, they'd stopped seeing each other. Sometimes they'd meet by chance, exchanging a nod of the head from a distance, but it was a rare occurrence. These days Massa almost never left Poggioreale, where he'd become the head of the guards at the prison there, with special responsibility for security. When Maione thought of him, he felt that vague pain one feels when an important feeling is allowed to wither away through neglect.

And so, when he encountered him on his way home that night, happiness clashed with guilt in Maione's heart, in a strange undertow of emotions. He was preparing for a joyful Christmas, but one without his son and without his best friend in the world.

Franco gave him a hug, full of the same love he'd always felt for him, and let the Bear wrap him in his arms, with Franco patting Maione's broad back, just as they'd embraced when they were little. But then Franco pushed him away and looked him straight in the eye. God, how he's aged, thought Maione. Franco looked at him for a long while, then he said:

"I have to talk to you, Raffae'. It's important. I need you to give me half an hour."

Maione was pleased and bewildered.

"Of course, Franco. When can we get together? Why don't you come over to our place, Lucia and the children would be happy to see you. I wanted to call you for Christmas; would you come eat with us on Christmas Eve? Lucia is making clams, you know what a cook she is."

Massa seemed to be thinking about something else.

"Christmas, right. Christmas. No, I need to talk to you right away. Let's go into that tavern, over there; I'll treat you to a glass of wine. Half an hour, no longer."

And he set off, without waiting for an answer.

XIX

From her kitchen window, Rosa Vaglio was scanning the street. The wind was chilly and her bones ached, but she feared neither one nor the other; she was from the high countryside. The mountains of Cilento, wild and treacherous, with snow that fell unexpectedly even on sunny days, clouds lurking behind the peaks, invisible until it was too late.

Once she had seen a wolf.

In the hope of bringing some color to the cheeks of his perennially pale bride, Luigi Alfredo's father, the Baron of Malomonte, had moved his family to a farm he owned in Sanza, at the foot of Mount Cervati. The green-eyed baroness, silent and smiling, had asked Rosa to accompany her on a walk in the surrounding countryside and they had been caught by a sudden rainstorm, cold and stinging. They'd taken shelter in a small shack that was used to store wood, and when it had finally stopped raining and they emerged, they'd found themselves face-to-face with that magnificent specimen, its fur practically black and its eyes a luminous yellow. The beast stood as tall as one of the ponies that the baron bred to race.

Rosa had immediately shooed the baroness back into the shack and turned to face the animal herself, staring it right in the eye, long and hard. She hadn't glimpsed anything savage in its gaze: just intelligence and curiosity, and great loneliness. Then the wolf had turned and trotted off, silently, moving up toward the peak.

Who could say why that memory had returned to her just

now, so many years later and so many miles away, as she was looking down into the street from the balcony, high above that city that she'd never really understood, awaiting the return of her young master, late for dinner, as he was every night. Perhaps the animal and the commissario had the same disease in their eyes.

When she'd first held him in her arms, more than thirty years ago, she'd stopped thinking of herself as simply his servant and had begun to love him. She had been the mother that the poor baroness, who died so young and had always been so frail and unhealthy, had never been able to be; but Rosa had never really understood him. Ever since he'd come home from the hospital, after she'd feared for his life, she sensed that he was more painfully alone than ever. It was just a feeling, but she knew she was right.

In her simple, uneducated mind, she understood that her boy was torn, tormented by some inner conflict, and she didn't know what it was.

She guessed that the Colombo girl, the eldest daughter of the haberdasher who lived across the street, had something to do with it. She'd stopped her, she'd spoken to her, she'd even had her over to the apartment when he wasn't there. She'd hoped that Luigi Alfredo's pathological solitude might finally come to an end with her; but then she'd vanished the day of the accident, to be replaced by that strange outsider, that widow who was too aggressive, too beautiful, too sure of herself, too everything.

She didn't like that Livia. She didn't seem right for her boy. "Wives and oxen from your own villages," the saying went; and if not from Cilento, which would have been ideal, at least a nice young lady from the south, serious and well-mannered, like Enrica had seemed to her. Certainly not that *signora*, a woman who smoked and swiveled her hips so that heads turned everywhere she went.

Rosa squinted into the wind as she saw Ricciardi approach in the distance, hatless as usual, hands in his pockets and his head bowed. She felt the usual tenderness touch her heart, and she decided that sometimes fate needs a little help.

There weren't many customers in the tavern. The week before Christmas, anyone who had a home and a family wanted to spend their time there, with them.

Maione and Massa found a corner table in a quiet spot and ordered half a liter of red wine to take the chill off. The brigadier tried to break the ice.

"How are you? As I was just saying, Lucia and I had been planning to invite you over for Christmas Eve. You know, things are better now; we're talking to each other again, and she's doing well. She's rediscovered her love for her home. And the kids, too . . ."

"Raffaele, forgive me. I have to tell you something that may cause you some pain. Forgive me."

Maione shut his eyes. He'd read the concern in his friend's eyes the minute he'd seen him; he knew the man too well, and there was no mistaking it. He'd hoped, coward that he was, that it was Massa's problem. He'd have done everything in his power to help him, but at least he'd have preserved his own peace, so fragile, so laboriously regained. But no.

"I don't really have a choice, do I? If I did, you wouldn't be here now. You'd have made the choice for me."

Massa took a long drink of wine.

"Yes, that's true. But I don't have that right, unfortunately. Listen: you know that since I was put in command of the prison guards I no longer make the rounds in the corridors doing direct prisoner surveillance. I work out the shifts, I assign the teams, that sort of thing. But my boys know that there are certain things I keep track of personally, and if there are any developments they come and report them to me right away. Last week there was a brawl among the prisoners, don't ask me what it was about, in the dining hall. For the most part they're brutes, forced to keep their violent impulses bottled up inside them. But sometimes all it takes is a look, or a word, or even a tone of voice . . . To make a long story short, they threw chairs, they kicked and punched, until finally my men arrived and restored order."

Maione waited, his heart pounding in his throat. Massa went on.

"But it was too late. One man was on the floor; he'd been kicked in the head after he fell. They took him to the infirmary, but it was immediately clear that he wasn't going to make it. You already know who I'm talking about, don't you?"

Maione shut his eyes. Him. Him. He was dead; fate had done its work. He almost stopped listening to Massa, who had gone on talking.

"They called me right away. They knew that everything about that man's health, the details of the life he led, every single sigh of unhappiness was to be reported to me. Every single day of his sentence was a gentle caress to my grief. Every single day."

His voice had lowered to a hiss, quivering with hate; his lips clamped, his gaze lost in the middle distance. With a surge of sadness Maione realized how much his friend must have suffered during the last few years, unable to find comfort in the other children and Lucia, as Maione had.

"I went right away, as you can imagine. I positioned myself right next to that bed. I wanted to watch him suffer, minute by minute. It was a huge wound, a boot to the temple; no one thought he'd ever come to. But then, he did."

Maione opened his eyes wide. What the hell had happened?

"He woke up, and he asked for a priest. That black soul of his, that demon wanted to save himself from hellfire at the last minute, with a sniffle and a benediction. He couldn't see anymore, so I grabbed a chair, I placed it next to his bed, and I became his priest. I became his priest, Rafe'. I became his priest."

He repeated it to himself more than to anyone else. Maione shook his head. He suddenly felt like crying.

"Poor brother of mine. Poor brother of mine."

"I'm not afraid, Rafe', believe me. I've already spent far too much time in hell, I've seen too many things with my own eyes, to be afraid of the afterlife. I wanted to hear from his own lips exactly what he'd done. I muttered a few words in fake Latin, and that illiterate cretin fell for it and started to talk. As you can imagine, I know his criminal record by heart, I've read it through so many times. He said the whole black rosary, theft by theft, robbery by robbery, and even the murders, one, two, three. Even one he'd never stood trial for."

Maione was hanging on his every word.

"But what did he tell you about Luca? Did he tell you how it happened, if he said something, if . . ."

"Wait. Let me tell you the whole story. At a certain point he stopped talking. I thought he must be dead, at last. Instead, he went on breathing, so I asked him, 'And Luca Maione?' He was silent, then he asked me, 'But Padre, how do you know what happened with the policeman?'"

Maione sat waiting, almost afraid to breathe.

"I answered him, 'You're at God's feet, and God knows all. Lying now won't bring you forgiveness.' He was silent again, then, in a voice so low that I had to lean forward to hear him, he said, 'It wasn't me who killed the policeman.'"

All around them people were talking, the music and the songs of Christmas wafted in from outside, and the wind rushing through the *vicolo* droned incessantly. But to Maione it was as if a profound silence, like the one you hear in church on a summer afternoon, had descended around him.

"What does that mean? What does that mean, Franco? What did he mean, he didn't kill him? Then who did kill him, who killed my Luca? He was lying, damn him. He was lying, in the very face of death!"

Massa had downed another glass of wine. From his bloodshot eyes and the red blotches on his face, you'd have thought that he had a high fever.

"I thought the same thing. But then I said to myself: Why would he do that? He's already confessed to the other murders, even one for which he was never tried, and he knows he's dying. What would be the point of lying? He can't hope to fool God Almighty."

"So?"

"So I thought to myself: I can't live with this doubt. I said to him, 'My son, I can't believe you unless you tell me what really happened. And if I can't believe you, I certainly can't give you absolution. I'm sorry, but hell awaits you for all of your sins.'"

"And what did he do?"

"What else could he do? He believed me. And he told me the story. That day he'd brought with him, along with his usual cohort, his little brother, Biagio. This kid had never done a thing; he'd always sheltered him out of respect for their mother, but that day Biagio had insisted. They thought the job would be a piece of cake, and the older brother had said, why not? But Luca tracked them down. He'd staked them out; he was good at stakeouts, he got that from you."

Maione nodded, lost in thought. He remembered the long hours he'd spent teaching his son all the techniques.

"Luca knew how many men there were, and he watched them go in, counting them one by one. He was good at what he did. Very good. When he determined that they were all inside, he raided them, with his gun leveled; that way none of them could pull a move on him. But he hadn't taken the kid into account, who'd gone to buy cigarettes. When the kid walked into the cellar, he found Luca with his back to him, Luca who had the drop on the whole gang. The kid panicked and, instead of taking to his heels, he pulled out the knife that his brother had given him to hold on to, and . . . he did what he should never have done."

Maione reached across the table and grabbed Massa's arm.

"So, it was the kid? The little brother?"

"That's right, it was him. The older brother heard the rest of the police arriving and thought fast. He took the knife and told his brother to get out of there, quickly but without running—nobody knew who the kid was anyway—and he took the blame for the murder. He had nothing to lose, he was bound to be convicted in any case, he was wanted for other crimes and other murders."

There was a long moment of silence. Maione had to assimilate a whole new order of thoughts about something very important that he'd only just managed to put to rest, deep in his heart, at the back in his mind.

"So the actual murderer, the man who killed my son, our son, is still at large. And he's been roaming the streets freely, maybe killing other people, for three years now."

Massa nodded.

"The news was upsetting to me, too. I just sat there, mouth agape, until that swine was finally dead."

Maione stared into the empty air.

"I can't believe it."

"But that's exactly how it is. That's why I came to find you, even though I knew that I would be ruining your holiday. But now we can finally settle the matter, and restore justice."

Maione looked at him.

"What are you talking about?"

Now it was Massa's turn to reach across the table. He grabbed Maione's hand.

"Don't you understand? It's so simple. We have to track down this Biagio and kill him like the dog he is, the same way he did to Luca. I'd have already done it myself, but I was only his godfather; you're his father, and you have more of a right than I do. If you don't want to do it, I'll understand; just tell me and I'll do it myself. I couldn't ask for anything better."

Maione felt as if he were suddenly drunk.

"Would you really do it?"

Massa laughed bitterly.

"Rafe', there hasn't been a single day, in these past three and a half years, that I haven't thought of Luca. I have no children of my own and I haven't wanted any: that boy was everything to me. I remember him the day he was born, as a toddler, as an adolescent, as a boy and and as a man. We understood each other at a glance, and you know I adored him. *Chist'ommo 'e mmerda*, that piece of shit, he stole the only real love I ever had in my life. For all these years, I've believed it was the brother, and I've watched him to make sure that he served his time in prison the way he should, and that's what I planned to do for the rest of my life, monitoring his punishment day after day. You chose to send him to prison, I would have bitten him to death, chewed him up alive, right there in that cellar. Now, you know the law: you can't try two different people for the same crime. And what evidence would we have? My testimony, the testimony of a man who pretended to be a priest, and who is also the victim's godfather?"

Brigadier Maione had to admit that his friend had a point. It was true: the murderer would go scot-free. But he couldn't let Massa destroy his own life. If someone has to do it, he thought, it should be me. I sent the wrong person to prison; it should be me.

"Let me take care of it, Franco. Let me find him, let me look him in the eye. If I can't bring myself to do it, I'll call you straightaway."

Massa studied him, grim-faced.

"Rafe', you know that Luca needs to rest in peace. And there can't be peace for him if his murderer goes unpunished."

Maione got to his feet.

"I know, Franco. And forgive me if after all this time I'd let myself forget about the grief we share. Thank you, thank you for what you've done."

Massa drained his last glass of wine and stood up in turn.

"I should thank you, for giving me the memory of Luca. It's been the only fine thing in my life. I'll wait to hear from you, Rafe'. Let me know."

And they went their separate ways, without saying good-night or exchanging wishes for the holiday season, or for anything at all.

But they both knew that this wasn't going to be a very merry Christmas.

XX

The Sunday before Christmas is a distinctly odd one.

In a way, it's like any other Sunday, because the church bells ring from early morning on; because it has the usual feel of a holiday, with all the rhythms and manners of those days that artfully pretend to make no demands on your time; because many of the shops are closed and some of the wealthier merchants allow themselves an extra hour of sleep; because the girls plot their clandestine assignations, taking advantage of the fact that Papa or Mamma might send them out to run some errand that they're feeling too lazy to run themselves.

But it's more than just a Sunday.

In a way, it's like a holiday, because the beggars swarm around the churches to put the self-rightous face-to-face with poverty, confident that it'll mean a few coins flung in their direction; because vendors of balloons and firecrackers occupy choice locations in the Villa Nazionale, with fingerless gloves and woolen rags wrapped around their faces to ward off the biting wind, attracting children with their merchandise while simultaneously frightening them with their appearance; because the smells of candied almonds, roasted chestnuts, grilled artichokes, and fried pizzas waft through the air to every corner of the city, making mouths water and stomachs growl.

But it's more than just a holiday.

In a way, it's Christmas, because the sidewalks are brimming over with articles of every kind for sale, laid out on old sheets, and everyone is selling something, legal or otherwise, the length of every thoroughfare and in all the adjacent alleys and lanes; because the potential customers are thus forced to walk in the street, earning themselves blaring horns and splashes of mud from the passing automobiles and carriages; because the shopkeepers selling fruit and cured meats have prepared huge arches of colorful products, and since it would take hours of work for them to break the displays down, they haven't shut their doors for days now, and they just stay up all night long chatting with one another, bundled to their noses in blankets and gathering close to the fires in the braziers at their feet; because the big *capitone* saltwater eels dart and wriggle in large basins painted seawater blue, all along Via Santa Brigida, and every so often one of them manages to slip out onto the street, where the fisherman chases it as it squirms between the feet of squealing women who run away in terror.

But it's not Christmas yet.

Enrica had decided to accompany her father that morning.

Taking advantage of the fact that it was Sunday, and preparing for the challenging pre-Christmas week of shopping that was about to begin, Giulio Colombo had decided to drop by the store to make sure that the gloves, hats, and canes in the stockroom were sufficient in number to keep pace with the hoped-for surge in holiday gift sales. Thirty years of experience in this line of work had taught him that when people were at a loss for a last-minute gift idea, these were often the kinds of products they turned to. It was therefore advisable to order plenty of stock, especially for the lower-priced items. People were struggling, and how: no matter how many articles claiming the contrary the newspapers liked to print.

And so there they were, father and daughter, behind locked doors in their shop, the metal roller blinds lowered halfway,

Giulio counting articles and Enrica checking off the stock numbers of each product on a list. The real reason they were there, though, as they both knew without ever putting it into words, was to escape the relentless nagging of Enrica's mother, Maria, who never tired of her one obsessive topic.

As Giulio well knew, Enrica had a very particular personality. The reason he knew this was that she was identical to him. Sweet-natured, courteous, never overemphatic, never raised her voice, never threw tantrums; but also stubborn, determined, neat and orderly to the point of mania, clear and precise in her ideas and in her movements. She was twenty-five years old now and not getting any younger, and still no fiancé, no young men asking her out or even asking her father permission to ask her out.

Not that she wasn't agreeable to look at, in her way, thought Giulio as he glanced at her out of the corner of his eye. But she discouraged any and all would-be suitors with a smile and a "No, thank you." This was something that drove her mother crazy, convinced as she was that by Enrica's age a woman ought to already have a home, children, and most of all a husband. She reiterated this concept an average of ten times daily, in the entire spectrum of tones, ranging from supplicating to imperative.

Enrica's reaction was to retreat into her shell. She would respond in nothing more than monosyllables, and went on doing her household chores or preparing lessons for the boys she tutored at home, prepping them privately for their school exams.

Giulio had a great deal of faith in his daughter. If she wanted to wait, then let her wait. If she wanted to spend the rest of her life living with him, so much the better, as far as he was concerned. Her younger sister, married to an enthusiastic young Fascist who held a position at his store, already had a child, and didn't she still live at home with them, too, after all? What would be so different? Times were hard, there'd been a war not that long ago, and the government's attitude was increasingly militaristic, as the liberal and well-read Giulio could hardly fail to notice. He felt more comfortable with the idea of his daughter living at home with her family than with some fanatical extremist, and there was no shortage of those around these days.

"Men's hat, felt, dark gray, with a black silk band," he said to his daughter, as if the words were actually "I love you."

"Article 15-26, one unit," Enrica replied, writing a check mark on the list. As if she'd replied, "And I love you."

Ricciardi had made a rough calculation: if he devoted his Sunday to interviewing Don Pierino and Dr. Modo, he'd get ahead in terms of timing. The priest and the doctor were the only people he needed to interview who saw one day of the week as pretty much like any other; that was the way Ricciardi saw things, too, for that matter.

As best he could tell, the personality of the late Centurion Garofalo was taking on unexpected and mysterious dimensions. The incorruptible straight-arrow militiaman who refused to take gifts from fishermen and projected an image of perfect family harmony to his neighbors was showing himself to be an unscrupulous careerist, a man who hadn't thought twice about ruining the life of his superior officer in order to take his job and his promotion.

This was hardly unusual; after all, they lived in a time when informers and spies reaped rich rewards. That's the way things worked at police headquarters, too, from what he'd been able to gather as a dispassionate observer, indifferent to the paths of ambition as he was. But it was one thing to steal a march on a rival by leveraging family ties or influential friends; it was quite another to send a man to prison for eighteen months and drive his wife to kill herself in shame.

As he strode down a Via Toledo that had been transformed

into a teeming market, heading for the church of San Ferdinando, Ricciardi visualized the nativity scene in the Garofalo home: the shattered statuette of Saint Joseph, clumsily concealed under the linen, and the one of the Madonna tipped over slightly, leaning against the statue of the ass. While reaching for the husband, they'd felled the wife. Too perfectly symbolic to have been pure chance. He miraculously managed to dodge an oncoming city bus, which emitted an indignant squeal of its klaxon. He was reminded of the phrase that Garofalo's shade kept uttering, his last thought: *I don't owe anything, not a thing.* What had the murderers demanded of him, what had the centurion refused to give them? The visit to the barracks had increased, rather than decreased, the array of hypotheses. Money, property; but also stolen years.

He needed to wait for news from Maione, about where this Lomunno might be, since he was certainly someone who had every reason to hate the victim. He wondered whether the brigadier would succeed, on this holiday Sunday, in tracking down his omniscient informant.

His thoughts went to Maione, and to his newly regained family harmony. Ricciardi, who'd been in constant contact with Maione's grief over those last few years, was happy for him. He knew how important the brigadier's family was to him, and he'd been gratified to see the smile slowly return to Maione's broad face.

Family, love. Enrica. The association of thoughts, as he pushed his way through the crowd in the vicinity of Piazza Trieste e Trento, was almost excessively linear. He knew that her father had a haberdashery and hat shop, and he remembered seeing her enter the establishment, somewhere in this very neighborhood. Maybe it was even the place with the roller blinds half-lowered. *Hat and gloves?* Signora Garofalo's corpse had asked, smiling with a downcast gaze as the black blood pumped out of the gaping wound in her throat. Perhaps the murderer or murderers to whom she had posed that question were customers of Enrica's father; they might even have been served by the hands of the woman he loved. Fate doesn't exist, Ricciardi told himself. But if it did, it would have a grand old time, pulling stunts like these.

He had reached the church, from which a stream of the faithful were emerging, following the ten o'clock Mass. He waited for the crowd around the entrance to dwindle and went in, continuing to think about fate, nonexistent though it was, and about Enrica.

Enrica was thinking about fate, and about Ricciardi.

To be exact, she was thinking how bitter it was to wait for months for a meeting and then, just when everything seemed to be moving in a positive direction, to lose him. Fate could be cruel.

She remembered for the thousandth time how happy she had been when she received the letter from the man for whom she'd waited for a lifetime, the man she'd fallen in love with from afar; and her interactions with the man's *tata*, his nanny, that rough-hewn but kindly woman who lived with him, and who had actually invited her into their apartment. She remembered the rooms in that apartment, how clean and tidy the place was, a strange scent that might have been his aftershave; the half-closed door to his bedroom, where he watched her from his window every night, during their regular evening appointment.

And then, when the natural next step was a tête-à-tête, a smile, their hands clasped together—the accident. As she checked off the articles on the list while her father dictated them to her, her mind found itself back in the hospital waiting room, with the slabs of stone that formed the pavement outside being pounded by the rain, on that Day of the Dead. It seemed a hundred years had gone by, but it hadn't even been two months.

She'd thought that he was about to die. She'd seen that beautiful woman, with her exotic accent, pacing back and forth, smoking and sobbing, perhaps every bit as heartbroken as she was. She'd felt like the wrong person in the wrong place. And she'd asked the Madonna of Pompeii to spare his life, vowing in exchange never to see him again. A moment later, the doctor had come out smiling; and it had also stopped raining.

Enrica had never been particularly religious, but that had struck her as an unmistakable sign. She'd leaped to her feet and left almost at a run, while the strange lady, the *tata*, and the strapping brigadier all rushed into Ricciardi's hospital room to see him breathing. She'd left with her heart torn between joy and despair; the joy had faded soon after, and the despair had been her constant companion ever since.

She'd never worried too much about her future, Enrica. She'd always believed that if there was someone she was destined to be with, sooner or later he'd appear and she would understand at first glance. If he never appeared, she wasn't interested in settling for someone else. She'd sooner have no one at all.

A romantic idea, a little girl's way of thinking, perhaps; but it was what she believed, and she clung tight to it. It had been confirmed for her when she realized that there was a man watching her, standing at the window across the way, more than a year ago: it was him, it was really him. He'd finally come.

But now she'd lost him. She'd cast him aside, of her own free will, delivered him into the talons of that beautiful outsider, without even putting up a fight.

For an instant her sense of frustration was overwhelming, and her eyes filled with tears. To hide her face from her father, she turned toward the shop door, which was halfway open, and saw Ricciardi walk into the church of San Ferdinando.

XXI

Don Pierino was doing his best to get rid of Signorina Vaccaro. She was a prominent and influential member of his parish congregation, a woman who was very wealthy and very, very elderly. Legends circulated among the faithful in the neighborhood to the effect that she was well over a hundred, but it seemed more likely that once she'd reached eighty, she'd decided to linger at that finish line, giving that as her official age for at least another ten years.

Periodically—every three days, to be exact—she decided that the time had come to update the higher echelons of the local church on her precarious state of health, and woe betide the hapless recipient of her report. The parish priest, Don Tommaso, had become a master of evasion, and always managed to disappear the moment before the signorina came hobbling down the main aisle. Actually Don Pierino suspected that his direct superior had assembled a network of scouts, and that some faithless altar boy must be delivering warning signals in the form of sharp whistles or some other piece of secret-agent tradecraft. The fact remains that it was always Don Pierino who fell into the arthritis-warped talons of that little old lady. Signorina Vaccaro, convinced that the accruement of all her earthly sufferings, along with her much-touted chastity, constituted a general fund of merits that would ensure her entry into a comfortable and everlasting Heaven, was determined that her Father Confessors should be promptly informed of every development in the progress of her countless maladies.

As he stood listening to Signorina Vaccaro tell of the debilitating effects of her most recent bout of dysentery, Don Pierino smiled and nodded. Short and stout, dark complected, with gleaming dark eyes like a pair of black olives, the assistant parish priest was much beloved by his flock, and especially by the great many poor and sick parishioners who lived in the populous city quarter that fell under the administration of the church of San Ferdinando. If there were hungry, sick, or parasite-ridden children, Don Pierino was always the first to offer to help, with his broad, contagious smile and the inborn optimism that characterized his faith.

Don Pierino possessed a cheerful faith, a faith that was filled with love of all creation and, therefore, of God. He also loved art, and especially music, for which he had a voracious appetite. He loved the countryside, though he was rarely able to return to it. And he loved the sea, which was far from his birthplace in Santa Maria Capua Vetere, but he'd quickly made friends with the waves and the salt air of Naples, unfamiliar though they'd been at first.

Signorina Vaccaro had just moved on to the effects of an especially uncomfortable gastritis attack, complete with graphic descriptions which Don Pierino would gladly have done without, when he thought he saw a familiar figure in the dim light of a side altar. A fond and familiar figure.

He'd first met Ricciardi during the investigation into the murder of the tenor Arnaldo Vezzi, a murder to which he'd unsuspectingly been a witness. The two men couldn't have been any more different in terms of personality, education, passions, and faith, but they'd established a relationship that, if not exactly a friendship, was at least a bond of powerful empathy. He was intrigued by Ricciardi's green eyes, which at first glance seemed cold: they were a window into an inner world of grief and suffering, of pain whose cause he could not confess.

The cheerful little priest sensed a heart imprisoned, trapped behind the iron bars of who knows what memory; but a big heart, a heart full of compassion for his fellow human being.

Ricciardi wasn't the kind of man who would come to see him if he didn't have a serious reason. And he felt sure that Signorina Vaccaro would survive both the gastritis and the interruption to their conversation. He told her that he needed to hear the confession of someone who, he was afraid, might have committed murder during an armed robbery in someone's home—knowing this to be one of his parishioner's special bugbears. Signorina Vaccaro's eyes grew round and, to keep the criminal from identifying her, she disappeared from the church at a surprising speed, evidently forgetting her debilitating arthritis for the moment.

Don Pierino hurried toward Ricciardi with his usual bouncing gait, mentally asking God's forgiveness for his white lie.

"Commissario, what an enormous pleasure! How are you? I heard about the accident and I immediately hurried over to the hospital, but you'd already gone home, in defiance of your doctor's orders. Did you feel what a fine chilly wind we're getting? Then again, what kind of Christmas would it be if it were hot out?"

Ricciardi returned the priest's greeting, with a brief handshake, after which he thrust his nervous hand back into his pocket.

"Don Pierino. It's a pleasure to see you, too, and you know it. And I'm sorry that I haven't been by to see you for a while, but . . . well, you heard about it. How are you?"

The assistant parish priest smiled, his fingers knit over his belly.

"Fine, fine. As the Lord wishes me to be. I'm certainly in no position to complain, don't you agree? You see worse cases than I do, on the streets out there. You know that none of us can really complain."

"In fact, quite true. I need to trouble you for some information, as usual. Can you spare a few minutes of your time?"

"Absolutely, of course . . . In fact, you just saved me from a long conversation, with that elderly signorina you saw when you came in, so I owe you my full attention. Ask, ask away."

Ricciardi registered the priest's willingness to help, then asked:

"Can we talk a little about the nativity scene, Padre?"

Don Pierino flashed a happy smile, like a *scugnizzo* who had just been offered a trip to the pastry shop.

"Of course we can! Come, come with me, *prego*."

He locked arms with Ricciardi, who though not a giant was certainly far taller than the priest, and walked him thirty feet or so to where, in front of one of the side altars, a manger scene had been set up. The construction covered quite a bit of floor space, at least eighty square feet, and it featured large antique shepherds in the foreground, declining in size toward the background, creating a remarkable illusion of depth. Ricciardi was impressed in spite of himself.

Don Pierino was bouncing up and down like a little boy.

"Beautiful, eh? Don't you think it's beautiful? I do it myself, with the help of a few of the boys who attend the parish school. Many of the figures are very old, they've belonged to the church for centuries; others have been donated more recently by our congregation, over the past several years. Others still we purchased ourselves, or else they were made by parishioners who are skilled at making clothing or working with terra-cotta."

Ricciardi studied them, fascinated.

"Impressive, very impressive, Padre. Really nice, my compliments. Tell me, is there a symbology to the figures? In other words, do they represent anything?"

Don Pierino nodded, never taking his eyes off the miniature landscape.

"Of course they do, Commissario. The manger scene is one

of our people's most venerable and well-established traditions. In it, throughout the various phases of this city's history, situations and characters have been depicted that over time have come to form part of our popular imagination. You see, each and every nativity scene, even the poorest and most rudimentary, has three levels: at the top is Herod's castle, there, representing power and arrogance; in the middle is the countryside, with the flock, the shepherds, and all the rest; at the bottom, and in the foreground, is the cavern with the nativity. And dotting the landscape are the ruins of the temple, symbolizing the triumph of Christianity over the pagan gods; the tavern, which symbolizes the human predilection for sin; and so forth. Each element of the manger scene has a meaning, and the principal elements have more than one."

Ricciardi listened, absorbed.

"Everything has one or more meanings, you say. Could you give me some examples, Padre?"

The priest cheerfully complied. This was his topic, and he was happy to be able to talk about it.

"Certainly. Let's start with the locations and the architectural elements. I've already told you about the temple and the tavern; concerning the tavern I'd also point out that the banquet you see under way here, inside, is a reference to the fact that all the inns and taverns refused accommodations to the Holy Family. It represents human wickedness and selfishness, which the advent of Christ is bound to illuminate. The oven, which you see there, is always present in the manger scene; not only does it illustrate one of the most ancient trades, it also refers to the bread that, along with wine, is one of the foundations of our Christian faith. The bridge over the river, which you see in the background, refers to an ancient legend according to which three babies, killed specifically for this purpose, were buried in its foundations, as part of an enchantment intended to ensure its arches would hold strong. It symbolizes the union—the bridge, in fact—between the world of the living and the world of the dead. The well is another element that is always included, and it represents a direct link to the underworld. As you can see, darkness and evil also play a part in the nativity scene. Just like in life, no?"

Ricciardi thought about it. A bridge joining the world of the living with the world of the dead. If he himself had been a shepherd in the scene, they would have placed him squarely in the middle of that bridge.

Those thoughts aside, in any case, the symbolism of the manger scene struck him as quite intricate. It would be much harder than he'd anticipated to understand just what the murderer had been trying to convey by breaking the statuette of Saint Joseph. Provided he had been trying to say anything at all.

"What about the characters, Padre? Do they have meanings, too?"

Don Pierino nodded.

"Naturally, Commissario. You see the market, in the background? Each character represents a month. January is the butcher, February is the man selling ricotta, and so on, all the way round to December, which is represented by the fishmonger. There are twelve of them. The gypsy girl, with her basket full of iron tools, predicts the future, while the iron symbolizes Jesus's fate, to die on the cross. The man sleeping on the ground by the flock of sheep . . . this story is a choice one . . . represents the fact that the coming of Christ woke us from the sleep of ignorance to the true faith. He therefore symbolizes the stupid, and he has always been called, by popular tradition, Benito. Well, these days, for obvious reasons, no one calls him that anymore. Now they just call him 'the sleeping shepherd.' But everyone knows his real name, and they all just cover their mouths and laugh."

This still wasn't the information that Ricciardi needed.

"Padre, what about the Holy Family? Does it have a symbolism, too: a significance?"

Don Pierino spread his open hands.

"Of course it does, Commissario. Forgive me if I've been rattling on, I could talk about the manger scene for hours. The Holy Family, naturally: Baby Jesus, childhood, wisdom, candor and innocence. The Madonna, motherhood, intercession, purity. Saint Joseph—"

Ricciardi bore in.

"Saint Joseph?"

"Saint Joseph, Commissario, represents a number of different things. He's the most human, being neither a virgin mother nor a son of God. He's a man, and in fact, as you can see, he's dressed as a shepherd. But he's also the putative father of Jesus, as well as a carpenter. For Christianity he represents, in addition to fatherhood, hard work, the labor that life demands of us so that we can raise our children, daily sacrifice."

Ricciardi asked the question he'd been wanting to put to the priest since the beginning.

"And, in your opinion, Padre, if someone profaned just that one statuette in a nativity scene, the one of Saint Joseph, what might that mean?"

Don Pierino raised his hand to his chin and stroked it, thoughtfully.

"It's certainly not a very nice thing to do, Commissario. I have no idea. I believe that the reference would have to be to work, and to fatherhood. Someone who wished to express their unhappiness at having been stripped of one of those two rights, especially the right to work, to earn a living. Saint Joseph is the patron saint of workers. That's all I can tell you."

The commissario stood for a long time staring at the manger scene of the church of San Ferdinando, illuminated by a thousand tiny lightbulbs and by the candles lit by the faithful. Graces asked and received, wishes, symbols, saints: what a complicated city, he thought.

"Thank you, Padre. I'm grateful. I may come bother you again, we're working on a rather complex case."

Don Pierino smiled at him, blissfully.

"It's always a delight to see you, as far as I'm concerned, Commissario. You know what I think of you: in your heart there's more love than you could even imagine. See you soon, come back whenever you like."

Don Pierino walked the commissario all the way outside, to the front steps of the church. Before taking his leave, Ricciardi turned to face the priest and said:

"Padre, one last thing: Why was Saint Sebastian killed with so many arrows?"

Don Pierino scratched his head.

"Saint Sebastian, did you say? One of the earliest martyrs. He was the head of the guards of Diocletian, a Roman emperor who was a terrible persecutor of the Christians. Sebastian converted to Christianity, and when the emperor found out, he had him tied to a pole and shot full of arrows by a platoon of archers. That's why he's depicted that way, with all the arrows sticking out of him. And that's why he's the patron saint—"

"Of the militia, yes, I know. Thanks again, Padre. Your help is always invaluable."

And he left, followed by the gazes of the priest and of a woman hidden behind a metal roller blind that was lowered halfway.

XXII

Bambinella went to Mass regularly.

He'd been going since he was a little boy, every blessed Sunday, and sometimes in the middle of the week, if for any reason he wanted to feel closer to God.

He remembered, in particular, a priest from when he was ten years old or so, and he already felt different from the other little boys his age. That difference was familiar and recognizable, something the city had always accommodated, but a difference nonetheless, and children, as we know, can be terribly cruel. Bambinella took refuge where the other boys lacked the courage to pursue him, and spent his time in the comfortable coolness, surrounded by the scent of incense.

That priest would sit beside him and talk with him as if he were a grown-up. He'd talk to him about life, about how hard life could be. Bambinella didn't understand at the time, but now that he thought back on it, he thought that perhaps Don Corrado— that had been the priest's name—was speaking to him about his own difference, even though the priest had chosen another way of living it. Bambinella had liked that priest. Maybe he'd even fallen in love with him, though nothing ever came of it.

It wasn't long after that that men first started reaching out to him, touching him, and Bambinella discovered that it was easier for her to be a woman than a man, easier than trying to conceal her true nature, which expressed itself forcefully in her graceful movements, her long eyelashes, her large brown eyes, and her tender heart.

Still, she continued to attend Mass, because of how comforting she found the dim light, the smell of incense, and the memory of that priest who would sit and talk to her for hours. She would go early, to the first service, the seven o'clock Mass. The other attendees were typically those who worked on Sunday and could not attend the later services, along with the elderly religious fanatics who started praying in the front pews and stayed there until nightfall, reciting countless rosaries between one Mass and another, and gossiping under their breath at regular intervals.

Bambinella knew everyone, and she knew everyone's personal history. Her profession was accepted as one of the facts of life, and in a microcosm in which social differences were determined solely by the ability to procure food at least once a day, she was even considered a privileged citizen. And since she was always willing to help those who were in serious trouble, she had eventually become a confidant to one and all, a spider at the center of an immense web of gossip that covered the entire city.

No one knew or remembered Bambinella's real name, because as a boy he'd lived on the streets, homeless and without a family, sleeping and eating wherever chance offered; but the song by Viviani that had given him his name was so beautiful and famous that it fit him like a second skin. Bambinella, from above the Spanish Quarter.

The people out on the street at seven in the morning on a Sunday were few and largely complicitous. The lanes and *vicoli* in the neighborhood, usually thronged with people and cluttered with goods, stretched out at that hour in a dim gray silence, broken only by the whistling wind and the sudden rays of sunlight momentarally released by the black clouds scudding across the sky overhead. Bambinella's clicking heels announced her arrival from afar, and here and there smiles appeared under the visors of flat caps pressed low or from behind the lapels of overcoats stitched and patched so many times that they'd become as threadbare as an old shirt. A wave or a nod from a distance, like in a small town, before the day began and the city starting spinning giddily like a whirpool, revolving around an empty center.

As she climbed the last flight of cold, dark stairs to her apartment, wrapped in the long overcoat from which only her black stockings and high heels protruded, Bambinella found herself face-to-face with a sight that she'd never have expected: sitting on the top step, his face in his hands, was none other than Brigadier Maione.

"Ooh, *Madonna mia*, Brigadie', what a fright you gave me! I thought you might be a thug or a hooligan! What are you doing sitting here in the early morning, in this cold, if you don't mind my asking? You're likely to catch your death! Up, up, come inside."

Maione's face was covered with stubble and showed all the signs of a night without sleep.

"Hey, Bambine', you're finally home. But where do you go this early on a Sunday morning, if you don't mind *my* asking?"

Theirs was an odd and confidential friendship. Once, years earlier, Bambinella had been arrested with a group of prostitutes who were trolling for customers not far from the Teatro San Carlo. Her beauty and youth contrasted clearly with the appearance of the other hookers, whose advanced age kept them out of the warm, safe authorized brothels, of which there were hundreds in the city. When the reason that Bambinella couldn't have hoped for such a position either became evident, Maione let her go, prompted by an impulse that he still didn't fully understand today. Perhaps it was a simple desire for consistency, since that strange long-legged creature was so different from the other whores caught in the sweep, with her broad shoulders and her slightly horsey features.

They'd established an odd friendship; Maione soon realized

Bambinella's immense potential as a source of information, and the *femminiello*, or fetching young transvestite, had become fond of the gruff policeman who was oblivious to his own weakness.

And so every time he hit a wall during an investigation into some crime, or whenever there was a sensitive piece of information that needed to be checked out, Maione endured the immensely fatiguing climb all the way up to the garret apartment behind Vicolo di San Nicola da Tolentino, with its terrace covered with pigeon guano, where Bambinella practiced her profession. The center of the spiderweb.

"Brigadie', what a romantic gesture: a suitor waiting outside the door of his lady love, early in the morning on the Sunday before Christmas. A girl comes home from Mass and who does she find? This strapping handsome man waiting for her. Not even at the moving picture house could I hope to see such a touching story!"

Maione rubbed his eyes, in an attempt to clear his head.

"And in fact you're not seeing it here either. Listen, Bambine', spare me the chitchat, this morning I have a headache you could photograph. I haven't slept a wink. I told my wife that I had something important to do for work and I went out, before she had a chance to start peppering me with questions."

Bambinella put her hands with their long painted fingernails over her mouth, in a gesture that couldn't have been more feminine.

"Ooh, *mamma mia*, then it must be something serious! I'd better make you a cup of ersatz coffee first thing; that'll help you to get over your headache. Have you already eaten your breakfast? I have a tray of *roccocò* and *mustacciuoli*, a client of mine who works in a pastry shop in the center of town brought them for me, would you like some?"

Maione grimaced.

"For Pete's sake, that's all I need now, a tray of *roccocò* first thing in the morning, you might as well just take me directly to the Pellegrini hospital. Just an ersatz coffee, please: it's filthy stuff, but at least it'll scrub the foul taste out of my mouth."

Bambinella snickered as she set to work at her stove.

"You're always so kind, *grazie*, Brigadie'. I know what you meant to say. 'Bambine', the way you make ersatz coffee, with those golden hands of yours, no one else comes close.' And if you only knew what else I know how to do, with these golden hands of mine; just think that a client of mine, who's a butcher in Torretta, says that my hand could wake up a dead man, especially when—"

"Bambine', please," Maione broke in brusquely, "I can take anything this morning, except for you confiding in me about your work. Moreover, if you make me think about what you do with your hands, then I'm going to have a hard time keeping this ersatz coffee down, so let's just drop it."

"Whatever you say, Brigadie'. It's just that a girl likes to share certain professional accomplishments, every one in a while, at least with her friends. Well, to what do I owe the honor of your visit, so early on a Sunday morning? I don't recall us ever meeting before on this day of the week. And we're almost in the midst of the Christmas festivities. Ah, let me guess: it's about what happened in Mergellina, is that it? Husband and wife, the man from the port militia, no?"

Maione shook his head, stunned.

"Incredible. But you're illiterate, and if you don't know how to read you couldn't have read it in the papers. Do you mind telling me how you found out?"

Bambinella scratched the hairs that kept sprouting up on the backs of her hands, which she'd so carefully shaved.

"Ah, Brigadie', by chance, purely by chance. I have a few girlfriends who ply their trade over at the Torretta brothel, you remember the place, one time you and I went over together to question one of them who happened to have some piece of information—I can't even remember what, but it was something you needed, I know that much. Well, they also work with fishermen sometimes, and with the local loan sharks. Of course, it's not like the fishermen can pay much, but they do bring them fresh fish and the girls eat them, even though the madam yells at them when they cook in their rooms because she says that a bordello ought to smell like roses, not fried fish . . ."

Maione lifted both hands in the air.

"For the love of all things holy, Bambine': just once, stick to the topic. I'm in a condition today to chase you through all the *vicoli* in the city. Let's just discuss the facts."

Bambinella put on a fake pout, pooching out her painted lips.

"Bad, bad Brigadier, why won't you let me talk the way I want to? Anyway, I met one of those girls and she told that all anyone's been talking about is the murder of this . . . what's his name . . . Garofalo, I think. And that people are saying lots of things about him."

"Well? What are they saying?"

Bambinella giggled coquettishly, her long fingers covering her mouth.

"Ooh, Jesus, how would I know? It's not like I took the time to ask about it, I didn't know that you and the handsome green-eyed commissario, the one who brings bad luck, were working the murder. If I had, I would have found out more, naturally."

"If I've told you once, I've told you a thousand times," Maione snapped, "I don't like it when you say that the commissario brings bad luck! First of all, it isn't true, and besides anyone who thinks that needs to come say it to my face, that way I can knock it out of their mouth, along with their teeth, once and for all!"

Bambinella fluttered her false eyelashes.

"But I say it on purpose just to see you lose your temper. *Mamma mia*, Brigadie', you know how much it excites me to see a manly man get angry like that."

"Bambine', you insist on kidding around but I'm here about very serious matters," Maione replied wearily. "Now listen to me carefully, we have no time to waste and there are two things I have to ask you. First, you need to go see your girlfriends at Torretta right away and find out everything they know or have heard about this Garofalo. Above all whether anyone had it in for him or had threatened him."

Bambinella listened, taking noisy little sips of her ersatz coffee from a Chinese-style demitasse, her right pinky extended, red fingernail protruding into the empty air.

"And the second thing, Brigadie'?"

Maione furrowed his brow. He didn't like what he was about to do, and it was something he'd never done before: use a professional tool for personal ends. He took a deep breath, then said:

"I need something else. This is highly confidential, Bambine', no one else can know, absolutely no one. I need you to find for me a certain Biagio Candela. He ought to be young, very young. I couldn't tell you what he does or where he lives, but I need you to track him down. But I can tell you that his brother, who was named . . . is named Mario, Mario Candela, is in prison, at Poggioreale."

Bambinella listened raptly, her eyes fixed on the brigadier's, her face expressionless. Then she nodded her head and said, in a low voice, free of her usual affectations:

"I know who Mario Candela is, Brigadie'. I also know that he was killed last week, in a prison brawl. And of course I know why he was in prison, among other things."

She paused, caressing the back of her hand against the grain of the hairs.

"You shave them, and you shave them, but they always grow

back, these hairs. That's just the way nature is, no, Brigadie'? You can't keep it hidden. A girl can fight it, but nature doesn't change. Are you sure that you want to track down this Biagio Candela? Have you thought it over carefully?"

Maione wondered how much and which things in particular Bambinella knew about his son's murder. He'd never given it any thought before.

"Yes, Bambine'. I want to track him down. And if you don't want to help me, thanks all the same, I'll find him on my own, you know I can."

Bambinella looked out the window. Curled up on the sill was a pigeon, head tucked under its wing, doing its best to find shelter from the chilly December wind.

"It'll be dead by tonight, poor little creature. And no one can do a thing about it."

She turned back to look at Maione, with a smile.

"We're friends, Brigadie'. Friends help each other, without asking and without limits. Don't worry, I'll find out where this Biagio Candela is and I'll let you know. Come back tonight and we'll talk. About both things."

Maione gulped down the terrible ersatz coffee, nodded goodbye, and set off, head down, to face the rest of his Sunday.

XXIII

Ricciardi had put in a call to the hospital, inviting Dr. Modo to lunch at Gambrinus at one. He'd taken a seat at his usual table, in the indoor dining room that overlooked Via Chiaia, and he'd ordered an espresso to kill time while he waited.

Gambrinus was the only place in town that Ricciardi liked to spend time in; the comings and goings of customers went on all day long, with variations in the clientele depending on the moment and time of day, offering an interesting cross-section of humanity. The stucco decorations and Art Nouveau frescoes, the diffuse lights, the discreet waiters. The stale scent of an ancient capital, now mothballed.

The red velvet chairs were comfortable, the music that came from the concert grand piano at the center of the room was excellent, and the sfogliatella pastries were outstanding: for the commissario this was more than sufficient grounds for appointing the historic café his office away from the office, and his personal lunchroom.

He'd been coming here for years, and not one of the waiters, who were accustomed to seeing him sitting off to the side, at his usual corner table, had ever ventured to greet him with any special familiarity. What Ricciardi appreciated more than any other quality was the gift of discretion, so hard to find these days and virtually extinct in that city.

Through the window he saw a steady river of people coming and going, loaded down with bags and parcels, gloves and hats, their noses and cheeks pink from the cold. Mute laughter, chatter that failed to reach him through the thick plate glass. It was like a film at the movie house, but in color, though those hues were dulled by the pale winter sun.

At the corner of Via Toledo, on the sidewalk, there was an old woman bundled up in blankets, her hand outstretched, begging for pennies. Every so often a passerby would drop a coin, and the woman would rapidly snatch the money away, hiding it under her tattered covers.

Standing just inches away from her, a little boy was playing a crank organ, wearing a half smile. The reason it was a half smile was that the rest of his face, as well as the leg and arm on that side of his body, was a shapeless mass of bloody flesh. Ricciardi, who had seen the image of that child every day for the past week, remembered the accident: a car had taken the curve at high speed late at night; the little beggar boy must have been trying to chase down one last munificent passerby and had instead intercepted the speeding vehicle driven by a short-sighted motorist. These things happen, Ricciardi thought to himself.

The child with the crooked half smile was calling: *Merry Christmas, Merry Christmas, Signo'. A couple of pennies for a song on the crank organ!* To the eyes of Ricciardi's soul, he seemed to be trying to attract customers for the old woman, since he didn't need them for himself anymore. He wished it could be the other way around, and that the little boy were still playing his crank organ with fingers deformed by chilblains. Without thinking, the commissario ran his hand over his wound, which was still healing.

"It hurts, doesn't it? That's too bad. That'll teach you to do what you're told and finish your convalescence next time, instead of hurrying out to bust the chops of honest citizens," said Dr. Modo, letting himself drop down into the red velvet chair next to Ricciardi's. The doctor doffed his hat and gloves, rubbing his hands together to warm them up.

"No, it doesn't hurt; it just itches a little, maybe. You know, I've got a really first-rate doctor, and then I was in no condition to listen at the time, so I just took the best and skipped the worst: listening to him talk, I mean."

"But that's what you like most about me, my brilliant conversation!"

Ricciardi grimaced in pain.

"I like it so much that I can't do without it even on a Sunday, as you can see for yourself."

As he was doing his best to catch the waiter's eye, Modo said:

"In fact I found the phone call from your lackey deeply offensive. First, because you groundlessly presumed that, even though it was Sunday, you were bound to catch me at the hospital; second, because you were right."

"As you see, Bruno, I'm the last man in town who could serve as a model of sophisticated amusement and the proper way to spend one's free time. But you know how important the first few days after a murder are in terms of gathering the necessary evidence."

Modo laughed heartily.

"A fine excuse, to avoid admitting that one has no idea what to do with himself on a Sunday. Now, I'm not complaining: I get to eat a delicious lunch for free, which seems fair and fitting for a poor underpaid doctor. Whereas you, who I've heard tell are fabulously wealthy and notoriously stingy, are going to have to foot the bill."

Ricciardi laughed in turn.

"Neither fabulously wealthy—at least I don't think I am, and in any case I don't particularly care either way—nor stingy. But the exquisite pleasure of having lunch with you is just one more indication of how accident-prone I really am. Come on, let's order; it's getting late and I have another appointment on this long working Sunday."

Out of the corner of his eye, Ricciardi saw the dog position itself comfortably not far from the beggar woman, out on the street. It sat down by the wall, where it was sheltered from the wind and able to keep an eye on the front door of the café. Its white coat with dark brown spots seemed shinier than before.

"Yes, I had him washed," said Modo, following the commissario's gaze. "After all, if I'm taking him into my home, then I can hardly afford the embarrassment of catching something infectious, can I? I'm still a doctor, after all."

"I'd never have thought it. So you've adopted him after all. You've become a dog owner."

Modo laughed.

"You don't know him. He's not the kind of dog a person can say he owns; he decides who he wants to live with. It's a temporary partnership that we have. There's no leash on him, and none on me. You don't know it, my solitary friend, but that's how all great loves are: no ball and no chain."

By the time they were done with their meal, the crowds on the street were starting to thin, in part because a hard, ice-cold rain had begun to fall. The old beggar woman had gotten to her feet with some difficulty and gone to seek shelter in an entryway. Ricciardi saw the image of the boy, with his horrendous smile, still perfectly dry as he went on asking for a couple of pennies for a song that he would never play again.

"So Bruno, tell me, what did you learn from the autopsy of Signore and Signora Garofalo? Did you find out anything new?"

Modo stretched, reclining against the backrest and extending his legs under the table.

"Ah, so now it's time to sing for my supper, I knew this was coming. All right then, the signore and the signora kept themselves in good shape. They were well nourished, in good general states of health, no serious illnesses. The signora had three gold teeth, while he was missing a couple; but he'd lost them long ago, nothing worth mentioning. The man's joints were starting to harden—if he'd been allowed to live another four or five years, then he might have started to complain about his hips or his knees. But overall I'd have to say that they were both in good health."

Ricciardi was waiting for more.

"Well, to tell the truth, when I saw them, they didn't really look all that healthy. What can you tell me about the way they died?"

"You're right," Modo agreed, "by that time they were no longer all that healthy. They died that same morning. I did a few tests on the tissues and the organs, and I'd have to guess they were killed a few hours before they were found, maybe at eight, nine o'clock. The signora died of blood loss. It couldn't have taken more than a few seconds: a severed carotid artery is always fatal. I can confirm that my initial impression from my first quick exam was correct: it was a single sharp blow from right to left. There are two possible scenarios: either the blade was very sharp indeed, or someone held her head still while they cut her throat."

Ricciardi listened attentively.

"So you found no signs of struggle on the body? I don't know: bruises, even small ones, ruptured blood vessels, lesions . . ."

"No, absolutely not. Those are the first things I look for, as you know. No signs at all. She wasn't expecting it."

"Was the killer right-handed or left-handed?"

Modo shrugged his shoulders.

"Impossible to say. You'd have to know whether her throat was slashed from the front, as I think it was, or from behind. The cut goes from left to right, from the victim's point of view. But there are no signs of a struggle. The woman put up no resistance."

In his mind's eye Ricciardi saw Signora Garofalo as she

asked, smiling and oozing blood from her terrible wound: *Hat and gloves?* graciously and courteously. From the front, I'd have to say, he thought. From the front.

"What about the husband, Bruno? You find out anything there? How can you explain the number of stab wounds?"

"That's something you're going to have to ask the killer, or rather I should say the killers, because to my mind—and I told you this when we first talked—there was more than one hand at work here. The fatal blow was the first one, straight to the heart. That blow alone would have killed him. While he was dying, and it couldn't have been more than a matter of a few seconds, he was stabbed at least five more times, between the ribs and the abdomen. I can tell you that for certain, because the wounds went on bleeding, though not for long, which means that the heart hadn't yet stopped. The other twenty-six . . . that's right, twenty-six . . . stab wounds were inflicted on an already-dead body."

Ricciardi committed the information to memory, remembering Garofalo sitting in a pool of his own blood, stating in no uncertain terms that he owed nobody anything.

"And you confirm that in your judgment there was more than one killer."

The Gambrinus pianist charged into the afternoon with a heartrending tango. A couple stood up from their table and began to dance.

"That's right, and I'll tell you why: the first wound is a clean, deep cut, inflicted with great power. The murderer first set the tip of the knife as if carefully taking aim, and then slowly drove it down, sure as can be, until it penetrated the heart. That's not an easy thing to do, you know; it takes a determination that you can imagine for yourself, but it also requires a truly strong hand, because there would have been none of the momentum you get when you pull back and bring the knife down hard from above. The other wounds are all much shallower, and they were all delivered from right to left."

Lost in thought, Ricciardi watched the dancing couple twirl and pirouette. The woman, under her breath, sang along raptly:

. . . *terra di sogni e di chimere*
se una chitarra suona
cantano mille capinere
hanno la chioma bruna
hanno la febbre in cor
chi va a cercar fortuna
vi troverà l'amor . . .

"So, forgive me, but what makes you conclude that there was another hand? If the direction was the same . . ."

Modo shook his head.

"Eh, no, *caro*, let me finish. I was just talking about the first group of stab wounds. Then there's another dozen or so that were inflicted in the opposite direction, from left to right, not as deep but more closely grouped together. A different arm, a whole other kind of strength. So I'd have to conclude a different hand."

The doctor was certain of his analysis, and Ricciardi knew very well how conscientious he was. The picture was starting to take shape.

"And so what's your conclusive impression?"

Modo knitted his fingers together behind his head. He followed Ricciardi's gaze and saw that he was watching the dancers. The woman went on singing:

. . . *e nell'oscurità*
ognuno vuol godere
son baci di passion
l'amor non sa tacere

*e questa è la canzon
di mille capinere . . .*

"My conclusive impression, as you say, my dear lord of the shadows, also known as Ricciardi of the Handsome Smile, is that the murderers started off with one idea and then let themselves get swept away by their passions, just like the warbling chickadees in the song sung by the lovely signorina, who by the way is a high-ticket whore, if you ask me. They wanted to see justice done, to take the law into their own hands and perform a formal execution, and then they went overboard and turned it into an orgy of blood, either each with his own knife or else passing the weapon around. You don't murder someone like this during a robbery or because of an argument that spun out of control. You and my beloved Brigadier Maione, who's now enjoying a pleasant Sunday meal with his family and a bowl of ragú—at least *he's* enjoying himself, lucky man—are going to have to find some powerful motive for this hatred. Because it took a lot of hate to commit this murder. Not for the woman; she was no more than an obstacle."

Through Ricciardi's mind passed first the statuette of the Madonna, tipped over against the figurine of the ass, and then the shattered fragments of the Saint Joseph. In the rain out on the street, almost deserted by now, the child stared into the middle distance with his bloody half smile, asking for a couple of coins to play a song on his crank organ.

Some ten feet away, the dog lay curled up, his coat ruffled lightly by the wind, one ear hanging and the other perked up, waiting for the doctor.

In the café, the tango came to an end with one last chord and a wobbly dip.

"Have I earned myself an espresso to top it off?" Modo said.

Outside, night had already fallen.

XXIV

Maione had waited for night to fall, engaged the whole time in a terrible struggle to conceal his emotional state from his family.

The news that Franco Massa had given him had demolished with a single fell blow the wall of the room in which, in his soul, he'd tried to lock away his perennial grief over his son's death. A wall he'd built day by day, brick by brick.

He realized only now how important it had been to know that the man guilty of the murder had been punished in accordance with the law in order to find an equilibrium, a state of resignation. Maione was a simple man, and he knew that he was: every action needed to be met by a reaction. Arresting the man that he believed guilty of the murder certainly did nothing to bring Luca back to life, but it had at least fulfilled his duty as a policeman.

He still had a vague memory of the days spent at the trial. At first he hadn't wanted to go at all, then Lucia had asked him to, because she couldn't bring herself to attend; she didn't want it thought that Luca's family had abandoned his memory. They had been days of confusion, altered states of mind, time passed in sleepless nights and blurred thoughts.

He remembered the courtroom in Castel Capuano, the smell of wood and dust, the chill in the room, the eyeless gazes of the busts and statues of the great lawyers of the past. He remembered the stentorian voice of the prosecuting attorney, who was demanding a conviction and a sentence that would set an example, and the pale, bloodless face of the man who he then believed had been Luca's murderer.

He vaguely recalled the mother, a woman who seemed much older than she was, and who wept incessantly, while someone comforted her.

Just as vaguely, he remembered the face of a boy who couldn't have been any older than Luca, arm in arm with his mother. Pale, light-skinned, fair-haired. He remembered thinking, and then saying to Ricciardi, who was at his side the whole time, that he couldn't imagine a man murdering a boy who so closely resembled his own brother. Ricciardi had replied that that's how it always was, after all.

That face, just barely emerging from the mists of the memories that he'd tried to erase, that face was the face of Luca's killer. Now he knew it. If only he'd known it then.

Playing with his children, listening to the radio, eating his Sunday meals, Maione had had that obsessive thought burrowing into his brain the whole time. Just have to get used to it, he told himself. Until I can start building that wall again. In the meantime, it's getting dark: time to come up with some excuse for Lucia and go see Bambinella.

He found Bambinella with her customary black kimono dotted with red flowers, tied closed at the waist with a silk sash, her long raven locks gathered in a ponytail with a large horn comb holding the hair together, and a black slip underneath, the lace trim peeking out from under her décolletage. On her chest and face, the dark shadow of mutinous hair and whiskers.

She was wrapping the corpse of the pigeon that had been struggling to withstand the cold just that morning in a newspaper parcel. Hot tears streaked her face, and she dabbed at them with a handkerchief into which she noisily blew her nose from time to time.

"You see, Brigadie'? It's dead. I knew it. I could see it was sick, when they start to tuck their heads under their wings, that means they're dying. *Puveriello!* Poor little thing!"

And she blew her nose again, producing the sound of a trombonist hitting a flat note.

"Buck up, Bambine', it was only a pigeon. Come on, what's it amount to? Human beings are born and die, and pigeons are born and die every day. Get over it."

"What can I do about it, Brigadie'. I'm tenderhearted; little critters just grab me inside, the same way little children do. There's no one to defend them. I bury dead pigeons in the dirt, out on the terrace. The thing is they won't let me keep them, and besides this is where I have to do my work, otherwise the place would be full of cats and dogs."

"That's all we need up here, a nice little zoo. Listen, forgive me if I'm hammering at you today, on Sunday of all days, but I need to know if you were able to find anything out."

Bambinella sat down gracefully in her low wicker armchair, knees together, arms folded.

"Brigadie', you offend my honor when you say these things. Do you think that if Bambinella makes a friend a promise, she's going to break it?"

"Let's drop this whole routine about what good friends we are. You give me information, and in exchange I don't throw you in jail. Do you really think a cop like me could be friends with someone like you? Come on, let's get to it; I told my wife that I was going out for a walk and I have to get back quickly."

Bambinella shot him a sly and fetching smile.

"You just say that to keep from seeming weak and silly, but we're friends and you know it. Of course, if you ever want something more, remember, for you it would always be free of charge. If you only knew how many of my clients tell their wives that they're just going out for a walk when they come here . . ."

Maione pretended to grab a vase and throw it in the *femminiello*'s direction.

"One of these days I'm going to crack your noggin, as God is my witness! Don't you dare, you hear me? And all this talk, the free this and the free that, I don't want to hear it again, is that clear?"

Bambinella shook her shoulders in annoyance.

"Well, all right then, there'll be no sentiment tonight either. It doesn't matter, besides, sooner or later . . . No, don't lose your temper. So, let's start with the guy from the port militia. How true it is that things aren't always what they seem."

"What do you mean?"

"I mean that behind all that respectability, that façade that said he was on the up-and-up, with no double life, no lover on the side, a man who never played cards, never did anything even remotely immoral, in reality he was *'nu bellu fetente*—a big stinker."

Maione was perplexed.

"Are you saying he actually did have a lover and he actually did play cards?"

Bambinella laughed.

"No, when on earth? The man really had no vices, as far as that goes. He was absolutely . . . how should I put it? . . . very serious. The way he was seen, that was the way he was."

"Then why do you say he was a *fetente*—a stinker?"

"Now let me explain: this girlfriend of mine who works at the Torretta brothel, not the Gilda you met the other time, this one is called Concetta, but she goes by Colette like that actress, the one, ah, what's her name? Oh, Madonna, I can't think of it . . ."

Maione motioned to reach for the vase again.

"Oh, all right, Brigadie', you know that I have to tell my story in my own way. So, to make a long story short, a number of this girlfriend of mine's clients are fishermen, she's always hungry so she's willing to take care of them in exchange for something to eat—when she doesn't have paying clients, that is, of course. In short, she says that this Garofalo, ever since he became the whatever it is, the commandant of the supervisors of the fishermen, he'd been threatening them."

Maione tried to understand.

"What do you mean, he'd been threatening them?"

"In the sense that he made them give him money or else he'd confiscate their fishing boats. I don't really understand the details, but apparently, if he wanted, he could just take their boats from them. And you know, Brigadie', a fishing boat is everything to a fisherman; if someone takes your boat away, they've just killed you and your whole family. Well, that's how this Garofalo was shaking them down."

Maione was baffled.

"But witnesses told us that he wouldn't even accept gifts of fish when they brought them to his apartment. They told me so personally."

Bambinella let go with a brief, shrewd laugh.

"That's right, I heard the same thing from my little girl-friend. She says that the whole thing was orchestrated, that he told the fishermen himself to bring the fish to his home and then he'd send them away, to show everyone that he was above graft. You see what he did, the sly dog?"

"I can't believe it. I can't believe that someone could go that far. Just how many fishermen was he shaking down?"

Bambinella shrugged her shoulders.

"Ah, that's not something she was able to tell me, my little girlfriend. But she did say that one of them couldn't pay him anymore, because he has a sick little boy, the kid actually seems to be dying, and he's had to pay for the doctor, and this Garofalo told him that he didn't give a damn about his problems, that the man needed to find the money or he'd confiscate his boat. And that this fisherman, sobbing in front of everyone, said that before he'd let his son die, he'd make sure that Garofalo died first—that he'd cut him open with his fish-gutting knife, his exact words."

Maione focused more intently.

"Is that what he said? With his knife? How long ago was this?"

"Three or four days ago."

"Do you know the name of this fisherman, by chance?"

Bambinella nodded.

"Yes, Brigadie'. His name is Boccia, Aristide Boccia, and he lives in Borgo Marinari, near the Castel dell'Ovo. But she told me that there were at least three others beside him, under threat of losing their boats."

Maione stroked his chin.

"I see. Another lead, then. *Grazie*, Bambine'. And listen, about that other matter . . ."

Bambinella smiled sadly.

"I already have that information, Brigadie'. But are you sure you want to know it, too? Don't you want to mull it over a little longer? In a few days it'll be Christmas."

Maione felt a shiver go down his back. He felt very weak; maybe he was even running a slight fever.

"I've already thought it over, believe me. Many times. So if you have any information for me, now's the time."

Bambinella sighed, then said:

"Biagio Candela, apprentice. He lives in Vico Santi Filippo e Giacomo, number 22. From the day that . . . from that day, the day that his brother went to prison, he seems to have broken off all his old friendships, he got married, and he had two children. And right now, just like so many other poor wretches out there, he must be getting ready for Christmas. Now if you'll excuse me, Brigadie', I have to bury this poor creature."

And Bambinella, her kimono fluttering in the wind, went out onto the terrace to give the deceased pigeon a funeral.

XXV

I remember when Angelina came out the door of the basso, and walked over to me here, by the sea.

The spray came almost to our feet, and the moored boats were riding and plunging. I looked out at the lights of the city, which seemed so close because of the clear, windswept air. It was so cold, Madonna mia. It was so cold.

She came to me because she knew that I'd come out here to cry. I don't want her to see it, her or the kids. Especially not Vincenzino. I know that he sees me, even if he sleeps all the time. The last time the doctor came he told me: he can see and he can hear, he's just too weak to speak.

I hadn't seen her coming, Angelina. Wrapped in her black shawl, so that it even covered her head; she frightened me. I was thinking about death, and she looked just like death, with her white face, her sunken eyes.

She was a girl, Angelina. Just a few months ago she was a girl, laughing all the time, filling life with happiness. Everyone knew the sound of her laughter, here in the Borgo. But she doesn't laugh anymore. She doesn't laugh anymore.

She was a girl and all at once she turned into an old woman, after Vincenzino fell ill. An old woman, who looks like death itself.

So she stands next to me, and she looks out at the city lights through the clear night air. You have to finish the nativity scene, she tells me. Christmas is coming, and you have to finish the nativity scene. Vincenzino really loves it, the nativity scene.

We don't have the money, I tell her. We don't have the money for food, or to take care of Vincenzino, much less for Christmas, for the nativity scene, for sweets and candy and all that nonsense. And it's so cold out here. But I can't go back in, because I'm still crying.

Angelina doesn't tremble, she just looks at the lights. Her voice is low and firm. But now, she says, now that we've rid ourselves of that tick, that parasite, we'll have the money. We'll be able to eat, and take care of Vincenzino the way the doctor said.

Are you sure of that? I ask her. Are you sure there won't be another to take Garofalo's place, and then another after him? And how do you know they won't demand even more, and more? I can't go on like this. You know I can't.

She turns to me and smiles. Her smile scares me; she looks like a skull, a death's head. I hadn't realized how gaunt she'd become.

Then if there's another one, the same thing can happen to him, no? He too can die choking on his own blood. Remember: he's dead, and Vincenzino is still breathing.

Someone has to die, in other words. Is that what you're saying?

She looks out at the lights again and pulls her shawl tighter.

If there's another one, then he'll die, too. If I have to save my son, he'll die, too.

By my hand.

XXVI

Before he could call an end to his long workday that Sunday, Ricciardi had one more thing he needed to do. So he headed out at quick walk to reach the Arco Mirelli before it got to be too late. He didn't know the schedule that the convent kept on days when there was no school, but he wanted to give it a try, just to see if he could get ahead.

This time the novice recognized him with a smile. Ricciardi asked for Sister Veronica, and waited until the young sister returned and told him to follow her.

They walked through the garden, where the wind stopped its lashing because of the high limestone walls that protected it from the outside world. Only the nearby sea was betrayed by the roaring of the waves. Otherwise, this was a place out of the world and out of time.

He was accompanied to the top of a stone staircase, and left to wait near a large painting of the Virgin Mary. It was beautiful, clearly quite old but in an excellent state of preservation. Ricciardi was fascinated by it; the woman's features were delicately rendered and very fine but they also conveyed a deep well of sorrow, the eyes uplifted to a heaven from which a cold light descended. On her head was a sparkling crown, in her chest an open wound in which could be seen a naked, palpitating heart, pierced by two swords. One of the Madonna's hands was raised upward in mute, heartfelt supplication, while the other hand gestured to her own chest and her suffering heart.

To his surprise, Ricciardi heard the sounds of children's voices and clattering dishes coming from a nearby room. He had expected the silence of a convent busy with its Sunday services, and instead it seemed like a school, now more than it had on his first visit.

In the distance he saw the ridiculous rotund, prancing figure of Sister Veronica coming down the hall, and she greeted him with her characteristic trumpet-like voice.

"What a surprise, Commissario. What are you doing in this part of town, on a Sunday and at this hour?"

Ricciardi greeted the woman, once again uneasily finding the clammy little hand in his own. He made a mental note to greet her from a distance the next time.

"*Buonasera*, Sister. I'm sorry to bother you, but I wanted to ask you something. If you're busy, of course, I can come back later."

Sister Veronica shot a glance down the hallway, which echoed with the shouts of children. A contented smile spread across her broad face.

"On Sundays we let in the poor children from the surrounding areas, for the most part children of fishermen and laborers. We give them something to eat, we keep them warm, we let them play. They aren't the same children who go to school here; this is an act of charity that the institute undertakes. And this time of the year, with Christmas on the way, many of them don't have the same kinds of treats that rich children do—candy and sweets, presents, the nativity scene. So we just do our best to make up for this disparity, as simple as that."

Ricciardi nodded.

"That's an honorable thing to do. First of all, I wanted to ask how the little girl is doing, your niece."

Sister Veronica heaved a sigh, and shot a fleeting glance at the painting of the Virgin Mary.

"What can I tell you, Commissario. She doesn't ask any

questions, she doesn't say anything. She's a sensitive, shy child. I'm with her all the time, I watch her sleep, and she's not having bad dreams, at least for now. I think that she still hasn't realized what's happened."

Ricciardi understood. A normal reaction.

"What about you, Sister? How are you?"

"I'm trying to cast out the anger from my heart. I'm trying not to think about my sister, how sweet she was, about the years of our childhood, how close the two of us were. I'm trying not to hate whoever did this. We can't hate, you know that? If She," she said, tipping her head in the direction of the Virgin Mary in the painting, "didn't hate mankind, who put Her son on the cross, and even interceded with Him on our behalf, then who are we to hate one another?"

Ricciardi felt himself struggling to reconcile conflicting feelings, the way he did every time he was brought face-to-face with the inflexible logic of faith. On the one hand, he felt envy for this ability to control one's emotions, and on the other this absence of human sentiments, however negative, such as rage and the thirst for vengeance, made him uneasy.

"My sister and her husband," Sister Veronica was saying, "have gone home to their Everlasting Father. Whoever did this must pay, and they will pay in the judgment that awaits them; and not only here on earth. What good does it do to hate?"

"I understand, Sister. But we must continue our investigation. I asked you, the last time we met, if your sister or your brother-in-law had confided in you concerning threats they'd received, or anything of that sort."

Sister Veronica remembered perfectly. She replied in her distinctive shrill tone, which was amplified by the echoing corridor.

"And I told you no, that they hadn't confided anything in me. I've thought it over since, yesterday and today, but nothing at all comes to mind."

Ricciardi decided to explain the reason he was there to see her.

"I understand, but I wanted to ask you, Sister, if I might, for just a few minutes, and in your presence, of course, ask the little girl if she remembers anything or anyone."

Sister Veronica made a funny face.

"Commissario, I don't know if . . ."

As she was talking, a small boy went racing by behind her, saying:

"Sister Vero', really gotta go."

Without even turning to look, the nun's hand shot out and seized the child's ear, bringing him to an abrupt, painful stop. Ricciardi was reminded of a reptile's prehensile tongue snapping a flying insect out of the air.

"But first, when we're in front of the painting of the Virgin Mary, what do we do?"

The child fell to his knees, hastily crossing himself. The nun, who still had him firmly by the ear, insisted:

"The reason we call them sacred images is because they're sacred; if I've told you once, I've told you a thousand times. When you see one, in church or on the street, you must stop and cross yourself, perhaps also reciting a short prayer. How does it go? *Ave Maria, gratia plena . . .*"

The little boy raced through the prayer in a single breath, crossed himself again, and was finally liberated, whereupon he shot down the hall toward the bathroom.

Sister Veronica smiled.

"They're like little animals, but they're innocent souls. All right, Commissario: I'll go call Benedetta. But please, no more than two minutes."

The little girl resembled her aunt more than she did her mother and father, Ricciardi thought to himself as he watched the nun come down the hall with her niece. The same bouncing gait, the same round, red-cheeked face. The commissario envied the girl her ability to hold Sister Veronica's perennially sweaty hand without disgust; he knew he'd never be able to do it.

The girl wore a serious, conscientious expression, which seemed out of place with her age and the smear of paint on the smock she wore. Ricciardi waited for her to rise from the requisite genuflection before the painting of the Virgin Mary.

"*Buonasera*, Benedetta. I'm a . . . friend of your aunt, and there was something I wanted to ask you."

The little one sketched out a curtsey, graciously holding the hem of her smock.

"*Buonasera*, Signore. Please, go ahead. My aunt told me to answer any question you might have."

Ricciardi was relieved to hear that the child's voice was normal, and not piercing like her aunt's.

"In the past few days, do you remember hearing your papa and mamma argue about anything? Did they ever seem worried or upset?"

The girl thought carefully, then shook her head.

"No, Signore. Papa and Mamma are fine, *grazie*. Whenever Papa comes home, Mamma and I kiss him and we sit down at the dinner table straightaway; then he listens to the radio and reads the paper, while Mamma does needlepoint and I draw. Then we all go to bed."

Ricciardi went along.

"Certainly, of course. Well, by any chance do you happen to remember whether anyone came to visit your parents? Someone unusual, someone you'd never seen before?"

The little girl furrowed her brow, struggling to remember. Ricciardi was reminded of the image of Signora Costanza Garofalo, smiling with her throat cut, and he felt a twinge of sorrow for that mother who would never see her daughter grow up.

"A while ago, though I couldn't tell you just when, a gentleman and a lady dressed in black came to see us. It was when

Papa was reading his paper, after we'd finished eating. I didn't like them. They talked loudly, and Papa was talking loudly back to them; my aunt doesn't like it when you talk loudly. Isn't that right, Aunt Veronica?"

Sister Veronica nodded, caressing her niece's head. Ricciardi, who wondered in passing just how Sister Veronica supported her argument in favor of whispering with the voice that God had given her, decided that he should drill in on this new piece of information.

"Do you remember anything about those two people? How they were dressed, or anything that caught your eye? Why didn't you like them?"

"The lady wore a black shawl over her head," the girl said. "And the reason I didn't like them was they smelled bad. They smelled like fish."

XXVII

There are some people who are very different from what you might expect judging them based solely on their appearances. Slender, timid young ladies who, once they're onstage, produce voices and aggressive demeanors befitting a lioness; corpulent gentlemen who spin and float as light as gossamer to the notes of waltzes and tangos; coarse, bad-mannered young men who, with a paintbrush in hand, are capable of creating the most delicate arabesques and the most refined landscapes.

Maione, for instance, was a master at stakeouts.

You'd never have thought it to look at him, big strapping man that he was, clumsy and loud, with his deep voice that reverberated indoors and his harsh, powerful laugh, metallic as an empty tin drum rolling down the stairs. And yet he had this talent, and he made constant and discreet use of it.

Perhaps it was because he knew and understood the city; perhaps in any other city he would have been incapable of literally vanishing from sight, merging into the ever-changing backdrop of Naples, endlessly diverse and in perennial movement. But here he could do it, and how.

He had his methods, of course. He showed up early, buzzed around the target location; he took in his surroundings, scouted nooks, vestibules, spots swathed in darkness and others that were bright or well lit. He ran his gaze over the walls, taking in their structure and texture. He'd sniff the air, identifying the lay of the wind, the directions of the drafts and breezes.

He'd pick his target, the things he wanted to see, and he'd look for the best angle, the ideal viewpoint. He'd take in the essence of the place. It was as if he were determining a note and then matching the frequency so he could fade into it and vanish.

It wasn't something you could explain in words; it was something more on the order of an instinct, a little like having an ear for music, that which allows someone who can neither read nor write music to play a complicated melody on an instrument they've never even held in their hands before. He was a born prodigy, the brigadier was, and he'd further honed his gift with professional technique, along with an innate bent for close observation and years and years of experience.

Thus he'd learned to tail a suspect for miles on end in the city, even in neighborhoods that were virtually deserted, without that suspect ever noticing or sensing a thing. Because he knew every dogleg and alley, and made use of shortcuts unknown to most, he could, on foot, tail even people in vehicles and never be left behind. Once, instead of chasing a robber fleeing aboard a horse-drawn carriage, he'd sensed from the man's accent where he was headed and had simply shown up there and waited for him to arrive, without even breaking a sweat.

But what he was best at was stakeouts. He could merge into the shadows of an atrium, the crowd in a café, the darkness of a movie house, becoming to all intents and purposes invisible; and he'd spend hours watching everything that happened in a house or an apartment, in a club or a bar, including the thoughts that swept over the face and through the heart of the person he was spying on.

And that was why Maione had shown up very early that morning on Vico Santi Filippo e Giacomo, in the neighborhood of San Gregorio Armeno.

He'd told Lucia that he had some important work to do; his wife was accustomed to Maione working the predawn hours when he was in the throes of an investigation, and he had already told her about the couple who had been murdered in Mergellina. Still, Lucia had caught a hint of a false note in his voice. It was nothing in particular—a slight hesitation, an unusual word—but it was something. Nothing that she couldn't easily put out of her thoughts, like a bothersome fly, with all the things she had to do to get ready for Christmas with a family of five children. Soon enough, she'd stopped thinking about it entirely, limiting herself to preparing the best ersatz coffee she could whip up an hour earlier than usual, so that her husband could step out into the streets while it was still pitch-black out.

There wasn't a place in all of Naples that was more Christmassy than San Gregorio Armeno. It was the street of the *figurari*, those artisans whose work came close to full-fledged artistry, making the terra-cotta figurines and statuettes that were used in nativity scenes. They fit into every category imaginable, from those who took months to craft a single head and a pair of hands—which, once they had been placed on a wire and cotton batting body and dressed up advantageously with an outfit made by the city's finest tailors, would complete the oldest manger scenes, to the point that the addition was indistinguishable from the original—to those who used molds to produce dozens of terra-cotta shepherds every day, all identical in shape, differing only in the hastily painted colors, sold for a penny apiece, to the delight of the city's poorest children.

Those artisans couldn't know it—and in fact they never would—but the tradition of that street had roots that reached down deep into the mists of time. This was the place where, when the world was so much younger, terra-cotta statuettes were made in honor of Ceres, the goddess of plenty, for whom a celebrated temple had been built; and those statuettes were the souvenirs, treasured and beloved, of long pilgrimages, and they departed for every corner of the earth in the sacks of the faithful as they returned to their fields.

More than a thousand years ago, a church had been built on top of that temple, followed by another. Naples had always been a sedimentary city, a city that laid one stratum on top of another, one for each era, all of them with the same spirit of place. The pre-Christmas industriousness of this street, in any case, was very convenient for Maione, with the steady stream of workers and suppliers coming and going, in the full hum of activity before the sun had even had a chance to rise, along with the occasional underhanded antiquarian waiting for the finest workshops to open in order to purchase beautifully made pieces, which he would then resell as genuine antiques in his exclusive shop back in Chiaia. The more people there were moving around, the better the chances of passing unobserved.

The street numbers went past: 12, 16, 20. He reached number 22 just as the heavy wooden door was swinging open to let someone out of the building.

Maione pulled back into the shadows, quickly and soundlessly. The wall of the building across the way was providentially furnished with a nook, which created a dark corner from which he could watch the street without being seen.

The person who emerged from the street door was a young man, little more than an overgrown boy. A few stray locks of fair hair peeked out from under the cap pressed down on his head, the undersized overcoat barely covered his legs. The young man took a few steps, then stopped and looked up: a dark-haired young woman looked out from a small balcony on the second floor; she was wrapped in a blanket and had something in her arms. The young man waved, and the young woman nodded back. A small arm darted out of the bundle, and a voice said:

"Papà, papà!"

The mother, smiling, carefully tucked the baby under the warm blanket, as the young man in the street below laughed and blew a kiss into the air.

That hand, thought Maione, murdered my son.

Rosa Vaglio was looking at her left hand. It was shaking.

She'd noticed it a while ago, but not that long, to tell the truth: a matter of months. And as soon as she had, she'd remembered that her father had suffered from the same malady. She'd gone home to see her birth family, after she'd been in service with the baron and baroness of Malomonte for a few years; she'd asked for a little time off, and it had taken a day to walk to the village where she'd been born. The baroness wanted the foreman to take her in his cart, but she'd said no. She was young, back then. She felt like she could walk to the far corners of the earth. Now she got tired walking to the fruit and vegetable stands in the Piazza di Capodimonte.

She found her parents very different from the way she remembered them; the damage inflicted by the passage of time clearly outweighed the advantages afforded by the money she sent them, month after month. Out of her eleven siblings, only three were left—the rest had gone off in search of greener pastures, or were dead.

Her father had that tremor in his hand, as if he were perennially gesturing to say: *mamma mia*, how astounding. In his eyes, however, she read confusion, like a mute cry for help.

When she left she had felt a flood of relief. She promised to come back soon, but she'd never gone back at all. She heard that her father had died a few years later.

And now she sat looking at the tremor in her own hand: slight, barely visible. It didn't resemble her father's yet, at least not the way she remembered it; but it was there, and it was getting worse, little by little, like a spreading weed.

It was a signal, like so many others: her backaches, the struggle involved in sitting down and standing up, the need for her spectacles whenever she needed to do fine handiwork.

I've become an old woman, she told herself. A drab, useless

old woman. My body's falling apart, and I can no longer do the things I used to be able to.

But her memory still worked, at least; and her thoughts were clear, crystal clear.

One thought was clearer than all the others: her young master needed to settle down and start a family. She couldn't stand the idea of leaving him alone, a victim of his own ghosts, his incomprehensible sadness, that abyss of solitude from which he seemed unwilling to emerge. Rosa knew that the right woman would bring a smile to that face. She could feel it. All it would take was the warmth of a home, the responsibilities of a family, and Luigi Alfredo would regain control of his life, his standing in society, and the administration of his property: all things he'd always turned his back on.

She'd identified the right woman, too, although she had the shortcoming of being even more shy and prickly than he was. Certainly she couldn't give that simpering out-of-towner with her chauffeur a clear shot at him.

Rosa took one hand in the other and held it still. Not yet, she thought. I've still got things to do. I have to give fate a push; if something isn't going to happen of its own accord, then I'm going to have to make it happen myself.

By my hand.

XXVIII

Christmas is warm.

From the windows of the apartments overlooking Via Toledo and Via Chiaia come candlelight and the sound of laughter. If you look inside those windows, you see cheerful faces, cheeks bright-red with wine and spumante, even though the actual holiday is still a few days away. There is a general sense of expectation, a swell of suspense. A holiday is coming, and everyone is going to be happy.

Christmas is cold.

The wind howls through the streets of the new quarters, where the poor in their hovels huddle together for comfort and warmth. If you listen carefully, you can just make out the sound of a child crying, but the cries grow ever fainter as the cold and the hunger grow stronger. Who can say which of them will make it through the winter. Who can say which of them will still be breathing, come January.

Christmas is warm.

Mothers smile as they tousle their children's hair, deciding whether to dress them in sailors' costumes like they did last year, or whether they're big enough now to be in the family photograph with everyone else on Christmas Eve, dressed in their first jacket and tie, sober-faced, hair neatly parted.

Christmas is cold.

The man comes home with a chunk of bread, the only food he's been able to find after a day spent looking for work at construction sites. He stole it from a delivery cart, then he ran himself breathless for an hour. There are six mouths to feed, waiting for him at home, and he's hungry, too. He stops, lowers himself to the ground, and eats a piece of it. He weeps in the wind.

Christmas is warm.

Grandpa turns eighty years old, right on Christmas Day. Sitting in front of the ceramic stove, sipping his after-dinner brandy, while his children listen to dance music on the radio and wonder what they can get him, since he already has everything he needs, with all the money he's earned in his career as a respected physician. So they laugh, and decide to buy him a new smoking jacket, just like they did last year. But Grandpa will die, unexpectedly, on December 23, and his smoking jacket will never be taken out of the box.

Christmas is cold.

Under the scaffolding at a construction site down near the waterfront, the old beggar woman draws labored breaths; she's dead to the world. Bronchitis, the cold, and hunger have won out in the end. She dreams she's singing a lullaby. She had sixteen children and they took them away from her, one by one. She doesn't even know if they're alive or dead; she only remembers that she sang a lullaby, once, to one of her children, or to someone else's child. She had sixteen children, and now she's dying alone under the scaffolding at a construction yard. Tomorrow they'll toss her, with her tattered rags, into a ditch in potter's field, full of others like her.

Christmas, warm or cold, brings a shiver.

Ricciardi was waiting for Maione, who was late: an unusual thing for him, especially given their unspoken understanding that when they were on a case, they always met very early in the commissario's office to bring each other up-to-date on the general situation and to plan out their day. Still, Ricciardi wasn't overly concerned; Maione had finally regained his emotional equilibrium, and it couldn't have been easy to drag himself away from his warm, welcoming home and go out into the cold and the dark.

Ricciardi was very fond of the brigadier, and Maione's well-being mattered deeply to him. In the past three years, the whole time they'd been working together, Riccardi had learned to read Maione's thoughts and emotions. The brigadier was a fair, strong, stubborn man; he wasn't afraid to work hard; and he was still moved at the sight of pain, grief, and suffering, and that gift of empathy was a gift that Ricciardi valued above any other.

He could remember all too clearly the afternoon that the two men had first become fast friends: it was the day Maione's son Luca was murdered.

He'd seen the young man a few times, a recruit who stood out for his energy and his desire to prove himself: fair-haired, blue-eyed, physically imposing. As he'd later see at the funeral, the boy resembled his mother closely.

Ricciardi had responded to the emergency call, getting there even before Maione, who was on duty elsewhere. He'd walked down alone into the cellar where the body had been found. He saw the young man standing there, next to the corpse curled up on the ground. He was leaning against the wall as if trying to hide from sight, even though Ricciardi was the only one who could still see him. A reddish foam oozed from the mouth, the bubbles of his last breath; the knife plunged deep into his back had punctured his lung.

I love you, you big-bellied old man. I love you.

That's all Luca's image was saying. Ricciardi understood immediately whom the specter was talking about. When Maione got there, he took him aside and, violating for the first and only time in his life a principle to which he'd always adhered, he told him. He told him the dead boy's words.

The brigadier never asked him how he'd known them, not then, not ever. But he became Ricciardi's human shadow.

The Deed, as Ricciardi called his curse to perceive the last sorrow and pain of the dead, almost never helped him to uncover the way that death took place. It was just an emotion, a simple manifestation of the dying person's suffering upon being removed from this life: the final separation. Like a scream, or a sigh, or a regret. Or all these things together.

Maione rushed breathless into the office.

"Forgive me, Commissa'. I'm a little late this morning."

"No problem at all, I just got in myself. Sit down, and let's go over everything we did yesterday."

They exchanged the information they'd gathered on their working Sunday. Ricciardi recounted everything he'd learned from the doctor and Don Pierino concerning the autopsies and the symbolism of the manger scene, as well as what he'd found out from his talk with the Garofalos' daughter.

Maione listened attentively, with his characteristic manner of concentration, his eyes half closed as if he were on the verge of nodding off. Then he told Ricciardi everything that he'd learned from Bambinella.

"So everything would seem to fit together, Commissa'. The visitors that smelled of fish, the broken Saint Joseph that represents the father who works to provide for his family, the two people who stabbed Garofalo."

Ricciardi looked pensively out the window at the piazza that was slowly beginning to fill up with people. The pane of glass, fogged over from the temperature differential between interior and exterior, shook with every gust of wind.

"You said it: everything would seem to fit together. That doesn't mean it's all true, though. First of all, we've got to figure out what this Lomunno, the militiaman who Garofalo got fired, is up to. And the fact that a couple who smelled of fish went and had an argument with Garofalo doesn't mean that they went back later and killed him and his wife."

Maione nodded.

"Ah, of course. All these hypotheses need to be checked out, as always. But Commissa'—and this is a solid fact—now there are at least two suspects: Lomunno and the fisherman, Aristide Boccia; and there could be others still, if the victim was extorting more than one fisherman. We can certainly say that our dearly departed pillar of honesty wasn't so honest after all."

Ricciardi went on looking out the window.

"The hardest thing, Raffae', is understanding such strong emotions. What drives a person, or more than one person—people who might have children, family, friends, a difficult, demanding job—to think: now I'm going to get a good sharp knife, go to Garofalo's apartment, and kill him, and his wife, too."

Maione said nothing, his eyes downcast. Ricciardi went on.

"It takes tremendous anger, I believe. Or a state of extreme desperation. In any case, pain, grief, sorrow. To decide to murder someone in cold blood, without the burst of madness that comes from an argument or a fight, you must be certain that you have no alternative."

Maione looked up.

"That's exactly right, Commissa'. It's one thing to kill someone who's standing right in front of you, and quite another to make the decision and then go kill him. You'd have to be truly desperate, without any alternative."

From the window came a prolonged blast of car horns: something was blocking traffic. Ricciardi sighed and stood up.

"Let's go look this desperation in the face and see what we see."

XXIX

They'll come, I know that they'll come. So what? I've been waiting for them for years, now that I think about it. Ever since that day.

I should have done it then. I should have done it so that the sun would never set on my shame, the sun of that same day. I should have extinguished that false voice, cut the throat that produced all that wickedness.

They'll come, and they'll ask me why. And I'll tell them that there's no difference between doing something and dreaming of doing it.

And if there's no difference, then I've done that same thing a thousand times. A thousand times I've spilled that blood, a thousand times I've seen it spurt from the hundred wounds, a thousand times I've driven the knife in deep.

They'll come, and they'll want to know why. I'll tell them that my mind has never moved from there, from where I saw my life rush headlong into the void. And that I died, too, when my angel took flight.

They'll come, and I'll have to hide the thousands of times that I've dreamed of it happening.

By my hand.

XXX

Enrica blinked as she stepped out through the street door. The wind was gusting cold and strong.

Her eyeglasses had fogged over; she had to take them off to wipe the lenses. When she put them back on, emerging from the blurry outlines of her nearsighted world, she found herself face-to-face with Rosa, who held her hat clapped to her head with her right hand while with her left hand she gripped a half-empty shopping bag.

The old woman's expression was determined: lips compressed, eyes narrowed, jaw jutting. She wasn't going to take no for an answer.

"Signori', would you be so good as to come with me to buy a few things for Christmas dinner? I'm an old woman, I need a little help."

The girl didn't even have the time to look around before a powerful arm hooked itself through hers and she was dragged out into the street.

Ricciardi and Maione reached the alley behind San Giovanni a Mare which corresponded to the address they'd been given at the barracks. Maione reread the little scrap of paper for what seemed like the thousandth time.

"This is it, Commissa'. It seems strange to me, but this is definitely it."

In more ways than one, the place was unsettling. Once they turned the corner, the two policeman left the world of

Christmas and entered a no-man's-land of squalor and misery.

The symbols of the holiday, even the cheapest and most miserable, had all vanished. Before Ricciardi and Maione stretched a dirt road lined by hovels tacked together with scraps of wood and rusted sheet metal. A few ragged children were playing, sitting on the ground in the muddy rivulets fed by the lack of a sewer system. The only sound, aside from the wind, came from a shutter banging against a window jamb at regular intervals.

They went up to the oldest child in the group.

"*Guaglio'*, do you happen to know where a certain Lomunno lives around here?"

The boy stood up, walked a short distance, and pointed to the door of one of the shacks. He stood there, motionless, one arm raised like a mannequin.

Maione knocked on the door. After a few moments, a man opened it. With a carving knife in one hand.

The brigadier instinctively took a step back, one hand jumping to his holster. Ricciardi grabbed his arm.

"Easy there, take it easy. He had no way of knowing who was at the door. You there, are you Antonio Lomunno?"

The man looked at them both, then he looked down at the knife he was holding in his hand, as if he'd never seen it before.

"Yes, that's me. Excuse me, I was doing some work at home. You are . . ."

Maione had recovered his self-control, but he kept looking down at the blade.

"Brigadier Maione and Commissario Ricciardi, from the mobile squad. We have a few questions we need to ask you. May we come in?"

Rosa stared back at Enrica with a look of resolve from the other side of the small round table in the café near home, where she'd steered her, practically by main force.

After a long, awkward silence, during which the girl had sat looking down at her hands folded in her lap, the *tata* said:

"Well, Signori': if you don't mind my asking, what's happened?"

Enrica blinked her eyes, looking up at the woman.

"What do you mean, Signora? Nothing's happened. I . . ."

Rosa had no intention of being put off that easily.

"Excuse me, but something's happened, and I know it. The last time you came to my home, we spoke, and it seemed to me that you were interested in my young master; there was certainly interest on his part. Then the accident happened. You even came to the hospital, and I remember the fear, the terror in your eyes. And then, when we found out that he was going to be all right, thanks be to God Almighty, instead of coming to see him, you vanished."

Enrica tried to mount a halfhearted defense.

"No, it's not so much that I vanished; it's more that I've just had so many things to do, Christmas is coming, my little nephew . . ."

Rosa swept away these excuses with an impatient wave of her hand.

"Signori', please, don't come tell this nonsense to me. You may be able to pull the wool over a man's eyes, but not another woman's. You even keep your shutters closed at night; that poor man looks out the window and he's denied even the pleasure of a nod in his direction. He's suffering, and I have to watch him suffer. So now I want to know: if you've simply gotten tired of him, if you're no longer interested, just tell me, and we'll be friends like before."

The young woman leapt up as if spring-loaded.

"What on earth are you saying? How could you even think such a thing? Do you take me for one of those fickle women who change direction with the wind, like a weather vane?"

Rosa leaned back in her chair, finally satisfied.

"No, I don't think you are. That's why I was so baffled. All right, then: tell me what really happened."

"I'd be lying if I said I didn't know why you're here."

The interior of the hovel mirrored the exterior and spoke to a terrible poverty. A little girl who might have been a little more than ten years old greeted them with a curtsy, and then went back to stirring a pot that was boiling over the fire. A heavy stench of cauliflower left no doubt as to what she was cooking.

Seated on the floor next to the table was a smaller child, a boy, bundled up in a sweater several sizes too large for him. The crystallized mucus on his upper lip told a heartbreaking tale of neglect.

The man had sat down at the table, without inviting the two policemen to take a seat, and so they remained standing. Lomunno had gone back to carving a piece of wood, from which he was extracting with a certain expertise what seemed to be a horse. Behind him, on a rough-hewn table, a handmade manger scene was taking form; it included several shepherds of superior quality. The man followed the commissario's gaze.

"The manger scene. I don't know why the creditors haven't laid their damned mitts on the shepherds in the manger scene. A few of them were lost, and I'm recarving them, making them myself, as you can see. This is the horse of Melchior, one of the three kings. The manger scene is what Christmas is all about, if you have children. You can have Christmas without a mother, but not without the manger scene."

He laughed a grim laugh, and the smell of soured wine on his breath reached all the way to Maione. The brigadier noticed that the little girl turned her eyes on her father, without the slightest expression.

"If you know why we're here, Lomunno, then tell us what we want to know," Ricciardi said.

The man gave Ricciardi a long stare. Then he looked down at the wooden horse that was taking shape under his knife blade.

"One day, I went into the office; I was highly regarded, esteemed. A party faithful, among the first to enlist. I was doing work that I loved, everyone respected me; or rather, I should say, that's how I thought things were. And in my office I found my boss, with two policemen and a man in civilian clothes. The man steps forward and says to me, 'You're a bribe-taking crook.' Then he puts his hand in my jacket and takes my money. The money I'd saved over a lifetime, little by little, squirreling away every raise, every bonus, and hiding it all under the mattress so that someday I'd be able to give my wife what she'd always dreamed of: a home of our own."

Outside they heard a seagull shriek, flying low, just over the shack.

"There was just one person I'd told this small, useless secret. Just one person who knew that that day I'd be going to get the money from my uncle and aunt, who I'd been giving my savings to every so often for safekeeping, and who were leaving for America. I tried to explain, but they wouldn't even let me talk. Coffee, they said. Coffee and cigarettes. You took money in exchange for letting smugglers bring in contraband merchandise. We have witnesses."

"What about these witnesses?" Ricciardi asked. "Were you allowed to confront them yourself?"

Lomunno tossed his head back and laughed a doleful laugh. The daughter shot her father another expressionless glance, then went back to stirring the pot.

"Then you don't know how it works, do you? The militia, the political police, the secret police—they don't hold trials; they promise immunity to those who'll testify, and then it's so long, nice knowing you. Lomunno goes to prison, the traitor gets a promotion. One loses, the other wins. Until the next round; but then there is no next round."

Ricciardi had never taken his eyes off him. The man's eyes glittered in the partial darkness. The stench of cauliflower and filth was intolerable.

"Really? It seems to me that there was a next round, and that Garofalo, in the present moment, is worse off than you."

Lomunno drove the knife violently into the tabletop, with a dull thunk. Maione took a step forward, his hand on the butt of his pistol. The little girl didn't stop stirring.

"You think so? You really think so, Commissa'? Just take a look around you; what do you see? A poor man, a useless man, dishonored, forced to live off the charity of his onetime friends, friends who are ashamed that they didn't rise to his defense when he needed defending. Two children who've grown old before their time, passed from one neighbor to the next until their father was released from prison, because their mother one fine day decided that she'd rather be dead than wait any longer. And you really think you can say who's better off and who's worse off?"

Ricciardi's tone of voice remained unchanged.

"A little girl has lost her parents. An innocent woman was murdered in her home, and a man—innocent or not—was butchered in his bed. We're the police, and it's our job to find out who did it. So let's return to the reason we're here: Did you do it?"

Silence fell. The girl stopped stirring, picked up her little brother, and hurried outside. Lomunno put his hands over his face and stayed that way. After a few long moments, he lowered them and replied:

"Sure, I did it. A hundred times a day, in my prison cell, in the most atrocious ways imaginable; but it was only him, never his wife, never his daughter, whom I'd seen as a baby and who had nothing to do with any of it. Then I did it a hundred times more, when I heard that my wife had killed herself, and I still had six months to serve and I had no idea what would become of my children. And then another hundred times when I was forced to bring them here to live in this shack, sleeping practically on top of them to ward off bronchitis, staying up all night to protect them from the rats. Sure, I did it. But if you want to know whether I did it outside of my mind, in reality, then the answer is no, I didn't. If my wife were still alive, if I had someone to leave the children to, maybe I'd have climbed those stairs and I'd have used this very knife. But things being the way they are, I might as well have killed them first, and then gone off to Mergellina."

The seagulls shrieked again. Maione shook himself back into the present.

"Excuse me, Lomunno, I have a question: How do you make a living now?"

"Day by day, Brigadie'. I don't have any skills, I've only ever worked as an official at the port, and after that, as a militiaman. Like I told you, I get a little help from my old comrades, each of them concealing what they do from the others. They come here at night, in civilian clothing, they look around furtively when they get here and when they leave. They're afraid, and I can hardly blame them; it wouldn't take much for them to be arrested as accomplices. In the past few days I've also started reviewing some ledgers for certain offices at the port: working under someone else's name, of course. And I've earned a little money, and for once I've decided not to drink it away at the tavern, but to use it to give my children a little taste of the Christmases they once had."

"Lomu', this is something we have to ask you: Where were you on the morning of the eighteenth, from seven in the morning until one in the afternoon?"

The man looked up at Maione.

"Out looking for work, Brigadie'. Searching desperately for work, pounding the sidewalks of this city. In the morning, I was down at the port, and I got a few doors slammed in my face, a few others closed more politely, and a few more left open just a crack. I can give you a few addresses, but each of them would only tell you what I was doing for five minutes: nothing that wouldn't have allowed me, in theory—I'll tell you so you don't have to tell me—plenty of time to go murder Garofalo and his wife. I used to be a cop myself, in a certain sense. I know how you have to think."

Then he took a step forward and laid his hand on Maione's arm.

"Brigadie', listen to me: it wasn't me. I'd have been happy to do it, and maybe I even should have. I'm sorry about the wife and the daughter, but the only thing I'm sorry about when it comes to that bastard is that when he died, it wasn't by my hand. If you have children, though, revenge comes at a price: a very great price. I couldn't possibly afford it."

XXXI

When she finally found herself recounting the promise that she'd made to the Madonna of Pompeii, Enrica assumed that she was putting an end to any worth she may have had in Rosa's eyes. A woman of her age, the girl thought, couldn't help but consider a sacred promise like hers to be final and unbreakable. But once again, Rosa surprised her.

"As far as I'm concerned, that promise is invalid," she decreed.

"What do you mean, it's invalid?"

Rosa counted the reasons off on her fingers.

"First of all, you had no idea what the young master's medical condition really was, and in fact you even said, 'If you save him, I'll never see him again.' But what was the Madonna supposed to have saved him from, if all he had was a bump on his head? Second, a vow to the Virgin Mary has to be made in a certain way, not the way you made yours, sitting in a chair in a hospital waiting room. You have to go to church, kneel down in front of a sacred painting, and you didn't do that. Third, a person can only renounce something they possess, not something that belongs to someone else. And with this vow, you've deprived him of something very important, too, and he never made any promises."

Enrica shook her head, again and again.

"But I did, I know that I made that promise. And I can hardly go back on a promise I made to the Madonna. And then . . . then there's that lady, the pretty one from out of town. I've already seen her with him, more than once even, enough times that I guessed that they were . . . that they were seeing each other, practically engaged, in other words. If he didn't like her, he'd tell her to leave him alone, wouldn't he? I just don't know what to do . . ."

Her eyes brimmed over with tears. Rosa shot a glance down at her own hand, which was trembling slightly: she couldn't afford to waste time on this nonsense.

"And that's why I sought you out. Let's speak plainly, Signori': Men are weak creatures. They think that they're the ones who decide, who choose, who make and do, but the truth is that they decide, choose, and make and do no more and no less than we women decide for them. But not all of us women: only the strong ones, only the determined ones. The lady that you're talking about, this signora from out of town—you say that she's pretty, but to me she just looks skinny and unhealthy, frankly—she strikes me as a determined one. So what are we going to do? Are we going to let her do as she likes? Are we going to let her decide, so she can scoop him up and carry him off to some town in northern Italy?"

Enrica's eyes opened wide.

"No, certainly not. No. You know, Signora, there's one thing I know for sure: I'll never love anyone else. No one. It's him or nobody."

Rosa shifted her substantial derriere in her chair and got more comfortable, adjusting her hat on her head with a bellicose expression.

"Well then, in that case, there are two things we've got to take care of: we need to go see a priest, to get the matter of the vow settled, so that we can put it out of our minds once and for all; and we need to decide what to do to get everything back in order, before that signora from up north starts putting her hands where her hands don't belong."

Enrica realized that she was no longer alone.

"About the priest—I may have an idea. I may know one who can tell us about the issues in question."

As soon as they turned the corner of the *vicolo*, Ricciardi and Maione found themselves back in the Christmas season, but that wasn't enough to dissipate the sadness from their encounter with Lomunno.

"Commissa', I don't know about you, but that chat with Lomunno made quite an impression on me. But I'm not sure I could tell you exactly what I think about him."

Commissario Ricciardi was walking with his head pulled down into the lapels of his overcoat, his eyes lost in the empty air.

"That's the way it always is when you see desperation, a life in ruins. He hasn't even started living again, and maybe he's just starting to try. But that doesn't mean it wasn't him who killed the Garofalos. Revenge, as you well know, is an ugly beast. It lurks in the shadows, sometimes for years at a time, then it lunges out and makes a bloody meal."

Maione thought it over.

"Sure, but what he said was true, too: revenge comes at a price. You have to be able to afford it. What would it have gotten him? Nothing but the complete and, this time, definitive ruin of his children."

"But revenge isn't rational. Maybe you're sitting there, just like Lomunno, half drunk, one night a week before Christmas; and it suddenly dawns on you how unjust it is that the one you love is dead, and that the guilty party is alive and happy and getting ready to enjoy the holidays. So you decide to take justice into your own hands. You pick up a knife, or a pistol, or what have you, and you set things right."

Maione felt his pulse throbbing in his temples.

"You set things right, sure . . . so the one who has to pay will finally pay. You set things right."

Ricciardi came to a sudden halt.

"It's just that that's no way to set things right, my dear Raffaele. You want to fix one wrong with another, and that's followed by another, and on and on it goes. Forgiveness is difficult, maybe impossible. But that's why we have laws, that's why we have justice: to set things right. Don't you agree?"

Maione felt confused.

"It's a human impulse, Commissa', revenge. Sometimes it's much harder to keep from taking revenge than it is to take it."

Ricciardi had started to walk quickly again.

"Yes, that's true. So in this case, we can't strike Lomunno from the list of potential killers. Among other things, he has no alibi, or at least he doesn't have anything that could exclude him from suspicion entirely, and his newfound tranquility, this sudden yearning for Christmas and family, manger scenes and pastries for his children, might very well mean that he's placated his conscience, precisely because he's finally taken revenge."

Maione nodded thoughtfully.

"True enough. But it's also true that Lomunno is alone, and so who would be the second hand that Dr. Modo says struck Garofalo?"

They weren't far from police headquarters now; they were almost run over by the cart of a pots-and-pans vendor, piled high with copper cooking vessels clanging together.

"We ought to go to the Borgo Marinari and delve into the matter of the fishermen who were extorted," Ricciardi said. "We might have better luck there."

They turned the corner and walked through the main entrance into the courtyard, where they saw Livia's car parked and she herself leaning against the vehicle, smoking, a smile on her face. Neither of them failed to notice that a good dozen of their colleagues just happened to be leaning out of the upstairs windows, in spite of the piercing cold.

The woman tapped the ash off the tip of her cigarette, with a gleam in her eyes.

"Just in the nick of time; a few more minutes and my nose would have frozen off. Ciao, Ricciardi. Welcome back."

XXXII

The murderous hands are finishing their work.
They've slowed down, because they'd gotten ahead of themselves, when really the preparation is more like choreography: there's a time for everything, step by step, leading up to the grand finale. And the grand finale is a gesture, nothing but a gesture.

The murderous hands are industrious. They never stop for a moment. There are a thousand little details to fix, a thousand things to move from here to there, a centimeter forward, a centimeter back.

You might think that once the bulk of the work is done, once you've created the panorama complete with grottoes, terraces, temples, and caves, you've almost finished the job. Nothing could be farther from the truth.

The murderous hands know perfectly well that it's the details that make the difference. Preparation is important, as is execution, but the details are what distinguish a job well done from a slipshod one.

The murderous hands arrange the fountain, with water that really flows. The children are overjoyed at the sight of the fountain: it makes the whole manger scene seem real, that stream of water moving in the midst of the stationary figures.

And they finish arranging the herbs and plants: the rosemary, the myrtle, the java moss, the butcher's broom. The murderous hands are familiar with the tradition: the greenery chases away the evil spirits that haunt people's homes from the Day of the

Dead to Epiphany. Need to chase away the evil spirits, for Christmas.

Because those who are dead are dead, and they need to stay with the dead. They can't come back, ever.

The murderous hands rub lightly together, pleased. It won't be long now, it won't be long at all.

Then everything will be complete.

XXXIII

Maione took advantage of Livia's visit to make himself scarce, in spite of the silent plea for help that he saw in Ricciardi's eyes.

"If you don't mind, Commissa', I'm going to go run a few errands for Christmas. I'll see you back here in an hour, then we can take that stroll over to Borgo Marinari."

"A wonderful place," Livia chimed in, "charming, with the houses of the fishermen and the boats beached just beneath the Castel dell'Ovo. I've been there in the summer, is it worth visiting in winter, too?"

"No, it's really not worth it," Ricciardi said to cut the conversation short. "We have to go there on a case, we have a couple of people to interview. All right, Maione, go ahead. But don't be long, we have work to do."

Trailed by the curious eyes of the headquarters staff, as well as by an unknown number of lawyers', Livia and Ricciardi walked toward his office. A man in handcuffs, waiting to be led to his cell by two police officers, let out a long low whistle of appreciation as he watched the woman go by; one of the cops smacked the prisoner in the back of the head, but he exchanged a knowing glance with his partner. She certainly wasn't the kind of woman who could pass unnoticed.

Ricciardi, however, couldn't stand being the center of attention, so he hurried his gait, and when he finally shut the door behind him, he heaved a sigh of relief.

"You could have spared me the theatrical entrance, couldn't you?"

Livia peeled off her gloves.

"And I'm delighted to see you as well, *grazie. Buongiorno* to you, too. How are you?"

The commissario picked up on the sarcasm behind the greeting.

"Forgive me: *buongiorno* to you. It's just that I don't like attracting too much attention, you know. Police headquarters is like a small town; there's gossip, mockery, all of which tends to undermine the work we do."

The woman took a seat, after removing her overcoat with its fur cuffs and collar.

"Of course, your work. The one thing that matters. Never giving yourself a break, never listening to what your heart is asking you."

"Livia, please. Don't make a special effort to make me uncomfortable."

"Uncomfortable. So I'm making you feel uncomfortable. Listen, Ricciardi, what if we spoke freely and clearly, just for once? If we looked each other in the eye and stopped beating around the bush, wouldn't it be better for us both?"

Ricciardi went to the window, looking down at the traffic in the piazza. On the bare-limbed holm oaks the few remaining leaves fluttered in the wind, and the strolling vendors hurried across the street to take their wares to the most heavily trafficked streets. In the distance, almost completely faded by now, were the images of a mother and a daughter killed in an accident some three months earlier. The woman and the girl, incongruously dressed in light summer dresses, were exchanging incomprehensible phrases: *Hurry, he's waiting for us*, the mother was saying, both her legs neatly shorn off. *My top, I lost my top, my top*, the little girl with her skull staved in was replying. She was in too much of a hurry to pick up her toy. You can't just suddenly turn around and go back, after you've crossed the street.

You can't go back.

"Livia, you know how I feel. We've talked it over many times. You're a beautiful woman, you see it yourself, you're well aware of it. You can have any man you want; and even if you weren't as beautiful as you are, you have plenty of friends, you're smart, you're wealthy. Why me? With all my problems, with all my quandaries?"

The woman considered the question seriously; it was one she asked herself frequently. She thought back on her suitors, both the ones who still called her from Rome and the new ones who sent her flowers and chocolates with fervent notes every morning.

"But you're the one that I want. You see, Ricciardi: I can sense two different people inside you, distinct and separate. One of them keeps the other one hidden, chained, like a hostage; and he forces him to suffer a long, involuntary solitude. Behind the facade of an apparent absence of emotions there's someone who needs to laugh, to open up to the sunshine. To be loved. And you know that I had proof of that, not long ago."

Ricciardi sighed and turned away from the window.

"You've had proof, you say?"

Livia laughed, with a nervous edge. That man disturbed her deeply, and for the first time in her life she didn't know what to do or say.

"I know what you're about to say. That you were sick, that you had a fever. That it was raining out, pouring down, and you were suffering over something you had inside. But I held you in my arms, Ricciardi; and a woman knows when a man is fully present and aware."

Ricciardi looked at her for a long time. His heart was touched by her brash attitude, her bold words, and the contrast with her bewildered gaze and her faintly trembling lower lip.

"I won't say that I wasn't fully present and aware. I won't say that I don't remember what happened between us that night. I was weak, yes, that's true, and I had a deep pain inside me. But for once the loneliness was too much for me, and I could no longer keep it to myself. I came to you, Livia, this I have to admit: even if I never knocked at your front door. I wanted warmth, I wanted hands and skin. Forgive me, I beg you."

Livia was caught off guard once again. She hadn't been expecting an admission of weakness from Ricciardi.

"But don't you understand that that's exactly what I want to give you? A little warmth, a little joy? Listen to me, Ricciardi: I'm not trying to lay claim to you; that's not the kind of woman I am. You came to me, and I was happy you did. I was very glad to have that time with you, but I'll be the first to say that it was a chance encounter," she said, running her hand over her eyes. "But it's also proof that a man like you can have a moment if not of happiness, at least of respite."

Ricciardi stood listening, hands in his pockets, his usual lock of hair dangling over his forehead, his green eyes expressionless. He could have been a statue.

"There are things about me you don't know, Livia. I'm not so . . . aloof, shall we say, by choice. Each of us has his or her own personality, and mine keeps me removed from certain emotions, certain sentiments." He closed his eyes halfway and heard the little girl, in the piazza behind and beneath him, searching for her toy. "And there's more. I do feel something, a strong feeling, I believe, for a person. I've told you that, once before. In other words, there's another woman."

Livia's head started spinning. Her heart raced in her chest. Fight, she told herself. If you really want this man, then it's time to fight.

"Does she know it? Have you told her that you feel what you feel for her? Have you felt her skin, laid your hands on her flesh? Has she felt your breath on her lips?"

Ricciardi opened his mouth, then shut it. He turned pale.

"No, she doesn't know. I haven't told her yet."

Livia laughed, but the laughter didn't reach her eyes.

"Well? That means that you have an extra something with me, no? That we might have shared nothing more than an instant, but share it we did. And the two of us are talking about it, at least."

Ricciardi looked around: his old wooden office chair, his desk with the worn olive-green blotter paper, the bare bulb hanging on a wire in the center of the room because the lampshade, which had broken more than a year ago, had never been replaced. The paperweight made from a fragment of mortar shell, the glass inkwell. His world.

"Look around you, Livia. What do you see? A beat-up old office. I live here—much more than I do at home, a place I hardly know. What can a man like me offer a woman? I don't know how many years I have left to live, but I'll be spending most of my time right here. Why would you want someone like me?"

Livia got to her feet. There was a sweet smile on her face, but a tear was streaking down her cheek.

"You just don't get it, do you? You don't understand. There's no reason why. People fall in love, just like that, for no good reason. Even a woman like me, who's lived an intense life, who's been very, very happy and very, very unhappy, can still fall in love. So this, you see, Ricciardi, is the gift you've given me, come what may, whether you want me or not: you've made me see that I'm still alive, that I'm still capable of falling in love."

She turned away, took a step toward the door, grabbed the handle. Then she turned back around and looked at him.

"And I want you to know: I'm willing to fight for this love. I'll stop at nothing, because I know that deep down you want me, too, that you want nothing more than to be led out of that miserable prison you've confined yourself to, God only knows the reason why. Never underestimate a woman in love, Ricciardi. I really wouldn't recommend that."

She walked out the door, and hurried downstairs to her car. Once inside, she collapsed in tears.

As the vehicle left the courtyard, a pair of eyes watched it discreetly from the lobby of the building across the way.

XXXIV

Immersing himself in Via San Gregorio Armeno, Maione could hardly keep himself from thinking of the shack where the Lomunno family lived, at least what remained of them. Just as Christmas seemed to have stopped at the entrance to that dirt road, abandoning those who lived there to whatever fate awaited them, here in contrast every single window, every door, every shop screamed at the top of its lungs that the year's sovereign holiday was on its way, and everyone should prepare for its arrival.

This had always been the place to find shepherds for manger scenes, decorations for the home, things with which to deck the halls. Sales began in late October and went on until the Twelfth Day of Christmas, Epiphany, on January 6. After that the street sank back into commercial lethargy, with the vendors specializing in the cloth flowers that were used to adorn the hats and dresses worn by the ladies of the city.

At least three pairs of *zampognari*, paid by the terra-cotta-shepherd merchants, were playing their Christmas melodies; even though it was still light out, every shop had turned on its luminous decorations to attract the eyes of the numerous pedestrians; and all the *figurari*, or figure carvers, had laid out their finest creations on the street, creating a particolored effect that enchanted and seduced the passersby.

Maione however wasn't looking at the shops' merchandise; he was thinking about what he intended to do.

He'd talked himself into believing that the boy wouldn't

recognize him if he saw him. Maione, after all, had attended the trial in civilian clothing and had hung back, blending in with the crowd of curious onlookers. Nearly four years later, he still clearly remembered the sense of alienation he'd felt, as if the trial were something that had nothing to do with him.

Now, years later, and with Maione dressed in his uniform, even if his son's killer saw him, he'd be unlikely to recognize him. The brigadier just needed to find out where the young man worked. He assumed that it couldn't be very far from the apartment he'd chosen, but of course he could be wrong about that; maybe Biagio worked at the Bagnoli steel mill, or at some construction site in Vomero, and that would require further investigation, and possibly another call on Bambinella.

Just as he was mulling over these thoughts, he spotted him. Hunched over a countertop, in the arched entrance of one of the largest *figurari* shops, the young man was intently shaping a wooden face with a palette knife. Maione noticed him because, on a street that seemed like a rushing river of people hurrying to and fro, there was a knot of people standing around him, raptly watching him work.

Maione stopped, hanging back at the rear of the crowd: he was tall enough to peer over the heads of the others. The boy was working with his head low, as if he were alone in the middle of the desert, blithely unaware of the commotion. He was putting the finishing touches on a face, what the *figurari* called a *testina*, a little head. It was an old woman, her hair pulled up in a bun, her cheeks hollow, her eyes wide open and slightly bulging.

The young man was really good; his sharp gestures gradually brought out a human expression, a look of wonder and surprise. On the counter lay two hands with curved, clawing fingers, reaching out as if trying to grab something. The hands had yet to be painted, but they already conveyed the impression of something fully alive. In the end, head and hands would be given a wire and cotton-wad body, in the old style, dressed in silk and lace.

He noticed that the young man, the tip of his tongue sticking out and his shoulders hunched, was putting the final touches on the *testina* with his left hand. With a sharp pang he remembered that the report on Luca's murder had identified a single mortal wound, under the left shoulder blade. It was a wound inflicted by a left-handed man, and the brother who was sentenced for the crime was right-handed. No one had given the matter any thought. After all, they had a confession; why dig any deeper? Maione himself hadn't thought twice about it, at the time.

The thought roused him from his state of wonder at seeing a woman's likeness emerge from a piece of wood, and brusquely reminded him of what he was doing there. He took a few steps back, picked a terra-cotta cow up off the counter, and went over to the proprietor of the shop who was standing, with a satisfied look on his face, behind the cash register.

"Hello. You're drawing a nice crowd today, eh?"

The man looked at the uniform with some mistrust, but smiled.

"Yes, Brigadie', at least the week before Christmas a few people come by; but for the most part, they're just looking, fine things cost money, they like to look but then they go and buy the cheaper shepherds."

Maione feigned sympathy.

"Certainly, there's not much money changing hands these days. People would rather buy groceries, no?"

The proprietor launched into a defense of his profession.

"Yes, and I understand that. But what's Christmas without a nativity scene? We survive, and that's fine; but it's a tradition in this city that every home, no matter how poor, should have at least a Holy Family. Of course, the shops that sell cheap items are doing better, with those clumps of terra-cotta colored in haste and hurry. But we, we make works of art."

Maione led the conversation where he needed it to go.

"Eh, I've seen that you have wonderful things. That young man, down there, for instance, who's working on the old woman: he seems truly talented."

The proprietor stepped around the cash register and stuck his head out, observing with satisfaction that the crowd around the young man had only grown.

"Yes, he's good. I've been doing this work for forty years, and before me my father did it, and I apprenticed with him; but I've never seen anyone so quick to learn. He does more things, and he does them better, than that idiot son of mine who's been here for fifteen years and still hasn't laid hands on a piece of wood."

Maione faked an interest just this side of good manners.

"Ah, and how long has the boy been working for you?"

"Biagio? It must be three and a half years now; this is the fourth Christmas. I remember when he first turned up here, he spent a whole day loitering in the street outside; he kept looking in but never came inside. At a certain point I called to him and said, '*Guaglio*', what are you looking for?' 'Nothing,' he said, 'I was just wondering if you needed someone to sweep the shop and mop up.' I said, 'All right, but just during the holidays.' Then one of the carvers got hurt in a brawl, he broke his fingers, and the boy sat in for him. And he hasn't left that seat since. He's a wizard with a knife."

Maione felt another stab of pain at those words. It's not an act of wizardry to drive a knife into the back of a poor unsuspecting young man, all the way to the hilt. That's not magic.

"So he's a help, and things are going well. And the boy seems to be honest, eh?"

It wasn't an uncommon question for a policeman to ask; the proprietor didn't seem suspicious.

"Absolutely, Brigadie', as good as gold. He's married, and he has two little children. After he'd been working here for a couple of months, he found an apartment right in the next *vicolo*. His wife, if you see her, is even better than him: a fine girl, a *bravissima guagliona*. She does some cleaning in the apartments around here, she leaves her children with a little old woman who looks after them, and she works hard. Everyone loves her here in the neighborhood. Right now she's doing some work for my wife, across the way. Every so often she looks out the window to watch her husband work. There she is, you see her?"

Following the man's gaze, Maione saw a dark-haired girl leaning out of the third-floor window of the building across the street, the same girl he'd seen that morning. It was a fleeting apparition, a smile and a blown kiss, to which the boy replied with a nod of the head, without a break in his work.

The proprietor looked Maione in the eye.

"It does your heart good, to see two young people so in love and working so hard. Certainly it must seem strange to you, Brigadie', accustomed as you are to seeing the worst class of people from morning to night, no?"

Maione shrugged his shoulders.

"I couldn't say. Sometimes people aren't what they seem. Not as good, and not as bad. I'm running late, I really have to go now. What do I owe you for the cow?"

Hustling back up the street in a hurry to get back to police headquarters, Maione felt a strong wind rushing through his head. A wife, two small children: it was the life that Luca could have had. There was that girl he liked, what was her name? That's right, Marianna. The daughter of Rosario, the mechanic who repaired bicycles.

His little brothers used to make fun of him, Luca has a girl-friend, Luca has a girlfriend, and he'd laugh and pretend to chase after them. By now, he might well have been married, I might be a grandfather. The grandfather of a little girl and a little boy. And this one, who's now showing off his bravura as a wood carver, would be a criminal, following after his no-good brother. He might already have met his unhappy end, killed by some other criminal on a street corner somewhere.

The voice of Franco Massa, Luca's godfather who had pretended to be a priest, echoed in his ears: we have to track down this Biagio and kill him like the dog he is, the same way he did to Luca. Kill him like a dog. Like a dog. If you don't want to do it, I'll do it myself.

In the midst of the sounds of the *zampognari* and the festive crowd preparing for the coming Christmas, Raffaele Maione was thinking about death.

XXXV

L istening to the sounds of the *zampognari* rising from the
street below, Lucia Maione was thinking about life.
And she was thinking that life is a strange thing, that no
one had ever understood it, neither philosophers nor song-
writers, much less her, ignorant as she was, who only knew
how to be a mother and a wife.

She thought back on her own life, as it had been until just
a few months ago. If you could call it a life. She just lay
sprawled on her bed, almost all day long and most of the night,
never really sleeping, in a state of waking sleep or sleepy wake-
fulness, a trance populated with images, broken thoughts,
memories. If you take a mother's son from her without warning, if she still has his shirts to iron, if she can still hear his
laughter echoing in her ears, then it's impossible to say what
will become of her.

She went on working busily in the kitchen. Her children
were playing in the next room. These are my children too,
she'd thought. They have a right to a mamma.

Still, that thought hadn't been sufficient for almost three
years. Nor had her home, or her husband, seemed like sufficient reason to start living again. The only thing that she
wanted to do was to stare out at the sliver of sky she could see
from her bed, waiting for a blond angel to come down and take
her away with him.

Then one day, without warning, she'd gotten up. There was
something in the spring air, a new perfume, or an unfamiliar

smell. And she'd leaned out the window and looked down. She'd seen the piazzetta, the *vicoli* running uphill and down. She'd seen life, flowing along as always, and she'd realized she missed it.

And just in the nick of time, she thought to herself, as she lined up her ingredients on the kitchen table. She'd come that close to losing her husband, and the love of her children. She'd run the risk of being left alone in an inferno of endless grief. And she'd realized that her handsome son, that fair-haired boy, his hair the same color as hers, who used to come home and lift her in his arms, spinning her around till she was breathless, who called her "my girlfriend," would never have wanted to see her in this pitiable state. So she'd brushed her hair and changed her clothing. And she'd tested out a hesitant smile in the mirror of the vanity table in their bedroom.

Since then she'd revived all the family traditions, one by one. And now that Christmas was once again drawing near, she was expected to lay the finest dinner table in the whole quarter, which meant that her husband and her children were the envy of all their friends.

Hands on her hips, her apron damp, she reviewed everything she'd laid out on the table, reciting the names of the items under her breath as if uttering a prayer: rinsed broccoli, with their broad dark-green leaves; *broccoletti*, with their long narrow leaves; chicory; cabbage; and *torzella*, a local curly-leafed cabbage. All the vegetables were present and accounted for.

It's easy to say *minestra maritata*. Married soup. And yet, for all its simplicity, it was one of the most challenging dishes of the whole year; but without *minestra maritata*, what kind of Christmas would it be?

Then after the vegetables came the meats: a prosciutto bone, pork rinds, salami, pork ribs, *pezzentella* sausage, fresh pork. To an inexpert eye, all these were scraps, the kinds of odds and ends one would feed to the family dog, but in fact they were the secret of a perfect soup. And, naturally, lard, fresh sausages to be crumbled into the mix, and dried cacio-cavallo cheese, a crucial ingredient. Then her own signature touch, a spicy red chili pepper and a glass of red wine.

She smiled as she thought of Raffaele, who loved her *minestra maritata* in particular. But her smile dimmed.

He'd been odd lately. There was a bass note, just barely detectable, in his expression, as hard as he might try to conceal it: a sadness or perhaps a hint of melancholy. Perhaps the impending holiday, or perhaps the thought of Luca, which kept her constant company, had snuck up unannounced on her husband, with the sound of the *zampogne* and the memory of Luca as a child, when he asked for gifts that were as expensive and unattainable as the moon.

Still, there was something that, as far as Lucia was concerned, just didn't add up: that dark shade in Raffaele's eyes had come on far too suddenly. It had already been there when he'd come home Saturday night.

The new investigation? His compassion for that little girl, suddenly orphaned in that horrible manner, which he'd told her all about? Perhaps. But it still didn't add up.

As she diced the lard on the cutting board, she thought back to the previous spring, when she'd suspected that Raffaele might be interested in another woman. This had been a wake-up call, the push she needed in order to regain her will and desire to reassume her place in her household. She'd never let anyone cast a shadow over her life again.

Because life is important. If you lose it and you regain it, to lose it again is a pity, but also a sin: a mortal sin.

She focused on Raffaele, singing as she diced the lard into neat, compact cubes.

Angelina took little Vincenzino's temperature, placing her lips on his forehead. He was burning up. Again.

The sea, crashing just a stone's throw from their home, went on incessantly roaring into the wind, but there was a different smell in the air: the old people had told her that the north wind was going to subside in the next few hours, and the cold would continue to rule alone.

That wasn't good news for Vincenzino. His lungs made a whistling sound at night with every breath, and Angelina listened to it as if it were a death chant. She couldn't sleep anymore.

The doctor had told her what medicines she needed to get, but if he'd asked for gold, myrrh, and frankincense—the gifts carried by the wooden silhouettes with the images of the Three Kings glued onto them—it would have amounted to the same thing.

Medicine is for the rich. Doctors are for the rich. Or else for thieves, like the centurion who had ruined her husband.

She thought about their large, luminous apartment. How warm it was in there, as if the winter were showing respect for those walls, as if the cold were afraid to come inside. All those lights, the glistening silver, the gleaming floors, the soft carpets like sand at the beach in summertime, when you walk on it barefoot and it feels like stepping onto a cloud.

And she thought about Garofalo's wife, her courteous, sarcastic, false smile. *Hat and gloves?* she'd asked. She'd asked them, people who'd never worn gloves in their lives; she'd asked her, who had the same black shawl her mother had worn covering her head; she'd asked Aristide, who was wearing a cap that smelled of salt water and of pain, of a thousand nights spent out on his boat praying for fish.

Suddenly, as she sat thinking about the pair of them, as if their black souls were somehow able to pull strings from down in hell like puppeteers, Alfonso, her eldest son, came in. *Mammà*, he said, excitedly and upset, *Mammà*, they're here. They're here in the piazzetta, asking about us.

Angelina thought about her husband, and about the contemptible dark sea that every night did its best to gobble him down, but which still gave them all enough—just enough!—to eat. She thought about Vincenzino and the way his lungs whistled, and how you could even hear it in the daytime now, and how his forehead was burning up. She thought about her mother and her father, who had taught her to be forthright and honest. She thought about groceries, medicine, carpets, and silver.

For a long moment she thought about doing nothing: about not telling anyone their name, not going out, not opening the door. About pretending that they were all already dead, as they certainly would be if they didn't do something to remedy their horrible situation. She thought about it for a moment.

Then she sighed and stood up. She took her shawl and wrapped it around herself and over her head. She glanced at herself in the mirror on the wall, perhaps the one luxury they had in the twenty by twenty foot room that was her home, and she was shocked at the sight of the old ashen-faced woman she saw reflected there. She ran her eyes over the cold fireplace, the brazier that she kept dangerously close to Vincenzino's bed, in the hopes of saving him from the death whose face was drawing ever closer to his, and the sad little manger scene that Aristide had carved and decorated with dried seaweed, so that even his children would have a little bit of Christmas.

She looked closely, but she saw no hope.

Then she walked out into the wind, to meet the policemen.

XXXVI

The road to the borgo from police headquarters wasn't particularly long, but it offered a panoramic view of unparalleled loveliness.

They skirted the Palazzo Reale, the royal palace with the portico of the church of San Francesco that bounded the Piazza del Plebiscito. From there they took Via Cesario Console, which turns downhill toward the sea. On the right were the large, luxurious hotels, with lines of vehicles waiting for fares and drivers standing smoking in the wind, holding their hats in place with one hand and shouting to make themselves heard as they conversed. Straight ahead was the sea, with high plumes of spray that reached the street, so that the cars and horse-drawn carriages leaving the center kept to the middle of the street and the ones traveling in the opposite direction drove right up along the sidewalk.

The massive bulk of the castle rose dark and menacing in the rapidly falling night. In this weather, though, it was less menacing, with its cannons and battlements, than it was protective, forcing the roaring wind away from the little lanes of the *borgo*.

The last fishermen had been moved from Santa Lucia to the low apartment buildings specially built for them here more than a hundred years ago. Many of them had opened small trattorias on the ground floors, which cooked freshly landed seafood in the summer and had even become popular with tourists, drawn there from their luxurious hotel rooms nearby by the mouth-watering aromas from the wood-burning grills. This seasonal diversification aside, the people of the *borgo* made a living the same way their fathers, their grandfathers, and their great-grandfathers had.

There were just a few dozen families, and over the centuries they'd inevitably all become interrelated, deprived of the best and most ambitious of their young, who'd chosen to book passage on the big three-stacked ocean liners that steamed to America, or else opted for the easier money to be found in the soft underbelly of the city. The ones who stayed behind were those who couldn't, or didn't want to, do anything else.

Ricciardi and Maione had walked along the road in silence; the wind was howling, it was hard to hear, and they were both caught up in their own thoughts.

There was a storm of confusion in the brigadier's heart. He was thinking about revenge, justice and the law, life and death. In his simple mind, made up of right and wrong, he couldn't allow a murderer—one responsible for the immense pain and sorrow that he carried within him and that for three years had reduced his wife to little more than a vegetable—to escape punishment for the crime he'd committed. That was one thing he was sure of, more than sure of.

But he thought: What, was he the judge? He was a policeman, accustomed to following principles established by others, in laws crafted by men more learned and intelligent than he was, and he wanted only to apply those laws. He apprehended the criminals, and then he handed them over. From that moment onward, and this was a rule to which he'd adhered all his life, it was no longer his place to concern himself with what became of those who had committed the crimes. Nor did he much want to be a judge; he'd always known that his conscience was a tender thing. He'd never be able to sleep at night.

But even he knew perfectly well that, by law, Biagio would get off scot-free. There'd already been a trial, followed by a conviction and a sentence; the dying brother's confession had been obtained fraudulently by Massa, who'd pretended to be a priest. In any case, there was no evidence, no proof.

Maione wondered what Lucia would have wanted. His instincts told him to talk to her, to share that terrible news with her, to ask her advice about what he should do, and how he should do it. Thoughts of his wife consumed him: her terrible suffering, the shadow he could still glimpse in the depths of those sky-blue eyes, her anguish in the days after it first happened. What pity could Lucia take on the one who'd caused her that pain? No, he couldn't revive those feelings in his wife. The responsibility for what he had to do rested on his shoulders alone. In the end, he'd become a judge after all, under circumstances he would never have wished for: in the most important trial of his life, with his own conscience sitting as jury.

Ricciardi walked at Maione's side, likewise caught up in a surging tide of thoughts.

Livia's visit had upset him, far more than he'd expected. He'd seen her more than once since the accident: she'd been the first to hurry to the hospital; he'd received visits from her several times at police headquarters, to the delight of the staff gossips and of Garzo, who was always ready to present his fat, smiling face to anyone who he thought could put in a good word for him in Rome. But he'd taken care to make sure he was never alone with her.

This time, however, he hadn't been able to get away. Not out of cowardice; he just couldn't bring himself to hurt her feelings. He knew very well—and things had turned out pretty much as he'd expected—that he'd end up saying exactly what he felt, word for word and letter for letter. He was incapable of verbal acrobatics; diplomacy was not one of his admittedly few virtues.

He doubted he loved Livia, but then he wondered if that was really true. His general disinclination for sentiment, not to mention his want of experience and the lack of any precedents for all this situation, made him dubious. He was gratified by the admiration everyone else seemed to feel for that exotic, feline woman; he liked her scent, a mixture of spices and something slightly wild; and he'd instinctively gone in search of her when his loneliness, fever, and suffering had become intolerable on that rainy November night. But was that love, Ricciardi wondered?

And then, of course, there was Enrica. Her calm gestures, the spark of good humor behind her tortoiseshell eyeglass frames. The strong feelings that the sight of her stirred in him, the sense of peace he felt when he spotted her through the window at night, his despair at seeing that same window shuttered in the past few days. But was that love, on the other hand?

But the question that most obsessed him was this: did he really want love to be part of his life?

After having recognized it as one of mankind's two chief enemies, even more treacherous and incomprehensible than hunger itself; having witnessed on an ongoing, daily basis its baleful effects, the blood, the pain, the sorrow, and the suffering; knowing the weaknesses that it brought in its wake, along with the pain of separation and the melancholy of loss; did he actually want this dangerous thing, love, in his life?

He'd always avoided it, sedulously. He'd always regarded it with mistrust, maintaining a safe distance, handling its effects with gloved hands to avoid potential contamination. And now he was actually trying to parse the distinction between the two emotions that he was feeling—not one, but two—in an attempt to understand their nature.

What the hell is happening to you, Ricciardi? he asked himself. Have you decided to jump out into the void, into the abyss along the rim of which you've always walked? Aren't you afraid anymore?

He tried to focus on the investigation. In a flash, the blood, the corpses, the stab wounds all appeared before his eyes; he heard the words of the Deed, what the dead said to him in their last breath before loosening their grip on life; the awkward caution of the militiamen, caught between the desire to cooperate and the fear that someone, in some secret room either in Rome or here in Naples, might not want them to air their dirty laundry; Lomunno's grief and despair, the misery of a man killed and not yet resuscitated, the sorrow of his children. The serious face of the little girl standing on tiptoe, barefoot, stirring that foul-smelling cookpot, and the grim determination that she'd shown when she picked her little brother up from the floor and carried him off, when rage had begun to seethe into her father's words. Something she was used to, evidently.

Ricciardi couldn't say whether Garofalo's former colleague was guilty of the double homicide. Experience told him that a killer generally chose not to express his regret at *not* having committed a murder. Lomunno seemed genuinely distraught at not having carried out an act of revenge that might very well have brought him a liberatory relief, and he openly said that it was only his love for his children that had kept him from doing it. And he had no solid alibi: a condition that would typically have led to his arrest, for lack of a better candidate, and probably in the end to a guilty verdict. Lomunno had so yearned to commit that murder that perhaps, in the end, he'd even come to believe that he really was the guilty party.

The lines of investigation that they were pursuing, then, had to produce some other—*any* other—hypothesis, otherwise they'd be forced to deprive Lomunno's children of the only parent left to them. Still, the commissario mused, he was clearly an aggressive man, filled with boundless rage and bottomless sorrow. He remembered the knife driven violently into the tabletop. Maybe he really was the killer, after all, he thought.

They reached the *borgo* almost without realizing it. Neither of the two, each lost in his own thoughts, noticed that they'd just walked for twenty minutes without exchanging a word.

The sea was howling in the wind.

XXXVII

They realized they'd been seen coming, as they always were. As soon as they rounded the curve in Via Partenope they realized that a messenger had broken off from the crowd of children loitering in front of the hotel in the hopes of receiving alms from the foreign tourists, and had rushed off down into the *borgo*.

Maione wasn't happy. It was like having a trumpeter going ahead and playing fanfares to announce their coming. Not that they really needed their anonymity; they weren't conducting a raid, nor were they planning to arrest anyone, unless it proved necessary. But it would have been at least a minor advantage to catch people off guard, so as to see their instinctive reaction to the visit from the police. But then they had become accustomed to losing that advantage by now.

The spectacle that greeted their eyes surprised them. At the center of a deserted, windswept piazzetta there was no one but a woman wrapped in a black shawl. Behind her stood two children, a little girl clinging to the signora's skirts and a slightly older boy, presumably the woman's daughter and son.

The figures remained motionless; if it weren't for the billowing of their clothing, they could have been a sculptural group, a statue dedicated to modern motherhood. They stood perfectly still, their faces turned in the policemen's direction. Ricciardi looked around, guessing at the eyes staring at him from behind the closed shutters of the surrounding buildings.

Maione sighed and stepped forward.

"*Buonasera*, Signo'. We are Brigadier Maione and Commissario Ricciardi of the mobile squad. We're here to talk to Signor Aristide Boccia. Do you know him?"

The woman stood still, in silence. Maione looked at Ricciardi for instructions. Had she heard him? Did she understand what he was saying? As he was trying to decide whether to repeat the question, the woman said:

"He's my husband. He's out on the water right now. Come with me."

She turned and headed for the front door of a *basso*, or ground-floor apartment, followed by the two children, Maione and Ricciardi, and many pairs of eyes, watching from behind the shutters.

The room they entered reminded them both of Lomunno and his shack. These people seemed to be living in even more dire poverty, but it was evident that there was a woman here at least. On the table lay a tattered piece of embroidered cloth; a curtain, patched but clean, hung at the hovel's only window; a hand-tinted photograph of a couple from the turn of the century, the woman sitting and the man standing, with a votive candle lit in front of them on a little shelf; and the aroma of fish chowder wafted through the air.

The little boy went running over to a cradle, in the corner of the room that was best sheltered from drafts and winds.

"This is my brother, Vincenzino. He's dying!"

He said it with pride, as if the infant in the cradle were about to perform a memorable deed of some kind. Maione looked down at his fingernails.

"Alfo'," the mother said to the boy, "go wait for Papa and tell him to come right away. Be careful not to get too close to the water. The seas are high tonight."

Then she turned to Maione.

"I'm sorry, I have nothing to offer you."

"Don't worry about it, Signo'. We're just here to ask a few questions. Maybe we'll wait for your husband."

The woman nodded. Ricciardi decided that she seemed much younger up close than he'd thought she was at first.

"Signora, one question: how did you know that we were coming to see your husband?"

The woman met and held the gaze of those strange, transparent eyes.

"Commissa', word travels fast. Policemen hear things, and so you come to talk to my husband. Well, we hear things, too."

Logical, thought Ricciardi. Logical, but she didn't actually tell me anything.

The door opened and Alfonso, the eldest son, came in, along with a man.

"I'm Aristide Boccia," the man said. "Were you looking for me?"

They looked at him. He was dressed like any other fisherman, with an oilskin raincoat and a large, shapeless hat made of the same material. He was carrying an unlit lantern, and he was dripping water.

"Yes, we're here to talk to you. I'm Brigadier Maione and this is Commissario Ricciardi, from police headquarters. We have a few questions we'd like to ask you."

Boccia made a face that could have been a tired sneer. His face was square and sunburnt. It was impossible to assign it an age.

"Well, here we are, as you can see. We haven't run off."

"Why were you expecting us?" Ricciardi inquired. "How did you know that we would come?"

Boccia stared back at him, expressionless.

"Because we went to see the Garofalos, my wife and I. We went two days before someone killed them."

A whistling sound came from the cradle, and the mother went over, moving something around inside it. The man continued, with an almost apologetic tone of voice.

"My youngest son, Vincenzino. There's something wrong with his chest; for the past few months he hasn't been breathing right, but now he's gotten worse, he has a constant fever. He's only four. I'm carving this manger scene for him. Who knows if he'll live long enough to see it finished."

Somewhere outside, the sea dramatically underscored what the man had just said with a roar.

There wasn't a hint of drama in Boccia's voice, no self-pity. It was as if he were talking about the conditions out on the water. He went on.

"It was on his account that we went to see Centurion Garofalo last week. If Vincenzino had been well, we'd have kept quiet and just muddled through."

"I don't understand," Maione said. "What do you mean?"

Boccia had taken off his oilskin rain poncho and placed it, with the rain hat, on a stool by the door. The boy moved quickly, grabbing the raincoat and depositing it in a cabinet next to the hearth. The well-established routines of an ordinary family.

"What do you know about the work we do? Do you know any fishermen, either of you?"

Maione shook his head no, Ricciardi said nothing.

"You can't make any money. You'd think that in a gulf like this there must be lots and lots of fish, but there aren't. There are times when you spend the whole day on the water and don't catch a thing. We move from place to place, we try different spots, we work together with others. But whatever we do, we barely make a living."

His wife placed a chair at the table near her husband, and he dropped into it, exhausted.

"I've been out since four. That's more than twelve hours. In heavy seas it's harder still, we shouldn't even go out at all, but then what would I feed my children? In this weather, we run the risk that the waves will carry off our nets. We don't even hoist our sails; we go out with oars. There's four of us, with a single boat."

Ricciardi listened attentively.

"You haven't told us why you went to see Garofalo the other day."

The man ran his hand over his face. Maione noticed that there were cuts on his hand, with thin, bloody strips of fabric wrapped around them. Boccia followed his gaze and said, dismissively:

"These are nothing, Brigadie'. They're just the little marks we get from handling the nets, cables, and oars. The worst damage is there, in that cradle."

The woman walked over and stood by her husband, her eyes leveled on the policemen. The man continued.

"As you know, there are laws for fishing. They're strange laws, and they don't really make all that much sense; still, we have to live with them. On a good day, we bring in four to seven hundred pounds of fish with our boat. On bad days, sometimes we come back completely empty-handed. We can't fish after the first hatching, so that means we can't even go to the areas where the fish lay their eggs in the sea. We can't go into private waters, as if the sea had fences and gates. We can't use explosives, and that's fair, I understand it. We have to have certificates and licenses, and we have to have receipts for all the taxes we pay."

The man was exhausted, and he spoke almost in a whisper. The room, along with its old, broken-down window and door frame, was illuminated by two lanterns, swaying in the drafts.

"Overseeing all those things is the militia's job. Even if you have everything in perfect order, there's always a little something extra to pay. It's what we've always done, none of us complain about it. As if it were just another tax. But then Garofalo showed up."

Maione nodded. This information matched what he'd been told by Bambinella.

"And what changed?"

"At first, he seemed better than the others, much better. He called all us boat owners together and told us, 'From now on, you don't have to give anybody anything. Nothing to no one. You can imagine how happy we were, it was a huge cost off our backs. That lasted almost a year.'"

"And then what happened?"

"And then one day he comes here, to the *borgo*. It was summer, we were out on the piazza, playing a little music and dancing. Sometimes we do that when it's been a good day; they can even hear us from the hotels, they lean out the windows and clap along. So he shows up here, alone, in uniform. He calls a few of us aside and says to us, 'Did you know that you've been fishing in the waters of Duke Thus-and-Such, off Posillipo?' We all look at one another, and we say, 'Centurio', when on earth? We're always careful where we fish, and we'd never fish there anyway, you can't catch anything.' And he said, 'You see? How do you know that you can't catch anything there, if you don't fish there?' And he fined us."

Maione and Ricciardi exchanged a glance.

"A fine? What's so serious about that?"

Boccia laughed sardonically.

"The fine is nothing. The serious part is that if you get a second fine of the same kind in a single year, then your fishing license is suspended for up to six months. They call it recidivism."

Maione nodded.

"Which meant you were at his mercy."

"Exactly, Brigadie'. If you deprive someone like me of his fishing license, then you might as well just take the whole family, put them in a boat, take the boat out to the middle of the sea, and sink it. Better a quick death than to starve."

"And what did Garofalo want?"

"He'd chosen his victims wisely, Commissa'. The ones who

went out most often, the ones with young children. The ones who could never stop working. He'd meet us at the market and take the money directly out of the wholesalers' hands. Ten, sometimes twenty percent. Depending on what kind of a day it had been."

"And it didn't ever occur to you to report him?"

Boccia laughed again.

"Report him? Our word against the word of a centurion in the militia, a Fascist? They would have thrown us in prison and given him a promotion, let me tell you. They'd have said we were just trying to get him out of the way for own ulterior motives. There was nothing we could do."

Maione was incredulous.

"So you did nothing? You just accepted the situation, you paid in silence?"

"We're used to it, Brigadie'. That's how it's always been: one time it's this one, another time it's that one, but it's always the same. But Garofalo could never get enough, he always wanted more. And I'd even have kept on paying, except Vincenzino got sick."

The wife took a step forward, emerging from the shadows.

"I spoke up; I told Aristide to stop. When the doctor left, saying that if Vicenzino didn't get that medicine, he didn't stand a chance, I said, 'Let's go and talk to him.' I thought, he has a daughter of his own, and he lives near the water; he must know how hard a fisherman's life is. Aristide said no. 'Don't fool yourself,' he said, 'what do those people care about Vincenzino and us.' But I insisted, I said that if we looked him in the face, if we talked to each other, maybe he'd leave us be, at least until Vincenzino got a little better. After all, he owed us that much."

Ricciardi thought back to the image of Garofalo, who kept saying, grim-faced, as he spouted blood from his many wounds: *I don't owe a thing, not a thing.*

"And in the end, you went to see him."

"That's right, Commissa'. We didn't bring anything with us, because he'd told us a thousand times never to bring anything to his home, since he didn't want his neighbors to think that he was taking graft. We just hoped that his wife, who was a mother like me, might understand and grant us grace, like the Madonna does, to us poor laborers."

Both Ricciardi and Maione were reminded of the sight of the shattered Saint Joseph and the Madonna tipped over onto the ass.

"What kind of a welcome did they give you?"

"The signora answered the door, with the little girl. As soon as she saw us, the child said, 'Mamma, these people smell bad.' The mother started laughing, and then he showed up. He didn't even ask us to sit down."

Her husband broke in.

"I'd prepared a whole speech, about our child and the medicine. A lot of good it did me: they looked at each other and burst out laughing. He said, 'If you don't get out of here instantly on your own two feet, I'll call some of my militiamen and have them toss you in a cell.' So then my wife spoke to the signora . . ."

". . . and I said to her, 'Signo', you're a mother; my son is sick.'"

Maione listened without wanting to.

"And what did she say to you?"

The woman's face was waxen.

"She smiled sweetly at me and said, 'Money is men's business, don't you know that? We women have to stay out of it. And after all, you have three children and I only have the little girl.' As if, since we have three, I could happily do without Vincenzino."

The sea thundered again. No more light was filtering in through the blinds; it was night already.

"So then what did you do?" Ricciardi asked.

Husband and wife exchanged a glance. He was the first to look away.

"What could we do? We came back home to await our fate."

Maione waited, then asked:

"Did you ever go back to the Garofalos' home after that?"

There was a silence that seemed endless, then the woman said:

"No, Brigadie'. We never went back. But when we heard the news that they had both been killed, I'll tell you the truth, it was a liberation for us both. Those weren't respectable people, no. They took no pity on people like us, in our condition. And a mother and father ought to feel pity for others. At least for their children. None of this should touch the children."

From the cradle came a faint, doleful hiss. The parents exchanged another quick glance. Ricciardi stood up.

"Let's go. Come on, Maione."

When he reached the door he stopped, then turned to look at the woman.

"Signora, a friend of mine is going to come take a look at your son. He's a doctor, a man with white hair, and he'll have a dog with him. He's the best doctor you'll find anywhere, and if anything can be done, he'll do it; and don't worry about the medicines, he'll take care of them. You're right: none of this should touch the children."

XXXVIII

That morning, suddenly, the wind dropped.

It was as if someone had flipped a switch, cutting the continuous winds that had been whipping the coast for many days down to nothing but still air. Those who were up and about early noticed it and looked up, bewildered, sniffing the air. From the balconies the capons and turkeys, who unbeknownst to them were living out their last few hours of life after a lengthy domestic breeding period, called to one another with renewed vigor, and the hens regained dominion of the *vicoli*, where they were no longer pursued by wind-crazed sheets of newspaper.

The vendors who had fixed locations immediately changed their strategy, hurrying off to the locations best for sales, which had been left empty thanks to the violent gusts of wind of the previous few days. The shoeshine boys took up their spots outside the Galleria, where they could accost lawyers and doctors who crossed the street at that exact point, and the newsies went back to waving their newspapers in the piazza, proffering their product to the gentlemen who no longer had to clap their hats to their heads with one hand.

The winter itself was caught off guard by the sudden death of the north wind. The temperature remained mild for a few hours, as if the weather were looking around indecisively, unable to remember the date and the season.

The army of the genuine strolling vendors, the ones who spread out across the city, moving continuously, immediately invaded all the main pedestrian thoroughfares. The calls of the vendors hawking their wares began to echo in the streets, as they offered their goods and their services to all those who might have need of them, as well as to those who hadn't yet realized that they had need of them The *carnacottaro*, or hot-meats man, displayed his tripe and pig's feet, to be eaten with pepper and a spritz of lemon. Competing with him for customers were the perennially boiling pots of the *maccaronari*, or macaroni vendors, and the pots of oil for the fried-pizza man, who also fried piping-hot *panzarotti* turnovers and potato croquettes, so hot that those who ate them cursed loudly as they burned their lips and tongues. The *acquaiole*, or water women, began to reappear in the streets with jugs—held in place with the aid of folded handkerchiefs—balanced on their heads, offering the cool and slightly rust-flavored water from the springs of Chiatamone. The kiosks retorted with *limonate a cosce aperte*—spread-your-knees lemonades—named for the fact that you had to lean forward as you drank them, since they would foam over the edge of the glass because of the pinch of bicarbonate that was added right before drinking.

Eat and drink without sitting down at the table, even first thing in the morning: that was the message broadcasted during the last two days before Christmas dinner. Plumes of white smoke rose like moving shop signs, to identify the fires over which the artichokes and piping-hot chestnuts were cooking. As well as walnuts, hazelnuts, lupini beans, and sun-dried pumpkin seeds.

Stunned by the sheer volume and variety of things on offer, the shoppers began to close the ranks of their armies: potential purchasers versus potential sellers. Soon the streets and piazzas were all a single teeming market, filled with transactions begun but never completed, shouting and staged arguments, interminable haggling sessions and precarious agreements.

It lasted a couple of hours. Then the temperature started dropping.

It occurred to Sister Veronica that children played a part in everything in life, if you really stopped to think about it.

Everything was done for them; everything was focused on them, and that was how it ought to be. After all, aren't our children our future? Aren't they our source of hope? This was why she loved the mission she'd been entrusted with, that is, teaching children.

She suspected that she'd been selected because she was short, and because of her shrill voice that sounded like a trumpet: qualities that made her seem like a character out of a fairy-tale, a fairy godmother with special powers. She'd been born to spend her life with children.

Even the Madre Addolorata, Our Lady of Sorrows, to whom her order was consecrated, had first and foremost been a mother, as her name suggested, and thus she had a child to take care of: a son who, through no fault of his own, had caused her—and would always cause her—perennial sorrow.

As she walked between the rows of desks, watching her students as they bent to the task of writing Christmas letters to their parents, it was clear to her that there was no nobler, no more demanding duty than that of caring for children; and that all children are really the children of those who love them, and not just those who engendered them. Otherwise Mary's heart pierced by swords would make no sense, would it?

Out of the corner of her eye, she glimpsed two young boys whispering pointers to each other, and she launched a resounding call to order.

"Watch out, I see you two!"

Immediately, from some unknown point at the far side of the classroom, came a perfect imitation of her voice, in the exact same tone but without words:

"*Pepepèpe, pepepè!*"

The whole class burst into irrepressible laughter, though the nun's stern gaze quickly doused that brushfire of hilarity. Deep down, however, the woman had to admit that it had been an impressive imitation, and she stifled a laugh of her own. What lovable scamps they were, after all.

She walked back to the last row, where her little niece, Benedetta, was sitting. Bent over the desk, the tip of her tongue sticking out, she was busy writing a letter that her mother would never see.

Sister Veronica felt a stab of sorrow pierce her heart at the thought of her unfortunate sister. Still, she thought, the little girl was luckier than so many others; at least she had her aunt to look after her.

The most important thing was to make it through Christmas. The holidays are the hardest period of the year, for people who've suffered a recent loss. But if the Virgin Mary was able to do it, with all those swords driven through her chest, then she and Benedetta would make it, too.

She benevolently caressed the head of a child. As soon as she walked past him, the little boy made a show of pulling out a handkerchief and wiping the place where the nun had placed her hand. The class once again burst out laughing.

Ricciardi and Maione met once again for their daily morning meeting in the commissario's office. They were both in foul moods, distracted and looking sleep-deprived.

Maione had brought two cups of ersatz coffee, as was traditional.

"*Mamma mia*, this morning this bilge is even worse than usual."

"Well, at least it's hot, no?" Ricciardi replied. "Now, tell me: what do you think of the fishermen?"

"Commissa', my feeling is that we're not making a lot of headway in this investigation. It could have been either Lomunno or the Boccias. In the case of the Boccias, now, there's also the fact that the woman could have taken part, and that would take the jackpot if you line it up with the findings of the autopsy and the theory that two different hands—one strong, the other weak—killed Garofalo."

Ricciardi added his own considerations.

"Who, it turns out, was a genuinely horrible individual, from what we can tell. And that means that the murderer or murderers could have been someone else entirely, extorted fishermen we know nothing about, for instance, or even some other colleague afraid he was about to wind up like Lomunno."

Maione nodded, setting the now-empty demitasse down on the desk with a grimace.

"I'm glad I'm done with that foul brew. In any case, it seems to me that we need to check out the statements of both the Boccias and Lomunno. The fisherman was out on the water in his boat when the murder took place, he said that they go out at four in the morning and come back at least twelve hours later, so we'll have to talk to the other three members of the crew. Lomunno on the other hand says he was going door to door looking for a job down at the harbor; maybe someone saw him and will remember him."

Ricciardi looked straight ahead of him, into the empty air.

"I wouldn't expect anything to come of it, though. What do you think Boccia's fellow fishermen are going to say? That he wasn't there with them? And even if you get confirmation that someone did see Lomunno, how could you rule out the possibility that he stepped away to commit the murder, and then went back down to the port? We need to check on these things because it's our administrative duty to do so, and we'll have to file the appropriate reports, I understand. But it's certainly not going to help us solve this murder."

Maione looked out the window.

"You see that, Commissa'? The wind has dropped. Maybe this will be a good day for the fishermen."

Ricciardi followed Maione's gaze and saw that the piazza was starting to buzz with foot and car traffic.

"But you should always know what it is that you're fishing for. Let's get moving: I'll go to the port, you go interrogate Boccia's crew. But first let's take another walk together over to the Garofalos' apartment, and see if we can find out whether our dead couple received any other visitors."

XXXIX

L ivia had just finished dressing when her maid knocked discreetly at her bedroom door.

"Signo', excuse me. There's a gentleman here who wants to see you."

That worried her; she wasn't expecting anyone, and if a man presented himself at the home of a single woman at that hour of the morning it could only be taken as a blatant discourtesy, or else it was something very grave and urgent.

"Show him to the drawing room, Teresa. I'll be right there."

Her suspicions were confirmed the moment she walked into the room. Standing by the window, well dressed and unruffled as ever, was Falco.

She didn't know if that was his name, or his surname, or neither of the two. She'd first met the man a few months earlier, when she was planning her reception for Edda Mussolini's trip south to Naples with her father, a party that was never held because of the accident in which Ricciardi had been involved. Falco had shown up at her home without warning, without being announced by anyone, and insisted on helping her plan the event.

He had told her that he belonged to a very discreet organization, one whose local branch was responsible for, among other things, creating conditions of the greatest possible security for the Duce and his family. Later, however, he had provided Livia with a detailed report on Ricciardi, making it clear that the anonymous organization he had said he worked for could be nothing other than a kind of secret police.

Even though she appreciated the usefulness of the information she'd been given, Livia continued to find that man disconcerting: his cold speaking voice, his in-depth knowledge of the details of other people's lives had left her with a sense of discomfort. She realized that no one who had any public stature could elude the close control of Falco and those like him. She'd felt only relief when he silently left her apartment the last time he'd come, and she'd fervently hoped never to see him again.

Instead, here he was, three days before Christmas, and first thing in the morning. As usual, he slipped through the front entrance, which was assiduously monitored, without the doorman calling up, the way he would for anyone else, even tradesmen. Livia was vaguely annoyed, and she had no intention of hiding it.

"*Buongiorno*. Did we have an appointment? If so, it must have slipped my mind."

Falco turned his gaze in her direction, with a half tilt of the head.

"*Buongiorno*, Signora. Have you noticed that the wind has suddenly dropped? How odd. Now, you'll see, the temperature is going to plunge."

Livia smiled remotely.

"So you even have that kind of information? Did you get it from a well-placed source with the Lord Almighty? Or does it come directly from God Himself?"

Falco smiled in response, though there was no change in the expression of his eyes.

"No, Signora. Quite simply, some of my kin were fishermen, and so I grew up with the ability to predict the weather a couple of hours in advance."

Livia felt a little foolish now, and decided to make up for it by making a show of hospitality.

"Ah, I see. Would you care to sit down? Have you already eaten breakfast?"

Falco remained standing.

"*Grazie*, Signora. Yes, I've been up for a long time now, I would say. And I apologize for the timing of my visit, but you know that we prefer to move around when the streets are relatively empty. Even though in these last few days before the holidays, there's always a lot of activity."

Livia waved her hand dismissively.

"But it's like that in this city all year round. Always lots and lots of people, of every stripe and color."

"Which often comes in handy for us, though other times less so. I imagine that in your city this kind of hubbub is uncommon, am I right?"

"To tell the truth, in Rome . . ."

"I meant Pesaro, where you were born. Though you haven't been back there for almost two years now, twenty-two months to be exact."

This level of detail about her life sent a sudden chill through her. She couldn't even have said herself how long it had been since she'd last been to see her parents, while that perfect stranger standing in her drawing room knew down to the day and the hour where she'd been over the past two years.

She understood that this was the man's way of telling her that idle talk and verbal fencing were pointless with him.

"To what do I owe the honor of your visit, Falco? I didn't expect to see you again so soon."

"I must admit, Signora, that of all the tasks assigned to me, this is one of the most agreeable ones."

"*Mamma mia*, what gallantry," Livia responded harshly. "I suppose I ought to cherish it, coming from a man of such a reserved nature."

Falco bowed his head once again.

"That's a familiar experience for you, to be paid compliments. I understand that you were even paid chivalrous tribute by a convicted felon yesterday morning."

Once again, Livia felt an ominous shiver run down her spine. She decided to stop playing along.

"Falco, let me ask you once again what you want from me. I have a number of things to do today."

The man seemed almost chagrined.

"That's too bad, I hate being forced to be unpleasant. It's a part of my job that I can never quite get used to. I know what you plan to do today, Signora. You're planning to go get two tickets to the theater."

Now he was going too far. She hadn't said a word to anyone about her intention to go to the theater.

"How on earth would you know that?"

"Let's just say that you were overheard yesterday, when you told your chauffeur to have the car ready for that purpose. I would imagine, though it's just a guess, that the theater in question is the Kursaal, on Via Filangieri."

Livia sat openmouthed; she could only nod her head yes. Falco smiled.

"That's not a result of any investigation, though. It's just that it's a very eagerly anticipated performance, a one-act play by this newly formed company of young actors that's gaining in popularity, two brothers and a sister, the De Filippos. I've heard they're really very talented."

Livia nodded, mistrustful.

"That's right. And this is a new play, written by the eldest of the three, who's the leader of the troupe and the playwright. It's about Christmas."

"And you're determined not to miss the premiere, which is tomorrow night. You intend to buy two tickets; one is for you. And the other?"

Livia shifted uncomfortably in her armchair.

"I don't believe that's any of your business, nor do I think that it's a matter of national security whom I choose to invite out for an evening at the theater!"

Falco looked down, running his fingers along the brim of the hat he held in his hand.

"Certainly, I understand. So let me explain: national security is a complicated matter, and it's intricately bound up with the press and propaganda. In other words, the public image of certain people counts a great deal. You are a very important friend to figures who occupy prominent places in the regime. They care for you; your well-being is of paramount importance to them. Your stubborn persistence in frequenting this man, I hardly need say his name, is starting to cause concern."

Livia clenched her fists to regain her self-control. Her eyes narrowed to slits, she hissed:

"That man's name is Luigi Alfredo Ricciardi, and he's a commissario of the Naples police force. It seems to me that his rank and profession are an indication that I'm in safe hands, wouldn't you agree? And whom I choose to see is a matter that concerns no one but me: certainly not my friends, no matter how prominent they may happen to be."

Falco sighed faintly.

"Of course not. And let me reassure you that we have nothing official against this person, though certain aspects of his personal life have aroused our concern. The problem is that everyone would be more comfortable, Signora, if you were to return to Rome. The man we're talking about comes from a different milieu; some of the people he frequents are, how to put this, ambiguous at best. There's that doctor, for instance, who . . . But I've already told you about him. You're traveling down a rather slippery slope, that's all."

Livia was almost tempted to laugh. There was no one, aside from herself, who looked favorably on her relationship with Ricciardi. Not even Ricciardi himself.

"Falco, if this is a warning, believe me, I appreciate it. But

I should tell you, so that you can report back to whomever the devil you like, that I'm a big girl, and I'm perfectly capable of making my own decisions. And I have no intention of going back to Rome; you may add that to your report as well."

The man hadn't stopped playing with his hat. He looked up.

"I imagined as much. I'd even told them in advance that this would be your response, Signora. To tell the truth, there's a part of me that's happy to have been correct in my evaluation. All the same, I'm going to have to insist one last time on this point: certain acquaintances, perhaps undertaken with the best possible intentions, without a second thought, can prove to be extremely harmful in the long run. And certain contacts, certain friendships won't protect you forever."

Livia snorted in annoyance.

"Falco, I've already told you that my friendship with Ricciardi is, for the moment, completely secondary and informal, and unfortunately the only one really keeping it going is me. If he were the one seeking me out, though . . ."

"I'm not talking about your friendship with him," Falco interrupted her. "I'm talking about his friendships with others. If you were to happen to tell him, say, purely in passing, in the context of a more general conversation, about a comment, or a trip being made by your . . . girlfriend in Rome, shall we say, and if he in turn were to mention the matter to a friend of his, that would become a matter of national security. And you, and he, and even we would be responsible for it. Is that clear to you?"

There was a long silence. Livia realized that with that elaborate example, Falco had meant to illustrate the level of surveillance she was under. She decided to express her appreciation.

"I understand. And I thank you for the information. I promise you complete discretion, you can rest assured. Please report back that I'd like everyone to stop worrying. I talk too little with Ricciardi to start with, and he talks even less to me. That's why I wanted to take him to the theater: at least there we wouldn't have to pretend to converse."

Falco grinned.

"It's just a matter of time, Signora. I can't imagine how or why anyone would hold out for long against a woman like you. Have a good day, and forgive me for the intrusion. I hope the two of you enjoy yourselves at the Kursaal."

XL

B eniamino Ferro, doorman of the apartment building at 2 Largo del Leone in Mergellina, takes a step back and admires his handiwork.

He's proud of the manger scene he's just finished. Considering that his work duties have prevented him from devoting the time to it that really was necessary, he's happy with the results.

To tell the truth, though, if he hadn't felt the frequent need to go and wet his whistle, he might have had more time; and if he didn't drop off to sleep every so often, as a result of the aforementioned refreshments, he'd have had even more time to spend on it.

But Beniamino tends to be self-indulgent: a single man, without a family, without a wife or children to lend him a hand, is entitled to take a break every now and then, he thinks to himself. And if, during one of those breaks, someone shows up and has sufficiently bad manners to enter without even announcing himself to the doorman, who just happens to be taking, in fact, a break, then it's certainly not his fault. Not the doorman's fault, that is.

The manger scene really is nice. It has everything: the moss, the herbs to keep away evil spirits; the two companions, Zi' Vicienzo and Zi' Pascale, one happy and the other sad, who represent respectively Carnival and Death; the virgin Stefania, who's concealing a rock under her dress to convince everyone that she's pregnant, and who will later miraculously give birth to Saint Stephen. And then there's Cicci Bacco, the vintner, his favorite, because the manger scene, after all, is about good cheer, too—*allegria!*—because the birth of the Christ Child is the best thing to ever happen to the world.

Right now, Beniamino's vision is blurry, because his eyes are filled with tears. He remembers his *papà*, and the ritual of building the nativity scene at home. He remembers how his father explained in intricate detail the meaning of every herb, every house, every shepherd. Why the manger scene represents the whole world, the world of the past, the world of the present, and the world of the future: Beniami', don't ever forget it. The manger scene is like the world: it seems as if it's all jumbled together by chance, but in reality everyone and everything has a specific meaning and purpose. And Beniamino, even if he has no children of his own, can appreciate the manger scene's beauty.

He puts away his razor-sharp carving knife, and his mind turns to Garofalo. *Mamma mia*, how harsh that man was, and always reading him the riot act: when he went by and found Ferro slumbering—because a man's allowed to catch forty winks every so often, you know—he'd shout and wake him up. And one time he even came over to the tavern to get him, one day when it was horribly hot and he'd just stepped away for a moment to get a little refreshment, because his throat was so dry that if he tried to spit, he'd wind up spitting twine.

He'd made him look like a fool, a buffoon, in front of everybody. He'd yelled that you can tell all you need to know about a building from its doorman, and that he was the bottom of the barrel, the worst doorman on earth. That sooner or later he'd make sure to get Beniamino fired, because he couldn't tolerate the thought that a man like himself, of his rank and his responsibilities, should live in an apartment building with a doorman like him.

So Beniamino really had hated Centurion Garofalo. He'd

really hated him, even though his wife was always smiling, and his daughter was sweet, and his sister-in-law, the nun, was friendly and made him laugh.

But Garofalo himself was a monster. A conceited, self-important bastard, and a monster. He's glad that the bastard never saw his manger scene finished.

Don Pierino, yet again, admired the manger scene of the church of San Ferdinando. He often went by it intentionally, taking the long way round from the sacristy to the confessional. It was a simple pleasure that he was glad to indulge in.

In these matters, he was no different than he was as a child: Christmas was the manger scene and the manger scene was Christmas, in the chilly, damp countryside of Santa Maria Capua Vetere where he had grown up. The town's parish priest, who had instructed him in the simple faith that still sustained him, used to build one that seemed enormous to him, full of characters, animals, and houses. He'd spend hours imagining he was a shepherd himself, wandering around in that enchanted world of peace and serenity.

At a certain point, he sensed that he was being watched, and he feared that it might be the Signorina Vaccaro with some new malady to inform him of. When he turned around, he was surprised to find the Signorina Colombo, the daughter of the haberdasher whose store was across the way from the church. He didn't actually know her very well. Her family was quite discreet, and although they attended the Sunday service, they didn't spend much time at the parish church during the rest of the week. He remembered that he'd once gone, in Don Tommaso's place, to bless the shop, and that on that occasion he'd met the father, a smiling middle-aged man, the mother, who struck him as something of a gossip and a busybody, and that tall and self-contained young woman, with her spectacles and a gentle, reserved air to her.

But today she seemed ill at ease. She stood there, some ten feet away from him, her purse clutched in both hands, as if she were caught between the desire to speak to him and the urge to run away. He decided to make up her mind for her.

"*Buongiorno*. You're Signorina Colombo, no? How are you?"

The young woman was visibly relieved that she could no longer make her escape. It was too late; she'd been seen and identified.

"*Buongiorno*, Padre. Yes, that's me. I'd like to . . . I have something to ask you, if you have five minutes for me. But if you're busy I can always come back another time."

Don Pierino looked hard at her; behind her eyeglasses, with thick lenses that showed she was nearsighted, the woman's eyes clearly expressed a raging internal storm of some kind. He was accustomed to recognizing the moments of travail indicative of a struggle, of a need for help and an inability to ask for it in explicit terms. To refuse that wordless request would be tantamount to abandoning a soul in need, and it could engender great pain and sorrow.

"No, no, I'm not busy. I'm at your service. Come, let's go to my office, where we'll be more comfortable."

What Don Pierino referred to as an "office" was really a sort of nook carved out of the large closet where the vestments of the sacristy were kept, a little corner almost entirely occupied by a desk and two chairs. It was used for his conversations with the faithful, that is, for those colloquies that were not full-fledged confessions but which still needed to be conducted in private.

Enrica sat down, a little stiffly. She was trying to find a way to bring up the topic she wanted to discuss, but she wasn't sufficiently at ease with Don Pierino to just start talking. The assistant parish priest, for his part, knew that he would have to help the woman to overcome her shyness.

"Now then, is everyone well at home? How are preparations going for Christmas? Have you set up your manger scene, have you already decided what to cook for dinner?"

An array of trivial topics, all woven together to put her at her ease. Enrica understood and appreciated it.

"My father is in charge of the nativity scene. A task that he won't let anyone else take over from him, but my little brothers gather round and watch him, and he pretends to let them help. Whereas we women are focused on the lunches and dinners, and it's very hard work. But it's work we enjoy."

Don Pierino assumed his customary posture, with the fingers of his hands knit together, resting on his belly.

"And spiritually? How are you feeling? Are you happy, with your heart at rest, at peace with yourself?"

Here we go, Enrica thought to herself.

"Well, actually, not really, Padre. I felt the need to speak to you. I need to . . . to ask you to explain something to me, to give me some guidance."

The priest nodded, seriously.

"That's why I'm here, Signorina. To help you to recover your peace of mind. That's all I'm here for."

"Yes, Padre, I know that. And I'd like to tell you a little story, if you'd have the patience to listen to it."

"I'm all ears."

And the young woman told the story.

She described a growing feeling, over the months and the seasons and the weeks and the hours, through windowpanes closed to keep out the winter chill or open to welcome in the warm summer air. She told him about interminable hours spent doing her left-handed needlepoint, slowly working under the cone of bright light cast by a lampshade, to the sound of dance tunes playing on the radio. She told him about a shadowy figure standing in the half-light across the way, arms folded across his chest, just twenty-five feet away and one floor below; and how difficult it was to bridge that distance, given all the social conventions that poisoned people's lives.

Then she told him about two fleeting encounters. One near a vegetable stand: a pair of desperate green eyes just inches away, and his hasty flight, and a trail of broccoli scattered in the street behind him. And a second encounter that she was more vague about: something to do with work, in the presence of a second person with whom she'd ended up exchanging a few words, while this other man sat there looking at her as if he were drowning, wide-eyed and openmouthed.

Last of all, she spoke of two letters, hesitant and awkwardly phrased, but letters she'd read and reread: one that absurdly requested her permission to greet her, and the other that granted him that permission, and how.

Then she fell silent, and with downcast eyes, she realized that at some point during her speech, she couldn't say when, she must have pulled a handkerchief out of her purse, and she'd been torturing it all the while with her hands.

Don Pierino had listened in silence, breathing softly and signaling his empathy and interest with the thousand lively expressions of his mobile face. He guessed that this was no straightforward tale of adoration from afar, and he waited to hear the rest.

When she resumed speaking, Enrica's voice had a different tone, more heartfelt, less evocative.

She talked about the thrill of being just one step away from an actual meeting, from the lowering of the barriers; about how she'd stood up to her mother who was trying to play matchmaker and push her into a relationship with another man, even arranging a date for her. And then the contact with a person from his family, an elderly *tata*, kind and determined, who regarded Enrica favorably. She also alluded to the mysterious, charming woman from up north who she'd seen with him; but she immediately added that the man's attitude toward that woman hadn't seemed especially intimate or affectionate.

At last, she took a deep breath, and told him about the accident. About the hospital, about the moments of horrific tension when she believed that he was going to die. About the ashen faces of all those who were present, a very small group made up of his *tata*, that lady, a colleague of his from work.

And she told him about the promise she'd made to the Madonna of Pompeii, that she'd never see him again if he survived.

From her very first words about the accident, a doubt began to stir in Don Pierino's mind. It all seemed too absurd: the similarities between this story and that of his friend Commissario Ricciardi were too strong. And, gradually, as Enrica went on, a hope sprang up in his heart that he could never have imagined, a hope that love and happiness might soon enter the life of that strange, forlorn green-eyed man. A lovely Christmas present, Don Pierino said to himself. In fact, Christmas had brought a beautiful gift.

Enrica went on with her story, as the priest's mind worked quickly: she was saying that she felt bound by that promise, even though the *tata* had gone to see her to try to persuade her not to exit his life for good; that in any case she felt uncertain, because she didn't know for sure how the man felt about her, and she had wondered whether the woman she'd seen him with might not be better suited to be near him; that nevertheless, even if she thought rationally about all these things, every night that she went without opening the shutters she felt herself die a little bit inside.

"Padre, what should I do? I made a promise, and you'll tell me that I have to keep my promise; I made it voluntarily, and I'd do it again. So why do I feel as if I'm dying?"

Don Pierino brought his hands together in front of his face and shut his eyes. Then he opened them again, and his gaze was one of absolute determination.

"Signorina, you promised something to the Madonna that

wasn't yours to promise. You promised the sacrifice of another person's love; you promised his loneliness, his unhappiness and your own. That's not what the Madonna wants; that's not what God wants, for His children."

Enrica listened, her eyes open wide and red from crying and insomnia.

"I'm sure that in your heart you know what's right and what's wrong. Our faith wasn't made to erect barriers, walls, or iron bars between us and love; it was made to increase the presence of love in our lives, so that we can give of ourselves and live in a state of communion, and start families that can help to keep us from feeling alone on dark winter nights. What kind of God would He be, if He wanted to lock those who can feel love in a cell of solitude?"

The girl listened to the priest, raptly.

"So what you're saying is that . . . in other words, I ought to . . ."

"You ought to fight for your own happiness, the way everyone else does, and always has. While respecting your fellow man, in the love you feel for your neighbor and for life, which is the greatest gift that has ever been given to us. You ought to speak and listen, smile and show all the love you feel inside to someone who, perhaps, lacks the strength to encourage you."

Enrica had begun to smile. Don Pierino decided that the girl was one of those people who completely change expression when they smile, as if they were smiling with every single part of their body.

"So what you're saying is that I should push myself; I should gather my courage, and fight for my happiness. Is that it? I should take the initiative."

The priest realized that the young woman was no longer talking to him; she was now talking to herself. He shifted in his chair until he was comfortable, once again with his fingers knit and resting on his belly, and a contented expression on his face.

"You've understood perfectly. Now if he happens not to want the same thing, if he makes a different choice, then you'll find another path to happiness, believe me; there are so many of them. But the important thing, for you, is to be certain that you've done everything within your power to attain happiness. Simple, no?"

Enrica stood up. From behind the lenses of her glasses, her eyes radiated with a new glow.

"Yes, Padre. Quite simple. That's what I'd never seen before, what I didn't know how to see. In reality it's all so simple. If you want to be happy, then you have to do what it takes to be happy. I thank you, I thank you from the bottom of my heart."

Don Pierino smiled.

"No, I thank *you*, for having chosen to confide in me. And, please, let me know how everything goes."

XLI

The air had turned chilly by now.

Maione and Ricciardi were numb from the cold by the time they reached the Largo del Leone, even though the wind had stopped blowing and they'd walked briskly from police headquarters in an attempt to stay warm. The brigadier had long since given up even trying to suggest they catch a trolley; his superior officer had taken off on foot directly, his head pulled down into the lapels of his overcoat, striding toward their destination at a rapid gait.

They had gotten a bite to eat along the way, a sfogliatella puff pastry for Ricciardi and two *panzarotti* turnovers for Maione: handheld foods chosen in order to save time and get as far ahead with their investigation as possible, since it wasn't long until sunset. They knew that when Christmas came, everything would come to a halt, and the sleepy twelve-day period leading up to Epiphany would lower a curtain of silences and closed doors on the case. It could provide a crucial advantage to the murderers, and enable them to get away entirely.

Maione couldn't see the reason for another visit to the crime scene. He thought it seemed like a waste of time: he still needed to go by the *borgo* to question the men in Boccia's fishing crew, and before nightfall he wanted to make another stop to take a look at what the hands that had murdered his son were up to, hands that were now occupied with the skilled work of carving faces on Via San Gregorio Armeno. Just as a way of drawing a little bit closer to the decision to ruin his own life and that of the murderer, in keeping with the absurd moral code by which he'd lived.

Ricciardi, however, wanted to see the doorman again. All right, the man was drunk more often than not, and he didn't seem especially efficient, but Ricciardi hadn't yet questioned him about the scene of the crime; and perhaps this time, if he was a little more sober, he might remember something else.

They were in luck: Ferro was at his post, and this time he looked more cognizant of his surroundings. He'd just finished putting up the manger scene in the building's lobby, and he seemed proud of himself. He was surrounded by a small knot of children, who were expressing their admiration with sharp whistles, sighs, and occasional bursts of applause.

When he saw the two policemen coming toward him, the man changed expression. His gaze became worried and mistrustful. He shooed away the children with a wave, as if they were flies, and walked toward Ricciardi and Maione.

"*Buonasera*. May I help you?"

The two men exchanged a look of surprise. The doorman didn't seem to have recognized them.

"Hello, Ferro. You have to accompany us into the Garofalos' apartment."

Ricciardi had been intentionally brusque; he wanted to see how the man would react. Ferro narrowed his eyes.

"Ah, Commissario, forgive me, the light was behind you and I didn't realize who you were. I just set up the manger scene; in the end I decided that, since it was done, I may as well put it up in the lobby. I was showing it to the children who live here."

Maione broke into the conversation.

"While you're showing us upstairs, Ferro, I'd like to ask you if anything has come to mind over the past couple of days. If there was anyone who came to call, whether you heard any discussions or arguments, that kind of thing."

Ferro had pulled a bunch of keys off a rack and was climbing the stairs ahead of them.

"Now that I think about it, yes, Brigadie'. A couple did come, a man and a woman, I'd say three, maybe four days before . . . before the incident, shall we say."

"What were they like, these two? Did they tell you their names?"

"No, they really didn't tell me their names. And I didn't ask, because I only saw them on their way out; when they went up, I . . . I had stepped away for just a moment."

"And how did you know that they had gone to see the Garofalos?"

"I asked them afterward. Out of curiosity."

All right, then, thought Maione: the Boccias' visit had been confirmed.

"Had you ever seen them before? Or did you see them again after that?"

"No, Brigadie'. Neither before nor after. Just that one time, and I couldn't tell you how long they were here, because . . ."

Maione finished his sentence for him:

"Because when they arrived, you weren't here yourself, right."

Ferro had opened the door and stepped to one side, without looking into the apartment. Ricciardi gave him a hard stare.

"Go ahead, Ferro, lead the way. We're right behind you."

The man looked at him with terror in his eyes.

"Commissa', I'd really prefer . . . I mean, I'll just wait for the two of you out here, on the landing."

Ricciardi met and held his gaze.

"No, you won't. You'll accompany us inside, and you'll lead the way."

His tone made it clear that he wasn't going to take no for an answer. Maione took a step toward the man, who closed his eyes halfway, opened the door, and prepared to enter.

The interior was steeped in shadow, with only dim light filtering in through the partially drawn curtains. On the entryway floor you could still clearly make out the stains from the blood that had gushed out of Costanza Garofalo's slit throat. Ferro staggered and grabbed the doorjamb to keep from falling, while Ricciardi was engulfed by the sight of the woman's translucent image, which smiled, eyes lowered, as it asked: *Hat and gloves?* Waves of black liquid oozed from the fatal wound.

"Jesus, but is that . . . is that blood, over there?"

Ricciardi studied the man's expression. He didn't seem to be pretending: he'd turned pale and looked like he was about to faint and slam face-first into the floor.

Maione stepped over to him and grabbed him by the arm.

"Come on, Ferro. Show us to the bedroom."

The man balked, running a hand over his face as if trying to conceal the sight of the blood from his eyes; then he headed toward the hallway at an unsteady gait. Ricciardi watched him, noticing that the doorman demonstrated a certain familiarity with the interior of the apartment. Leaving aside how upset he was, he moved with a fair degree of confidence. The commissario noted that he was very careful where he put his feet, avoiding the spatters of blood that marked the way between the two corpses, even though those drops were scarcely visible in the dim light.

Once they reached the bedroom, at the sight of the large black stain on the sheets, Ferro let himself drop down into a chair with a faint lament.

"Oh, Madonna. Holy Virgin Mary, help us all."

Ricciardi turned his back on the image of Garofalo repeating: *I don't owe a thing, not a thing*, and spoke to the doorman.

"I wanted you to see it with your own two eyes, Ferro. And now I'm going to ask you whether you have any idea, any idea at all, as to who could have done this."

The doorman began to weep, softly. He murmured, as he stared at the bloodstain:

"No idea, Commissa'. If I knew anyone who could do this kind of thing, I'd run away from them as fast and as far as I could, believe you me. And that poor little girl, she was so pretty the other day, with her braids . . . and now she'll never see her mamma and papà again as long as she lives. Centurion Garofalo was . . . well, he had a very particular personality, God rest his soul. Maybe not everyone loved him, maybe he could make you angry sometimes, but to kill him like that . . . No one, Commissa'. No one on earth would be capable of it."

But in fact, evidently, someone on earth had been capable of it, Ricciardi thought.

"Let's take a little walk through the other rooms. That way we can see if they took anything that you remembered but that we couldn't know about."

The point of this was to see whether the man's reaction betrayed anything. They'd checked everything during the first on-site investigation, and if anything were missing, they'd be able to tell from the empty space on the item of furniture or on the walls.

Ferro seemed relieved to be getting away from the scene of the murders, and he led Maione and Ricciardi through the other rooms in silence, walking robotically. When they walked past the nativity scene in the room next to the bedroom he sighed, but he didn't seem to notice Saint Joseph's absence, or the figurine of the Virgin tipped over against that of the ass.

They finished their tour of the apartment and met up back at the front door. The doorman held his breath at the sight of the marks left behind by the woman's corpse, stepped over them, and walked out onto the landing where he loudly inhaled a chestful of air. He pulled a crumpled cigarette out of his pocket; he tried to light it with a match but couldn't because his hand was trembling too violently. And so he gave up, and finally vomited in a corner of the staircase.

XLII

They decided to take the waterfront route. It wasn't any colder there, and there was no wind blowing that the trees in the Villa Nazionale might help to break; they might as well enjoy the sight of the sea, finally placid, embracing the falling darkness.

Ferro's reaction and the few additional bits of information they'd gathered during their interview with the doorman were the subjects of the sporadic phrases that Maione and Ricciardi exchanged along the way.

"Commissa', as far as I could tell, he was truly upset. He really couldn't handle it; you could see he wasn't used to the sight of blood."

Ricciardi, on the other hand, had some misgivings.

"His reaction seemed a little theatrical, don't you think? And besides, today he was stone-cold sober; the things that happen to you when you're drunk seem different when you revisit them after sobering up. I don't know. But when he walked past the manger scene, he didn't even change his expression."

"That's right. And he admitted that he'd seen the Boccias when they came to talk with Garofalo. For the moment, that's the one sure thing we have, eh, Commissa'?"

Ricciardi nodded, walking along with his head down.

"True, the visit from the Boccias. And they're a couple, so that would provide an explanation for the two different hands that killed the centurion, except for the fact that the 'light' hand, the one that inflicted the shallower wounds, was a left hand, according to Modo, and it looked to me like Signora Boccia was right-handed. But that doesn't necessarily rule her out. And Lomunno could have had an accomplice."

Maione agreed:

"And our friend the doorman, here, could have done something stupid when he was drunk that he can't even remember now. It could mean everything and it could mean nothing. *Mamma mia*, there are times when I get really sick and tired of this job."

They skirted the beach, with the sea on their right and the road with cars and carriages moving past on their left. The pedestrians were few and far between, and the ones they saw walked hunched over from the cold.

The fishermen who had no fishing boats of their own had gathered in small knots on the sand. It was the time of day when they brought in their nets. This time of year, it was an operation that had to be done twice daily.

Small one-oared dinghies headed out some six hundred feet from shore, leaving one end of the nets onshore and tossing out the large swathes of mesh, which the women repaired early in the morning and at night, stitching up the rips made by the currents. Once the nets had been cast, the dinghies returned to shore, unrolling their cables on the sidewalk that ran along the beach. At this point the men, barefoot and with their trousers rolled up to their knees, hooked the cables of the nets to a canvas shoulder strap and, in groups of four or five per side, began hauling first on the cable and then on the net, walking back into the area reserved for strollers and then advancing gradually as the net came in to shore, bringing with it the hope of another day of survival for all the men's families. As they hauled in, the children would wrap up the cables around large spools on the beach.

At other times of the year, when demand was lower than at

Christmas, this grueling task was performed only in the mornings; but now a crowd of potential customers in search of affordable fish—which they knew they could get here because there was no markup for wholesalers and retailers—was waiting on the street, so the additional effort was likely to be worth it.

Maione, slowing his pace, turned toward Ricciardi.

"They certainly put in a hard day's work, these fishermen. And these are the ones who fish off the beach. Look at that, Commissa', as cold as it is, they're barefoot in the water; their legs are black from the chill."

"Yes, it's tough for them," Ricciardi agreed. "But even the ones who go out on the water, like Boccia—you've seen what a hellish life they lead. And then someone like Garofalo comes along and eats you alive, and suddenly you can't even make ends meet."

They'd come even with the *borgo*, in the shadow of the dark and imposing castle. Ricciardi nodded his head in Maione's direction.

"This is where we split up. You see what you can find out from Boccia's fellow fishermen, who at this time of day are probably returning from their day out on the water. I'll go down to the port and ask around about how Lomunno spent his morning on the day of the murder. But you go directly home once you're done; there's no point in dropping by police headquarters again. If we come up with anything new, we can write our reports tomorrow."

Maione nodded.

"At your orders, Commissa'. Tomorrow's already the day before Christmas Eve. Christmas is upon us."

"Yes, the holidays are here. And I'm afraid we haven't accomplished much so far. Good luck."

Christmas is upon us.

That thought prompted the usual mix of feelings in Tata

Rosa: anxiety about the things she still had to get done around the house, anticipation for the festivities, worry about the year that was coming to an end and the year that was about to arrive in just a matter of days.

She needed to prepare for the Christmas Eve supper, of course; even if it was only the two of them, she was determined to see that the traditions of her homeland be respected. Let some memory of their roots survive, at least, in that higgledy-piggledy city that she would never become entirely used to.

Getting everything taken care of would be no simple matter; the Christmas traditions followed in the Cilento region were fairly strict. On Christmas Eve, the menu was rigorously meatless: *scàmmaro*, homemade spaghetti served with anchovies, olives, capers, and red chili peppers; cauliflower, potatoes, and broccoli as side dishes; and *baccalà alla salernitana*, stockfish breaded, fried, and baked under a cascade of white onions, cherry tomatoes that had been hanging on the balcony for months just waiting for the day, and green olives.

Christmas dinner was quite another matter: for that meal they made fusilli, rolling them out one by one around a square umbrella rod, and then dressed them with a dense meat sauce and covered them with grated aged goat cheese; next, veal flank in broth; and then *scauratielli*, funnel cakes fried in boiling oil, in the shape of little intertwined snakes, which would then be drizzled with honey and eaten on the spot.

It was hard but gratifying work. If things went as well as she hoped with the Colombo girl, she'd be able to teach her every last detail, so that the memory of those things wouldn't be lost in that family.

Food wasn't the only thing, though. Christmas was significant for other reasons. The young baroness, Luigi Alfredo's mother, who'd been dead for many years now, had brought with her from the city a nativity scene; it had once belonged to her family, and included a small set of very old statuettes: the

Holy Family, the Three Kings, a few sheep, and a couple of shepherds. Rosa remembered the baroness clearly, the way she would arrange the figurines with her slender, childlike hands on a table a few days before Christmas and then remove them after Epiphany, carefully putting them away in a flowered box. It was an important tradition to her, especially when the young master was small; she used to say that for children certain images represent the holiday, and they carry those images in their hearts for the rest of their lives.

The box covered with painted flowers had come to the city with them, and Rosa made sure that every year when Christmas came it found the Baroness Marta di Malomonte's little manger scene waiting for it, on the side table, like a mother's caress for her son from the afterlife.

Who would see to these things—the Christmas dinner, the manger scene—when she was no longer around? She looked sadly at her right hand, which was trembling slightly. She felt a need to tell her stories, describe, inculcate events, anecdotes, and traditions; otherwise, once she was dead and forgotten, her young master would find himself celebrating Christmas Eve in some barren trattoria, all alone. With nothing left to remember.

She wondered whether the Colombo girl had finally decided to take action and decide her own fate; she certainly hoped so, after the conversation they'd had the previous day. There really wasn't anything more she could do.

She went to get the flowered box. As long as she was around, the traditions were going to be upheld.

All of them.

XLIII

Maione headed straight for the *borgo*'s little wharf, where the fishermen tied their boats up. It was a narrow wooden pier, anchored to the seabed by heavy rocks.

He settled in for a wait, hiding in the shadow of the warehouse of a neighboring yacht club. He wanted to get a look at Boccia's fellow fishermen, so he could then approach them one by one and compare their stories. Not that he had high hopes: he knew the kind of solidarity he could expect to encounter among fishermen who were trying to protect their friend.

The fishing boats came in, one by one, furling their sails. The brigadier could tell immediately that the day's catch had been a good one: the men sounded cheerful and the big baskets they were unloading were filled to overflowing with fish, many of them clearly still alive, a cascade of silver that glistened in the long low shafts of light from the setting sun.

Boccia's boat was one of the last to dock; clearly he had taken advantage of the good fishing to the last possible minute. The crew unloaded and unrigged the boat, lowering the sail and shipping the oars, then folding away the nets.

Maione waited, noting as he looked on that two of the men were clearly a father and his teenaged son, while the third man aside from Boccia was wiry and dark-complected, so much so that Maione wondered if he was African. Waiting on the pier was Alfonso, Boccia's son, who had come to get his father as he had the previous evening. The man said goodnight to his fellow fishermen and glumly followed the boy; Maione thought that he might be worried about his younger son, but he might just as easily be troubled by the ghosts of his conscience.

The other three parted ways soon afterward: the father and son walked together toward the door of a small building nearby, while the skinny dark-skinned man strolled off smoking a cigarette toward a tavern not far off. Maione decided to go for the two men.

He knocked vigorously at the front door, and the boy came to answer. No fear, no uneasiness: just curiosity, then a flash of realization; Boccia must have told them about his visit from the police.

Maione was invited in; he was offered a glass of wine, which he courteously refused. With the two men was a very old woman, perhaps the younger man's grandmother. Maione explained the reason for his visit, but got the impression that there had been no need.

"Yes, Brigadie', you can be sure of it: Aristide was out with us," the man told him. "Otherwise we couldn't have gone out at all."

"Why not?" Maione asked.

The man smoked, holding the cigarette with the tip inside his cupped hand, accustomed as he was to smoking in the wind.

"We use a trawl net. Do you know what that means?"

Maione shrugged his shoulders.

"I'll explain it for you. Now then, a trawl net has two ends: one is lowered into the sea, secured to an anchor so that the net remains in place; the other end stays in the boat, which sails around in a circle, pulling the net along with it. You need two men on each side, and another to keep an eye on the scraps of colored cloth tied to the cables, to make sure everything is going smoothly, otherwise the net will get all tangled up. We make do without this fifth man, because there's not enough to divide it five ways, so one of us, usually Aristide, keeps an eye on the cables while he's holding up his end of the net."

"Which tells me what?" Maione asked.

The men threw their arms open wide.

"Which tells you that if it's already hard for four men to do it, it would be impossible for three."

"But couldn't you have found someone to take his place? I'm not saying you did—let me be clear—but I'm asking."

The young man laughed and said:

"You think so? Who would want to come out with us, to work as hard as we do? Besides, all the others have their own boats to look after."

The brigadier had no more luck with the other man, who was busy getting drunk in the one tavern in the *borgo*. The fourth member of the crew, the skinny individual with very dark skin, in fact answered only in monosyllables, confirming that Boccia had been present in the fishing boat on Friday, "as on every other blessed day that the Almighty gives us here on earth."

But as Maione was leaving, he said:

"Brigadie', Aristide is a truly good man, and that Garofalo was a bastard of the very worst sort. If he'd done the same thing to me, I'd have chewed the heart out of his chest with my teeth."

The harshness of that phrase, spoken by that mouth set in a face so browned and weatherbeaten that Maione could hardly distinguish it from the surrounding darkness, made the policeman shiver.

"There is such a thing as justice, you know," Maione replied. "It's not something a man can create with his own two hands."

The man nodded and said:

"Sure, there's such a thing as justice. But when it's about someone taking your son away from you, you take justice into your own hands. Take it from me."

He was talking about Boccia and his little boy, but Maione felt his stomach lurch at the words.

The thought of Vincenzino, and the horrible shrill whistle coming from the cradle, made him feel the need to stop by the fisherman's house before he left the *borgo*.

Outside the door that opened onto the piazzetta was Alfonso, the older son, playing with a brown-spotted dog with a familiar appearance. Inside, in his shirtsleeves and leaning over the little bed, was Dr. Modo.

"Oh, my dear Brigadier. Now it's come to our making house calls on police orders, can you believe it? Your friend the commissario issues directives and all I can do is take off at a run."

"Okay, okay, Dotto', but at least this time we didn't call you to look at a dead body, no?"

Modo ran a hand over his forehead, sweeping back the white hair that hung down in front of his eyes.

"No, but we're dangerously close, I'd say. This child is in critical condition; it looks to me like I got here just in the nick of time. He had a raging fever, it's a good thing he has a robust constitution."

Off to one side stood the child's parents, clinging to each other and clearly terrified. The mother's face was pale and showed the signs of sleepless nights, and the father had not yet changed out of his work clothes. Maione did his best to bolster their morale.

"You have nothing to worry about. Doctor Modo, here, like the commissario told you, is the only physician in the city of Naples capable of working miracles."

Modo pretended to throw a little fit of annoyance.

"If you want miracles, ask your God; after all in a few days it's going to be His birthday. I'm a scientist, and as a scientist I say that it's a crime to let a child slip into this state, when all that you needed to do was to give him a simple treatment when he first got sick, and he would have been fine."

Boccia spoke in a somber tone:

"You're right about that, Dotto'. But medicine is expensive, and if you have to make a choice between feeding your children and medicating them, then you just have to pray that the child gets better on his own."

Modo felt a surge of irritation.

"Well, you're wrong to think that way! At least take him to the hospital, no? Find out how serious it is, get some information!"

Maione smiled at the Boccias.

"Don't worry, this doctor's always spouting off like that, he shouts and loses his temper, but then he fixes everything. Rest assured."

The physician glared at him, then he turned his attention back to the little boy. After a few minutes he stood up, pulling his suspenders back up onto his shoulders and tightening his loosened tie.

"His fever has broken. We'll have to wait for the medicine I gave him to take effect. In six hours or so, you'll need to give him these pills, and in eight hours, these others. If he coughs or you hear that whistling sound again, Signo', give him a spoonful of this syrup right here. Are you clear on that?"

Boccia took a step forward and looked at Modo with pride in his eyes.

"Dotto', I can't pay you for these medicines. And I can't pay for your house call, either."

Modo looked at Maione and then replied:

"Who ever said anything about you having to pay me, or having to pay for the medicine? Haven't you heard that I'm a physician in the personal service of Commissario Ricciardi and Brigadier Maione, here? Don't worry, you don't owe me a cent. I'll come back tomorrow night to see how he's doing."

Maione watched the parents' eyes as they looked over at

Vincenzino, finally sleeping quietly. Outside the window, the sea slapped slowly against the tillers of the moored boats.

The woman's expression relaxed; it was the first time that the brigadier had seen her with an unlined face.

"Dotto', then at least allow us to bring you a little fish. Tomorrow is the day before Christmas Eve."

Modo looked at her contentedly.

"Ah, now you've found the way to my heart. *Grazie*, Signora, I'll accept gladly."

He whistled softly, and out of the shadows came a silhouette with a wagging tail, which followed him into the cone of light from a streetlamp.

And he walked off, raising the collar of his coat and pulling his hat down tight on his head.

XLIV

Ricciardi felt chilled to the bone and his head was spinning with confusion.

He had made the rounds of the few import-export companies working in the port area, but he'd come up with nothing: the managers he'd spoken to had had a vague recollection that Lomunno had come by in search of work sometime in the past few days, but none of them could have said exactly what day, let alone what time. Some of them had even refused to see Lomunno entirely: there were no jobs, or else they were afraid of turning the militia against them for having hired someone whom they'd given a dishonorable dismissal. Still, all of them had confirmed that, in the contact they'd had with Lomunno before he was fired, they'd always had a very positive impression of him, and they'd been surprised at the accusations and the arrest. One man, the chief administrative officer of a shipping company, told him that he'd actually had the impression that not all the members of the militia were convinced of Lomunno's guilt, and that there was a general dislike of the late Garofalo, whose façade of irreprehensibility also failed to convince his colleagues.

That last conversation drove Ricciardi, on a sudden impulse, to take another stroll over to the Mussolini barracks, perhaps in part just to warm up a little.

The militiaman at the door was the same as the last time, and in fact he showed that he recognized Ricciardi by saluting him with his usual overly enthusiastic heel-click. He asked for the consul in person this time and, after a brief exchange over the intercom, the soldier who stood at the desk outside the commandant's office door showed up and led Ricciardi in to see his boss.

He was given a reasonably cordial welcome; the consul came to meet him, striding across his immense office.

"Commissario, nice to see you. This time I wasn't given advance notice of your arrival. I wonder why?"

Ricciardi smirked in dour amusement.

"*Buonasera*, Consul. They would have had to read my mind; I just decided a couple of minutes ago to come by and say hello."

Freda laughed heartily.

"Ah, of course: the one sure way of forestalling informers. What can I do for you? How is your investigation proceeding?"

"Not all that well. We've run down, and are still running down, a couple of leads. Unfortunately, or perhaps fortunately, having an excellent motive to murder someone doesn't always mean that a person will act on it."

The consul dropped into his desk chair.

"I see. And I'm aware of some of the challenges. Certain situations can be very difficult to decipher."

Ricciardi leaned slightly forward.

"Signor Consul, there's something I need to ask you. And I need to ask you in a nonofficial capacity, in much the same way that I'm not officially here with you this evening. Why did you point us in Lomunno's direction? When we came by the other day, you made sure that we knew about the background of what had happened, why Lomunno had been expelled from the militia and Garofalo was promoted. Why?"

Freda turned to look out the window, despite the fact that it was already dark outside. He seemed to think his answer over for a long time.

"When we learned about Garofalo's tragic demise, everyone here thought of Lomunno first thing. He certainly had a strong motive, you have to admit, to . . . to do this thing. And those of us who had, unofficially, met with him after he got out of jail, reported that he was a man coarsened by rage and grief, over his dead wife, his lost career, and the conditions in which he is now forced to live with his children. Make no mistake, Commissario: no one here has even the slightest bit of evidence against him; but the idea that Lomunno did it could certainly stand up. But the thing is that when you work with people in here, side by side, you get to know them. And all of us liked Lomunno, but we felt the opposite about Garofalo."

Ricciardi waited.

"And so?

"And so," the consul went on, "we preferred to have you learn about the situation from us, rather than from some impersonal judicial report or stray piece of gossip. That's all."

Ricciardi did some quick thinking: It was crucial for him to find out whether the consul, and therefore the militia at large, suspected that Garofalo had other dirty business dealings, that he was shaking down the fishermen. Steering the investigation toward Lomunno might well have been a way of covering up something that was a further source of shame for the corps.

"From our investigations so far, we haven't uncovered any other motive that might have led someone to kill Signore and Signora Garofalo. As things now stand, therefore, Lomunno is the sole suspect."

What looked to Ricciardi like genuine disappointment appeared on Freda's face.

"In that case, please, Commissario: keep looking. Here we're all pretty certain that poor Lomunno has more than paid for his mistake, which was really just the mistake of trusting a disloyal subordinate. We don't believe that he did it. I'm not asking you this as the commandant of the legion, nor as a long-time naval officer. I ask you as a man and as a father: make sure that Lomunno is brought up on charges only if you're absolutely sure that it couldn't have been anyone other than him."

Ricciardi looked Freda straight in the face for a long time and became convinced that this was all he knew about Garofalo's life. And he also realized that if he accused the Boccias, he'd make a lot of people happy, there in those barracks.

"All right, Consul. You have my promise. We'll go on looking. But for now, we have nothing in hand. If by any chance you were to think of something, or if some new information were to emerge, please, don't hesitate to let me know."

For the tenth time now, she went into the drawing room to look at the old pendulum clock which was loudly marking the passage of time. Lucia Maione was uneasy, and every single second only added to her anxiety. He's on an investigation, all right. The first few days are the most important ones, granted. If you have a lead you have to stay on it, sure enough. The world is a safer place without murderers, even for our own children, of course. But the absences, the gazes into the empty air, the unanswered questions, those are signals: and I'm no fool, I don't ignore clear signals.

And so she summoned her eldest daughter, little more than a child, heaven knows, but sufficiently adult to take care of her little brothers for an hour or so, and she gave her some basic instructions; after which she grabbed her overcoat, her hat, and her gloves and hurried downstairs, furtive and determined.

Never assume that your day is done until you close the front door of your home behind you: that was a cardinal principle of an old boss of his. Ricciardi was thinking back on his scratchy, hoarse voice, the result of a lifetime of cigarettes, when, swinging back by police headquarters just to see if there was any news, he found himself face to face with a smiling Livia, looking radiant in a brand-new outfit.

"Well, here you are, at last. I thought I was going to have to hire one of your colleagues, here, to get them to go track you down. If we don't hurry up we're going to be late, you do realize, don't you?"

Ricciardi was stunned, even as he kicked himself mentally for his excessive zeal: if he'd just gone home directly from the port, he wouldn't find himself in this awkward situation now.

"Late for what? Forgive me, Livia, but I'm very tired; it's been a grueling day."

The woman's smile didn't drop a millimeter; she was determined to enjoy the evening she had planned.

"Listen, Ricciardi, I don't want to hear excuses. God only knows what it cost me, in terms of time and money, to get these two tickets to the Kursaal; I had to claim connections I don't even have to get them, and I intend to go. And this time you're coming with me."

"Really, Livia, I don't think it's a good idea. Look at me, I've been pounding the pavement all day long, I'm grimy and a mess. I'd only embarrass you."

The woman's eyes filled with tears of frustration. Her lower lip began to tremble, and she turned and looked away.

"You know, I don't think I deserve these continuous slaps in the face from you. I'm not asking you for anything, really: just to go to the theater with me. That's not asking so much, is it?"

Ricciardi lacked the necessary experience to stand firm against one of the most powerful forces of nature: that is, a woman's tears. Moreover, he knew how to read, and between the lines of Livia's words was clearly, if invisibly written: *When you needed me, I was there.* Last of all, an involuntary thought went out to the stubbornly closed shutters of the window across the way.

He heaved a sigh and said:

"Fine, I'll go with you. But after the theater I have to go straight home; I've got another horrible day awaiting me tomorrow."

XLV

He knew that he should return home, where his wife and children were waiting for him. He was hungry and the chill, which was increasing from one minute to the next, was penetrating his bones.

Nonetheless, Brigadier Maione found himself, at dinnertime, just as the shops were closing their shutters, on San Gregorio Armeno, drawn like a moth to the flame of a lantern on a summer night.

He had gone to police headquarters on his way back from the *borgo*, to check in and see if there was any news; the commissario hadn't yet returned, but in the courtyard he saw Signora Vezzi's car awaiting him. He thought to himself that perhaps, just this once, the commissario might even be able to enjoy the company of a beautiful woman, seeing as he was young and single.

He'd glanced at the watch he kept in his jacket pocket: his shift was over. It was time to head home. He'd even started homeward, up the hill that runs from Via Toledo toward Concordia and the blue eyes of Lucia.

Lucia. The thought of her had summoned him, like an accusation he'd have to bear, to turn his thoughts once again to Biagio Candela, the man who had killed Luca. His feet then changed direction of their own accord: they'd headed toward Piazza del Gesù, and from there across Via Tribunali toward the street of the *figurari*.

What are you looking for? he asked himself. What do you hope to see? What do you hope to find out?

The thing he loved about his job was its simplicity: illegal acts took place, and it was up him to find the perpetrators and make sure they paid for their crimes. It was easy. But this time he felt as if he were caught in a maze, sentenced to go round and round, in circles, in search of an exit that might not even exist. He didn't know what he was doing.

He envied Franco Massa, who had no doubts: the boy had to pay, because he'd committed the most horrible crime imaginable.

But there's need for more than a policeman here, Maione mused. I'm being asked to be policeman, judge, and executioner. It's one thing to cuff a criminal, it's another thing to see him live, work, and love, and then wish him dead.

He'd reached the workshop where he'd seen Biagio do his carving before a small but admiring audience. Now there was no one on the street, even if the lights and decorations still adorned the walls—those wouldn't be removed until after Epiphany, according to tradition. He sought out the shadow of an entryway, and stood watching to see what was happening.

The shutters were half closed, but he could make out the proprietor, the man with whom he'd spoken earlier, sitting at the cash register and counting his money, visibly satisfied. Some ten feet away, the fair-haired young man was sweeping wood shavings off the floor. His heart lurched: from a distance, just for a moment, he'd taken the murderer for the victim; Biagio's hair was the same color as Luca's, which in turn had been the color of his wife Lucia's.

His well-trained eye noticed, even before they entered the light of the streetlamp hanging over the center of the street, three young men striding briskly toward the shop. At first they had been walking at a leisurely gait, like layabouts who were out late; then they'd begun to move at a more determined pace. The eyes of the one leading the trio were focused on the cash in the hands of the workshop's proprietor.

Maione realized what was about to happen, just as he saw

the blond young man's wife appear, holding a little girl by the hand and their baby in her arms.

He looked up and down the street: there was no one coming. Instinct pushed him to intervene, but he knew that if he did, in those very particular circumstances, he'd have given away the fact that he was there on a stakeout, and he'd be forced to explain. He hesitated for a long minute.

The young toughs had reached the front door of the shop. Two of them positioned themselves on either side of the shutters, while the third started to step inside.

The events that followed unfolded extremely rapidly: the robber pulled out a knife and headed for the cash register; Biagio leapt in front of him and blocked his way, waving the blade he'd been using that morning to carve the old woman's head; the robber lunged at Biagio with his knife, but he dodged the blade; Biagio's wife, who'd realized what was happening, screamed loudly, so that faces began to appear at the windows; the two men at the door exchanged a glance and vanished into the shadows.

Maione realized that even though Biagio was brandishing his knife much more skillfully than his adversary, he was only dodging the blows, making no effort to wound the man in turn. Maione decided that he'd seen enough and, from the shadows where he was lurking, he pulled out the police whistle that he used to alert others to his presence, took a breath, and blew hard. At that shrill sound, the robber jumped back and fled, running off up the *vicolo*.

The proprietor was shaking like a leaf, looking around in bewilderment and wondering where the policemen who had blown their whistles could be. The young woman, in tears, had thrown herself into her husband's arms; he was deathly pale in the light of the decorative lightbulbs. He hurled the knife away from him, as if it were burning hot, and the blade rolled along the floor and out the shop door.

The whole thing had lasted no longer than two minutes.

All of a sudden, Maione felt an overwhelming yearning for home. He emerged from the shadows and headed back, his heart heavier than ever.

Ricciardi was surprised to see so many people, as cold as it was, lining the sidewalks in front of the Kursaal theater and movie house, on the elegant Via Filangieri. You could feel the excitement in the air: everyone was very well-dressed, smoking and stamping their feet in the cold, exchanging comments on the weather.

In the car, Livia had explained to him that the two brothers and sister were an up-and-coming troupe, who were beginning to make a name for themselves even outside the city. They were three very different individuals, she had told him, but they were perfectly compatible onstage: the sister was homely but magnificent, capable of making her audience laugh or cry as she chose; the younger brother, who had an instinctive, scathing comic gift, was just at the start of his career but could send the audience into overpowering gales of laughter; the elder brother, head of the troupe and the author of that night's play, was a theatrical genius, though it was said that he had a thorny personality.

Ricciardi had asked Livia why on earth they were premiering a show on such an unusual date, just two days before Christmas. Livia told him that that was exactly the point: the play, a one-act, was in fact a portrayal of a Christmas in a bourgeois Neapolitan family.

Livia was excited, but it had nothing to do with the play they were about to see: she'd managed to drag that man to the theater despite his aversion to all forms of social activity, and his acquiescence, even though she'd practically had to beg him to bring it about, touched her. He was here, with her, by her side. That was enough, as far as she was concerned: at least for tonight.

They took their seats, as usual observed with curiosity by many. Livia's exotic beauty and her circle of prominent friends had made her a focus of gossip among the city's high society; people wondered, in all the drawing rooms in Naples, why on earth a woman like her didn't have a husband or at least a couple of lovers, seeing as there were so many candidates offering their services, paying court on her with suffocating insistence. And the more she graciously declined her suitors, the greater the number of men sending her bouquets and boxes of bonbons, and the greater the number of women claiming to have seen her here and there around the city in questionable company.

For these reasons, to see her in male company constituted a show within the show; and to see her with that peculiar individual, too, whom no one in high society had ever seen before, and whose very name was unknown. Dressed in a nondescript manner, absurdly without a hat, with a dazed air about him and a diffident stance, the man triggered everyone's curiosity; it was assumed that he must be from out of town, possibly from Rome, and thus deeply involved in the Fascist regime. With those strange green eyes glowing in that angular face, he even struck a vague fear into people, as if he could see things that others could not.

The play was good fun and even Ricciardi, tired and distracted as he was by a thousand different thoughts, smiled at certain points and, at others, felt a pang of tenderness. Certain elements, moreover, called him back to the investigation he'd been working on, such as the constant references to the nativity scene: just one more indication of how important the artisanal portrayal of the birth of Jesus was for the people of that city.

He thought about what Don Pierino had told him, amid the heavy odor of incense in the church of San Ferdinando: Every figure, every construction is a symbol. Nothing is accidental, everything has a meaning. And he thought that the same thing might be true about this city, which he imagined as seen from on high, atop the Piazzale di San Martino, with thousands of tiny illuminated windows, all of them seemingly identical, but each with a story, a family, and a drama all its own.

After all, he reflected, this city is nothing more than a manger scene that they keep up all year long. An immense living manger scene, teeming with love affairs, hunger, hatred, and resentments, a city that shields itself from the cold and the heat as best it can as it ponders what it can do to better its terrible condition. A manger scene where the shepherds are ruthless and capable of anything.

A manger scene of which a certain part, a significant part, was visible to him and him alone: the part made up of the cries of those who had been torn unwillingly from their lives, lives that, however hopeless they might have been, were the only good things those people had.

The play ended to a standing ovation. Ricciardi caught the two brothers glaring at each other as they stepped forward to the footlights for one more bow, but perhaps that had just been an impression of his. It saddened him to think that he had become, as a result of his occupation, someone who spotted negative emotions, such as jealousy, even when they weren't present.

Livia, radiant as she clung to his arm, tried to talk him into going out to dinner with her, following the stream of theatergoers who had no intention of ending the evening there, but he managed to resist; besides, the woman could see the signs of weariness etched into his face, and she decided not to overplay her hand. For tonight, that was quite enough.

When they were outside Ricciardi's apartment house, on Via Santa Teresa, he told her goodnight and turned to get out of the car. She put her hand on his arm and said:

"*Grazie. Grazie*, Ricciardi. You gave me a wonderful gift, tonight; I won't forget it."

Before he could reply, she pressed her lips against his in a quick kiss.

Instinctively the commissario, the minute he was out on the street, turned to look up at Enrica's window, and for the first time he was glad to see that the shutters were fastened tight.

The old Enrica would have waited, just as the new one was doing, behind the fastened shutters for the man she loved to return home, worried at the darkened windows across the way and the lateness of the hour.

She would have glided silently, just like the new Enrica was doing, between her bedroom and the kitchen that overlooked the street, to keep from awakening her parents; and she would have held a glass of water in one hand, so as to have a convenient explanation to give any other family members she might encounter up and about so late at night.

The old Enrica, who had existed until that morning, would have watched with her heart in her mouth as the glistening automobile pulled up at that late hour, and as it stopped outside the front entrance of 107 Via Santa Teresa. Just as the new Enrica did.

Much like the new Enrica, the old one would have narrowed her eyes behind the spectacles hurriedly grabbed from her bedside table, to see what was going on in the car idling below, its engine purring in the dark, like a tiger in the jungle in an adventure novel by Emilio Salgari; and she'd have seen, in the backseat, illuminated by the streetlamp, the smaller silhouette move closer to the taller one, the better to speak to him. And then she'd have seen the smaller one dart her head forward suddenly, like a venomous snake, drawing close to the taller one in what would unequivocally look to both Enricas very much like a kiss.

And the old Enrica, much like the new one for that matter, would have seen the man she was head over heels in love with get out of the car and, as it pulled away and finally vanished from sight, she would see him turn and look up, straight at her, where she stood, invisible in the dark, behind the locked shutters. And then she would have watched as he sighed and opened the front door, his head hanging low, to go inside and upstairs, to bed.

The old Enrica would have felt a wave of despair wash over her, and perhaps she'd have locked herself in her room to cry her eyes out in silence. But the old Enrica was gone forever.

The new Enrica narrowed her eyes to slits, clenched her jaw, and smiled, catlike. Then she murmured: All right, then. All right.

And she went to bed.

XLVI

The morning of December the twenty-third told the world that there would be no more kidding around: Christmas had arrived.

The sky was the color of lead from the heavy cloud cover hovering in wait, which had pushed down from the north overnight, determined to play some role in the festivities, though for now that role was known only to it.

The air was almost hanging in place, chilly and inhospitable as it ought to be to make it clear to one and all that the proper place for human beings was indoors, bundled up and warm, with the sounds of songs and of laughter, in the warmth of the heating stoves and the fireplaces, and in the light of the thousand lamps and lightbulbs that decorated the banquet halls, opened specially for the occasion.

The streets were crowded with the same pedestrians, but they seemed to be seized by a different anxiety. Time was up: the gifts had to have been purchased by now, or at least selected, the menus decided, the ingredients by now had to be in the pantries, and the decorations all in place. Those who had not yet finished their shopping wandered around grim-faced, in the grip of a vague sense of guilt, resigned to spend more money and get less for it than the farsighted ones who had taken care of things well ahead of time.

And yet the merchandise was still there, luring in shoppers for one last, desperate, seductive struggle.

The shops were competing to outdo each other with displays rich in imagination, offering walls of salamis dangling over mountains of dried figs and dates, adorned with silver and gold tinsel; spilling over onto the sidewalks with sacks of almonds and walnuts and chestnuts, beneath arches of braided fronds and leafy branches.

The butchers, too, were playing their last cards, laying out all their remaining merchandise, so that the backdrop in their shop windows consisted of sides of beef and pork, carefully trimmed and misted with water from time to time to give the impression of freshness and quality, in front of which would be a vanguard of capons, turkeys, hens, and rabbits, with plumes and fur, or else skinned, to terrify little children with their glassy eyes.

The shop windows of the confectioners and pastry shops were especially spectacular, and at the center, enjoying pride of place, was a Christ Child made of spun sugar. Surrounding him was an overabundance of cookies and cakes, small hillsides of *struffoli*, balls of fried dough dripping with honey and colorful candy pellets, *cassata*, along with the traditional pastries and confectioneries that no Christmas in Naples could do without, from the brightly colored almond pastries arranged on specially cut biscuits to the hard almond-dough *taralli* also known as *roccocò*; from the rhomboid-shaped Neapolitan Christmas cookies known as *mustacciuoli* covered with a chocolate glaze to the spicy, aromatic *quaresimali*, or Lenten almond biscuits; from the crescent-shaped, pine-nut-encrusted *pignolate* to the *susamielli*, the delicate S-shaped cinnamon-flavored holiday cookies. And then there were the *raffioli*, or mini-cassatas, and the *sapienze*, covered with whole almonds, and little pastries filled with chestnut and clove cream, all of them desperately seeking one last banqueting table that would be willing to take them in, like their fellow pastries that had been sold by the hundreds of pounds over the last few days.

December twenty-third is the last chance.

The *verdummari*, the fruit and vegetable vendors, know it, sitting with their weary, worried gaze in the center of their elaborate installations. They've stood guard for the past week, taking shifts with their wives and children at night, to make sure that the street urchins, the *scugnizzi*, didn't pilfer any of the merchandise they kept out on display. They've built make-believe Grottoes of the Nativity, weaving together lemon and orange branches from which the fruit still dangles, cunningly mixing the green of the broccoli, the orange of the tangerines, and the yellow of the large Sorrento lemons, flanked by clusters of melons and tomatoes, and crowning the pyramids of pears, prickly pears, and apples.

The chill is welcome, because it wards off the scourge of insects, but what hasn't been sold by the twenty-third runs a serious risk of lying there and rotting; that's why the sales are being called out to the passersby in such pleading tones, in sharp contrast to the triumphant calling of their wares on the past few mornings, when the vendors' voices resounded cheerful and bright, summoning the housewives to make their purchases.

Now they're begging, supplicating: Come buy, come buy. Take pity.

Because December twenty-third is the last chance.

Maione and Ricciardi met in the commissario's office, over cups of the brigadier's ersatz coffee, well aware that they had come to a decisive crossroads in their investigation into the deaths of the Garofalos. The information that they had gathered, each on his own, one in the *borgo*, the other in the port, had neither added to nor taken away from the precarious condition of the suspects, just as they'd anticipated.

Maione was the first to speak.

"So all things considered, Commissa', we're back where we started from, just like we were yesterday, and the day before. Lomunno and the Boccias—that is, unless it was some other fisherman who hasn't come to our attention yet, because let's not forget that the only reason we found the Boccias at all is because they went to the Garofalos' apartment a few days before the murder. If the real murderers staked out the building and waited for the doorman to step across the street to the tavern, then they'd have been able to get in without being seen by anyone. How would we ever know?"

Ricciardi was in agreement.

"Quite true. If we were the kind of cops who are determined to throw someone in jail no matter what, just to move a case along, then we could just as easily arrest Lomunno as the Boccias. Lomunno might well have done it in a moment of despair, and the Boccias would have no way to defend themselves because the testimony of the boat crew is not all that credible. But you and I both know that the fact that a person might have committed a murder, and might even have had some excellent motives for doing so, doesn't mean that they really did it; and we're not the kind of cops who toss potentially innocent people in jail, are we? Otherwise, we'd have chosen to be judges, not policemen."

Otherwise, we'd have chosen to be judges, Maione thought to himself.

"Well then, Commissa', what do we do now? We need something to lure them out, to make them give themselves away. Something unexpected."

Ricciardi stood there thinking, in his characteristic pose, his hands joined in front of his mouth, his eyes lost on the surface of his desk.

"Something unexpected. You know, Raffaele, last night I went to the theater: Livia practically dragged me there. I saw this one-act play about Christmas, the one with the two brothers and the sister."

"Of course, Commissa', I know the one you mean, I hear they're really talented, the whole city's talking about them."

"Well, it's true, they're talented, though I don't know much about theater, as you know. Anyway, at a certain point, they're all together, and that's when the issues boil to the surface. Maybe that's what we need, to bring them together, face-to-face."

"We should be able to find them all in one place. Today is December twenty-third, the last day of the fish market on Via Santa Brigida."

"Last day? How so?"

Maione smiled.

"I always forget that you aren't really from Naples and so there are a few city traditions you might not understand. In practical terms, during the Christmas season, for the convenience of the customers and the vendors, fish is sold all on a single street, to be specific, Via Santa Brigida, right near here. They all set up there, with their big wooden basins painted light blue to give the impression of seawater, and people go there to get fish for the Christmas Eve dinner and Christmas lunch. It's a kind of warfare: the vendors want to sell fast and at high prices, while the customers want to wait until the last minute to buy at lower prices, though at the risk of there being nothing left."

Ricciardi listened.

"Well? Why do you think that they'd come face-to-face?"

"Because everyone who works in the fishing business, including the part-time seasonal workers, will be there. Boccia and his crew will be there, no doubt, to earn extra money by selling their fish directly, and possibly even Lomunno, working for some merchant who needs extra hands."

Ricciardi nodded.

"In fact, yesterday down at the port I heard one guy say to another that they'd see each other today at the market. So what he meant was this sale on Via Santa Brigida."

Maione agreed:

"He couldn't be referring to anything else. Let's stroll down there, Commissa', maybe in the early afternoon, when we'll find the most people there; right now we'd run the risk of the fishermen taking advantage of the opportunity to get out on the water one last time. There might even be a squad from the port militia, keeping an eye on the sales."

Ricciardi briefly scratched his wound, which had finally closed up.

"To tell you the truth, I'm still stuck on the symbolism of Saint Joseph. What on earth could they have meant, by breaking that figurine?"

Maione shook his head.

"We won't know that, Commissa', until someone confesses."

Ricciardi made a disconsolate face.

"*If* anyone ever confesses."

XLVII

I'm a policeman, Maione thought to himself. A policeman.

That night, in the agitation of incoherent dreams, he remembered his own hands. He remembered that he found himself in a deserted *vicolo*, a place he didn't know; and he traveled the whole length of that twisting alley, uphill and down, only to find himself back at the exact point he'd started from.

And so he started walking again, and as he walked he felt a mortal sense of weariness, and especially a numbness in his hands.

He looked at his hands over and over again in his dream: he couldn't recognize them. They seemed like extraneous body parts, two animals endowed with a life of their own, completely separate from his arms and his will. Anxiety seized him, and he started walking again, in fact running, and Franco Massa was chasing him, calling him *Orso*, Bear, the way he had when they were children, and saying to him: You have to kill him, you have to kill him. It has to be you. It has to happen by your hand. By your hand.

And in the dream, his heart was breaking; he kept seeing the two children and the pretty dark-haired wife, as well as Biagio, but never his face, only his blond hair.

By my hand, he kept saying. By my hand.

But I'm a policeman, he told Massa in his dream. A policeman, not a judge, not a hangman. How can I do it?

And at the far end of the alley, which ended in a downhill slope, he saw the two children, laughing as they came toward him, calling him grandpa. And he ran up to Biagio from behind, and Biagio didn't turn around, and his hands, independent of his will, reached up and began throttling Biagio by the neck. By my hand, the voice in his head kept saying. And Biagio turned around in his death throes, and Maione realized that it was his son Luca, dying a second time, but this time by his hand.

He'd woken up with a jerk, drenched in sweat. Luckily, Lucia was sleeping soundly by his side.

Taking advantage of the fact that he was meeting the commissario in the early afternoon to take a look at the fish market, instead of going home he decided to go once more to San Gregorio Armeno. The shop where the young man worked was closed to the public, but the wooden door stood ajar.

He stuck his head inside and saw that there was no one there but the proprietor.

"Brigadie', *prego*, please come in. It's a pleasure to see you again."

Maione took a thorough look around.

"Excuse me, I wanted to buy a couple of sheep, but I see you're closed. Why is that? Is something the matter?"

The man heaved a theatrical sigh.

"You can't imagine, we came this close to a genuine tragedy!"

"Why, what happened?"

At this point, the proprietor came around the cash register and took up a stance in the middle of the empty shop.

"Last night, as we were closing up, I was here counting the money from the day's sales, and it was a lot of money, too, because as you know this is a particular time of year, when we have to bring in enough to keep us going all year long. Well, I was standing here, you see, when four masked individuals burst in, with knives in their hands!"

Maione feigned horror at the news, smiling inside at the sudden proliferation of bandits, now wearing handkerchiefs as masks, like in a movie with cowboys and Indians.

"Really, you don't say? And they robbed you?"

The man put on a dramatic air.

"It would have been a tragedy, the receipts of two whole days. I thought it was all over for me. But then Biagio jumped in, you remember him?"

Maione denied all knowledge, with a baffled look.

"No, who's that?"

"What, the young man you said was such a good carver, don't you recall?"

The brigadier pretended he had only just remembered.

"Ah, right, the fair-haired boy."

The man nodded his head.

"That's right, him. He ran over, right where I'm standing now, between the bandits and the cash register, with the knife he uses in the mornings to carve, and he fought a duel with those criminals, just like on the stage in a melodrama, you know what I mean, in the final scene? Exactly like that."

"So then what happened?"

"What happened is that the hoodlums, since things weren't looking as easy as they'd hoped, took off down the *vicolo*. Chance would have it that at that exact moment Biagio's wife and children arrived, and if the thieves had decided to run off in the opposite direction, they would have run right smack into them. A huge danger averted."

"So it was a close call."

"That's right. We were also helped by the fact that, right when those robbers were all in here, we heard a whistle like the ones the coppers . . . I mean to say, that *you* all use. But then there weren't any policemen around after all . . . Odd, don't you think?"

Maione put on an uncertain expression.

"You know, there are kids who can imitate a police whistle so well you'd swear it was real."

"Add to that the Fascist squads, which make the rounds in the neighborhood, too. They're worse than you, no offense, Brigadie'; they tend to beat you up first and ask questions later. But it's the same thing with them: they're never around when you need them."

Maione looked the man in the face with a slightly grim expression. He'd been there, all right, but he couldn't have shown himself.

"So then why are you closed today?"

The proprietor flashed a broad, magnanimous smile.

"I decided to give the young man half the day off, partly as a reward for what he did yesterday. He went off to the Villa Nazionale, to take his children out for a little fresh air and a few roasted almonds, I gave him a little cash. Then later today, after lunch, we'll reopen."

The Villa Nazionale, Maione thought. A happy little family, out strolling on the day before Christmas Eve.

He went over to the counter and picked up a terra-cotta Saint Joseph, very similar to the one they'd found shattered in the Garofalos' home. He hefted it, feeling its weight.

"Nice, eh, Brigadie'? Our products, if I do say so myself, are refined, not like the trash they produce around here, where you can't tell which part is the face and which is the body, they're painted so badly. Look at the features, the beard, the staff."

Maione furrowed his brow.

"In your opinion, what does Saint Joseph represent?"

He would have guessed work, carpentry, craftsmanship. Instead, the man replied:

"The father of children, that's what he represents, Brigadie'. All the love and all the pain that a father carries with him in life. Because everybody always says: the mother this, the mother that. But what about us? We sweat blood without complaining, all day long, from morning to night, and who do we do it for, if not for our children? But no one ever thinks about the fathers. So that's what Saint Joseph represents, a father who sits quietly off to one side, working away in the shadows and in silence for a whole lifetime, for the good of his children."

Maione listened, surprised. Then he said:

"We do everything for our children. They're what matters most, aren't they?"

"Yes, Brigadie'. Last night, when I found myself face-to-face with those knives, that's what I thought to myself: that all a man wants is to be left alone to work in peace, for the good of his children."

The policeman was suddenly overcome by an immense anguish. The good of the children, yes. But whose children?

"*Grazie*, be well. And take my advice: At night, close up shop when everyone else does. The thieves love an empty street."

XLVIII

One last trip out, onto that ice-cold sea that looks like a slab of black glass, pressed down under a sky as heavy as marble.

One last trip out, in defiance of the weather, to tear another breath of life from the salt water. In the hours in which the day battles against the night, when the lights quiver in the still air and hands numb from the cold can no longer grip ropes and oars.

One last trip out, a shorter one, and thus more desperate, with emphatic gestures rendered frantic by the weather and by necessity.

Your only choice is to run from one side of the boat to the other, to make sure there are no tangles or knots in the net, so that down beneath the black surface the meshes don't twist up and catch nothing but themselves, or else all the tugging and hauling on earth will yield nothing but a mass of cords and seaweed, after all that careful planning, all that exhausting work.

Just one trip, and in half the usual time, to see what we can carry away in our wicker baskets to the market, to display before the eyes of people whose only thought is what to cook for Christmas dinner.

One last trip out, with our aching bones, sure to confine us to a chair by the time we're fifty or a little older, paralyzed by pain, watching young men who will wind up the same way. Just one last trip, in this icy dawn the day before Christmas Eve, so different from all the others.

Dreaming of pulling up a net full of picarels and calamari, meagre and silver-bellied gilthead sea bream, lobsters and salt-water eels, so many that they fill the deck of the boat, and we can feel their tails slapping around at our feet, their lives for our lives and the lives of our children.

One last trip out, life against life, for a pocketful of change. And for another Christmas.

Ricciardi decided to swing by home, instead of remaining at police headquarters until the afternoon or going to Gambrinus for his usual quick sfogliatella.

It was a fairly rare occurrence. Normally he wasn't willing to give up the time that it took to walk to Via Santa Teresa and back, more than an hour all told, time that he didn't like to take away from his work duties, and the tedious bureaucracy that went along with them.

But this time he wanted to go home. The crowds filling the street in spite of the cold would have invaded the café, forcing him to stand and wait for a table for God knows how long, so that his lunch hour would be more work than break. But that wasn't the main reason.

The main reason was Rosa. In the past few days he'd noticed that the background noise of the woman's complaints about the lack of routine in his life, the unpleasant soundtrack of his evening hours, had faded to the point of vanishing entirely. His *tata* had something on her mind, and she seemed irritated, almost preoccupied.

At first, it had been nothing more than a feeling, but with time it had become a certainty. He wanted to ask her how she was, if she was having any trouble with her health; he wanted to ask her, even though he knew it would inevitably lead to a long tirade about him being alone, the importance of starting a family, that usual line of conversation: in other words, Rosa's favorite hobbyhorse.

He reflected, as he made his way through the mass of people that crowded Via Toledo, on the fact that he actually already had a family. And that family consisted of one person: that very same old woman, strange, energetic, and simple, fragile and incredibly strong at the same time, who had been with him since the day he was born. Always present, always vigilant in her rearguard position, more of a parent than his father who died when he was young, more than his mother who was always sick, more than anyone else had ever been. His family, which was much dearer to him than he'd be willing to admit, much more than he was capable of showing.

Along the street, the crowd of the living was punctuated here and there by the dead. A young man who'd fallen from a scaffold, his neck broken, who called out for his mother; a man who had been beaten to death, and who inveighed against a certain Michele through his shattered jaw; a woman run over by a car in the middle of the road, who recited like a prayer the list of items she was going to buy, while blood from her leg, shorn clean off, pumped out into the empty air.

Here I am, thought Ricciardi. Just another face in the crowd. Neither fat nor skinny, neither tall nor short; small active hands plunged deep into the pockets of an overcoat, a rebellious lock of hair dangling over the forehead. Just another face in the crowd.

The only real difference, he reflected bitterly, is the crowd itself. My crowd is made up of the living and the dead, indifference and sorrow, cries and silences. I'm the sole citizen of a city made up of people who are dead but think they're alive, or of people who breathe but think they're dead.

When he got home he opened the door and realized that someone, in the drawing room, was crying.

The Villa Nazionale was teeming with people, in spite of the cold.

It was full of people because the Villa Nazionale was yet another one of the battlefields of December twenty-third, where opposing armies of vendors and purchasers of all manner of merchandise squared off and clashed. Every square inch of open ground was occupied by stands and stalls, behind which the merchants huddled, fighting off the cold and the damp that came in off the water, bundling themselves in every item of clothing imaginable, all the way up to their eyes.

The playful experience intrinsic to the Villa Nazionale also influenced the selection of merchandise on display: balloons, wooden and tin toys, candies and sweets; but also conversation pieces, ceramic items, chinoiseries, and cooking utensils. The result was the usual particolored cacophony of wares-hawking and feverish haggling, under an increasingly dark sky that promised only bad weather in the offing.

It took Maione a little while to identify the people he was looking for, a family like so many others, a young couple with two small children. He adjusted his pace to match the gait of the Candela family, three hundred feet or so ahead of him, shielded by a curtain of strollers preparing for Christmas with one last walk among the trees, down by the sea.

They couldn't afford a perambulator; the little girl held her mother by the hand, and the little boy rode on his father's shoulders, with the man holding both the boy's tiny feet. Maione noticed that, unlike most of the children there, Biagio's weren't constantly pestering their parents for a piece of candy or a toy. They'd been brought up to resist temptation, or else they were simply happy to go for a walk in the park and didn't feel the need for anything more.

After a while the little family stopped in a clearing and sat on the lawn, not far from the bandshell where a chilled, haphazard little orchestra sat playing operatic arias without vocal accompaniment. Out of her bag the mother pulled a little bundle containing some pieces of bread, which she gave to her husband and daughter, then sat breaking something into small bits and feeding them to the toddler. Maione lurked behind a tree, about seventy-five feet away.

What am I doing here? he asked himself. What do I want from these people? Why do I keep watching them, memorizing their gestures and expressions? It's not as if by spying on their lives I'll be able to figure out what I want to do. Or what I ought to do. It'll just make things worse, when the time comes. Knowing how the man smiles at his son and daughter, having seen him roll around on the grass with his daughter the way he's doing now, or watching him carve with his left hand, with the tip of his tongue protruding between his teeth like a little boy, or seeing him risk his life to protect money that doesn't belong to him from a robber—none of that's going to help me. Not one bit.

All around him, the Villa Nazionale was teeming with excitement, expectations for the future, enthusiasm and optimism. The expressions on people's faces were cheerful; poverty and desperation seemed far away, when in fact they were right here, just below the surface of the holiday that was fast approaching and would be over all too quickly.

Maione was confused and frightened. For the first time in his life, right and wrong kept changing places before his eyes, losing their proper outlines and transforming into floating, elusive concepts, like the balloon that had just escaped the hands of its young owner and was now flying off into the gray sky.

He could feel a chill, and he realized that it was coming from within. He wished there were someone close to him who could help him. He passed his hand over his eyes, disconsolate.

"You could talk to me about it. There was a time when you used to, and you could do it again."

He turned around with his heart in his mouth. Just a few inches away from his own, he saw the blue eyes of his wife.

XLIX

Ricciardi rushed into the drawing room and found Rosa sitting in her armchair in tears, with something in her hand. As soon as she saw him, the woman tried to get to her feet, wiping her face with the hem of her apron, but she soon gave up that effort.

"What's happened?" asked Ricciardi anxiously. "Are you hurt? Did you fall?"

Rosa didn't even try to control herself. Between sobs, she choked out:

"Useless, I'm useless . . . a useless old woman . . . You should just commit me to an institution, one of those places where they keep old people like me . . . I can't stand it, being unable to take care of things myself . . ."

Ricciardi looked around the room, trying to guess the reason for all this drama. In all the time he'd known her, which is to say as long as he'd been alive, he'd only seen Rosa in tears once: when his mother had died. He'd accompanied her to the funerals of several of her brothers and sisters, and they'd experienced sad moments together, like when they'd left once and for all the home in Fortino where he'd grown up, but he'd never seen her cry again.

But now here she was, dissolving in unstoppable sobs in her armchair in the drawing room.

"Rosa, please, stop crying. I don't know what to do. You're starting to worry me! What are you saying, you're not useless, I need you. Please, stop talking nonsense."

As he said it, he realized that every word was true, and that what he'd been thinking the whole way home had been this, and nothing else: the elderly *tata* was all the family he had, and without her he'd have been infinitely more lonely than he felt now.

"No, I'm becoming a burden to you. Before long I won't even be able to dress myself, let alone cook, iron, and take care of the apartment. I'm an old invalid woman, and all I do is cause trouble . . ."

Ricciardi kneeled on the floor next to the armchair. He reached out hesitantly with one hand and placed it on the woman's head, as she covered her face in despair, and he gently stroked her gray hair, gathered into a bun.

"Now stop it. You're not useless—if anything, I'm crazy for making you work so hard at your age. You know what we'll do tomorrow? We'll hire a housekeeper, that way she can do all the hard work and you can direct her. What do you say?"

Rosa jerked her head up, staring Ricciardi in the face with a warlike glare.

"Have you lost your senses? An outsider in our home, robbing us blind? It would be more work supervising her than it would be to take care of things myself. Ah, but I almost forgot, you don't care a fig about your own money, and if it weren't for me the peasants back home would have taken the clothes off your back by now."

At last, the Rosa he knew.

"Whatever you say, Rosa. Maybe we could send for someone from back home, what about that? Then you'd be comfortable with her around, maybe one of your nieces, the daughter of one of your brothers or sisters. Just to lend a hand."

Rosa waved one hand irritatedly, as if she were shooing away a mosquito.

"We'll see about that later; it's out of the question for now."

Ricciardi nodded, continuing to stroke her hair all the while. It seemed to have a calming effect on her, and he would have done anything to make her stop crying.

"Well, in any case, will you tell me what the dickens started all this? What happened to make you cry like that, as if your heart was broken?"

Rosa heaved a deep sigh and lifted her clenched fist until it was right in front of Ricciardi's face. She opened it slowly, and he glimpsed shards of something that seemed vaguely familiar.

"Well? What is it?"

Rosa put on a despairing expression.

"You don't even recognize it . . . It's the Baby Jesus that once belonged to your mother, the baroness. And I dropped it, because I can't even hold things in my hands anymore!"

The tears started streaming down her face again, and Ricciardi felt a stab of pity in his heart.

"Please, don't start crying again! It's nothing, just an old piece of porcelain, you'll see, we can fix it. All we need is some glue, no? You had me thinking it was something really serious, and instead it's just a trifle."

"No, it's not a trifle. I'm really upset, it's an antique, and it was so important to your mother that I put up the manger scene every year!"

Ricciardi felt like smiling, but he didn't want to seem dismissive about something that was clearly important to his old *tata*.

"All right, we'll buy another one. They told me that a real manger scene is like that, you always have to add pieces, one or two every year."

Rosa said nothing, staring at her hand. Suddenly she held it up and said:

"Look. Just look at this."

Ricciardi noticed the tremor, with a new stab of concern, this one sharper than the first. For a short time he said nothing. Then he took Rosa's hand and kissed it tenderly.

"Easy there, don't worry about it, calm down. You'll see, it'll turn out to be nothing. And I want you to write a letter back home first thing to send for one of your nieces. I don't want you to be alone anymore, you understand? We can afford it, and that's what I want."

The woman looked down. Then she murmured under her breath:

"If you had a family of your own, the way nature intended, there wouldn't be any need for a niece."

Rosa was Rosa; nothing could change her, not even a trembling hand. And that was a good thing.

"Still, it'll be faster to bring your niece up here, trust me. I'm a little slow when it comes to this kind of thing. Now get up, come on; I'm hungry and I have to get back to work."

Antonio Lomunno sat looking at his hands. He thought about how inadequate they were given his new situation.

He'd lulled himself into the belief that he'd spend his life working at a desk, enjoying a steady climb up the rungs of a brilliant career, toward an increasingly prosperous future for himself and his family; but then everything was gone in an instant, and now he wished he knew how to do something that was humble but useful.

When he was a boy he loved carving wood, but he'd never pursued that passion because, his father told him, it distracted him from his studies. He used to carve little armies, and he'd make them fight one another for hours, on rainy Sunday afternoons when he couldn't go out and play in the courtyard. Now that old talent was good for only one thing, carving a manger scene for his children.

He looked at it: an absurd luxury for a shack that lacked

everything. His children never complained, not even when that damned cheap wine was blurring his heart and he started shouting at them about some ridiculous trifle. They'd stare back at him, but they wouldn't cry or run away.

He was all they had, and they were all he had, too.

He'd clung to the thought of his children during those long, terrible months in prison; and the love he felt for them had saved him from madness, after the warden informed him of what his wife had done.

His children, no question: and his thirst for revenge.

Two conflicting emotions, equally powerful, equally intense. During the nights he spent staring sleeplessly at the ceiling of his cell, watchful as rough hands reached out for him, as cockroaches scuttled across the floor, those two passions worked together to keep him alive.

But the minute he was released, those two emotions became enemies: if he wanted to provide for his children, if he wished to preserve a shred of hope for them, he'd have to renounce his thirst for revenge.

As he was getting ready to go out for the day of temporary work he'd managed to secure, he thought about the blood that had been shed; and his own blood, which flowed in the veins of those two children who'd become old too soon, who watched as he dressed.

Again, he looked at his hands, and he decided that loading and unloading fish at the market was certainly a job he could do. It wasn't that hard, after all. And anything was respectable that was good for his kids.

He reached his hand out toward the manger scene and picked up Saint Joseph. The original figurine, the one he had owned in the beautiful home he'd lived in in his previous life, had been lost; he'd carved this one out of wood, coloring it with a little paint. You were a father, too, he murmured. A father who had only one thought, to work for his

son's good, without a lot of talk, without a lot of philoso-
phizing.

He put the figurine back, amid the others, and smiled sadly.
Among the many houses in the manger scene, there was room
for little shacks like the one he lived in.

He stood up, gave his children a kiss, and went to the market.

Maione gaped, opening and then shutting his mouth twice, like a fresh-caught mullet wriggling on the deck of a fishing boat. He was experiencing a sense of bewilderment, as if Lucia had suddenly materialized before him in response to a mystical invocation. As if she'd been transported to the Villa Nazionale on his own thought waves.

He stared at her, her hat fastened to her head with a ribbon, her overcoat with the fur collar, the one he'd bought for her so many years ago and that she kept in perfect condition, her cheeks red from the chilly air, her blue eyes turned in the same direction he'd been gazing until just a few seconds ago.

"Luci', what are you doing here?"

His wife didn't answer; she just looked at him with her lips pressed firmly together and a determined expression on her face. Then she said:

"You're not working. Don't even try to tell me that you're here on a case, that you're tailing some criminal the day before Christmas Eve. Those people aren't fugitives; they're just a normal family, out for a little fresh air in the Villa Nazionale. Don't you dare try to lie to me, Rafe'."

Maione knew his wife. Joking around at home, back when Luca was still alive, they used to say that she was the real policeman in the family. All the same, he tried lying to her anyway.

"What's that supposed to mean? If you only knew how many people seem normal, harmless, but then it turns out they've done things that you can't even imagine. Believe me, people aren't always what they seem."

Lucia, without taking her eyes off Biagio's family, replied:

"Nonsense. A minute ago you put your hands on your face; you only do that when you're confused, when you don't know what to do next. And you never have doubts or uncertainties about your work. There's some other problem here, and I want to know what it is."

Maione didn't know what to say. The woman went on.

"I've been following you for two days now. Ever since you came home that night three days ago, your mood has changed. You've seemed sad, distracted, pensive. You try your best to seem normal, but I know you: you can't pull the wool over my eyes. When an investigation gets under your skin you bring it home with you, but there's always been a limit. This time it's different, and I want to know what it's about."

Her tone of voice brooked no objections.

"Come here, Luci'. Let's sit down on that bench and I'll tell you all about it."

A few shafts of sunlight slanted down, making their way fitfully through the thick black clouds, hitting the sea here and there. The bench was cold, but the fact that there was no wind made it tolerable. The strollers were thinning out as lunchtime drew near, but the orchestra played on heroically, keeping the Christmas spirit flying, like the banner of a regiment fighting in the trenches.

"Do you think that certain things can ever end, Luci'? Do you think that it's possible to put an end to certain sorrows, and start living again?"

Signora Maione sat stiffly, her face sunk deep in her fur collar. The brigadier couldn't see her expression. All the better: it would make it easier for him to find the strength to tell her everything.

"I think that pain and joy both leave their marks. And you

have to deal with the marks they leave. They never end, no; they leave you a different person. But you have to provide those who depend on you with an explanation of some kind. That's something that took me three years to learn—you know. And we never talked about it; one day I smiled at you, and you wrapped your arms around me. That's what I know, and that's all I want to know."

Two seagulls shrieked at the winter weather. Candela's wife was telling the children something, and they both listened, spellbound; he sat on the ground, looking out at the sea and smoking a cigarette.

Lucia and Raffaele, sitting just some fifteen feet away from the man and woman and their children, watched them and, beyond them, watched the sea, pierced here and there by shafts of sunlight. Christmas was looming over everyone, midway between a promise and a threat.

"Tell me. Tell me the whole story. I can tell that it's not something that's yours alone, that it concerns me as well. If that's true, and I know it is, then you have to tell me everything."

It was true, and Maione knew it. His simple mind grasped the fact that he ought to have shared what was happening with Lucia, but his terror at the thought of shattering the fragile equilibrium that they'd only recently managed to recover after Luca's death was overwhelming.

He suddenly realized that he'd crossed that line at the very moment he had learned that that fair-haired young man, so gentle and inoffensive in appearance, who was sitting in the grass mere feet away, was their son's murderer.

Maione heaved a sigh. And he started to tell her the story.

He told her, and his voice sounded like the murmuring of the waves on the deserted beach. He told her, and his hushed words carved a groove as deep as hell itself. He told her, and as he told her he told himself as well, creating order among the vague and rebellious thoughts that had been traveling between his mind and his heart, giving him no peace.

He told her, and it seemed as if a century had passed since that evening just three days ago, when he had found Franco Massa standing on a corner on Via Toledo, ghostlike, waiting for him.

He told her about the scratchy voice pouring out of the broken heart of a father who'd never had children of his own, and through that voice he told her the story of a confession extorted through a last act of deception, and the final truth that had come out of that confession.

He told her about a man who was guilty of many crimes and murders but innocent of one, a man who had died in the belief that he was cleansing his soul in the presence of a priest, and about that fake priest who had decreed the death sentence for a man who was guilty of nothing except that one murder. And how that death sentence had been entrusted to his hands, the hands of a father who'd once had a son but no longer did.

He told her about how he'd climbed all the way up to Bambinella's garret apartment, of a name and address whispered in a setting of silk curtains and dying pigeons. And about the walk to San Gregorio Armeno, in the midst of a Christmas that seemed like an empty collective charade surrounding the song of death that played to him in his heart.

He told her about the hollow feeling in the pit of his stomach and the way his head spun, when in the light of dawn he'd first laid eyes on that hand, the hand that had changed everything for him, the color of the sun and the very taste of happiness. He told her about the horror he'd felt when he saw the same blond hair, the identical youth of both the murderer and the victim.

Lucia sailed silently over the waves of the story her husband was telling her, as if in a dense fog. She felt as though she were listening to a story that didn't concern her, as she observed from a distance events and characters like those you could watch in a movie house.

Maione went on talking, staring straight ahead of him, following the flow of his own emotions. He felt as if he'd been crushed, but was slowly climbing out of the rubble.

He told her about the hand that still gripped a knife, but now only to give shape to a piece of wood, not to pull it out of their son's back. About the shop owner's pride, the smiling young wife on the balcony of the building across the way, the joy of the little girl throwing her arms around her father's neck.

He told her about the robbery, the young man's instinctive reaction, the bandits who ran off as fast as their legs could carry them, but he didn't realize that almost within arm's reach his Lucia had witnessed the same scene, and had wondered why her husband had failed to intervene, hoping that the reason was just an instinctive aversion to risk.

Then he stopped. But he started talking again, in the same tone of voice, whispering into the cold, still air of that December twenty-third, as the city held its breath in anticipation of Christmas; and he told her about the tempest that was raging in his miserable soul, the soul of a policeman who wanted to be a father but whom circumstances and Franco Massa seemed determined to transform into a judge and executioner.

He told Lucia about Lucia, about how her sorrow, her days sunk in the abyss, lying in her bed staring at the sliver of sky, were the chief responsibility he felt in his heart, driving him to carry out that death sentence. About the burden he felt pressing down on his shoulders, the weight of the suffering that they all carried, day after day, without ever speaking of it.

Finally, he fell silent. And in that silence they both realized that they were staring at the back of the neck of the man who'd murdered their son, who in turn was looking out at the sporadic shafts of sunlight on the dark sea. The two seagulls called out and responded to each other.

Lucia spoke. Her voice was harsh and spare and it came from the depths of a soul that had never stopped dying. Listening to her, Maione realized just how false his impression that she had emerged from the abyss really was, and he understood that his wife had merely learned how to live with her sorrow, had simply stopped struggling against it.

"You know, there are times I think I can still feel him suckling at my breast. That's absurd, no? I saw him all grown-up, strapping and tall; I used to iron those immense shirts he wore. He'd pick me up in his arms and whirl me around until I was breathless, you remember the way he'd spin me through the air? And I've had five other children, and I love them all dearly, you know how much I love them all. But I can still feel him suckling, sucking the life out of me. My firstborn, Rafe', there's no replacement. He's the one who tells you who you are, and who you'll be for the rest of your life. A mother. A mother, and nothing else."

Maione fought back his tears. He nodded his head, but his wife wasn't looking at him.

"I married the only man I've ever loved in my life. I married him because he made me laugh and because I cared about him. I married him because he's hard-headed and honest, because he's a policeman. Because he fights against evil, and especially because he knows how to recognize evil, and he teaches my children how to recognize it, so they'll know what good is. And what the difference is between the two."

Maione heaved a deep sigh. It all felt like a dream. Candela's little boy scampered over to his father and sat down beside him, running his tiny hand up and down the man's back. The man didn't stir. Lucia's voice went on.

"My love for my son. My love for my husband. That's all I

am, Rafe': nothing more, nothing less than my love for my son and my love for my husband."

She turned to look at Maione, and her eyes looked like a window over the summer sea.

"It's Christmas, Rafe'. At Christmas Luca used to write us a letter, you remember? He'd put it under your napkin, and you always pretended to be so surprised when you found it, the same way you do now with the letters from the other children. Do you remember the things he used to write to us, in those little letters? I still have them all; I kept every last one. He told us that he wanted to be a good boy, good just like you."

Maione felt as if he were on the verge of dying, then and there on an ice-cold bench in the Villa Nazionale, just a stone's throw from the sea. About to die of heartbreak and regret.

"It's Christmastime, Rafe'. Luca's not coming home for Christmas. I'll set a place for him, the way I always do, with a plate and silverware. But he's not coming home. He'll never come home again. And after a whole lifetime, you want to tell him now, now that he's in the world of almighty truth, that you're willing to commit this horrible crime, to take a father away from his wife and his two innocent children? Whether they're our children or someone else's, they're still children."

The brigadier looked uncertainly at his wife.

"What should I do, Luci'? What should I do now?"

From the sleeve of her overcoat emerged a hand, slender and pale. It rose toward her husband's face and caressed it, drying a tear that Maione hadn't even realized he'd shed.

"I'll tell you what we ought to do. It's Christmas. We ought to stand up and go away from here. I still have to cook the second dish for tonight, and you have to finish your shift. And then we'll celebrate, because it's Christmas and we have five children who want a smiling mamma, and an honest papà to write their little Christmas letter to."

In front of them the little girl had fallen asleep, and the

father had picked up the little boy and was holding him as his gaze, lost in the distance, continued to follow the phantoms of his conscience.

Lucia stood up and took her husband by the hand, turning to leave the Villa Nazionale, while behind them the orchestra went on playing and the sea lay calm beneath a few shafts of sunlight and a great mass of black clouds.

The city above them, climbing up the hillside, slowly turned on its lights. And it looked exactly like a nativity scene.

LI

Christmas accosted Ricciardi and Maione, shouting at the top of its lungs, the second they turned the corner of Via Toledo. By longstanding tradition, December twenty-third transformed one of the city's most historic thoroughfares, the street that ran from the venerable quarters of the army of Aragon all the way down to the port, into a vast open-air market selling the monarch of all the foodstuffs that grace the holiday banqueting tables of Naples: His Majesty the Fish.

Dozens of wooden crates painted light blue to give the idea of salt water and fresh fish had been arranged on the sidewalks, the way they were every Christmas, decorated with fishnets, sea urchins, seaweed, and even sea horses. Inside, lying in eight inches of water that was constantly being replenished, wriggled fish of all colors and sizes, eels, anchovies, and all other manner of freshly caught seafood.

The street, short but very broad, lent itself perfectly to the displaying of the merchandise and the passage of the much-courted shoppers. The fishmongers had set up their own stalls, with raised setbacks that slanted toward the street, offering the greatest possible surface area to the potential buyers' view; on these were arranged, in perfect symmetry, a series of low woven wicker baskets swarming with clams and tellins, mussels and lobsters with their claws tied shut with twine, their feelers in perennial motion, and gaping gray and red mullets.

The stalls were lit by acetylene lamps, which cast an almost blinding light out into the rapidly darkening afternoon. All around, the decorations that had been painstakingly put up by the hands of the women that very night: flowers, seaweed, seashells, and colorful stones, to reinforce the impression of the sea come to visit the city for Christmas.

And the scent of the sea was intense, not only because of the marine vegetation and fauna present in such considerable quantities, but also because of the salt water that was continually being sprinkled over the seafood to accentuate the impression of freshness, and especially because of the dark, leathery faces of the fishermen, sunburnt and wind-tanned, their trousers rolled up over their muscular calves and their triangular hats flopping against their shoulders, worn pulled back. All of them ready to flash welcoming, toothless smiles, with a jacket thrown over one shoulder and their scales in hand, a challenging look in their eyes, as if to say: You can try, but you won't find better seafood than what I have to sell.

The noise was almost intolerable. The steady buzz of the immense crowd of bargain hunters was offset by the calls of the vendors:

"*Mo' l'ha pigliato 'a rezza, frícceca ancora!* Freshly caught fish, still wriggling!"

"*Chesta è 'a pesca nova, 'a pesca nova!* This is fresh fish, fresh fish!"

"*Facitevíllo co' 'o limone, 'o pesce frisco!* Cook it with lemon, this fresh fish!"

And then there were the vendors who boasted about the specific locations the seafood they were selling came from:

"*È Marechiaro, chiaro chiaro!* The bright waters of Marechiaro!"

"*Vene 'a Pusilleco, frisco 'e Pusilleco, vi' che addore!* It comes from Posillipo, fresh from Posillipo, come get a whiff!"

"*L'anema 'e Mergellina, tèneno 'sti cozze!* These mussels hail from Mergellina!"

When it comes to seafood, as everyone knows, you can't

buy too far in advance, but no table could do without it. And so the desperate game that the fishermen of Naples had to play for Christmas was decided entirely in those few hours, in that one spot. As a result, everyone was involved, wives and children, relatives who normally had other things to do, and the fishmongers hired extra workers for the day, hoping against hope that there'd be money enough at day's end to pay them their wages.

The two policemen stood there in silence, each lost in his own thoughts. The commissario, worried, kept wondering what could be responsible for the tremor in Rosa's hand. He made a mental note to talk to Dr. Modo about it, and he felt a twinge of guilt at having left her alone, in the condition she was in. He had made up his mind to make her accept a helper; at her age she couldn't keep up with all the work she demanded of herself.

Irrationally, his thoughts kept turning to Enrica, to what he thought of as her calm and unruffled way of dealing with life. He wished he could ask her advice. Then his mind took him back down the long, sad road of how impossible it was to make her a part of his life, and that thought crushed his spirit.

Livia was different. She was aware of his sudden bouts of sadness, the imprint of solitude that weighed on him heavily, and she still seemed convinced that she could take that burden on herself. Who knows, Ricciardi thought: perhaps in the end it's fair to let everyone pick for themselves the life they prefer.

Once again, Maione felt as if there were a strong wind blowing through his head. His conversation with his wife at the Villa Nazionale, just a few minutes earlier, had left him in tatters.

Forget about codes of honor, forget about handing down sentences and carrying them out, Lucia had told him; all that mattered was the life they had to live, the five children they had to raise. Every action had its consequences, and a person needed to be aware of that fact, at all times.

The brigadier should have felt a sense of relief, and to some extent he did: but deep inside a voice went on asking if he'd done the right thing, if he could live with the idea that a killer, whether of his son or someone else's, should live his life in peace, without paying any price for his actions.

But, Maione asked himself, couldn't it be that this itself is the punishment? To live with perennial remorse, as well as the regret of knowing that your brother died in prison for a crime you'd committed with your own hand?

He'd glimpsed a deep sadness in Biagio's eyes that morning at the Villa Nazionale. Holidays, as he knew all too well, are also family and childhood memories. If the man had continued with his criminal ways, the brigadier wouldn't have hesitated to arrest him and take him in; but the honesty of his present life was as good as many years served in prison, and not wanting to go back there at any price.

He knew, deep down, that he'd continue to monitor Biagio Candela's life from a distance, that no one else would suffer any harm at that young man's hands if Maione had anything to say about it. He was glad to take on that responsibility, as a father and as a policeman. He'd go talk to Franco Massa, reason with him for as long as it took, and persuade him to underwrite that decision—a decision that had been Lucia's even more than it had been his. Enough sorrow. Enough suffering.

With some effort, both Ricciardi and Maione brought their minds back to the investigation then under way: the corpses of the Garofalos and the solitude of their little girl demanded their undivided attention, also because Christmas was upon them and would soon bury everything under the trappings of the holiday, guaranteed to keep them—and everyone else—from working for many days to come.

They wandered for a while, disconsolately, in search of some familiar face. After nearly fifteen minutes spent trying to make headway through the river of people, they caught sight of Lomunno, who was unloading crates of fish from a horse-drawn cart and carrying them to a fishmonger's stall on the sidewalk. His face was red with sweat and strain, he wore an expression of sheer concentration, and he was taking extreme care not to drop anything. He moved stiffly, showing how unaccustomed he was to this kind of work.

Maione elbowed the commissario in the ribs, pointing Lomunno out. As they walked toward him, they glimpsed a squad of militiamen crossing the street; they had come to make sure that the market was operating properly, and as they came through, the crowd parted, as if to avoid any contact with them.

Among them Ricciardi recognized Criscuolo, the platoon leader with the dancing mustache who had told him the story of Garofalo's promotion. Criscuolo looked around, circumspectly, as if he were looking for someone.

The commissario held Maione back by one arm: he wanted to watch this situation unfold without being seen. He pulled the brigadier aside, the two of them withdrawing from the flow of the crowd, and he stationed himself next to a calamari vendor who was tossing an enormous squid from one hand to the other, boasting of its freshness and flavor.

Some fifteen feet away from him, Criscuolo stopped near the stand that was being stocked by Lomunno, who was over at the horse-drawn cart at that moment. The fishmonger recognized the militiaman and greeted him respectfully, doffing his cap and bowing his head; the officer replied brusquely with a nod of the head, and his mustache quivered as a result. There was an exchange of glances, an inquisitive one from Criscuolo, a sly winking look in response from the fishmonger, who tilted his head in Lomunno's direction, just as he was approaching the stand.

The eyes of the militiaman and his former colleague locked. Lomunno reddened visibly, ashamed at being seen working as a simple roustabout by his one-time inferiors, while at the same time aware that he owed his friend a debt of gratitude for having obtained this job for him. Criscuolo, with a twitch of his whiskers, having completed his favorable inspection, decided to spare Lomunno the mortification of being recognized by the other militiamen and ordered the little group to make a rapid about-face and head elsewhere.

Ricciardi and Maione exchanged a glance, having understood this additional dynamic in the relationship between Lomunno and his former colleagues: life had made other decisions, but certain ties of friendship had remained intact. Even if they thought that he'd killed Garofalo, the militiamen believed that Lomunno had paid his debt to society.

They swung back out into the middle of the stream of people and let themselves be pushed along, in search of the other figures of interest to the investigation. They didn't have to go far: in fact, only about thirty feet. There they all were, the Boccias, husband and wife, the three fellow crew members, a couple of female family relations, and even little Alfonso, who was in charge of sprinkling the merchandise with water he carried in a bucket, a task he performed very conscientiously.

They were painstaking and professional at their work, and their expressions, it seemed to Ricciardi, betrayed their fear that they wouldn't be able to sell all the fish they had on display. They called out to passersby in loud voices, trying to gauge the prices that they would be willing to pay, and showing themselves amenable to discussions of discounts.

The commissario watched them, and he also watched Lomunno, who was tirelessly loading and unloading crates of fish a few stalls away. All around, the noise of the vendors' cries and the haggling was deafening, almost intolerable. Just a few feet away a boy was swearing to a woman, on the Madonna no less, that he was losing money at the price he was giving her for a sack of clams: Signo', as God is my witness, these aren't just clams, this is the freshness and the salt air of the Gulf of Naples that you're carrying home to your kitchen.

Ricciardi thought about the profiles of the suspects, Lomunno and the Boccias, and how neither one fit perfectly with the findings from their investigation. Lomunno had the strength, the motivation, and the rage to account for the savagery of the crime, as well as the knowledge to have wanted to destroy the Saint Joseph as a way of saying that stealing a father's living was a mortal sin. But he was alone, while it seemed that there had been two pairs of murderous hands, and taking his revenge would have been mortal to his children as well as to Garofalo. Really, he didn't seem the type, to Ricciardi, to kill the informant who had ruined his life in his home, killing his wife while he was at it. If he had to guess, he thought that Lomunno would probably have ambushed him somewhere else, so as to be able to carry out his intent with greater ease.

Now the Boccias had an even more powerful motivation: the life of their son. And they'd already gone once to the Garofalos' home; they'd been seen leaving, they knew all about the doorman's habits, and they could easily have sneaked back in. Moreover, there were two of them, and if they had wanted to commit that murder they'd necessarily have had to get rid of the woman as well. But Ricciardi just couldn't see them inflicting all those wounds on an already-dead body; and they were certainly not likely to have attributed a special symbolism to Saint Joseph, or to have left that kind of signature on the crime scene, staying longer than necessary to do so.

Standing motionless on the sidewalk, being shoved and tossed about by the crowd, as was Maione, Ricciardi once again realized that something wasn't quite right with either of the two hypotheses, but that he had no other theories to go on.

Just then, from a crate ten feet away, a large saltwater eel made its escape.

And as if by enchantment, every tile in the mosaic suddenly fell into place.

LII

If fish is the prince of the Christmas table, the saltwater eel is certainly king.

The big eel with its jutting jaw, fat and slippery and perennially on the move, brought home partially stunned by the brown paper in which it's wrapped, comes back to life the minute it's tossed into a bath of fresh water for a wash, and becomes very much like a snake, wriggling before the fascinated and terrified eyes of the children who stand watching the whole bloody preparation, never to forget it as long as they live. In fact, the cut-up pieces of eel continue to move in the blood as if possessed of a life of their own, as if the animal were capable of defeating death itself, until finally, coated in flour, they land in the frying pan and become the main dish of Christmas dinner, served with a traditional laurel-leaf garnish.

On Via Santa Brigida the basins with saltwater eels were virtually under siege, more and more so as the time passed and the hour to return home drew near. One of the most active vendors, a dark and handsome young man with a charming smile and a deep voice, drew women to his stand by picking up clusters of eels and swishing them around in the large basin before him, shouting:

"They're dead and they're alive, authentic saltwater eels, the tail of the Devil himself!"

The symbolic phrase, the reference to the Devil's tail and life and death, attracted the commissario's attention and he moved away from Maione through the crowd. The brigadier stayed behind, keeping an eye on the Boccias, who seemed to be having good luck with their sales.

When Ricciardi was near the eel tank, as one large eel was being moved from the scale to a paper wrapper, it suddenly twisted and lunged and flew into the street.

The girl who'd just bought it watched it hurtle through the air, as surprised as the fishmonger by the eel's sudden spurt of energy as it landed at the feet of a couple who happened to be passing by. The man noticed it first, and he darted to one side, knocking flat to the ground a little boy who was walking by and holding his mother's hand. The woman, in turn, screamed and hiked up her skirts with both hands, breaking into a sort of propitiatory dance around the poor creature as it writhed on the stone slabs of the sidewalk.

In the space of a few seconds, the place was a madhouse: some people were screaming, while others were laughing; a few little girls burst into tears because they'd suddenly been separated from their parents; and everyone was diving forward at once in an effort to catch the huge eel, which, slippery and contorted as was its nature, managed to slip through all of their hands.

Ricciardi watched, openmouthed, the only person to remain motionless amid all the confusion.

He stood staring at the elusive, uncatchable eel. He watched it slither through one outstretched hand after another until suddenly, with a forward lunge, the very same fishmonger who had let it get away seized it, restoring it to its fate.

But by that point, Ricciardi had vanished.

LIII

He kept asking himself how he could have missed it; it was suddenly all so obvious.

It had been, from the very first, as clear as day.

As he ran through streets still packed with people, stalls, stands, food, and merchandise.

As he ran through the cold, hurrying past the living and the dead, all so wrapped up in what they were doing that they didn't listen, capable of looking at only their own, tiny worlds, capable only of not seeing, not understanding.

That was the same mistake that Ricciardi had made. He could see that only now. He'd looked closely, where they'd told him to look. He'd stopped at the first station, then at the second and the third, without stopping to consider that the train might also have gone a long way round to fetch up exactly where it started from.

He was furious with himself for having allowed himself to be distracted by his own concerns. A step back, damn it, he told himself as he hurried along Via Chiaia, pushing past people still lingering to gaze at shop windows, through small knots of strollers laughing and talking loudly without exchanging any information at all, past pedestrians trudging along with their heads bowed and their foreheads furrowed, in the silence of their own thoughts. If only he'd taken a single step back, he would have been able to see everything in its proper perspective, read all the signs.

He thought about Rosa, her tears, her malaise, her sense of

uselessness. Once again he cursed himself and his mind's inability to make the proper connections between the clues that he had gathered. And he hoped with every fiber of his being that he could complete the circle before any other terrible things happened. He trembled at the thought of the terrible risk they'd run over the past few days, chasing after will-o'-the-wisps. And yet everyone had told him, in one way or another, both the living and the dead; and Modo had been right, two different hands had wielded the knives, with different degrees of strength, and from different angles.

The murderous hands.

He started running even harder.

Maione found himself alone in the swirling mob that was pushing through Via Santa Brigida. He'd been standing there watching the Boccia family and their desperate struggle to sell every last bit of seafood; then his eyes had locked for a moment with those of Aristide's wife, Angelina, and she had nodded her head in his direction without breaking off her negotiations over the purchase of two gray mullets with a mustachioed gentleman clearly reluctant to buy. The brigadier was fascinated by the sense of timing and choreography that seemed to guide everyone's movements, and by the sheer determination that he could see in the people's faces, even in the face of Alfonso, the Boccias' older boy, even though he was really still just a child.

Then his attention was caught by the upheaval attendant upon the eel's escape, and he realized that he'd lost track of Ricciardi. He looked around, but he was nowhere in sight. He wondered where he had disappeared to, then he noticed someone in the distance, pushing his way through the stream of people pouring into the market, and heading for Via Chiaia. Baffled, Maione wondered what could have driven Ricciardi to run off like that, and he tried to reconstruct his superior officer's thoughts.

The eel, he thought; the Boccias' little boy; Lomunno; the militiamen.

With a sinking feeling that danger was imminent, he started shoving his way through the crowd.

LIV

He was ushered into a room on the ground floor that he hadn't seen on any of his previous visits. It was dark by now, and the air was growing colder by the minute.

At first he couldn't see anyone; the room was dimly lit, with a pair of low-hanging lamps emitting a yellowish glow that left darkness in the corners. At the center of the room, dominating the space, was one of the largest manger scenes Ricciardi had ever seen: a full-fledged miniature city, which sloped down from the hilltop toward a crowded city quarter in the middle of which, in a large grotto illuminated by a series of small light-bulbs concealed from view, was the Holy Family.

Even caught up in his thoughts as he was, the commissario was entranced by the construction. There were distant houses with windows glowing in the darkness, flocks of sheep, grazing cattle, wandering shepherds and peasants; inns, taverns, and shops of every kind on the intermediate level, with goods laid out for sale, and shopkeepers and shoppers engaged in mute but realistic conversations; and at the very front, angels, the Three Wise Men come to adore the Christ Child, all portrayed by figurines of extraordinary beauty and evident antiquity. Ricciardi was certainly no connoisseur, but he felt sure that the value of that manger scene and the work that had gone into its creation must certainly have been quite considerable.

As he gazed at it, openmouthed, a voice as shrill as a piece of chalk screeching across a blackboard made him start.

"Our manger scene is famous throughout the city, Commissario."

Sister Veronica emerged suddenly from the darkness, a smile on her round red face.

"There are shepherds from the eighteenth century, and every year some pious soul from the neighborhood, returning home to the Almighty Father, leaves us a donation in their will, so that we can complete the scene and make it grow even more. Or rather, so that *I* can; for the past seven years, that task has fallen to me."

Ricciardi walked over to the nun to greet her. She extended her little hand, as usual clammy and damp with sweat. The policeman continued to let his gaze range over the miniature panorama.

"Very impressive, indeed. And you do it all on your own, Sister?"

The woman gazed in satisfaction at the fruit of her labor.

"This room is dedicated to the nativity scene, which is closed off all year long until the Feast of the Immaculate Conception on December 8. The structure is left intact, but the shepherds are removed after Epiphany and put away in their boxes, carefully packed, of course; some of these pieces are very valuable, you know. My work consists of arranging and adding a few pieces every year, so that the children and my sisters have a surprise every time they come to see it, when the door is opened on December 8."

"So what's new this year?"

The nun was thrilled at this display of interest on Ricciardi's part.

"I go on working on it until Christmas Eve, even when it's already open to the public. This year, working with the materials and tools you see on that workbench, I added a hill. I arranged sheep here and there on it, and I added three houses, with two lightbulbs, you see them? I'm still not done. I'm finishing gluing on the moss, but we're almost there."

As she danced on tiptoe pointing to the places she was describing to Ricciardi, Sister Veronica seemed like a little girl. Her voice, already piercing, had risen even higher, accentuating the impression that she'd regressed to a child's age. Suddenly she stopped and regained her composure, seeming to remember whom she was talking to.

"Forgive me, Commissario. Whenever I talk about the manger scene, I lose my head a little bit; it's just that I love it so. It represents the triumph of faith in everyday life, with the symbols of our beliefs mixed in with everything that happens around us. It helps us to teach children that God, the Madonna, and all the saints can see us at any time, no matter what we do, and therefore we must act in accordance with their will, even when we think that we're alone."

Ricciardi listened, his hands in the pockets of his overcoat, his eyes fixed on the face of the diminutive nun. He could still feel the fingers of the woman's sweaty hands on his own.

"You're quite right, Sister. Everyday life conceals any number of things. We know that all too well ourselves, sadly, dealing as we do with the things that human beings do to their fellow men. In fact, that's why I'm here. I have a few questions I'd like to ask you; I have a theory about just who might have done this terrible thing to your sister and her husband. Is the little girl all right? Where is she right now?"

Sister Veronica shrugged.

"She's sad, some of the time. She doesn't talk about it, but it's clear that she's thinking about her home, and her parents. But as long as she's here—with me, with my sisters in God, who all love her, and with her classmates, with whom she plays and has so much fun—she's perfectly safe. Of course, now it's Christmas, the holiday of the family. She even wrote the little Christmas letter to her mother and father; she thinks they're traveling, and we pretended to mail it to them."

Ricciardi heaved a sigh of relief. At least he wouldn't have to carry that burden on his conscience. The nun went on speaking.

"But you were telling me, Commissario, that you have some idea about who could have been responsible for this horrible crime?"

The commissario walked over to the manger scene, so that he was standing next to the Grotto of the Nativity.

"The other time, when I came here to talk with your niece, you scolded a little boy who hurried past an image of the Virgin Mary without crossing himself. Do you remember?"

The woman was standing by the workbench where tools and materials were laid out and, as she went on talking to Ricciardi, she started to test the thickness of a piece of cork glued down less securely than the others. She smiled.

"Certainly I remember. That was Domenico, a little rascallion, he always runs in the hall, though I've told him a thousand times not to do it. He's not bad, though; he's just a child."

Ricciardi nodded, his eyes fixed on the Holy Family.

"Of course, a child. Still, it made me think about the importance of sacred images, about their worth. The failure to honor a sacred image, as you said on that occasion, is a terrible sin."

Sister Veronica had changed her position somewhat so that she could go on handling her tools and still look at Ricciardi. She was closely following everything he said.

"That's right, exactly right. But they're just children, Commissario; it's hardly right to punish them past a certain point, don't you agree?"

The commissario picked up the figurine of Saint Joseph and hefted it in his hand.

"But what if an adult intentionally failed to honor a sacred image? Or what if, worse still, they deliberately destroyed one?"

The woman watched, petrified in horror, as the policeman threatened the safety of her Saint Joseph.

"Commissario, what are you doing? Put Saint Joseph back immediately! You have no idea how much that piece is worth!"

Her voice had become even more shrill than before; it was if the nun had shards of glass in her mouth.

"What would you think of me, Sister Veronica, if I were to hurl this statue to the ground and shatter it into a thousand pieces?"

"Don't you dare! Don't you dare! You don't even have the right to touch it! Put it back this second!"

Ricciardi didn't bat an eye.

"But that's exactly what I intend to do. I can do it, seeing as you did it yourself."

The nun, her face disfigured by rage, emitted a high-pitched scream that sounded like a sharp blade scraping across a slab of sheet metal. With a sudden lunge, she grabbed a long, well-honed knife from the workbench and drew it back to launch herself at Ricciardi, but a strong hand seized her arm.

She turned around and found herself face-to-face with two hundred and sixty-five pounds of out-of-breath police brigadier.

"I wouldn't do that, Sister. If I were you, I wouldn't do that."

LV

Now she's calm. She's talking, and her voice and her thoughts are at cross purposes, and they echo in the minds and hearts of Maione and Ricciardi.

I didn't break it! I didn't throw it to the floor, you understand? I'd never do such a thing, and since then I've prayed day and night that no one up in Heaven should ever think that I did it intentionally.

To break a sacred image, me of all people—why, I'd never do such a thing. It fell, I dropped it, because of these cursed hands of mine. It slipped through my fingers, it hit the ground, and it broke, may God in Heaven forgive me.

Only for that one thing do I ask the Lord for forgiveness. Not for the rest. The rest was justice. The rest was the right thing to do. The Madonna in person told me so; even with all the pain from the swords in Her heart, She told me Herself that the time had come to do it.

You must listen to me. I have to tell you everything, down to the last detail. I'm not interested in your forgiveness, let me be clear about that: or even your comprehension, as far as that goes. I just want to tell you my story so that you understand what happened, so that you learn how a respectable person ought to behave.

Because I'm a nun, you understand? I'm Sister Veronica. I'm the nun who makes the manger scene, the little nun with the big brassy voice like a trumpet; I'm like a fairy godmother, the chil-

dren all adore me. And I adore them back. Children are my mission, that's why the Madonna summoned me in the first place.

*Suddenly, her face is transformed; it becomes sweet and
devout, like the faces of the saints on the saint cards that women
kiss and men keep in their wallets.*

I wanted children of my own when I was young. I wanted a
family, with lots of children, born of true love. And I waited to
meet the right man, I wrote poetry in my diary, and I even drew
pictures of him, as best I could imagine him, because I
dreamed about him from sunrise to sunset.

My mother always used to tell me, wait and you'll meet him,
the father of your children. I'd say to her, Mamma, tell me,
how will I know it's him when I meet him? And she'd say, don't
fret, you'll hear a little voice inside you that'll tell you: it's him,
he's really the one.

I waited. I spent every day preparing myself to be a good
wife, learning to sew, wash, iron, and cook. If I never found
him, I wouldn't settle for anyone else. I'd much sooner have no
one at all.

My sister, on the other hand, thought only of herself; she
brushed her hair and strutted around in front of the mirror like
a peacock. That's the way she was, my sister.

And then one day I met him. My father worked at the port,
he had a small company, I used to take him lunch when he
couldn't get away to come home to eat; and that day, talking to
my father in his office, there he was. Emanuele.

*Ricciardi sees her regret, her melancholy. And he sees love,
the ancient enemy.*

He was an official with the port authority; the militia wasn't
something they'd dreamed up yet. He was so handsome, you

know? So handsome. He looked at me, I looked at him, and I heard that voice deep inside me, the little voice that my mother told me I'd hear: it's him, the voice told me. It's him, I said to myself.

My father didn't like him, he thought he was just a grabby careerist and a social climber. That he seemed far too comfortable handling other people's money. But I'd heard that voice inside, and from that day I thought of nothing else.

We would meet in secret. He'd tell me that I seemed like a little girl, and he'd smile. I was happy, like I'd never been before, like I'd never be again.

Then one day I came down with a fever. My sister went to take lunch to my father that day.

A cloud passed over her face. Not remorse, not displeasure. Annoyance, rather. A bump on the road, an inconvenient mishap. The vain sister, the stupid sister. The sister who won in the end.

I don't know what happened. I hadn't told anyone about him, because my father was opposed to him. My mother didn't know, my sister didn't know. But he knew, he knew perfectly well. But he pretended not to. He avoided me for the next couple of months, and then one night there he was, at the dinner table: my sister's fiancé.

I'd always said it: either the man that fate had chosen for me, or no one. The next night, as I lay in bed sobbing, I heard a voice deep inside me saying: then come to me.

It was the Madonna. That was Her voice: now I knew. She wanted me, even if no one else did, She wanted me. I entered the convent as a novice just a week later, and my parents put up no objections. But my sister had plenty to say: Didn't you want lots of children? she asked. And I told her: Yes, and in fact, I'll have lots of children. Lots and lots.

She was scary now, with that shrill little-girl voice and a grim expression, like a hundred-year-old woman. A shiver ran through Maione, who was standing behind her, ready to immobilize her again if necessary.

Several years went by, at least five. I went to their wedding, but I never went to see them. To see them happy together—no one could ask me to do that, except the Madonna, but She never did. My father died, my mother fell sick, but we nuns say that our family is the convent.

I learned that my sister was expecting a child. I went to see her. She was annoyed, angry, worried. She told me that she would turn into a cow, and that her husband's eye would wander, that he'd find someone else. That was all she cared about.

I told her that she'd surely end up in Hell, thinking and talking that way. That a child is the greatest possible blessing, that it was sheer sacrilege to complain. And she said: Fine, if you like children so much, why don't you raise it. And I said: Of course, I'll be happy to raise her. Because I knew she would be a little girl, and so she was.

The smile, a chilly, frightening smile. Or perhaps it's just the lights of the manger scene which looks like a distant city, and the air that's growing colder minute by minute.

It was a little girl, sure enough, and from the very beginning she spent more time with me than with her mother. My sister, you see, wasn't born to be a mother. She would always smile, she was courteous, and she liked to look at herself in the mirror, but she was good for nothing else.

You've seen Benedetta. She's like me. Serious, well-behaved, intelligent. She'd rather be here than at home; that's what she always tells me.

Everything was all right, no problems. I saw him only rarely, he pretended not to see me, the only reason he even said hello to me was to keep my sister from getting suspicious. Once or twice she told me: My husband doesn't want the girl to spend all her time at the convent. But he was working all the time and she was happy to be able to have the hairdresser come over or to go out window shopping.

Do you know that song, the one that talks about toys and perfumes, *Balocchi e profumi*? The one that makes everyone cry when they hear it? My sister was like the mother in that song.

But in the song, the little girl is alone and she falls sick, but I'm there for Benedetta. And so everything was all right.

Until, in mid-December, that devil in human form gets it into his head to make a manger scene.

She looks at Ricciardi, as if that were an explanation. As if that were enough to explain all that blood, all that pain. As if that were enough.

The manger scene, you understand? The manger scene, in that home. A depiction of the family in its holiest form, a depiction of faith and love, right there in that apartment. I said: A manger scene? Why on earth a manger scene?

My sister laughed, she laughed right in my face. She said: You're asking me why, you who spend the whole year thinking about nothing else, going around begging for donations, you who build yours piece by piece? And anyway, it's your fault that we're doing it, the girl is so in love with your manger scene at the convent that Emanuele has finally decided to put one up here. In fact, he told Benedetta that he's going to buy her one even more beautiful than yours.

She's started crying, a terrible sight. The tears are streaming down that face of an aged little girl, reddened and furious. Her voice continues scratching the blackboard.

*

I waited, and I prayed to the Madonna to pardon this blasphemous act. How could a man like him depict the Holy Family, a man who had discarded me, who had brought a daughter into the world who he didn't care about, a man who pretended he had forgotten everything that had happened between us? How could he? I prayed for her to forgive him, to forgive them. Believe me, I really wanted to save them. But one night the Madonna told me no, that the sin was too great. That the world couldn't be soiled like that, that the world had to be cleansed.

Here we go again, thinks Ricciardi. Here we go again. Love, the old enemy, degenerates and turns into madness.

I waited till Saturday, when he goes to work a little later; I know their habits. I went in the morning to pick up Benedetta. I hoped that that drunk of a doorman would be at the tavern as usual, but instead he was in his booth, in the lobby, half asleep at his desk.

My sister was getting ready to leave; he was still in bed. I told her that I was running late, I took the girl and left. When I got to the bottom of the stairs, I pretended to realize how strong and cold the wind was blowing, and that I'd forgotten the child's hat and gloves.

Then I left her in the entryway and I went back upstairs.

Ricciardi feels a surge of anger at himself for not having figured it out right away. Ferro had remembered how lovely the little girl's braids had been that morning because he'd seen her without a hat; the image of the murdered woman was saying: Hat and gloves? not because she was asking for them, but because she was offering them, the hat and gloves of her daughter; and she was looking down either because her sister was so short, or else because she was looking for her daughter. I'm an idiot, a miserable idiot.

The Madonna had told me to do it, but I didn't know how. Then it occurred to me to bring the knife I used to cut the cork with me, the one that's razor sharp. The minute she opened the door, handing me the little girl's hat and gloves, I grabbed them from her and I did it. One blow, a single slash. That was all it took. I just wanted to make sure she stayed quiet.

One blow, a single blow. From right to left, just like the doctor said, with strength and determination. The Madonna had told her to do it.

And then I went inside, to the bedroom. With the knife in my hand. I had to be quick, because the child might catch cold, without her little hat and gloves. She's very susceptible, you know that? Her throat is delicate. Every winter she gets a fever, at least once.

He was sleeping peacefully. I placed the tip of the knife right over his heart, and I waited. At a certain point he opened his eyes. He didn't say a word. Maybe he thought it was a dream; maybe he'd been dreaming of me, the way I still dreamed of him, after all these years.

You have to get rid of the manger scene, I told him. You owe me that.

He made a cruel face, and he said . . .

I don't owe a thing, not a thing, he said. And I thought he was talking about money, thinks Ricciardi.

. . . that he didn't owe anyone anything. And then I sank that knife deep, into that heart black with sin. And I stabbed him, I stabbed and stabbed and stabbed. His protector was

Saint Sebastian; perhaps he wanted to die that way. My hand, my hands get sweaty, they never stop sweating. And when I'm nervous they sweat even more. I switched to the other hand, and I kept stabbing. He needed to be punished, he had to go to hell. And he had to go there by my hand.

There were two hands, the doctor had that right, too, thinks Ricciardi; with different degrees of strength because of the sweat and the different angles. The murderous hands. And the blood that sprayed in all directions remained invisible because the nun's habit is black. The only way to leave without attracting notice while covered with blood. And the murderous hands.

Then I wiped the knife on the sheets: I still needed it, you understand. I still needed to add a hill, over there, you see it? There's still moss to be added. I needed the knife.

But before I left, there was one thing left to do, and so I went into the other room. I wanted to take away the Saint Joseph, because a figurine like that didn't belong in a home like theirs. A father who lives for his child's sake: the complete opposite of that man. I grabbed it, but it slipped out of my hand; did I mention that sometimes my hands get a little sweaty?

That's why I suddenly understood. Rosa told me, when she dropped the Christ Child, and then there was the eel, the way it slithered through the fingers of all the hands that were trying to catch it. The Christ Child fell; it wasn't hurled to the floor, it wasn't shattered intentionally. And the eel was wet and slippery, just like the knife in the murderous hand. He had to die, she'd said. By my hand.

You have to believe me, I'd never have intentionally broken a sacred image. You can't think that of me, please. Tell me that's not what you think. I would never break a sacred image, never. The Madonna wouldn't talk to me for two whole days, even though She knew that I hadn't done it on purpose.

I kicked the broken pieces, I kicked them under the tablecloth. I just hoped no one would see them. I couldn't touch them, not with hands that had just done what my hands had done.

Tell me that you believe me, I beg of you.

You do believe me, don't you? Do you believe me?

LVI

Eventually, finally, Christmas Eve comes around; and after all the waiting it still catches everyone slightly unprepared. The dining room tables seem a little inadequate to the mistresses of the house, always a little barer than they'd imagined when they'd planned the meals; the gifts never seem quite abundant enough, you always seem to have forgotten an uncle, a good friend's wife, or one of the nephews; you worry that there aren't enough pastries and candy, but with what they cost, you certainly couldn't have bought any more.

In the morning, the fireworks start going off, at regular intervals, as if marking the hours left to go till midnight, when the city will explode like a giddy powder keg of happiness, inundating the streets with smoke and light. And the hospitals will overflow with men wounded in this war of happiness; a couple of fingers gone, a missing eye—just so many souvenirs to remember the holiday by.

Eventually, finally, Christmas Eve comes around.

Deputy Chief of Police Angelo Garzo looked around, satisfied only in part.

He'd so badly wanted to host that Christmas Eve dinner at his home, and he'd invited a number of prominent individuals, but almost no one had taken him up on it, understandably preferring to remain at home with their own families. But it didn't matter, because a few people had come and he felt gratified by those who had.

His wife, with the help of their maid, had laid a beautiful table, with flowers, candlesticks, silverware, and crystal. The manger scene, a small one but an antique, had been given the place of honor, under a bell jar.

Among his guests, in fact, was none other than Duke Freda di Scanziano, the consul of the second legion of the port militia. He at least could hardly refuse the invitation, after Ricciardi brilliantly solved the murder of that centurion, whose name Garzo no longer remembered. A solution that had not implicated any other militiamen, an outcome that Rome had been dreading.

The deputy chief of police had adroitly taken advantage of the thank-you phone call to extend an invitation to the consul and his wife that night: what a windfall.

Certainly, as soon as Epiphany was over, Garzo expected a phone call of complaint from the bishop for the rude and unannounced incursion into the convent, even though the nun had ultimately confessed. But what could he do about that?

Of course, a nun: damn that Ricciardi, never once could the man catch a criminal who looked like a criminal. But he'd worry about that after the holidays; right now he needed to tend to his very important guest. One day, sooner or later, he'd turn out to be useful to his career.

He walked over to him and said, with that dazzling smile he'd tried out a thousand times under his new mustache:

"Consul, care for another *roccocò*?"

Eventually, finally, Christmas Eve comes around. And amid all the disorder, it even manages to settle some things.

Lomunno looked around, and for the first time the interior of his shack seemed a little less squalid.

He'd managed to find a couple of candles and a tablecloth, and the money he'd earned at the market had helped him to put something on the table that was a little better than their usual fare. And to reward him for his hard work, the merchant had given him some fresh fish.

The children were eating hungrily; every so often, for some reason known only to them, they laughed together. Just like they used to do, in that other life, a thousand years ago, when Christmas was a celebration for another family, a family that no longer existed.

Lomunno decided that the human mind was a very odd thing indeed. He'd never have had the strength to take revenge on Garofalo: the fear of what would have become of his children, left on their own, would have stopped him every time. But the knowledge that the man was still alive, enjoying the comforts he'd stolen from him, that he was laughing and growing fat without a twinge of trouble from his conscience, had been ruining Lomunno's life.

Now that the man who had devised his ruin was dead, maybe the time had come to think of something else: how to reconstruct a life for himself, for instance, and a decent existence for his children.

Lomunno reached out his hand and caressed his daughter, who stood up with a serious expression on her face and kissed him on the cheek.

Sometimes, Lomunno thought, good can come from evil in this life. And after all, today is Christmas Eve.

Christmas Eve comes around and it has fun putting together things that couldn't be any more different one from another.

Dr. Modo dried his hands and turned to Vincenzino's parents.

"The fever has subsided. No question, this child is weak; but as the inflammation recedes, little by little, he'll regain energy and, I assure you, appetite. Boccia, I think you're going to have to redouble your fishing from now on; this little wolf is going to devour a lot of food, to catch up on lost meals."

"Dotto', believe me: I'll empty the sea of fish for my little Vincenzino," Aristide answered passionately. "I thought we were going to lose him. You can't imagine how many of our children we lose around here to illnesses like these."

"I believe you. As damp as it is, and the food the poor creatures have to live on, only the strongest ones are likely to survive. But our little Vincenzino, here, is strong indeed."

Angelina turned around, stopping her stirring of the pot on the fire for a brief moment.

"Dotto', if I may? This evening, on Christmas Eve, where are you going to eat? Are they expecting you at home?"

Modo sighed as he put on his jacket.

"No, no, Signo', no one's expecting either of us, neither me nor the dog, here. We'll go for a nice walk and see if we can find a trattoria, we'll have a little wine, just me, not the dog, and then we'll go to sleep. That is, if they don't keep us awake with this idiotic custom of shooting off Christmas firecrackers, a custom that does no good except to fill the hospitals with mutilated citizens."

The woman shot her husband a glance and signaled to him imperiously with her eyes. He turned and said:

"Dotto', if you're not offended by my asking, why don't you stay and eat dinner with us? It's a custom with us to cook everything we didn't sell at the market, and luckily it's not that much this year, and we eat it all together with the families of the others in the crew. Then we play a little music, we dance, and we laugh. We're penniless, but we have a good time. What do you say, would you care to honor us with your presence?"

Modo pushed back his hat and scratched his head. He looked at the dog, curled up at the threshold with one ear cocked.

"What do you say, dog? Do we want to spend Christmas Eve with these new friends of ours?"

The dog barked just once, and wagged its tail.

"It's his decision. Thank you, glad to accept. And what are you making that will no doubt be so delicious?"

Christmas Eve comes around, and it fills all the seats.

Maione had said nothing all morning, and Lucia was worried again. She hoped with all her heart that her husband had forgotten once and for all about his plans for revenge, which, she felt certain, would ruin their lives for good. She'd already lost too much, in terms of happiness, hope, and a future. She wasn't willing to plunge back into a nightmare. She knew Raffaele, she knew that if he acted according to a moral code any different from his own, the best possible outcome would be that he'd be tormented by his conscience for the rest of his days.

At a certain point, as if he'd finally come to an irrevocable decision, he'd gone out, saying that he needed to get something he'd forgotten. She'd done her best to keep him at home—the idea of him leaving just a few hours before the meal she'd put so much work into preparing; the idea of leaving the children—but he'd smiled at her and left.

Lucia had clung to that smile for the next two hours while she waited for him to return, and the time had stretched out until it seemed like two years. Then she'd heard the sound of the key in the lock, and she'd braced herself for anything and everything: except for what greeted her eyes.

Standing next to Raffaele in the doorway was a person, a little person. With her little hand in his big paw, her face red from the cold, and two braids poking out of her little wool cap, was a girl wearing a bewildered expression.

With his eyes, her husband signaled to her not to ask him anything. He summoned his eldest daughter, just a year older than their diminutive guest, and told her to take the girl to her room and show her her dolls. Only when he was sure he wouldn't be overheard did he speak to his wife.

"Luci', I couldn't celebrate Christmas with this thought on my mind. In just a few days, this little girl has lost both her parents and now her aunt; she has no one left. She'll have to stay at the convent, for now, then they'll see. But the thought of her spending Christmas Eve all alone, surrounded by nuns, just made me feel bad. I talked to the mother superior, and she gave me permission to keep her here with us until after the holidays. Forgive me for doing it without telling you."

That was Raffaele Maione all over: the man she'd fallen in love with, the man she'd married, the man she loved. The father of her children. A man who was such a father that he even felt he was the father of other people's children.

She stroked his broad, worried face.

"You did the right thing. Exactly the right thing. In fact, let me tell you this: that empty chair at the table, from now on we'll make sure that there's always someone sitting there at the holidays, at Christmas, at Easter. The good fortune that this family of ours enjoys, we're not going to keep it all for ourselves. That wouldn't be right. And you'll see, the original proprietor of that seat will be glad."

Christmas Eve comes around, and it tosses everything in the air.

When he realized he was the last one at the office, Ricciardi decided it was time to go home for the night.

He shot a look out the window: the piazza below was practically deserted by now. Every so often the boom of a firecracker would resound in the distance: they were test-firing the fireworks that would inundate the air at midnight, to greet the birth of a Child who they hoped would bring them peace, health, and prosperity. That's a little too much to ask, the commissario mused, from someone so young.

He headed off, walking at a fast pace along the sidewalk finally clear of stands and stalls and beggars. Everyone had found somewhere to spend those hours, many of them with someone to embrace.

He thought of Rosa and her shaky hand. For the first time in his life he'd felt a twinge of anxiety as he glimpsed the specter of a future of loneliness, deeper and darker than the loneliness he felt now. He should have demanded that she take better care of herself; it was his duty to protect her, as she had done for him from the day he was born.

Now there was no one left on the street but the dead, and their unexpected, painful last thoughts; them and the occasional hurrying straggler, racing against the clock.

At the corner of the archaeological museum, where the road started uphill toward Capodimonte, Ricciardi heard the sound of his name coming from a car.

"*Ciao*, handsome detective. Can I offer you a ride home?"

The interior of the car was nice and warm. Livia's scent washed over him.

"I happened to be passing by police headquarters. The sentinel told me that you'd just left. I know the route you take to go home, and here I am. Don't get ahead of yourself, eh? I went out because I chose to, I had invitations from my friends, since it would never occur to you that I'm all alone on Christmas."

Ricciardi fumbled for an excuse of some kind.

"I assumed you'd go to Rome, or to be with your parents. I had no idea you were still here."

Livia laughed.

"What would you have done otherwise, would you have invited me home for dinner? Come on, Ricciardi, don't make me laugh."

"Livia, you know my situation: I live with my *tata*, she's an old woman and she's not really well. And anyway I've told you before, you shouldn't expect the same kind of behavior from me that you get from . . . from other men, the usual kind. I'm always happy to see you, but I have my own life and my own things, and they're not the sort of things you can easily share."

The woman's tone of voice shifted, suddenly turning softer.

"I know that that's what you think. And deep down I also know you're wrong, that all you'd have to do is open the door a crack and let me in, and it would make you happy and me happy, too. There are two reasons I wanted to see you tonight."

They'd already covered the short distance to Ricciardi's home. The driver pulled over in front of the street entrance.

"And just what would those two reasons be?"

From the slats in the shutters over a certain window, two eyes, which had been waiting, saw what they wanted to see.

"First of all," Livia replied, "I have to tell you that for the first time in my life I've lost all confidence. I've always believed, ever since I was a young girl, that I could get anything I wanted from men. Then I met you, and it was like knocking my head against a brick wall."

She looked to Ricciardi like another woman entirely: her lower lip was trembling, and it was obvious that she was making a tremendous effort to keep from crying. She clenched her hands in fists in her black velvet gloves, and resumed in her normal tone of voice.

"Second: yes, I could have left town. But I'm happy even just to be in the same city as you. That's enough for me. For now, it's enough."

In the darkness, her dark, liquid eyes glittered from their veil of tears.

"Merry Christmas, Ricciardi."

She leaned forward and kissed him.

The eyes that had been watching dropped from the shutters to the front door of an apartment building. From the black clouds that had continued to grow heavier and darker all day there fell, swirling slowly, a single snowflake. Then another, and another still.

The car door opened, and a man stepped out and headed toward the apartment building across the way. The car drove off.

As he was searching for his keys, Ricciardi sensed a movement behind him.

He turned around and froze in astonishment as he saw Enrica walking toward him.

From her stride it seemed that she had lost every trace of uncertainty; she wore neither overcoat nor hat: the flakes of snow, which were coming down faster now, were falling in her hair. Her eyes, behind lenses that were slightly fogged from the chilly air, glittered like black stars.

Ricciardi understood in a flash that she couldn't have missed the sight of Livia bidding him farewell with a kiss. He felt himself die a little bit. He shut his mouth with a loud snap and tried, desperately, to come up with some way to keep from losing her yet again.

"Signorina, I . . . I don't know what you think, but you have to believe me: that car didn't . . ."

Enrica walked right up to him and stopped just inches away. She took his face in both hands and gave him a long, passionate kiss.

Then she turned around and went home.

Ricciardi stood there in the snow, with his keys in his hand and an earthquake in his heart.

All around him, the city was an immense manger scene.

A Meeting with Enrica
by Maurizio de Giovanni

I t's no simple matter for a man to be allowed to speak alone, unchaperoned, with an unmarried young woman from a respectable family these days. You run the risk of looking like a fool, and, even worse, of putting her in a gravely awkward position. People will talk and they want nothing so much as an opportunity, an excuse to stick a label of flighty flirtatiousness on some young woman; for the neighborhood gossips, an irreprehensible reputation is no fun at all.

I was therefore compelled to get in touch with her in the only way I knew how that would shield her from nosy neighbors, while also allowing me to explain the reason I wanted to meet her: I wrote a letter.

Even this wasn't easy. What I had to do was tickle her curiosity, making her understand that I wasn't entirely a stranger, that I had some insight into certain matters concerning her but that I wouldn't meddle, that I wanted to know more about her and that I'd like to meet her, perhaps to offer some advice. I was cautious, straddling a narrow boundary line, well aware that all it would take was a single word too many to frighten her off, and one too few to leave her indifferent. Last of all, since I could hardly ask her to write back, I had no choice but to suggest that we meet at a certain time and place without having any way of knowing whether she'd come.

Enrica, as I've learned from writing about her, is far more unpredictable than one could imagine. Her lack of inclination to indulge in spectacular gestures, her quiet nature, her calm manners, the measured way she has about her all give only a partial and incomplete idea of her true personality. She can be instinctive and abrupt, and without raising her voice, she can even be quite cutting. And like many women, she takes odd approaches to expressing herself, with some surprising results.

And so I'm relieved, though hardly astonished, when I see her walk into the waterfront café where I asked her to meet me. I already know that among the few customers on this chilly January afternoon there's no one who might recognize her. Outside the waves and the wind are quarreling, with the sound of a mournful symphony. The summer heat and the street urchins leaping naked from the rocks of Mergellina seem like a distant island, the product of a storyteller's imagination.

I bend briefly over her gloved hand, she pulls out the hat-pins and removes her hat. Her cheeks are bright red, perhaps from the cold outside or possibly from the emotion of the meeting. She peers at me through her spectacles, fogged from the warmth emanating from the ceramic stove, and her gaze is level, her eyes curious.

"Here I am. I came, as you can see. Tell the truth: you didn't think I would."

I try to look at her objectively, as if I didn't know certain of her thoughts, or her recent personal history. A young woman who tries to undercut her excessive tallness by wearing flat shoes, dressed nicely, if a little somberly, in good clothing that makes her seem a bit older than her actual age. Her features are symmetrical, perhaps a little nondescript but still pleasing. Her hands are long and lie motionless in her lap, folded over her handbag. Her head is cocked slightly to one side, and her dark eyes glisten with a faint spark of curiosity. One of those women who seem more appealing every time you look at them, if you'll only give them a second look.

"I'm delighted you came, Signorina. A strange appointment, with a stranger who can't tell you much about himself, or about how he knows what he knows about you."

A sudden dazzling smile lights up her face.

"I know, I understood that. Perhaps I sensed it. But from your letter I could tell that you know a great deal about me, more than my own parents do; and that you want to know even more. And you promised me that after this one meeting, I'll never see you again, even though we'll still be in contact in some fashion. That caught my interest and made me want to know more. All right then: what would you like to know?"

I study her. Agreeing to meet a stranger, in an out-of-the-way place. Once again, she has surprised me.

"You just mentioned your parents. Do you talk to them much? Which parent are you closer to?"

"They are two very different people, my *mamma* and my *papà*. I think I'm like my father, at least that's what everyone tells me; my mother says it quite a lot when she gets angry and accuses me of never telling her what I think, what I feel. With *papà* . . . well, we just understand each other at a glance. We don't even need to speak. That's how it's always been, ever since I was little. He doesn't pry, he minds his own business, and I know that he'll be there if I ever need him. He's a safe haven in my life, and we get along very well."

"What about your mother?"

She shakes her head.

"My mother, she . . . What she wants is for me to find a man and settle down; she's afraid I'll wind up an old maid. She's constantly reminding me that when she was my age she had two children already, that my younger sister has been married for years and already has a son, that my aunt had her first child when she was just seventeen, that the lady who lives on the fourth floor and has three children is the same age as me . . . I've gotten very good at pretending to listen to her while think-ing about the things I care about. Still, of course, I love her dearly. And she teaches me lots of useful things. She's a sorceress in the kitchen."

The kitchen. I smile back:

"But so are you, from what I've heard. You often make dinner for the family, don't you?"

She nods, with a hint of pride.

"That's what they tell me. My father, for instance, says that my *genovese* is even better than the one my mother makes. I don't know if that's true, but I can tell you that I like to cook. It's just one more way of embracing the ones you love, don't you think?"

I most assuredly agree, just as I know that if I had the time, I'd happily eat a heaping bowl of traditional *genovese*, the kind you never find these days.

"In your family, there's a militant member of the Fascist Party, isn't there? Your brother-in-law, your sister's husband, if I'm not mistaken."

She shrugs her shoulders.

"People are free to think what they like, is the way I see it. He's a good kid, he's very young and he really believes every word that Mussolini says. He and my father, who's a liberal, have endless arguments, they raise their voices, they pound their fists on the table, and in the end each of them sticks to his own convictions. My mother and my sister get upset every time, but I just feel like laughing. Besides, Fascists or no Fascists, nothing will ever change. Life will go on like always, right? What could ever really happen?"

Nothing will ever change. I try to conceal a shiver by asking another question.

"You say that nothing will change, but according to your mother the years are passing for you, just as they do for everyone else. How do you see the future?"

A simple, all-too-ordinary question. But Enrica blushes and looks away.

"The future," she murmurs. "Impossible to predict the future, impossible to plan for it. Still, you can dream. If hearing my dream is enough for you, I can tell you that the future is simple and wonderful, just like the present, but with me in my mother's place. A modest apartment, nothing grand, in a new neighborhood, like Vomero or Posillipo, where they're building all the new apartment buildings. At least two children, or as many as happen to come; I like to think of them as angels flying over my head even now, eager to come into the world. A man who loves them. Who loves me. And then joys and sorrows, as many as are needed so that when it's all over I can say that I lived. And moments of melancholy, and of happiness, the joy of seeing my grandchildren grow up. I dream of living, you see. That's all, just living. And that's the most ambitious dream there is."

The wind underscores the silence that follows, with a short howl that rattles the windowpanes.

"A man who loves you, you say. And yet, I know that you've been asked out by more than one young man, that you've received letters and flowers, and that, a few months ago, your parents even introduced you to someone they wanted you to see more of; but you chose to let the matter drop."

She smiles and says nothing, looking off into the distance. Then:

"So you know that, too. Yes, it's true. There have been signs of interest, and one or two of them might even have been worthy of consideration. But I, I don't feel that I can . . . I don't feel that I'm free, you understand. It's as if I were suspended, waiting for something. For someone. A woman knows when the moment has come, don't you think? And perhaps, when mine comes, I'll know it."

Now it's my turn to smile.

"Signorina, nice try, but you can't hide anything from me. I know all about you. And I know that when you refer to a man, you don't mean just any man. And that your moment arrived some time ago."

She looks at me, unruffled. Her eyes are deep and dark, and they glisten like the eyes of a doe. I believe that certain beauties swim just under the surface, emerging now and then, only to dive back into the depths.

"Ah, then you know. You know about the eyes that I felt watching me for months, every time I sat down by the window in the kitchen to do my needlepoint at night. You know about my encounter with those eyes, the desperate appeal for help that came out of them, at the fruit stand in the street, at police headquarters when the old fortune-teller was murdered, at Gambrinus. You know about the emotions that I sense, that I can see in the gestures, in the expressions. And you know about my apprehensions, the uncertainty that I feel. Perhaps you even know things I don't know, things I don't understand."

"You see, Signorina, I . . ."

She raises her hand, as if to silence me.

"You can't tell me anything; I understand. I don't really want you to, either. I want him to decide on his own that he wants me, or rather I want him to realize it, because I know that he loves me. I know it, I can feel it. And I can also tell that there's something stopping him, keeping him away, and that this something has nothing to do with the power of what he feels for me. Something dark, something outside of him. An obstacle, which must be removed or overcome. And I'm sure that he'll do it. He'll do it for me."

Determination: I can feel it, strong and calm as a tide.

"But you know how to wait. You have the right character for it. In the meantime, you've already met Signora Rosa, haven't you? And it seems to me that she's an important ally."

She laughs graciously.

"An ally, you say? What an odd word, as if there were a war

in progress. Signora Rosa is a lovely person, who even welcomed me into her home, of course it was when . . . when she was alone, that is. We speak, certainly; she's very concerned about what will become of her 'young master,' as she calls him. He's like a son to her, or perhaps something more. And she wants to see him happy, or at least less troubled than he is now, because his welfare has been the prime consideration of her life. She wanted to meet me, to see if I was the right person, and I believe that she thinks I am. Which makes me happy. Let's hope she's right."

I nod, with conviction.

"It's true, she thinks you are. And you are certainly much closer to her idea of a wife and a mother. Much closer than . . . Well, let's just say that she's very convinced of it."

She watches me in silence. She's suddenly become sad.

"Thank you for your concern, but you needn't worry: I already know about . . . I know about that other woman. I've seen her, on more than one occasion. An extraordinarily beautiful woman, wealthy, charming. She wears all the latest fashions, a different outfit for every occasion, and she's always the height of elegance. She has a luxury automobile, with a chauffeur who drives her all around town. Yes, I've seen her. And I've seen her adoring eyes, the way she looks at him. And I've seen the way men look at her: when she walked into Gambrinus, that time last summer, everyone was left openmouthed. I know that she's not from Naples, that she has close friends in high places, and that she's a widow, unattached and childless."

Livia. I haven't met her yet, but I know her, and the description jibes perfectly.

"A formidable adversary, from what you say. What do you think of her?"

Her hands grip her handbag tight.

"I'm jealous; of course I am. I'm a human being, I'm made

of flesh and blood, too. And I understand that for most men a woman like that constitutes everything that can be desired: beauty, luxury, social advancement. There's no comparison between a woman like her and an average girl like me. Still, there's something. Something I know, something that makes me think that matters are at least still up in the air."

"Something, Signorina? What exactly, if I may ask?"

The wind shakes the window.

"A man doesn't look at a woman the way he looks at me if he has feelings for another. There are certain looks you don't give a woman if you want to anchor your ship in another harbor. I've seen those longing green eyes, Signore. I've seen them and I've felt them on me, night after night, day after day; and I know what's in those eyes. And so I must cherish that feeling, I must cultivate it. And wait for it to emerge, because emerge it will. I know it will. And I know how to wait."

Her voice quavered at the end. Only a little, but it was unmistakable. She's a determined young woman, and she knows how to wait, but she's afraid. Who knows what fate awaits her.

Outside the window, the wind howls. As if *it* knew.

ACKNOWLEDGMENTS

The reason that Ricciardi exists at all is because Francesco Pinto wanted him to, so the first thank-you goes to him, as always; and Ricciardi walks down the streets conceived by Antonio Formicola and Michele Antonielli, as always. The atmosphere around him, the people he meets, and the air that he breathes were built with the fundamental, loving assistance of Dr. Annamaria Torroncelli and Dr. Stefania Negro.

For information about the magical world of the Neapolitan manger scene, Ricciardi owes a debt of gratitude to the extraordinary expertise of Michele Nevola, who spoke to him through Don Pierino. For Rosa's Cilento cooking, gratitude is owed to the clear and rigorous information provided by the magnificent Sabrina Prisco, of the Osteria Canali in Salerno.

A heartfelt thanks to the magnificent De Filippo siblings, and I hope they'll forgive me for moving the premiere of their play *Natale in casa Cupiello* by a few days for considerations of plot.

The author must also express his thanks, once again, to the wonderful group of the Corpi Freddi, who turn solitary activities like writing and reading into a fantastic collective experience. Ricciardi's heart beats for these young people and, through them, echoes back, amplified and more profound.

My last thank-you goes to a little girl who, at the end of the 1930s, told her stories to a little rag doll, imagining that it was her child.

And those are the stories, Mamma, that I tell here.

ABOUT THE AUTHOR

Maurizio de Giovanni lives and works in Naples. His Commissario Ricciardi series, including *I Will Have Vengeance* (Europa 2013), *Blood Curse* (Europa 2013), *Everyone in Their Place* (Europa 2013), and *The Day of the Dead* (Europa 2014) are bestsellers in Italy and have been published to great acclaim in French, Spanish, and German, in addition to English. He is also the author of *The Crocodile* (Europa 2013), a noir thriller set in contemporary Naples.